ler Anne Snell genuinely loves all genres of the itten word. However, she's realised that she loves oks filled with sexual tension and mysteries a little ore than the rest. Her stories have a good dose of both. ler lives in Alabama with her same-named husband d their mini "lions." When she isn't reading or iting, she's playing video games and working on her g, *Almost There*. To follow her shenanigans, visit rannesnell.com

A TODAY bestselling and RITA® Award-winning hor **Marie Ferrarella** has written more than two ndred and fifty books for Mills & Boon, some under name Marie Nicole. Her romances are beloved by s worldwide. Visit her website, marieferrarella.com

D1353636

Also by Tyler Anne Snell

Also by Marie Ferrarella

Discover more at millsandboon.co.uk

CREDIBLE ALIBI

TYLER ANNE SNELL

COLTON 911: COWBOY'S RESCUE

MARIE FERRARELLA

MILLS & BOON

Cotton 911: Cowboy's Rescue © 2019 Harlequin Books S.A.

Special thanks and acknowledgement are given to Marie Ferrarella for her contribution to the *Colton Search and Rescue* series.

ISBN: 978-0-263-27428-8

0719

CREDIBLE ALIBI

TYLER ANNE SNELL

This book is for Lissanne J., Marci M. and the Bat Signal crew.

Thank you for loving Madi and Julian and thank you for the continued support, critique and constant hilarity.

This book is also for Madi Rice. I named a character after you only to realize I never knew your real first name.

Chapter One

Julian Mercer didn't know this woman from Eve and yet he knew exactly three things about her the moment her baby blues swung his way.

One, she was hanging on to something that was heavy. As she made her way across the yard, following a path of mismatched stones embedded in the earth, there was an almost imperceptible drag to each step. Like there was an invisible weight on each shoulder that threw off a normal, happy gait. She was thinking of something and that something was difficult, whatever it was. Her polite, welcoming smile, which was required as the owner of the bed-and-breakfast, even had a tightness about it.

Two, someone or something had hurt her. Not just physically—though Julian clocked the small but noticeable scar that broke the smoothness of her skin above the left cheekbone. In addition to the subtle, weighted steps she took toward him, there was a hesitation. So small, yet he was as sure as his own scars lining his body that it was there. It was like she wanted to meet him but at the same time wanted nothing more than for him to leave. Halfway between fight and flight. It intrigued and perturbed Julian all at once.

And that third thing he knew about the golden-haired stranger making her way toward him?

She was beautiful.

Long braids thrown over each shoulder shone in the Tennessee sun and complemented a complexion formed by a life out in the elements instead of tucked in front of electronic screens. Crystal-blue irises took him in as his gaze dropped to the freckles dusting her cheeks. Those freckles, he had no doubt, probably made several other appearances across the skin of her arms and legs as well, but for now were hidden beneath a long-sleeved dress and a pair of black tights. It was a modest outfit, yet Julian didn't miss the pleasant curves beneath the clinging fabric. She wore flats but only had to tilt her head up a fraction to see into his eyes as she came to a stop in front of him.

"Well, you sure are punctual, aren't you, Mr. Mercer?" She held out her hand.

He shook it. "Is that a problem?"

"Absolutely not." Her polite smile stayed just as polite. "It's just not that common around here. Most guests end up stopping along the road to take pictures. One time a couple showed up an hour late because they spotted a black bear hanging out in a tree." She glanced down at her watch. It was one of those smart watches made for exercise. The time popped up on the screen as she moved her wrist slightly. "You said you were going to be here at eleven on the dot and here you are."

"You can thank my military training for that," he said with a wry smile. "I don't think I could be late for something if I wanted to."

She laughed. Julian made sure not to trace the scar against her cheek with his eyes again.

"Well, either way, I'm happy you made it." She angled her body and spread her arms wide toward the house. "I'm Madeline Nash, and this is the Hidden Hills Inn."

The bed-and-breakfast was aptly named. Near the heart

of the very small town of Overlook, Tennessee, the road to the inn wound its way through fields, forests and hills. Mountains crested in the distance. No sound of cars or city life broke through them or the land they were boxing in. Julian had gone from big-city Tennessee to small-town Tennessee to this rural beauty. The inn was in the center of it all yet felt a world away from everything else.

Julian appreciated the quiet, just as he did the privacy.

"Let's get you all signed in and then we can start the tour," Madeline continued. He followed her up to the long covered porch. She paused before opening the front door. "I'm sorry but it wasn't clear on the phone, are you expecting to meet someone here or are you traveling alone?"

"It's just me. I'm alone."

Madeline kept smiling. Customer service was in her wheelhouse and it showed. She kept to small talk without it ever feeling like small talk. After Julian signed in, she took him on a tour of the wide two-story house with all the best efforts of a seasoned host. From the common rooms to the private suites to the small bar that made up the surprisingly comfortable lounge at the back of the house, Madeline Nash made every space interesting and somehow intimate.

When the tour concluded at the bottom of one of the two sets of stairs the house offered, his golden-haired tour guide fixed him with a grin.

"I'll leave you to it," she said, already taking a step back. "If you need anything, don't hesitate to call the number on the card in your room. Breakfast and dinner are served every morning and night at seven. There's a list of activities and sights you might consider during your stay in a packet on your bed."

Julian had a flash of impulsive bravado. He almost asked the innkeeper if she ever considered accompanying guests to those sights and activities when a car door slammed outside. They both turned to the entryway window. A man with dark hair and a cowboy hat started up the walkway.

Madeline didn't say it out loud but she wasn't happy to see him. Her already-tense body tightened. Yet her smile stayed where it was.

"Again, if you have any questions, don't hesitate to ask."

Julian tipped his head in acknowledgment as Madeline left through the front door, greeting the man. Instead of coming inside, they moved across the yard and disappeared from view. A part of Julian wanted to follow, to make sure she was okay, but then his senses came back.

He didn't know Madeline and thinking he had to protect her was foolish. His mother would have scolded him for his presumptions that the innkeeper was some kind of hurt, damaged woman in need of saving. For cripes' sake, he'd only just met her.

Julian knew from experience that there were more people walking the earth with scars than with smooth, untouched skin. That didn't mean he had to try to save them all.

That didn't mean they needed saving in the first place.

First impressions were tricky like that.

The first smile was easy.

It was everything after that got a little murky when trying to decipher them.

His room was in the far corner of the second-floor landing. It was a big difference from the hotel rooms he'd been frequenting and, if he was being honest, the apartment he'd been living in the last several years. The room was spacious and stretched much wider than he thought was possible. Not only was there a king-size bed, there was an adjoining sitting area and a desk and a three-piece bathroom. He was surprised and happy to note that the showerhead was high enough to allow him to stand up straight beneath it, a luxury his apartment had never afforded him. In his Special Forces unit he'd been known as the Lumberjack. It wasn't that inventive of a nickname but it was apt. Julian was built tall, wide and muscled like his father before him. Most times it translated into unintentional intimidation. Other times it meant he had to hunch over in the shower.

Julian threw his bag down just as his phone started to ring.

The caller ID read Chance Montgomery.

"Mercer," Julian greeted. He walked to one of the windows that ran along the room and looked through the blinds. He spotted Madeline at the table where she'd been sitting when he'd pulled up earlier. Her male companion stood across from her. Julian couldn't get a read off of him.

"You know, we've been friends for a few years now," Chance said in his Southern twang. "Answering with a 'hello' or even a 'howdy' instead of your last name would make our conversations a little more casual and a little less like I've just accidentally called my old high school math teacher and she's still mad about the gum I put on her chair that one time."

Julian chuckled.

"Old habits die hard," he responded, actively loosening his shoulders by rolling them. "Brevity and precision have been my friends in the military for a while now."

"Luckily for you, the private sector has a lot fewer friends." He paused and then laughed. "Well, you know what I mean."

"It means I need to say 'howdy' apparently."

Chance laughed again.

"You can't see it but I'm giving you a type of salute you

also wouldn't find in the military. It has to do something with a certain finger."

They joked around for a few more minutes before Chance finally circled back to the reason for the call. Julian didn't mind the chatter; in fact, it was one of the reasons he was headed to Chance's workplace in Alabama. Chance, a cowboy by upbringing but, lately, a surprisingly skilled bodyguard, was one of the few civilian friends Julian had kept through his marine service over the last ten years. Julian not only liked him but was confident he could work alongside him, which was why he was interviewing at the private protection firm Chance's uncle owned.

"I just wanted to make sure you were stopping to smell the roses in Overlook and not rushing here," Chance said, losing his earlier humor. "The interview isn't until next week and as long as I've known you, you haven't had a vacation, one that actually counted. So I'll reiterate one more time and then let it go. Enjoy yourself, go watch a sunset, sleep in, buy a lady a drink. You'll thank me for that advice when you're out in Germany away from all the Southern hospitality you've been hitting on your way here."

Julian knew Chance was right. His last deployment before he officially left the military started the week after his interview. Then he would hopefully return to Alabama and finally, finally stay put for a while.

"I'll make sure to smell the roses," Julian promised. "I'm here for two days and then on to Nashville for the next three. I should be at your place after that."

Chance must have thought this was acceptable. He ended the call without any more constructive criticism. Julian stayed at his spot by the window, admiring the curve of the mountain in the distance. Then his gaze dropped to the innkeeper.

Two days here and then he'd be one step closer to a new life.

"I'M NOT TRYING to destroy the family, Des."

Madeline Nash watched as her brother tried to save face moments after showing his backside. He took his dark gray Stetson, pressed it against his thigh and blew out a sigh she recognized as frustration.

"I didn't say that and you know it."

Madi pulled out her long braids, tamed the waves with her fingers and then sectioned her hair again. She separated it into three parts. Ever since she was a little girl she did what her eldest brother, Declan, had dubbed "angry-braiding." It wasn't like she could correct him. The evidence throughout her thirty years of life was fairly damning. Every scowl or frown captured in photographs or home movies was accompanied by long braids down her back or across her shoulders.

Some people counted to ten to cool off; she made her hair more manageable.

"You didn't have to say the words, Des. You gave me that look and then that tone. Don't for a minute deny it, either. Even outside our triplet telepathy I know your moods."

Desmond rolled his eyes. It was his trademark move for their disagreements.

"All I asked was if you had been to the ranch lately," Des countered. "I didn't suggest you were destroying anything, let alone our family."

Madi tried not to let the guilt move into her gut again.

Instead she channeled her irritation. Her hands went across her chest and her chin rose a fraction.

"And why would you ask that? You've never asked about me going to the ranch before."

"Because up until three months ago, you lived on that ranch."

If Desmond had been anyone else, Madi would have blushed at how childish she knew she sounded. But he was her brother. So she huffed and pretended there was nothing wrong with what she'd just said. She finished the braid over her left shoulder, then looked at anything but him.

"For your information, I had lunch with Ma and Nina a few weeks ago and it was lovely."

Desmond gave her a pointed stare.

"And was that at the ranch or in town?"

It was Madi's turn to roll her eyes. It didn't matter that she was an adult who had opened and currently ran her own business; Desmond still found a way to make her feel like she was a child again. A child who was perpetually in need of a guide to help her through the life he thought she should be living. It was at all times frustrating; seldom was it touching. In those few instances, a voice deep inside Madi would remind her why Desmond was protective of her more than he was with her brothers.

Now wasn't that time.

"You're making it sound like I've abandoned my family," she said. "As you said yourself, I've lived on that ranch for basically all of my life. I don't have to set foot on the property every day, you know."

Des rolled his eyes again. They were bright and ever-changing blue, just like hers and Caleb's. Madi felt another jab of guilt looking into them. He'd been the first person she'd told about her dream of running a bed-and-breakfast and the first person who had encouraged her to follow that dream when the old Richman house had gone up for sale.

Even now, after her childishness, he kept to the high road.

"I'm not saying you are obligated to check in. You don't have to go to the ranch at all, but you need to at least own up to the reason why you're currently not making any appearances there." His expression softened. "You're avoiding Mom and you know it."

Madi did know it but she didn't dare admit it. Thankfully, she didn't have to find a way to avoid the truth he was pointing out to her a moment longer. Like she knew his moods, she had to concede that he knew hers. Des took his cue to leave with grace. He walked around the table, gave her a kiss on the forehead and smiled. Then on went the Stetson.

"I really am proud of what you've done here, Madi. So are Mom and the others. Give them a chance to prove it to you."

Madi watched him leave without another word.

In the small town of Overlook, Tennessee, there were no hotels or motels. If you wanted a place to lay your head, then you'd have to leave town limits to get it. The Hidden Hills Inn was Overlook's quick and easy option for tourists who'd rather not bust their budgets by trying to rent one of the few cabins deeper in the forest and near the mountains. Or at the Wild Iris Retreat.

There was that flare of guilt again.

Her family owned the retreat. One Madi had left to open her own version of a hotel.

They're different, she reminded herself. The retreat was for guests seeking an authentic experience of living on a ranch and staying on the land. Hidden Hills was just a cozy, less expensive place to spend a night or two. *I'm not stealing anyone from Mom! They have more business than I do!*

Someone cleared their throat behind her. Madi jumped clear out of her seat.

"Whoa there!" Julian had his hands out as if he could steady her despite the distance between them. "Sorry! I thought you heard me."

Madi put her palm against her chest and gave him an embarrassed smile.

"No worries. I was just stuck in my own head." She motioned to the road that Des had just driven away on. "My brother has a habit of making me think too hard."

Julian took the joke with a good laugh and what almost looked like a dose of relief. Though maybe that was a touch of wishful thinking on Madi's part. There was no denying Julian Mercer was a handsome man. His hair was as black as night and cropped close, neat. His eyes were dark, too, but held a softness to them as they moved to hers. While he was a tall, obviously muscled man, the sharp angles of his nose and jaw were an elegant kind of ruggedness. Madi placed his age around her own and noted on reflex that his ring finger was very much bare.

"Family has a funny way of doing that, don't they?"

Madi nodded. Heat surprised her by moving up to her cheeks beneath the man's dark gaze. It inspired an offer she didn't have time to think about before saying.

"Would you like to join me, Mr. Mercer?" She waved to the table behind her; the lemonade pitcher on its surface had more than enough for two more glasses left in it. "Unless you would prefer to be alone, which is absolutely fine."

The man's smile only stretched.

"You can call me Julian," he said, moving around her to the other chair. Its dainty size made him look even more rugged and muscled. Still, there was a softness to his eyes. One that, despite herself, intrigued Madi.

"And you can call me Madi. Madeline was my grand-mother."

Julian nodded and watched politely as she flipped a cup right side up from the serving tray and filled it. He chuckled before taking a drink.

"What's so funny?"

"My friend just told me I need to learn how to enjoy myself more. One thing he suggested?" He tipped his glass toward her. "Buy a lady a drink. I was wondering if this counts?"

The heat in her face started to travel south, propelled by the glint in his eye. Madi knew it was probably just her imagination and yet...

"I wouldn't say that it doesn't."

Julian's eyebrow arched but his smile stayed.

"I can work with that."

They lapsed into a pleasant conversation. It stretched into a walk along one of the trails. Then that became dinner. A proper drink came after.

Madi was too wrapped up in the unexpected great time to notice that the figure out in the woods that night wasn't just a shadow between the trees. It was a man.

Watching.

Waiting.

Chapter Two

Six months later, Madi was standing on the back porch, trying really hard to convince herself that she wasn't thinking about Julian Mercer. There wasn't time, and even if there were, she had already gone down that particular road so much that her tires were absolutely bare. Her metaphorical tires. Her real tires were in fine condition and attached to the van she hadn't wanted, but needed, to buy.

She replaced the mental image of smiling Julian Mercer with one of her behind the wheel, gunning in the direction of Loraine Wilson. She knew it wasn't polite, but it made her smile to imagine wiping the smug look off that wealthy woman's face.

Madi knew a murderous rampage was taking her irritation too far, but she could blame it on her hormones.

Being pregnant, in the Tennessee summer heat no less, had stretched her patience and politeness thin.

"How are you doing it?"

Jenna Diggins—Hidden Hills' chef, bartender and occasional cleaner—nodded toward the stone pathway that led from the backyard and forked between the rental cabin and a small nature trail. Loraine, one of three guests currently booked at Hidden Hills, was pacing across it, immersed in her phone conversation.

"How am I doing what?" Madi asked, feigning innocence. Jenna wasn't just the only other employee—she had been Madi's friend for a decade.

Jenna giggled. She bumped her shoulder against Madi's. "How are you destroying Mrs. Pearls and Coiffed Hair?"

Madi swatted at the woman but didn't deny anything.

"*Destroying* seems like such a harsh word. What I'm doing is simply giving her a love bump with my new mom van." She paused, then grinned. "Over and over again."

Jenna laughed and handed her a bottle of water from her backpack. Madi took it, grateful.

Summer in Tennessee was just about Madi's favorite time. Every tree and flower was teeming with life; every stream, creek and river was asking for companionship; and the skies stayed a shade of blue that had a way of making Madi appreciate life all the way down in her bones.

Or at least that had been her feeling about the sunny season before she'd been pregnant.

Now the sun made her already-hot body hotter, the trees and flowers stood by as the mosquitoes and bugs dive-bombed her every chance they got, and the blue of the sky was a reminder that she wasn't the same woman she had been the year before. Just like she wouldn't be the same woman next year, either.

The water was the only part of summer that Madi remained fond of, which was why she was getting ready to show the guests to the creek in the nearby forest that stretched across the property line. Madi had grown up taking advantage of the creeks and ponds and rivers to cool off. Not even Loraine's passive-aggressive comments could derail her plans to enjoy herself today.

Someone cleared their throat behind them. Heat instantly flooded Madi's cheeks. Ray Cutler, the guest staying in the rental cabin, gave them a humoring look.

"Don't worry," he said. "After listening to her go on and on about how she had to let her dog nanny go because she was positive he was watching her Netflix, I can appreciate your frustration."

Jenna laughed but Madi still felt shame at being caught bad-mouthing a guest. After her whirlwind romance earlier that year she'd made a vow to never stray into unprofessional territory again. She should have known better. Yet there she was prattling on about how she'd like to run over someone less than two yards away.

"It's the hormones making me cranky," she said, knowing it was a lame excuse. "That and the heat, and I can't stop babbling nonsense." Jenna snorted. Madi pushed on. "Are you ready to go, Ray?"

Ray was what Madi's mother, Dorothy, would call a middle man. He wasn't short but he wasn't tall. There was no myriad of muscles filling out his clothes but he wasn't bone thin, either. He had one of those faces that seemed to be universally familiar, pleasant to look at but not knee-buckling handsome. His hair was a dirty blond, cut short and wavy, and for the last two days he'd been sporting a pair of glasses across his dark eyes. His personality so far had fallen in the middle, too. Polite and quiet but vocal when you hit the right topic. Madi liked the man because—unlike Loraine and her husband, Nathan—his love for the outdoors and Overlook seemed genuine. He cracked a broad smile.

"Two lovely ladies taking little ole me out to the creek on a hot summer day? This day would only get better if I could go back and tell my fifth-grade self about it."

Madi and Jenna laughed and soon they were off across the stone path. Loraine ended her call but didn't seem interested in focusing on her husband. Instead she breezed past him and matched Madi's pace when the stones ended and the dirt trail began.

"Sorry about that," she started, waving her smartphone around. "You'd think our gardener would know what we want by now. Do I like succulents? Yes. Do I want them in my bedroom? No. Roses are the only flower I'll allow in there, and only on special occasions. You'd think after working for us for over a year he'd know better." She let out a long, dramatic sigh. "But I suppose it isn't his fault. His daughter is trying to become some kind of interior designer. She's been trying to use me for practice. Stick with what you know, little girl. I'm not running some kind of weird work charity."

Loraine gave Madi a look that clearly said she was waiting to be agreed with. Madi begrudgingly flexed her customer service muscles.

"Working relationships are hard to navigate sometimes. I used to work with my family before I opened Hidden Hills. It definitely can be tricky."

Loraine nodded emphatically. Her hair, a teased-out red that matched her shade of lipstick and her purse, barely moved at the motion. A look of disgust flitted across her impeccably made-up face.

"My Nathan is a wonderful man in the boardroom but I barely can stand him at the house sometimes. I can't imagine working alongside him, either. He's been talking about retiring early and staying at home and that just makes my skin crawl." Loraine let out a laugh. It wasn't a good one. From Madi's experience with the socialite during the past two days, she knew what was coming next. "Maybe I should do what you did. Buy a funny little house out in the middle of nowhere to keep myself busy. How fun would that be?"

Madi couldn't blame the pregnancy hormones on the

rage that kicked up in her chest. Luckily, she didn't have the time to regret anything she might have said. Loraine prattled on without a care in the world.

And right onto the worst subject she could have prattled about.

"Though I suppose you won't be doing this for much longer. Once that baby of yours is here you won't have time to be a single mother and run your little inn." Madi must have made a face. Loraine adopted a look of concern. Madi doubted it was real. "Oh, honey, just remember, there's no shame in raising a kid all on your own. Whoever the father is, I'm sure you had nothing to do with him abandoning you. Try not to beat yourself up about it, okay? It isn't healthy for you or the baby."

Every part of Madi tensed. Her shoulders, her jaw, her fists. Her heart. Good customer service and good manners became just words in her head. Loraine Wilson continued to smile. There was a pointedness to it. An edge. Sharper than she'd expect from the wife of a rich businessman from Portland.

Loraine was intentionally trying to rile her up.

Why?

Was she that bored? Was she that unhappy in her own life that she had to tear down others?

"Hey, Madi! Could I steal you for a second? I have a question about tonight's dinner."

Bless her heart, Jenna appeared at Madi's other elbow like a guardian angel. She gave her a squeeze that brought Madi out of her angry haze and back to reality.

"Sure, let's talk." Madi pointed a small nod and an even smaller smile at Loraine. "Just keep following the path. If you'll excuse me a moment." The woman seemed put out that the conversation was ending and let her husband,

Nathan, who had been trailing behind them deep in his business call, walk alongside her.

Madi and Jenna waited until there were a few feet between them and started walking again.

"That was uncalled-for," Jenna said in a harsh whisper. "Want me to go get the van?"

Madi didn't mean what she said next but her heart was hurting. And she was sure that Loraine had done that on purpose.

"Forget the van. I'd like results faster than that."

Jenna's expression softened. She put her arm around her friend. They walked the rest of the way to the creek without saying a word.

The pain in Madi's chest only grew once she dipped her feet into the cool, crisp water.

Madi felt no joy in it.

And that was Loraine's fault, too.

THE DAY CRAWLED into night. After showing the guests the creek, Madi busied herself with chores around the inn. For the first time since opening Hidden Hills, she skipped dinner with the guests. Not that it was required of her or even asked, yet she had thought it was a nice touch. Tonight she couldn't stomach sitting there and pretending everything was all right.

It wasn't.

Even before Loraine showed up.

It had been almost five months since Madi had found out she was pregnant. In that time a lot of things had gone right and wrong. The inn had hit its stride for a few months and made Madi money rather than just breaking even. She threw herself into work and welcomed the distraction that kept her thoughts away from the fact that Julian Mercer was nowhere to be found.

The number he'd given her was disconnected. The emails she'd sent bounced back. His social media existed but wasn't active. They'd spent two amazing, surprising and magical days together that had turned into a week. One blissful week she had never imagined would be as great as it had been. Yet the moment Julian's SUV had disappeared down the road on his way out, it was like the man had vanished completely.

Since then the burn of anger and embarrassment had cooled. The drive to be the best parent she could be had taken its place. Along with what she had thought was acceptance. Never seeing the father of her unborn child again was a harsh reality, sure, but what had she really expected? What they'd had was, to her, once-in-a-lifetime hot, but once in a lifetime nonetheless. Julian had been a ship passing in the night. A momentary escape.

Though that had been her decision, hadn't it?

Could she be mad at him for being radio silent after she'd been the one who said their week together was all they should have?

Madi ran her hand over her naked belly. The water from the bath had never been that warm. Now it was cold. She was only fooling herself. Almost every single time she felt her stomach she thought about Julian. Where was the mountain of a man who had rocked her world? She felt an emptiness that let Madi know she hadn't accepted anything. At least, not with any enthusiasm.

The music that had been playing from her phone lowered. A rhythmic sequence of beeps filled the bathroom as a call came through. Jenna's name scrolled along the screen. Madi wasn't about to ignore her friend, even if she'd asked not to be disturbed.

Madi sloshed water out of the tub and with wet fingers answered the phone.

"Hello?"

"Sorry to mess up your quiet night," Jenna said, diving in. "But, uh, I have Nathan here with me right now and—" There was a rustling sound as she must have moved away from the man. She lowered her voice as she continued. "He wants to know if you and Loraine are done talking."

Madi gave her reflection in the mirror over the sink a dubious look before grabbing her towel to dry off.

"Come again?"

"Right? That's what I was thinking when he asked but he said that you called Loraine an hour ago and asked her to come up to your room. He tried calling her to come to dinner but the phone went straight to voice mail. He didn't want to come up there because he didn't know the rules."

Madi felt her eyebrows fly high.

"Why would I do any of that? I wanted to not be disturbed because of Loraine. She was two seconds out from getting popped in the face."

"Nathan seems adamant."

Madi sighed.

"Tell him to go ahead and call Loraine again. She was probably just tying up the phone line with her gardener complaining about life."

Jenna repeated the suggestion while Madi bent down awkwardly. She felt around for the drain plug and shouldered the phone. When a song started blaring from the next room she nearly dropped both.

"What in the world?"

"What?" Jenna asked, voice still low.

Madi pulled the drain plug up and placed it on the counter. She shook her hand off and looked at the door separating her from the small living area. A weird knot started to tighten in Madi's stomach. She slipped into her robe.

"What's going on, Madi?"

"I think Loraine might really be in my living room," she whispered. "A phone is going off."

Jenna said something, but for the life of her, Madi couldn't pay attention to what it was. Her focus narrowed to pinpoint precision. She opened the door, ready to confront the woman who was still managing to ruin her day, but found it empty. Or, at least, no one was around.

A cell phone continued to play music from the coffee table. It wasn't the only thing out of place. A shotgun sat next to it. Madi's blood ran cold.

"That's Dad's."

"What's going on, Madi?"

Madi felt like she was falling down some wild rabbit hole. She knew that shotgun. Her father's initials were carved into the grip. Right next to her grandfather's. It was supposed to be at the ranch.

Not on her coffee table with a phone that wasn't hers.

The phone finally stopped ringing. Madi touched the gun, running her finger over her dad's initials to make sure it was real.

"I'm coming up," Jenna said, no longer trying to be discreet.

Madi heard the concern, knew she should say something, but another detail caught her attention.

Her bedroom door was closed.

With steps that felt like wading through water, Madi went to the door and swung it wide.

"Oh my God."

She saw the pearls around the woman's neck first. The dark red, tight-fitted dress second. The Louboutin pumps third.

Finally, as though her eyes had been reluctant, Madi saw the woman's red hair. It flowed around a disfigured face covered in blood.

She was dead.

And if Madi were a betting woman, she'd wager that the gun lying on her coffee table had been used to murder Loraine Wilson.

Chapter Three

"And you think *this* is a good idea?"

Chance Montgomery gave him a look filled with skepticism.

"I never said it was a *good* idea," Julian admitted. "I just said it *was* an idea."

They were standing on the side of the road, their cars parked in front of the town of Overlook welcome sign. It was as quaint as Julian remembered. Worn but filled with charm. Two small spotlights lit up the hand-painted letters. It sent a warm glow bouncing off the hood of his truck.

It probably would have been better to come back during the day but the pull of seeing the Overlook innkeeper had tugged Julian right off the road to his new life.

Chance took his cowboy hat off. He'd been finishing up a personal matter in North Tennessee and had met up with Julian to caravan on the way back to Alabama. He sucked on the toothpick between his lips. He'd gotten it from the diner where they'd eaten an hour ago. In another hour they were supposed to be stopping at a hotel. The next day, Tuesday, they'd be in Alabama at the security firm. Next Monday would be Julian's first official day as a private bodyguard.

His first official day in his new life.

Yet there they were.

"Well, I can't really tell you not to do it," Chance said. "Just that you might want to think it over a little. I can't say my track record with women has been outstanding but even I'd be a bit worried about rolling into town unannounced. You haven't talked since you left. That's a lot of time between then and now. A lot could have changed."

Julian knew better than anyone how different life could be from one moment to the next. He knew how just one second could irrevocably change everything. He also knew that dropping in after all this time could be construed as too much.

"Listen, I'm not going to go there and stand outside in the rain with a stereo over my head and hearts in my eyes," Julian deadpanned. "I'm just going to see if there's an opening at the inn for the night and, if there is, see if she wants to grab a quick meal to catch up. Last we talked she was worried about the inn doing well and I was on the way to a job interview." He shrugged. "Nothing more or less than a conversation or two. Then I'm back on the road tomorrow. No harm, no foul."

"And if she doesn't want you there?"

Julian shrugged again, though he had to admit he didn't like the thought.

"Then I'm back on the road tonight."

Chance nodded, conceding to the logic. Plus, he was right, there wasn't much he could do to stop Julian from taking the detour.

"Well, here's to hoping she's not married and keeping your time together a secret from her husband," Chance teased. He clapped Julian on the shoulder and went back to his truck. Before he got in he paused and grinned. "And if she's happy to see you, well, then I guess I'll see you Monday morning."

Julian watched his friend take off down the road before

he got back into his own truck. There he sat and stared at the sign for a moment. It had been over half a year since Julian had seen Madi Nash. For all he knew she *could* absolutely be married. She could have sold the inn. She could have moved.

She could be happy to see him.

She could wish he hadn't shown up at all.

Julian scrubbed a hand down his face and exhaled. He'd been deployed six times in his career, three of those in combat zones. He'd set boots down in the dusty heat of Iraq. He'd navigated the islands of Japan with little more than a partially busted radio. He'd even, to the chagrin of their spec-ops commander, fought his way through a bar brawl in Germany. And yet here he was, in small-town Tennessee, actually nervous that a golden-haired, freckled-skinned bed-and-breakfast owner was going to put him in his place.

How the mighty had fallen.

Not that he'd counted himself as mighty.

Julian finally turned the engine over and got back onto the road. He marveled at the fact that he remembered the town as well as he did. The streetlamps across the main strip cast light on the same businesses he remembered, just as the moonlight shone across the houses and landscapes he'd passed before. Not much had changed. He knew plenty of people, including those he'd served with, who would have been bored by the lack of change. Julian welcomed the familiarity. It was everything he was hoping to have for himself when he finally got settled in his new job. Roots. Ones that grounded him. Ones that centered him.

A life that would start after the detour.

The GPS on his phone remained off as the houses turned to fields, the fields turned to trees, and the trees started to open up to the inn's property, which he'd recalled countless times in the last half year. Despite all of his resolve, he was starting to feel something like nerves when the drive curved, indicating the inn was almost in sight. In his mind Julian had already pulled into one of the spots, gotten out of the car with calmness and determination and bounded up the stairs with a smile on his face.

However, what really happened when the road straightened and the inn came into view was drastically different.

Blue and red lights were strobing from the tops of two parked deputy cruisers. One had two uniforms standing next to it. They were talking to a man Julian recognized from pictures in Madi's room as one of her triplet brothers. A truck was pulled up on the grass next to him, and in the far corner of the lot was something that made Julian even more uneasy.

It was a coroner's van.

Julian coasted to a stop far enough away from the closest cruiser so everyone could still drive around him. By the time he cut his engine, one of the deputies was on his way over. The other seemed to be in deep conversation with Desmond Nash. Neither of them looked his way.

"Howdy there," the deputy greeted. His voice was tight. As was his body language. "How can I help you?"

Julian wished he were a people person, but he knew better. Sure, he prided himself on being a good friend, but putting strangers at ease had never been in his wheelhouse. He didn't have the patience, especially now.

"I'm here about a room," he stated without any preamble. "What's going on?"

The deputy looked like a man who very much did not like what was going on. His jaw hardened.

"There's been an incident that we're investigating." He cast a look back at the inn. Jenna, Madi's friend and employee, shut the front door behind her with enough vigor to draw the attention of everyone outside. She didn't look sorry for the force. Though when she swept her gaze across her onlookers as she stepped off the porch, she stopped with obvious surprise at Julian.

Neither had a chance to explain.

The door behind Jenna opened. A dark-skinned woman with a badge swinging against her chest came out. Her face was impassive, frown set so deep that Julian tensed even more than he thought was possible.

That was when he saw Madi.

In the distance between them the glow of moonlight mixed with the whirls of blue and red. It was unsettling.

But what put fire in Julian's gut the most?

Madi's hands were handcuffed in front of her.

A uniform led her out, hand against her back. Her eyes stayed on the porch as she walked to the steps.

"What's going on?" Julian asked, his voice becoming an octave too low. The deputy tensed in return. His hand moved near the butt of his service weapon. Julian made sure not to move another inch, but couldn't stop himself from yelling when she was waiting for her escort to open the back of the closest cruiser. "Madi?"

For a moment Julian was worried she hadn't heard him. But then she turned, first her face and then her entire body. From the side Julian noticed something he hadn't seen when she'd first walked through the front door.

Her stomach.

Her *pregnant* stomach.

Part of Julian's mind went into overdrive; the other, cool-under-pressure part gave him the patience to stay still.

Madi's eyes widened in surprise, just as Jenna's had.

"I didn't do it," she yelled. "I swear!"

Then, in a movement that was neither harsh nor easy

to watch, Madi was ushered into the back seat. When the door closed behind her, all Julian could do was stare.

GRANDMA MADELINE NASH had always said a person was never given more than they could handle in life. She'd said it when their house was destroyed in a flood, when the ranch fell on hard times, after her husband passed away, when the triplets were abducted and right through the aftermath of the attack, leading up to her only son's death.

Madi put her head in her hands. She had a hard time believing she could handle everything like her namesake had. She'd been at the Wildman County Sheriff's Department for almost five hours. In that time she'd been handcuffed to a metal table in the interrogation room before being uncuffed and brought a rolling office chair because it had more padding. During those five hours she'd only spoken to three people.

The first had been Detective Santiago, her brother's partner. Jazz was a family friend but treated Madi with short, clipped questions. Where had Madi been in the hours leading up to dinner? Why had she called Loraine? If she hadn't done it, then why did the call log on her phone say she had? Where did she get the shotgun?

How badly had she hated the woman?

Madi had gone over her afternoon and night several times before Jazz excused herself. Her brother Caleb never came in.

Declan, the sheriff and Madi's eldest brother, eventually did and explained why.

"Caleb can't work this case because he can't get his emotions in check," Declan had said. He hadn't sat down across from her. His body was riddled with tension, his face pulled down in a frown. Madi didn't need any triplet connection to know he was trying his best to keep his own emotions in check. "Him working this case is a big-time conflict of interest. Jazz will take over as well as a detective from the local PD in Kilwin down the road."

"She's teaming up with the police department?" Madi had been stunned at the news. The two only ever worked together on emergencies like high-speed chases that crossed the town limits or manhunts that spanned the county. Now they were doing the same with her?

It made her already-knotted stomach quake.

Declan had sighed.

"It was at Mayor Harding's suggestion, and honestly, it took all I had to convince him to keep us on the case. You have two brothers on the force. Our family history doesn't help. This is only going to rock the boat on public perception of us."

"Family history? Do you mean the abduction?" she had nearly shrieked. "We were eight! How is that our fault?"

"I'm not blaming any of you for that, and you know that. I meant what happened with Caleb last year. I think the mayor would like the Nashes out of the spotlight for a while. Even though you know as well as I do that the town has never really let go of what happened when you were kids."

Madi did know that Overlook was incapable of forgetting one of its biggest unsolved mysteries. It wasn't every day that three children were attacked, abducted and held for three days before escaping on their own…and that, to this day, no one had ever been able to ID the man responsible. Never mind understanding his motive.

As far as what had happened with Caleb, talk had gotten out of hand quickly but had died down.

Or so Madi had thought.

"The mayor thinks it's best for you, the department

and the town if we're extra careful with how we move forward," he continued, as if his words were scripted.

"And that means what exactly?"

Declan let out another long sigh. This time Madi saw the defeat in it.

"That means that my chief deputy will run point on this case while I handle the rest of the department and try to keep this in-house as much as I can. Past that, Caleb and I will have nothing to do with this case. We can't afford anyone blaming us for favoritism or being impartial."

Madi felt the tears spring to her eyes before they ever fell down her cheeks. She was angry. She was scared. Caleb being taken off the case made sense. Declan stepping away hadn't crossed her mind as a possibility.

Pain twisted his expression. His face softened.

"I know you didn't do it, Madi," he said, voice low. "But the evidence against you is pretty damning. I can't dismiss it, even though I know you're innocent. Hell, I think everyone in this department knows it, too. We just have to do our jobs and do them carefully, or we could end up hurting your cause instead of helping it." He reached out and touched her hand. "Jazz is great at her job. So are the rest of my people."

Madi wiped at her cheeks. She nodded.

"I understand."

He smiled but then let go of her hand. Then his face went stony.

"Are you sure there's no one who could corroborate your side of the story, though?"

Madi shook her head. She brought her hand down to her stomach.

"It was only the two of us."

Declan left soon after. Another hour went by. Madi's

thoughts went between everything that had happened and the other surprise she'd gotten that night.

Julian Mercer.

In the flesh.

This might be too much for me to handle, Grandma, she thought ruefully.

The third person to visit her finally was Caleb. He moved into the room like they were teens again and sneaking out of the house to go to the barn loft to meet their friends. He hurried to her side and crouched down next to her. There was an undeniable excitement in his movements that she didn't understand.

"Why did you lie to us, Madi?" he asked in a rush. "Pride be damned, you're looking at murder charges!"

Madi felt her eyes widen. Did Caleb really think she killed Loraine?

"What are you—"

"You should have told us about your alibi the moment we showed up on scene!" Madi didn't know what he was talking about. She said as much. Caleb looked exasperated. "I know you didn't want to get him in trouble with his boss, but my God, Madi, this is serious."

"His boss?"

"Julian Mercer. Your alibi." He thumbed back to the door. "He just wrote his official statement about you two being together. I mean, yeah, I have some personal questions I'd like to ask—for instance, who the heck is this guy—but right now he could be that creep you dated in college and I'd be happy as punch."

Madi didn't have time to correct her brother before the door opened and in walked Declan and a man who must have been the lawyer.

They expressed the same sentiment.

Madi should have come clean about being with Julian

during the afternoon and leading up to the discovery of Loraine's body, instead of trying to cover for him so he didn't get into any trouble with his boss. No one's job was worth the risk of her being suspected of murder.

Now they couldn't charge her. Which meant they couldn't hold her there any longer.

The air in the interrogation room became lighter. Her brothers' shoulders were no longer sagging. There was new life behind every word and movement. The entire mood had changed.

It made Madi realize how dire her situation had been before Julian's lie.

And that was what it was—a lie.

Yet with one hand resting on her pregnant belly, Madi realized it was a lie she wouldn't correct.

Not until Loraine's real murderer was caught.

Chapter Four

"So I've been downgraded to lead suspect instead of a shoo-in for murder."

Madi was as beautiful as Julian remembered but undoubtedly tired. Her eyes were red and swollen. She rubbed her hands together, fretting with nervous energy. They stood outside the Wildman County Sheriff's Department. A hint of the sunrise colored the distance. The air was cool and seemed to add to her discomfort.

Julian wanted to reach out and take all of the concern and worry away, but truth be told, he was out on his own limb of uncertainty.

He'd just lied to the authorities. In a big way, too.

"They're going to find the real person who did this," he said, hands shoved into his pockets to curb the urge to tuck a loose strand of her hair behind her ear. "Now that they aren't focused on you they can do that."

Madi shot a nervous look toward the front doors. They were standing next to the sheriff's truck in the parking lot. Declan and Caleb were still inside. This time with the husband of the murdered woman. He'd been out-of-his-mind angry and had to be kept in a separate part of the building.

I don't care if she's pregnant! She killed my wife! She killed my Loraine! She needs to pay!

The man had been so certain of Madi's guilt, so incensed by it, that he had spit as he'd yelled. His fervor had solidified Julian's urge to help Madi.

He knew without a doubt that Madi was innocent. He'd felt it in his bones the moment she'd yelled out to him that she didn't do it. He'd jumped into his SUV and flown to the station, ready to watch as the rest of the department believed her, too.

Yet it didn't happen.

Or at least, the evidence forced their hands.

The looks across the local deputies' faces changed as the hours wore on. Julian stayed in the lobby with the flimsy reasoning of being a friend of Madi's. He waited to be questioned but no one ever came for him. In all the uproar he'd seemingly melted away into the scenery. He'd only had the chance to talk to Jenna to get the quick and short story of what had happened before she'd had to leave. The sheriff and Caleb could be seen, angry and whispering. The entire department's mood went from determined to find the alternate story to souring. Then on edge. When Julian had seen the lawyer come in through the lobby, wearing a suit and an expression that meant he was in for a rough ride, the need to help Madi had punched through Julian's gut until he was standing in front of her brother and lying through his teeth.

Now he was standing in front of Madi and telling the same lie.

"I sneaked in an hour before Jenna called you, parking my vehicle off the road and hiding in the trees so no one knew I was there. That's why you didn't want to eat dinner with the guests, which is unlike you," he spelled out. "I was with you in the bathroom when Jenna called. You found the body, but I was next to you. Realizing the cops were going to be involved, I went out the window and made it to my car. Then I pretended to come in for the first time so no one would suspect I'd been there at all."

Madi's eyes were wide and blue. Oh so blue.

"And the reason I didn't want to be caught up in an investigation was because I was worried that it would get me fired before I ever started my job next week." Julian shrugged. "Not a noble story, but everyone in there knows you didn't do it so it made sense to them."

The innkeeper ran a hand over her belly. Her pregnant belly. Julian wanted to ask how far along she was but getting their story straight here, now, was the most important thing they could talk about. As she'd already said, it was a lie that had made the difference between murderer and lead suspect.

"Why?" she finally asked. "You... Well, you don't know me. This could absolutely get you fired *and* jail time." She lowered her voice and took a step closer. Julian could reach out and touch that baby bump between them if he were so inclined. "Why take that risk? Why lie?"

Julian gave her the honest truth.

"You said you didn't do it and I believe you."

A look he couldn't interpret crossed the innkeeper's expression. Then it transformed back into exhaustion.

"And am I to guess what we were doing together in secret last night?"

Julian felt the heat of their earlier intimate memories burn through him. Just as they had been throughout the last several months. Like lighter fluid thrown into a low flame. Hot, alarming and just a dangerous taste of what else could happen.

"The same thing we did last time I was here," he answered. "Apparently, Caleb had no idea you and I had been romantic then. I had to tell him otherwise to give credence to my story now."

Again, Julian wanted to search her expression to find the reason why she'd ended things, why she'd kept him a secret then and the time after he'd left, but he had to focus. Not that he could have gleaned the truth from the woman standing so close to him. Her expression was as guarded as her brothers' had been when they'd brought her in. Maybe it was a Nash family trait.

"And why did you show up? Outside the fiction you've been spinning about our romantic encounter."

Julian tried to smile, tried to downplay the eagerness he'd hidden from Chance when he'd decided to visit Hidden Hills. This time he lowered his voice.

"I just wanted to say hi before I went on to my new life."

Madi was quick to comment. She wasn't smiling.

"And now you're my alibi in a murder investigation where I'm the lead suspect. If that's not good—or bad—timing, I don't know what is."

Silence stretched between them for a few moments. Madi looked down at her hands on her stomach. Her expression was knotted in thought. When she met his eyes again there was a fire behind them. However, before she could speak, the door to the department swung open.

Caleb took the stairs down two at a time. When he got to them, he clapped Julian on the back and smiled for all he was worth.

"While I'm not exactly happy you waited so long to do it, I'm sure as hell glad you came forward," he said, reiterating what he'd told Julian earlier. He gave his sister an equally enthusiastic smile. "I'm just glad we can all go home now."

Madi didn't share in his exuberance.

"My home is a crime scene," she pointed out.

Caleb nodded, deflating slightly.

"Good thing that's not the only home you have here."

Madi looked like she wanted to say something else but Caleb wasn't having it. The earlier stress had lifted. Now he was reveling in the lightness. Julian had been there before. He became reacquainted with the feeling at the end of every deployment.

Caleb motioned to his truck and addressed Julian directly.

"Why don't you two follow me?" he said, already digging out his keys. "Mom and Nina have some beds made up and some breakfast going, depending on how you're feeling."

Julian's eyebrow rose high.

"And where exactly are we going?"

The detective gave them both a grand smile.

"The Nash Family Ranch! Where else?"

THE SUNLIGHT MET them and followed them across town and right up to and through the entrance to the Nash Family Ranch. The last time she'd talked to Julian, Madi had been avoiding the ranch and her mother out of guilt.

Things hadn't gotten much better. When she'd announced her pregnancy her mother had been happy, but also angry.

It had created a rift between them, one Madi's brothers had tried to repair, but they found no easy way to soften either woman. Because even though her situation wasn't ideal, Madi wouldn't allow any negativity. No matter if it was a passive-aggressive comment or a wayward glance that held an edge.

Now, though, as the fields passed by on either side of Julian's SUV and the ranch at the end of Winding Road became closer, Madi wanted to avoid her mother for an entirely new reason. Dorothy Nash had been through the wringer in the past three decades. She'd faced and dealt in heartache like she'd been cursed with bad luck. She'd seen needless violence and pain much more than any one person should have to bear.

And here Madi was, adding another heartache alongside the father of her child, who'd just committed a crime to keep her from being charged as a murderer.

Madi pressed her forehead against the cool of the window. It sounded like the plot to a movie where Harrison Ford would eventually be jumping out of an airplane or from one skyscraper rooftop to another to save the day.

"So, *this* is the famous family ranch?"

Julian's eyes had been swiveling as he'd driven through the front gate that ended Winding Road. He was observant, that much Madi knew of the man. She had appreciated this skill during their week together. He'd noticed the shifts in her mood and thoughts with ease. He understood her.

Yet maybe that hadn't been something special between them. Maybe that was just who Julian was. An observant man who had come into town, flashed his smile and then disappeared.

Then again, she'd been the one who said leaving was okay.

So what that Julian hadn't reached out? He hadn't picked up a phone, hadn't sent an email, and the mailbox had remained free of any letter bearing his name.

That was what she had said she wanted, right?

Never to see him again?

Yet here he was.

It, along with everything else, filled Madi's head like rising water. There wasn't time to sort out what didn't make sense. All she could hope to do was survive it. To keep swimming. To escape the flood.

So she held her tongue back from asking why Julian had gone silent and why he was back. Instead, she tried to answer him like she would a guest. Forced jubilance and pride. Polite but not overly expressive. A good middle ground.

"Yes, this is it. The Nash Family Ranch. Home to several generations of Nashes throughout the many years it's been here." She motioned to a road that forked off the straightaway. "That leads to the Wild Iris Retreat, the stables, several trails and Caleb and Nina's new house." She hesitated before detailing the rest of the ranch's geography. The customer service lilt to her speech drained away. She couldn't hide the weight of what had happened pressing her next words down. "You know, I don't know if Mom has anyone staying at the retreat right now. If so, this could really hurt business. Maybe I shouldn't be here."

Julian shook his head. For a moment she thought he was going to reach out to her, but he kept his hands firmly on the steering wheel.

"I don't know your family but I have a feeling, just by what I've seen in the last few hours, that there's nowhere else they'd rather you be." This time his gaze swept over to her.

And then down to her stomach.

Madi ran her hand over it, as if she could shield herself from his questions. For months she had tried to tell him the very same thing she was trying not to bring up right now.

What if he reacted poorly? What if he decided to recant his statement? Madi now knew how bad things had looked for her with Loraine's murder. What if she was actually convicted?

She'd lose her daughter.

From there Madi's thoughts of the future spiraled. Fear and uncertainty pricked at her eyes, blurring her vision. She didn't realize they were at the main house until Julian cut the engine.

"Madi." His voice had gone low, a sound that normally put the fire of longing beneath her skin. This time, however, it wasn't the sound of lust she heard. It was severity. Like a moth to a flame, she met his stare. She was unable to look away as he continued. "There is nothing you can tell me that would make me take back the alibi. Okay?"

Madi shouldn't have been surprised that once again, Julian Mercer had read her like a book. He had a knack for that sort of thing. She nodded. He kept on.

"There's no ring on your finger. You're not married or engaged," he continued. "Are you seeing someone?"

"No."

Julian nodded, more to himself than the conversation.

Caleb's truck door slammed shut near them. The porch light flipped on, bathing the SUV's cab in an eerie glow. Julian wasn't done yet, but Madi wanted to finish what she'd been trying to do for months.

Because as ridiculous as it was, Madi realized she trusted that Julian would keep his word. That even if he didn't like the news, he wouldn't betray her.

At least, she really hoped he wouldn't.

"Julian," she said, cutting him off just before he could say anything more, "she's yours."

Madi might have trusted the man, but in that moment, it was startlingly clear to her that she didn't have his gift of observation. She couldn't read his book. Not a single word.

Julian was a mystery to her.

And Madi was afraid he always would be.

Chapter Five

The low buzz from the air-conditioning was comforting. So was the softness of the sheets. The fabric softener's scent wrapped around Madi's senses like a warm embrace. She stretched her legs out and, for the briefest of moments, felt peace settle across her.

Then her bladder reminded her that not only had she just woken up, but she had just woken up pregnant.

She couldn't lounge in her bed.

And she wasn't in *her* bed.

That was when the insanity from the inn came back in full force. Madi groaned and struggled to sit up. The sheets might have been soft and smelled good, but they weren't hers. She was in the guest bedroom at Desmond's house. Through the open slats in the window she could see the roof of the main house in the distance. The house they'd all grown up in. The one their mother still lived in now.

Madi remembered how the Nash matriarch had looked at her when she and Julian stepped out of his SUV. Right after she'd told him the truth about the child she was carrying.

Right after neither had said a word once that truth had spread between them.

Dorothy Nash was an optimistic woman but Madi had seen the cracks in her armor in the light of dawn. No one in the Nash family was a stranger to how hard it could be to carry on. Still, her mother had worn her brave face with conviction as she'd embraced Madi. That affection had transferred to Julian, a man she'd never met, before ushering both inside for food.

Over that meal, Caleb had done most of the talking, laying out everything that had happened while Madi and Julian kept quiet. Madi knew she could tell her family anything without fear of being exposed as a liar but she didn't want to make *them* liars. So she ate her food and then accepted the room at Des's for a nap. Julian had been offered the other guest room, and she'd all but run to her bed before seeing if he had accepted it.

Madi felt for her phone on the nightstand before remembering she didn't have it. Her bladder's urgency became louder than the vulnerability she felt creeping in. She didn't stop to see who was or wasn't in the guest bedroom as she fled to the hall bathroom. It was only after she was finished and cleaned up that she paused at the closed door.

Hesitation wasn't just a word. It was a full-body experience for Madi, whose fist hovered next to the wood of the door. The twisted, horrible image of what had once been Loraine's face entered her mind.

If everything happened for a reason, Madi hated to know what the reason was.

Movement downstairs pulled Madi's attention. Her hesitation to talk to Julian turned into a resolution to avoid him for as long as she could. She hurried down the stairs, already pulling up a smile that sold the fact that she was okay.

That smile, fake or not, wavered when her mother bustled into view. Madi angry-braided. Her mother everything-braided. Today was no exception. She sported a tight silver braid over each shoulder and had her best pair of overalls on. She held up her late mother's outdoor serving platter, topped with several cups and a pitcher of tea.

"Hey, sweetie," she greeted, expression softening so much Madi could have used it as a pillow. "I was about to come up and wake you after I put this out." That soft expression started to harden. Madi followed her through the house, feeling the concern transfer.

"Why? What's going on?"

Her mother paused just before the front door. Her voice lowered.

"Caleb just showed up in a huff. I don't think any news he has is good." Madi fought the urge to gulp. Her mother leaned over to bump her shoulder. The ice cubes in the pitcher clinked against the glass. "But don't you worry, we're all going to get through this. We just need to band together and figure it all out."

Her mother flashed a reassuring smile and pushed through the door. Madi followed, hand already rubbing her stomach.

Between the main house and Desmond's was a small dirt path, a picnic table along with extra seating and a driveway that led to the main road that cut through the ranch. Their family was big on outdoor living. That always included eating and tea drinking. So a gathering at the table wasn't an unusual scene for the ranch. What *was* unusual was the company sitting at the table.

Julian stood as they got closer. Caleb was already on his feet, pacing the dirt beside the table with a phone against his ear. Neither man looked pleased.

"Hey."

Madi was ashamed at how Julian's baritone sang to her body, even in the most innocent of settings. She slid into the seat opposite him with a small "hey" of her own. He settled back in and smiled politely as her mother set a cup in front of him. His eyes remained grim.

"What's going on?" she asked, looking to her brother. He wasn't as tightly wound as he had been the night before but there was a definite weight there. Julian answered while Caleb finished up his call.

"Apparently after they let us go last night it was implied that the sheriff's department had already crossed the line and was playing favorites."

"That's ridiculous," her mother interjected.

"That's a direct quote." Julian looked apologetic. He thumbed toward Caleb. "The local police department has been asked to completely take over the investigation." He gave Madi a pointed look. "Which Caleb wasn't happy about, to say the least."

Madi's stomach twisted.

"We're going to be questioned again," she realized.

"Sadly, that was going to happen no matter what," her mom said. "This town is small enough that no one can be that easily dismissed." She grabbed Madi's hand and squeezed. "Even when they're innocent."

Madi knew that was true but that didn't stop that stomach twist from mixing in with a little dread. She might not have killed Loraine but she'd still been complicit in a lie to the department. Her brothers' department. If all of this blew back it wouldn't just hurt her and her child, it would hurt the rest of her family, too.

And Julian.

Even with the table between them Madi felt him against her skin. Felt his body heat enveloping hers, comforting and strong. Immovable. Was it what she wanted now or just a memory dredged up thanks to worry and pregnancy hormones?

Once upon a time, Julian Mercer had made her feel safe.

"What about Hidden Hills?" she asked. Jenna had taken over locking up, but Madi realized now with more than a dose of regret that she had lost sight of what would happen next with the inn. "What about the other guest, Ray? I completely spaced about him in all of the chaos."

"Desmond went to relieve Jenna this morning," her mother answered. "As for Ray, he's in a cabin at the retreat."

Under normal circumstances, Madi would have been riled up. After announcing her pregnancy to her mother, her concern that she was competing with her family had been pushed low on her priority list. Now Madi was just grateful. Hidden Hills *was* a crime scene after all.

"Good," Madi said. "Though I still want to head over there myself."

Caleb was shaking his head before he ended his call.

"You can't go snooping through it yet."

"I don't want to *snoop*," Madi countered. "All of my clothes and things are there!"

Caleb rolled his eyes and addressed their mother.

"Jazz just got out of a meeting with Declan and two detectives from the local PD. Like we thought, they want to conduct interviews all over again, plus add a few. Declan offered the conference room in the department for convenience's sake and they finally agreed. It probably would look better if we all headed there now. Show that we're not trying to avoid anything."

Madi's gut twisted. Her mother stood, Julian rising in sync. Madi had a little more trouble. Her baby belly was relatively small, yet she still wasn't graceful.

"Let me run and get some things from the house and I'll be ready," her mother said. Caleb started to dial another number.

"I need to touch base with Nina and Desmond."

Julian reached out and helped Madi stand. His hand was warm, strong. Distracting. She was grateful when he looked down at his phone and not into her eyes when she was standing tall again.

"I need to call Chance," he explained.

"Chance? Your friend from Alabama?"

He nodded. Then his voice was low.

"He's the only person who could prove I wasn't with you before the body was found."

Madi felt her eyes widen but he didn't give her more than that. Instead she was left next to the table as the three of them scattered. It made her feel even more helpless.

And that was when it hit her.

A detail she hadn't focused on fully yet.

Something that had fallen through the cracks as the shock had paved over everything.

The shotgun.

She hadn't heard the shot that ended Loraine's life.

Someone hadn't just killed the socialite; they'd done it somewhere other than Hidden Hills.

Why would someone go through the trouble of bringing her back?

And putting her in Madi's bed?

Madi rubbed her stomach, chewing on the thought. It was a sour taste.

"I think we need to go over a few more things before we head out," Julian said after a couple of minutes. He sidled up to her, close enough again that she was enveloped by his scent. "Especially if we're about to be put through the wringer."

"Agreed."

The main house's back door swung open. Madi's mother hurried over to them, brow creased.

"This is probably more madness," Madi muttered.

"Someone's driving up the road but I don't recognize the truck," her mother said without preamble. It was enough to pull Caleb off his call. They turned as the sound of crunching gravel preceded an old black two-door Ford. Madi didn't recognize the vehicle, either. It came to a stop on the side of the road between the houses.

The man, however, she did recognize.

Madi's triplet telepathy flared to life. Caleb gave her the briefest of glances before squaring his shoulders. Their mother lost any and all signs of a polite, hospitable woman. Madi felt ice in her veins.

"What's wrong?" Julian asked at her ear.

Madi didn't have time to hold up the walls around her that guarded her. Not when *he* was walking across the grass toward them, badge glaring at them from his belt.

"Remember last time you were here and I told you that everyone in the county likes at least one of us Nashes?" she said, voice low. "So much so it's like a running joke in town?"

"Yeah."

"You're looking at the one man who hates all of us."

"The feeling's mutual," Caleb threw in despite the distance between them. Their mother didn't deny either accusation.

Julian's jaw hardened.

"Why?" he asked.

Madi didn't take her eyes off the approaching man. She hadn't told Julian about her past—why she had the scar on her cheek—but now wasn't the time to be coy with the information. She had to bullet-point it for him. He needed to be on the same page when it came to the man.

"When my brothers and I were eight, a man abducted us from a park. We were held for three days in a cabin in the woods before we managed to escape. The guy who took and held us got away, never to be seen again. My dad had a theory that someone paid him to take us for whatever reason, but died before he could prove it." There was steel in her next words. "You're looking at the only suspect my dad ever had."

THE CHANGE IN all three Nashes was more than alarming. Madi's hurried explanation of why was enraging. Julian pictured the scar across her face and replayed the small limp that Desmond walked with. He'd never asked about either but now wondered if both were born from that trauma.

The man of the hour closed the distance between himself and their group.

The mood hadn't just gone cold, it had plummeted into arctic waters. Even the Nash matriarch was as stiff as a board.

"Good morning, Nash family," the man greeted. He smiled but it was as off as the surrounding mood. His eyes roamed to Julian. "And guest." He reached his hand out, bypassing Caleb and Dorothy until he got to Julian. "I don't think we've met. I'm Christian Miller. Lead detective from the Kilwin Police Department."

Julian shook. The man's grip was a little too tight.

"Julian Mercer. Nice to meet you."

Miller didn't seem to share the sentiment.

He stepped back to face them as a group.

Julian placed him in his upper fifties. He was bald on top but had a salt-and-pepper beard shaved close. It highlighted the frown that had deepened at the sight of them. He wasn't a big man, but there was a severity to him. He was also easy to read. He held no love for the people he was around and they held no love for him.

Not that Julian expected anything less after the bomb

that Madi had just dropped. That was one more conversation he wanted to have with the woman with balled fists at his side.

"Well, I'm assuming the sheriff has already informed you about us handling the case," he started, voice gruff. "I just want to let y'all know there are no hard feelings. This investigation is going to be conducted in a professional manner. That's what Mrs. Wilson deserves and that's what she's going to get." His eyes wandered to Madi's. Julian had never seen her so rigid. It inspired an almost primal reaction within him.

He wanted to protect Madi. He wanted to protect all of the Nashes. Even if he didn't understand all the nuances to the situation, Julian knew beyond a shadow of a doubt that Christian Miller was a threat. And he had made a career out of assessing and dealing with those.

"So…" The detective's demeanor changed. He smirked and waved between them. "I know how tight this family can be so we're going to go ahead and have Madeline come with me. I think it's a damn shame how this case has already been handled. The department shouldn't have even responded. All it did was give you time to get your stories straight. Really a damn shame, if you ask me. It's just another example of how the Nashes always seem to get their way. That stops today."

"I'm not going anywhere with you."

Julian wouldn't have believed the words came from Madi had he not seen her speak them. Each held a knife's edge, sharp and biting.

The detective's demeanor changed yet again. This time there was no smirk.

"A woman was found in your bed, killed by your father's shotgun, which was found on your coffee table," he said. "A witness claimed to have heard you talking about wanting that same woman dead several times that day. The call that you claimed not to have made to the victim was found in your phone log. And let's not forget the glaring detail that everyone seems to have glazed over because you just happen to be pregnant—" His eyes narrowed to almost slits. A new wave of tension moved across the Nash matriarch and her children. Julian took one small step forward. "You have violence in you, Madeline. You may smile, you may say nice things, but at the end of the day I know you're more than capable of doing exactly what was done. And this time, this family is going to pay the consequences for their actions. Pregnant or not."

Caleb looked ready to lunge. So did Dorothy. Julian moved closer before either could.

"Watch out there, Detective," Julian ground out. "I think your bias is showing."

The man laughed, an embittered sound.

"If I were you, buddy, I'd cool my jets," he said. "You just so happened to be the perfect alibi for the Nash daughter, but I'd bet my badge that everything you've said so far has been a lie. You want to know what else I think? I think you didn't come to see her at all. You just happened to be in the right place at the wrong time." His voice dipped into a sharpness that rivaled Madi's. "That's when she convinced you to lie. That's when you broke the law. And that is what I intend to prove."

Caleb started to rally but Julian spoke over him.

"You're right. I didn't come to see Madi."

The innkeeper placed a hand over her pregnant stomach, eyes wide in confusion. Julian hoped what he said next wouldn't hurt their case more than it helped. Then again, whether or not they would admit it out loud, everyone in that yard was nearing the edge of a cliff. One that they could be pushed off at any second, whether it be by a murder with no leads, a rich and recently widowed husband on the warpath, or a lawman with a grudge. If they didn't start building a bridge soon, what hope did they have to get on the other side of it all?

Julian might have lied about the alibi but Madi was innocent. He was going to help her the best he could. So he aimed to control the one part of the investigation that he could at the moment.

If Detective Miller was accusing him of being a stranger, then Julian needed to correct him.

He looked the man right in the eye and spoke clearly.

"I came to see my daughter."

In front of God and everyone there, Julian placed his hand over Madi's. Both were resting against her stomach.

Against their daughter.

Chapter Six

Madi had to hand it to her family—their poker faces were fantastic.

No one, not even her triplet brothers, had known who the father of her unborn child was. She'd decided not to tell anyone after realizing she might not ever see Julian again. It had been the sore spot between her and her mother. Dorothy Nash was a fierce protector when it came to her children but she couldn't protect them without all of the details. Madi had taken a stand after another round of questioning from her mother and brothers. She would tell them who it was when the time was right.

Now? So close to a man she'd loathed for years and hurtling toward an investigation that made her look like a murderer? It certainly didn't feel like the right time.

Though it was effective.

Detective Miller hadn't been able to hide his surprise as well as her mother and Caleb had. His smug and righteous attitude had zipped away, replaced by a critical look split among her, Julian and the stomach they were both touching.

"You're the father," Detective Miller said.

Julian nodded.

"And I'd be happy to confirm that during my interview." He dropped his hand from her stomach. Its heat went with it, leaving Madi in want. His admission that he was the father had shifted something inside her. Sure, she'd known—and for much longer than him—yet now it felt different. It made the guarded part of her heart feel even more vulnerable than it had.

Julian motioned to the detective's truck. His expression wasn't giving anything away.

"Which I think it would be more professional to do at the department instead of out here in the yard," he continued. "So why don't we all head that way now? That SUV parked at the main house is mine. You can follow us there if it'll make you feel better, but unless you have something to charge her with right now, I think it'll be better for all of us if Madi rides with me."

Julian was absolutely thrumming with authority. One second he'd been the quiet yet hard-to-miss man at her side. Now his words carried more power than anything Detective Miller had said. It had affected her mother and Caleb, too. The first had loosened her shoulders; the latter had unclenched his fists. With a few sentences Julian had managed to flip the tables.

Now it was Miller who was on unstable ground.

"Fine," he said, not at all sounding like it was fine. "I'll follow you but if you do anything, and I mean anything, that seems even remotely suspicious, I'll call the whole county on you. On all of you."

He didn't give them another word. Madi and her family didn't speak, either. No matter how badly she wanted to say a few words that might have made Grandma Nash roll over in her grave.

Caleb was the first to break their formation.

He turned to Madi. His eyes dropped to her stomach before going to Julian.

"Was that the truth?"

Madi nodded. There was no point in keeping the secret any longer.

Caleb seemed to assess Julian with new attention. What conclusion he came to, Madi couldn't tell.

"The longer we wait to go to the department, the more ammo we give Miller," he added. His face twisted in anger. "I get why the case was moved to another agency but giving it to him? That's on the far side of the professional spectrum. But don't worry. Declan and I will fix this."

Her mother still hadn't moved. Madi couldn't tell if she was angry at Miller's sudden reappearance or if there was something else moving beneath the surface.

"Mom?" she tried. "Do you want to ride with us?"

Dorothy Nash kept her expression unreadable.

"No, dear, but thank you. I think I'll take my own car."

Madi tried to smile, tried to give her something that would make everything better, but there wasn't much she could do. She felt no joy in the wake of one of the Nash family's ghosts of tragedies past.

Julian and Madi went straight to his SUV. Detective Miller lurked in his truck, waiting. Julian was a cool cucumber. Only belatedly did Madi wonder if that was because of his military experience.

"I bet you're sorry you came to visit me this time, huh?" Madi asked after they were moving down the ranch's main road.

Julian shrugged, eyes ahead.

"Sometimes things happen," he said. "You can either hang on for the ride or jump off before it gets anywhere good. You just have to adapt."

"Adapt," Madi repeated. "That's a word I used to hear a lot." Absently she brushed her fingers across the scar on her cheek. Most days she forgot it was there; others it was impossible to pretend it wasn't. "Adapting or not,

Miller isn't going to back down," she added on. "There's too much bad blood there."

"And he's not making it a secret that he holds some serious anger for your family. I can't imagine it's ethical for him to be the lead investigator."

Madi sighed. Her ankles were starting to swell. The heat never helped.

"I need to go to Hidden Hills after the interviews. If I'm not charged with anything, that is. Everything I own is in that house."

Julian nodded to the road.

"We'll get you there."

Madi didn't like that his words made her feel better, but there was no denying that they did. She let out another long, deep breath and rubbed a hand over her stomach. There was so much they could talk about that it muted them. Silence filled the vehicle.

Which topic would they even focus on?

The murder? The lying? Their reunion? Their daughter? The weather?

"Madi?"

They were moving down the county road toward town. The sun was shining. Madi longed for a normal summer day. Swimsuits, sun and carefree fun. No mystery. No Miller. No death. "Madi," he repeated again. "Something's happening."

His eyes were on the rearview mirror. Madi turned, worry flooding her system. Caleb had broken their caravan. He sped around them, flashers on. Detective Miller had his on, too, but was motioning through his window for them to pull over. When they were on the shoulder, Miller stopped on the road next to them.

He didn't get out.

"You go straight to the department right now or so help

me God I'll send a manhunt after you two," he yelled. "Got it?"

"Got it."

Julian didn't get a chance to ask what was wrong. The detective floored it after Caleb. Madi's mother pulled up behind them, brow knit. She threw up her hand in confusion. Madi shrugged.

"Something happened," Julian said. He steered them back onto the road and turned on the radio. "I don't like this."

"It seems to be a theme lately."

Madi turned on the radio and searched until she was on the local station. The hair started to stand up on the back of her neck.

The Morning Rundown radio show with hosts Micah and Calhoun should have been rolling through the usual spiel with prank calls, talk of viral videos, relationship blunders and fart jokes. Instead, Micah's high-pitched, nasal voice was strained.

"...avoid County Road 11. Take Jackson Road to the highway to get to Kilwin or reroute through Rockport Landing. Again, if you plan on using County Road 11, detour instead. The road has been shut down due to what appears to be a large motor vehicle fire. Authorities are currently blocking the road and trying to get a handle on the situation. Do not take County Road 11."

Calhoun, his cohost, spoke in a more reserved fashion than her normal radio persona. A car fire didn't seem to warrant the change.

"For those of you who have called in about it, thank you. We'll be back after this commercial break."

Madi tilted her head to the side a fraction, confused.

"Surely that's not where Caleb and Miller are going," she said. "County Road 11 is on the opposite side of town from us. The department is closer than we are. Plus, Kilwin's volunteer fire station would be, too."

"Maybe they went out on another call," Julian pointed out. "Or maybe the deputies at the fire needed more help?"

Madi didn't hear any conviction in his voice.

"Maybe." She didn't hear any conviction in hers, either.

When they got to the sheriff's department, that niggling feeling of dread was confirmed. It was not as simple as not enough hands on deck or another call that needed their response.

Desmond met them at the front stairs. He was in one of his best suits, his black Stetson on and his cell phone in his hand. He was also rattled. It was a look that set Madi's already-fraying nerves to ribbons. When he set eyes on Madi, the concern was palpable.

"Where were you just now?" he asked without segue.

Madi was taken aback by his demanding tone.

"I—I was at the ranch. Talking to Christian Miller. Why?"

Des sagged in relief. Which was telling in itself. He disliked Miller just as she did. The detective's reappearance in their lives should have had more of an impact.

"Thank goodness," he said. "I didn't think you did it but was afraid you wouldn't have an alibi this time."

"Come again?" she asked just as Julian repeated, "This time?"

Des motioned them to follow him.

"I want to make sure as many people see you as possible, just in case. Declan said for us to meet in the conference room for the interviews but let's go ahead and get in there now. Then I'll explain."

Their mother pulled up and with her they followed him inside the faded and chipped brick building with a collective and mounting worry. Declan was the sheriff; Caleb was a long-standing detective. Desmond might not have been law enforcement but his work and charm had made connections with almost everyone in town. Madi knew the faces that turned toward them as they passed. She'd been to their weddings, given their kids birthday presents, talked to them in the aisles at the grocery store, knew their embarrassing stories from adolescence and could give at least one fun fact about each. She knew the department and the people who worked inside its walls.

Yet as several pairs of eyes set on her, Madi had no idea what her friends were thinking.

What had happened?

The conference room was right off the bull pen, visible through the glass windows that lined the shared wall. Des didn't close the blinds over them but he did turn his face away.

"What's going on, Des?" their mother asked, hands wrapped around her cell phone like it was a lifeline. Madi fought the urge to wrap her own hand around Julian's.

"Does it have to do with the car fire out on County Road 11?" Madi followed up.

Des nodded.

"Yes and no. It wasn't just a car fire." He placed his hat on the table in the center of the room. Madi sank into one of the chairs. Everyone else remained standing. "Carl Smith, the county coroner, was transporting Loraine's body to Kilwin this morning. Lee Holloway, the junior detective working at the police department, was accompanying him. He made a distress call yelling that someone was trying to run them off the road." Des paused and looked back at Madi. "He said it was a blonde woman."

Madi felt her eyes widen.

"But there are more blonde women in this world than Madi," Julian said. "They can't think it was her anyway.

I'm assuming this all happened while Detective Miller had an eye on us."

"Which is the only good news about this whole situation," Des continued. "Miller may hate us, but that hate can't put Madi in two places at once."

"What happened to Carl and the detective?" their mother asked. "Are they okay?"

Des's face became even more grim.

"The van was engulfed last I heard…and there was a body inside. Not just Loraine's. That's all I overheard in here before someone said you all had pulled up."

Madi shook her head.

"I don't understand what's going on. We went from normal to crazy in less than a day!"

Julian agreed with the sentiment.

"Whatever is happening, it's nothing good."

"Oh God, I can't believe you shot me!"

The man wrapped the strip of his shirt he'd torn off around the bullet hole in his hand. He'd already gotten sick just looking at it, never mind the pain. The man who had taken the shot was glaring at him above his duct tape gag. His look promised more than pain if he ever got loose from the cuffs around his wrists. Or the binding around him.

He wouldn't.

And if he did? Well, where would he go?

"Make sure you wrap it up tight."

The sweet voice often caught him off guard. It preceded a woman he believed was made from fire and steel. Looks were definitely deceiving with her.

But again, that was the point.

"Do you think they bought it?" he asked, trying to knot the cloth tighter.

The woman laughed. It was dark and calculated. How he loved the sound.

"They better have. I don't want to stick my neck out anymore. This was the last big splash." The smile crept across her lips, resembling a lioness preparing to go on a hunt. Despite the pain he was in, it rallied him. "But if they still don't think Little Miss Perfect is capable of such horrors, then we'll just have to convince them. Until then—"

She picked the gun up and walked over to their captive. He lashed against the ropes around him. There wasn't anything he could really do beyond that.

"Have you heard the phrase 'an eye for an eye'?" she asked. She walked her index and middle fingers down his chest. The duct tape muffled his anger. "It's a really big thing for me, an eye for an eye. It's a principle I learned at an early age. One I truly believe in. One that applies to everyone." She stood back to full height, moved around his back and pressed the gun against the palm of his hand. He thrashed around again. It did nothing but make her smile grow. "No matter if they're a young man wearing a badge or a pregnant innkeeper."

She pulled the trigger.

Not even the duct tape could muffle the man's scream.

Chapter Seven

Julian hung by the conference room door. His legs were stiff from standing in one spot but he wasn't going to sit. The closest available chairs were in the lobby. That was too far away.

He wasn't going to leave Madi. Even now with the door shut between them, Julian couldn't help but feel uneasy. He wasn't going to lengthen that distance.

"She's a tough one, you know." Dorothy Nash walked up with a small smile. She motioned to the door. "Madeline may look fragile on occasion but I tell you what, sometimes she gives all of my boys a run for their money."

Julian hadn't had time for a one on one with any of the Nashes, Madi included, since they'd made their way into the department. He knew it was only a matter of time before the pregnancy was brought up. Along with why he hadn't been around through it. Still, he wasn't going to be the one who dived into that topic first. Not with everything going on.

"That I don't doubt," he said.

Dorothy took the spot next to him, lining up her shoes inside the large square tile. After her statement and interview with another Kilwin PD detective named Devereux, she had moved to the sheriff's personal office for privacy. Declan was at the scene with most of the department, but those left behind hadn't made one peep of protest as she'd gone in and shut the door behind her. It was clear that, despite everything that had happened in the last twenty-four hours, it took more to lessen the respect for the Nash matriarch.

She crossed her arms over her chest and let out a long breath. They had been at the Wildman County Sheriff's Department for several hours. Two of those had been spent waiting, wondering what was going on. Then Detective Devereux had shown up. Julian had read the tension in the man well before he spoke. Worry had folded a line into his forehead; his eyes had jumped around as he took them all in, unable to settle.

"Detective Holloway appears to have been taken by force by whoever attacked the coroner's van," he had said, barely able to hide the anger and concern there. "Our only suspect is a blonde woman." He had focused on Madi, and Julian felt relief when there didn't seem to be any malice toward her. "Detective Miller puts all of you within eye-sight before and during the incident." He'd pulled out a small spiral notebook. "Does anyone have any information they'd like to share before individual interviews?"

The room had quieted as Julian, Madi, Dorothy and Desmond had shaken their heads. No one knew what was going on, local or not.

Past that, their interviews had started with Dorothy before ending with Madi, who was still inside now. Julian was glad Detective Miller wasn't around. His questions might have delved further into their lie. As far as Julian could read through Detective Devereux's body language, the investigator believed what he had to say.

Julian hoped the same went for Madi.

"Madi said you were here before?" Dorothy's words were low but pointed. "I mean here in Overlook?"

"Yes ma'am, but then I had to leave." His answer was curt, but he didn't know the extent of what Dorothy was privy to when it came to Madi and the pregnancy. A thought that made his skin crawl. Everyone here had known about her pregnancy while he had been clueless. What if he had decided to keep driving instead of taking his detour?

Would Madi have been sent to prison?

Would he have ever had a chance to meet his daughter?

These questions had been springing up too often in the last few hours. He was going to talk to Madi at length about everything when things died down. That was for sure. Until then he wanted to keep all of his cards close to his chest.

"You had to go back home?"

Julian shook his head. So Dorothy didn't know about him being in the military. Which meant Madi hadn't told her mother about him.

Or the fact that she'd been the one to end things between them. No matter how short their time together had been.

"I had to get things squared away for a job after my next deployment ended, which it just did."

Dorothy's eyes widened in surprise at the information. She didn't voice it. Instead she let out another sigh.

"Well, I suppose we're all lucky for your sense of timing," she said. "Madi and the baby don't need this stress. No one does."

Her expression darkened and the conversation stalled out. Julian was good at silences, so he lounged in theirs until, finally, the door behind them opened. Detective Devereux with his flame-red hair came into view, looking more world-weary than he had when he'd first walked into the department.

He wasn't a local in Overlook but he knew to address

Dorothy with respect. Another deviation from what might have been had Miller grilling them.

"For now you all are free to go, but I'd appreciate it if no one left town and you all kept your phones on you just in case we need to get ahold of you." He moved out of the doorway so Madi could make her way out, too. She smiled but it was tight—channeling her customer service skills, Julian had no doubt. Devereux didn't care one way or the other. His gaze swept the room behind them. He found no relief in what he saw. "You can return back to your home," he said to Madi. "We have everything we needed from the crime scene." Then he was charging across the room, phone up to his ear.

Julian felt for the man. He was worried about the missing detective—his colleague, most likely his friend. He also knew the overwhelming worry of leaving a man behind. How it could drive someone to great lengths to get him back.

Which was why Julian directed Madi and her mother out of the department and to their vehicles as fast as he could. It was easy to see the department and Kilwin PD were looking for someone to blame. He didn't want that urgency to make them point fingers at someone they shouldn't.

Still, both women hesitated in the parking lot. Madi cut her glance between Julian and her mother.

"How you doing, Ma?"

Dorothy surprised him by cracking a smile.

"Oh, you know me. Focusing on one thing I can do and not all the things I can't."

Madi rubbed her hand across the older woman's back. Julian had noticed the tension between them earlier and hadn't been surprised it was there. Dorothy had been a sore topic when he was at Hidden Hills all those months ago. Yet for that one moment, he saw nothing but love between the two.

"Dad might have talked a lot, but that was my favorite piece of advice." She turned her smile to Julian. "There's never enough time to do everything, so focus on the one thing you can."

He nodded. "Definitely good advice."

Madi dropped her hand, along with her smile. She glanced at the department behind them.

"I need to go back to the inn and see how everything looks," she said, voice hard. Resolute. "If it's all good then I'll call Ray and, if he's willing, tell him to come back to his cabin."

A look Julian couldn't place flashed across Dorothy's face but she nodded.

"Let me know what he says. I can help."

They hugged and Dorothy said goodbye. She hung back where only Julian could hear her. Her words held more of a wallop than he cared to admit.

"You make sure nothing happens to my baby, Mr. Mercer. Yours, too."

MADI FELT DISMAL. Take away the stress and confusion of what had happened to Loraine and the missing detective, and take away the mountain of handsome that was the man driving her home, and there was still a fact that blared like an unending alarm. She was almost seven months pregnant.

Her ankles were swollen. She was hot and hungry. Halfway through the questioning she'd caught a whiff of Julian's cologne and spent the next half hour trying to not be as turned on as she was. But, as she'd been learning the last few months, being pregnant was a wild, unpredictable ride. It was marked with things such as hormones running rampant, love that knew no bounds and stretch marks. My goodness, the stretch marks.

Now as they stood in the doorway of her bedroom at Hidden Hills, Madi waited for her hormones to knock her down. To pull out tears that would rival the creek flowing through her property. Yet nothing came.

"She was in your bedroom?" Julian asked, moving past her to the coffee table in the living space. It was cleaned off.

"Yeah, on the bed."

Madi cringed as the image of the body thrown across the foot of the bed flashed through her mind. She moved back to the hallway like she could escape it and what had happened. Julian went in the opposite direction. He stepped into the bedroom and cracked the door behind him. Madi didn't try to see around it.

After a minute or two he came out, done with his inspection.

"Uh, how attached are you to your mattress?"

Madi cringed.

"I didn't even think about it with everything going on. Is it that bad?"

"Let's just say that I'd feel more comfortable getting that thing out of there while you're somewhere else." He shook his head. "It's not pretty."

Madi sighed.

"I don't think I could sleep on it again, anyways." Anger surged from the tips of her toes out to the roots of her hair. It was so sudden and violent that she took a step farther back into the hallway, as if her body were trying to keep Julian from seeing that side of her before her brain had the chance to stop the words that poured from her mouth. "Whoever killed Loraine did it somewhere else and then brought her here! To my home, into *my bed*, and for what?

To make it look like I killed her? Why? Why do this?" That anger burned holes in her calm. Tears leaked through. She balled her hands. "I didn't like Loraine but I didn't want *that*. Why would someone do this?"

Julian walked over to her slowly. Each step was calculated. Every movement controlled. It only made Madi feel even worse. She was the one who needed to get back some control.

"We'll figure this out," he said. "But first, let's tackle what we can." He tried on a grin. It was weirdly reassuring. "I'm sure I'm not the only one who needs to eat something. Come with me to the kitchen?"

Julian held out his elbow. Madi wiped at her tears, then took it. His skin was warm against hers. A Band-Aid to hold closed the wound. His presence was something Madi had longed for ever since he left. Even before she'd found out she was pregnant.

There was something about the man that calmed her. Yet at the same time, excited her beyond reason.

Why had she turned him away?

Madi felt the heat of shame slither up her neck.

She knew why.

It was the same reason she'd never had a long-term relationship in her thirty years of life. The same reason her friendships were limited to Jenna and few others. The same reason she wanted to deal in a profession that brought in strangers who *left* as strangers.

The same reason she was terrified of being a mother.

Madi hadn't just been hurt as a child, she'd been broken. Some of those pieces that had been shattered would never be put back together again. She didn't want them to be.

You can't do everything, so just focus on the one thing you can.

Michael Nash had said that countless times but it was

only now, walking arm in arm with the father of her child, through the inn that was her home, that Madi finally realized she'd taken the advice further than she'd realized.

Instead of moving on from her fear, she'd just removed herself from the world as best she could.

Yet somehow, fear had found her again.

This time, it brought death, too.

Chapter Eight

Nathan Wilson was staying in a hotel in Kilwin. Ray had opted to stay at the Wild Iris Retreat on the ranch until the next day. Jenna had also had a long night before and would wait until further notice to come in. As for the Nash brothers? Julian didn't know yet.

Which left him sitting across from Madi, eating peanut butter and jelly sandwiches in silence.

She had her feet up on a chair in the eat-in part of the kitchen, gaze firmly out the window. It looked into the backyard, but in the waning light after dusk, the view was slowly being snuffed out. The change sent shadows that dulled the strands of gold splayed out across her back. For once they weren't braided. Another change in a long list of differences between this visit and his last.

Julian prided himself on noticing details. The little things. The small movements. The subtle shifts. It had been his bread and butter in his military career, helping him better the world by understanding it just a bit more than most.

Right now that skill was telling him three things, just as it had the first time he'd seen Madi months ago.

One, Madi was uncomfortable and not just in the emotional sense. Every few minutes she would readjust. The briefest flash of annoyance would move across her expression. She'd stroke her stomach and then settle again. Only to do it all over again. Julian couldn't deny every time it happened his concern went from normal to all-out alert. He came from a small family. Loving parents and a sister, Bethany, only one year younger than him. He'd never had the chance to be around someone pregnant before. Certainly not six months along and wrapped up in a murder investigation. He didn't know what was normal in either situation, never mind combined.

Two, something had changed between their walk from Madi's room to the kitchen. Julian had felt it through their touch and then seen it in her face. Or, really, hadn't seen it. Madi had gone from a rush of emotions to closed off. First she'd been angry at the senseless act of violence, then she had cried. Even now Julian could feel the need to comfort her pulsing through him. The tears that had traveled down her beautiful tanned skin had only reminded him that as much as he wanted to, he couldn't protect her from everything. That included whatever had prompted her to surround herself with the invisible walls that were keeping him out. Julian couldn't blame her for her caution, but that didn't mean he had to like the idea that she had retreated away from him. Again.

And the third thing he knew without a doubt was that, despite the time that had passed since they'd seen each other, he still found her impossibly beautiful. Exhaustion? Stress? Worry? They might have changed the way she was holding herself but they hadn't changed the way Julian marveled at her. There was an effortless way about her beauty. It drew him in months ago, just as it beckoned to him now. Julian wanted to reach across the small table and tuck a strand of her hair behind her ear. To look into those sky blue eyes before pressing his lips to hers. Before he could police those thoughts, parts of him started to wake up in excitement. Memories of doing that, and more, started to flood back in.

It wasn't like the first day he'd met her all over again, wondering what she felt like. Tasted like.

Those were questions that had turned into memories and he'd be lying if he said he didn't want to revisit those moments.

Even after the fact that she had kept something from him. Rather, someone. A daughter.

Which would make him a father.

Julian prided himself on understanding and recognizing the small things in life. The details that made up every day. Yet, when he thought about his future before he'd met Madi? Before he'd found out he was going to be a father?

Well, he'd imagined thousands of little details that his future might be made up of and having a daughter hadn't been one of those details. At least, not like this.

He wanted the job with Chance to be the start of growing roots, of staying still. Eventually he knew that would turn into his own family. A wife. Children.

But now the details he'd imagined of his future were different. Not only had he found Madi after months of being apart, he'd found more questions than answers surrounding her.

Did she expect him to leave again?

Did she want him to?

Did she regret that he was the father?

Sitting across from the golden-haired innkeeper as she stroked her pregnant stomach, Julian found that despite the questions he had there was one answer that was clear.

He would love and protect his daughter for the rest of his life.

No matter what.

The realization rocked through him in such a profound way he nearly said it out loud.

Madi, unaware of his influx of paternal love, shifted in her chair again. She winced, took the last bite of her sandwich, and then stroked her stomach again. This time she kept her hand resting there.

Julian also realized he wasn't the only one trying to protect someone.

He opened his mouth to speak, but Madi beat him to it.

"I don't share this story a lot, or really at all, but everyone in town knows it." Her gaze swung to his. "It's only fair I catch you up."

Madi let out an unmistakably defeated breath.

"Okay," he said. "I'm listening."

For a moment Julian didn't think she'd continue, but then she looked out of the window again and did just that.

"When Desmond, Caleb and I were eight we sneaked out to a local park. We were bored and you know how mob mentality works? Well, that was us when we were together. Triplet terrors." She smiled. It was brief. "The park was really just trails in the woods with a picnic area thrown in the middle. Nothing too fancy but, for us, it was a fun place to play. That day, we decided to play hide-and-seek. Des and I went to go hide while Caleb counted… For the life of me, to this day, I can't remember what I first thought when I saw the man. I just remember screaming."

Julian's hands fisted beneath the table. It was hard to hold his anger in. It wouldn't help eight-year-old Madi or her siblings now.

"He grabbed me before I could run. When Des and Caleb showed up he had a gun on me and told us that we were coming with him. All three of us." She shook her head. "My dad was a detective at the sheriff's department, before that a deputy for years, just like his dad. He'd made sure that all of us knew that there were bad people in the world and if those bad people ever tried to take any of us anywhere to fight like hell."

"Chances of survival go down tremendously once a person gets into a car while being kidnapped," he stated, already knowing the statistic. Madi nodded.

"As soon as he said the words, that was all I could hear," she continued. "Dad just telling us over and over again to fight. To escape. To not be taken even if there was a risk we'd get hurt. So I did what I could." She fisted her hand but didn't mimic any movement. "Caleb called it a throat punch but I just hit the first thing I could with how he held me. I didn't even realize it was his throat until he let me go. But it wasn't enough." Madi turned her head. She ran a finger across the scar on her cheekbone. "He pistol-whipped me. And that's all she wrote on my end. It knocked me out cold and left a constant reminder."

Julian swore. There was no way he could hide his disgust for a man who would hit a child. Madi waited until he was done to continue. She didn't turn toward the window again but her eyes were averted. Julian recognized the past glazing over them as she replayed what had happened for him.

"Apparently this incensed the boys. The man shot at them to keep them away as he tried to get his bearings back. A bullet grazed Caleb's arm pretty deep, blood went everywhere, or so I'm told. That only revved Desmond up even more. He managed to jump on the man. That didn't work out, either. He was thrown to the ground, where the man then stomped on Des's leg and broke it. And just like that, he was three for three. He took me to the car and the boys followed, Caleb dragging Des along, both bloody and broken. They didn't want to leave me." Madi paused, collecting herself. Julian realized his adrenaline was surging, building along with his rage at their attacker. She cleared her throat after a moment and finished the story. "He used the threat of hurting me to get the boys to comply with being blindfolded and to behave as he took us to a cabin out in the woods near the town limits. He locked us in the basement apartment. Three beds, a bathroom and no earthly idea as to the why of it all. He held us for three days."

Julian shook his head.

"Who the hell would do that?" He seethed. "You were children."

Madi let out a long breath.

"The man only ever spoke to us to threaten us to behave. He'd bring us food, tell us he'd hurt Desmond even more if we tried to escape, and then would leave. So we listened… Until we didn't."

Julian had thought the end of the story was nearing before but now he could read the ramp up to the climax in Madi's expression. Memories bled through people's guarded walls sometimes, even if they didn't want them to. Madi couldn't hide the anger, anguish and defiance that flashed across her face in quick succession as she spoke again.

"Des was in so much pain, even before we got into that basement. The man knew it and so we used that against him. Caleb and I yelled that Des had stopped breathing while Des tried his best to pretend. I can still remember how hard I cried, yelling out for him. Caleb at my side doing the same. One minute we were trying to fool the man, in the next I believed our lie. It helped us sell it. The second the man bent over Des to check on him, Caleb and I attacked. Then Des joined in. We worked like a unit, one mind between three little bodies, but it worked." She let out another, smaller breath. Relief, even though it was an old one, flitted over her causing some of the tension she'd been holding in her body to visibly lessen. In turn Julian felt himself calm down a little.

"We managed to lock him in the same place he'd locked us up before escaping into the woods," she continued. "A Good Samaritan found us and took us to the department."

"And the man?"

"Gone by the time Caleb led them back to the cabin. No clues. No leads to follow. My father tried his hardest to find him, even sacrificing his health through the years to do so. He passed away without uncovering anything."

"But he thought Detective Miller was involved?"

Julian had already disliked the man. That had only intensified hundredfold. Madi nodded.

"I never knew all the details," she said with regret. "Dad tried his hardest to keep us out of it, but whatever he found made him look at Miller. Eventually he stopped the accusations but you could tell he was still bothered by it." She took another deep breath. Her baby blues met his stare. "Which is the point of this story. The Nash triplet abduction is one of the most famous cases in Overlook history. The story of what happened has changed hands so many times that I've even been told about it with a few details completely wrong. It's like an urban legend here now… but before it evolved, it was a real, living and breathing mystery that ate at the town. When my dad started investigating Miller, it didn't matter that Dad didn't have evidence—it ate Miller up, too. His marriage ended, he left the department, left town and was only hired at the Kilwin Police Department after Dad passed. Whether or not he had anything to do with what happened—it didn't matter. The damage was more than done."

Her expression softened.

"Which is why I have to warn you about being with me.

Being around me," she amended. "Our last name carries a lot of weight in this town, most of it good, but when it comes to Christian Miller? I'm sure he already has a cell with my name on it that he'll do anything to fill. I don't want you to get caught in his cross fire."

Relief, more powerful this time, seemed to deflate her rigidness. That was it. That was the end of her speech. There was still tension there but Madi appeared to have said her piece.

Julian understood why the woman had walls now…and she was giving him an out while she stayed behind them. Pain, trauma. They changed everything. A stone in the water with ripples moving out and touching every part of your life, even those around you.

Julian had seen pain. He understood trauma. He could empathize with how both affected a person and why Madi might need those invisible walls more than he needed to knock them down.

What he didn't understand was why Madi hadn't discussed her swollen belly or his daughter now or at any time in the last several months. A child was a game changer. One that didn't just affect Madi.

A daughter. His daughter.

With a start, sitting there in the kitchen, darkness creeping through the windows splaying shadows across the face of a beautiful woman, Julian realized he felt those words again. The meaning.

Pure, unyielding love slammed into Julian's chest like a Mack truck. No matter what happened between him and Madi, he knew, without a doubt, that he would be there for his child.

Sitting to his full height, he made sure to keep Madi's eye as he asked the question he'd been waiting to ask.

"Were you ever going to tell me about our daughter?"

To her credit, Madi didn't skip a beat. Her jaw hardened.

"I tried," she said, words clipped.

They also hit hard.

"You tried? How—" Julian cut himself off by swearing. One moment he was feeling a love unlike any he'd ever felt before, the next it was loathing. "I had to get a new number when I switched phones right before deployment. Which means the number I gave you was useless," She nodded. It was also a clipped movement. "And I didn't give you the new number," he finished.

She nodded again.

He felt like an idiot.

"It was hectic right before I left," he continued, knowing it was a lame excuse. He reached out for her hand just as she backed her chair up and stood. Still he finished the thought. "I should have called. I'm sorry."

Madi shook her head. Her expression had gone impassive again. The walls were up and reinforced.

"Why would you call me with a new number?" she asked, though it was rhetorical. "I'm the one who said we should go our separate ways. It's fine, really. I'm fine. This—" she motioned to her stomach "—was a surprise. One we're going to have to talk about at length, but… well…can that talk be tomorrow?" She smiled. It didn't reach her eyes. "If we don't get this inn under control, how am I supposed to get anything else under control?"

Before Julian could respond, her demeanor shifted.

"I mean, unless you want out of all of this? I know it's a lot of madness."

It was Julian's turn to stand. He made sure to keep eye contact this time, too.

"We can talk tomorrow," he said. "I'm not going anywhere."

Chapter Nine

The air had been cleared between Madi and Julian, at least somewhat. They were going to talk about the future in the future, and until then he was staying. Madi tried to keep the flutter of excitement in her stomach under control but the feeling lasted right up to Loraine and Nathan's room.

Julian whistled.

"It looks like a tornado tore through here."

Madi had to agree.

The guest suite was smaller than her personal one and, as a result, had only the necessary pieces of furniture. Those very same pieces had been either moved, flipped or otherwise disrupted. The desk chair was on its side, the dresser had a few of its drawers on the ground, the mattress had been mostly pulled off the bed and several towels had been thrown around the room.

"Looks like Nathan took some of his anger out in here," Julian said, not moving from the doorway.

Madi sighed.

"In his defense, he thinks I killed his wife." She went to the closest towel and tried to pick it up. It was like navigating around a yoga ball. A warm hand went to the small of her back right before Julian bent down and grabbed it instead. The contact was surprising. It made quelling the flutter in her chest even harder.

"I feel for him, I really do, but I'm glad he's staying somewhere else tonight." He went to the next towel and picked it up. "I don't want his misplaced aggression falling on you or this place. He needs to focus on figuring out who really killed her and why."

Madi's heart ached for the man. Loraine might have been a pill but Nathan had been nothing but kind and respectful to her. If not always on a business call.

"What I don't get is why she was killed in the first place," she said. "Here, I mean. It couldn't have been random. Someone brought her into the inn and into my room. Why? Was it a crime of opportunity and they brought her here because they panicked? Or did they follow her to Overlook and then do it when the time presented itself?" Madi felt like her head was going to explode with questions. "And what about the blonde woman who attacked the coroner's van? I'm not a detective but that's oddly coincidental since it had Loraine's body in it."

Julian moved around the room, picking up the rest of the towels. His lips were downturned in thought.

"And don't forget the cell phone bit."

"The cell phone bit?" she repeated.

"Your phone had a call to Loraine's phone logged in it. Plus Loraine's phone was placed on your table. And so was your father's shotgun, the supposed murder weapon."

Madi groaned. She pulled a section of her hair over her shoulder. Her fingers nimbly began to braid.

"Do you know how hard it is to keep all of this straight? Especially while you're nearing your third trimester?" she asked, voice raising. "One second everything is fine and the next I need a flowchart just to keep my sanity! Do you know the other day I had to make myself three cups of tea? Three! I kept forgetting where I put them or that I already had one cup in the other room. Finally I just gave up on trying to drink a whole one." She finished the braid and threw her hands wide. "Now I feel like I've been dropped into a really awful *Twilight Zone* episode where we find out at the very end that I did do it somehow!"

Julian closed the space between them, towels in his arms.

"I'm not almost seven months pregnant and I wouldn't mind a whiteboard to track all of this," he stated matter-of-factly. "This is a bizarre situation but one that, I'm sure, will make sense soon. Until then we can check off one fact we do know."

"What? That even though I just peed, I have to go again because this kid thinks my bladder is a trampoline?"

Julian snorted, then he was smirking.

"I was going to say that you didn't kill Loraine Wilson. But if it makes you feel better we can add 'baby uses bladder as a trampoline' to the list."

It shouldn't have helped her feel better but Madi couldn't deny that his words did the trick. If only enough to focus on the task at hand. Wordlessly the two moved around the room, straightening up. Julian took on the big-ticket items while Madi tackled the easier pieces. She'd already had a long talk with Desmond and the lawyer he hired about Hidden Hills. To play it safe she'd had to agree to shut the place down until the investigation was over. Not that she'd been thrown by that exactly, but it still had stung.

Hidden Hills wasn't just how she paid the bills, it was a purpose that focused her. That distracted her from the fears of being a mother and the loneliness that sometimes rocked through her.

Shutting down the inn, even temporarily, hurt. Plain and simple.

A heavy knock sounded on the front door as they finished up in the guest suite. The dull sound traveled up the stairs and right along Madi's spine. She shared a glance with Julian. He'd gone tense.

"Were you expecting anyone?"

"No, but I wouldn't be surprised if it were Miller. He didn't get a chance to grill us earlier."

Julian led the way down, careful to stay in front of her. That didn't change when he got to the door. Luckily, the face they saw on the other side was familiar.

"It's Des."

Julian opened the door and was met with a hardy handshake. Then Des was hugging her. It surprised Madi. While he could be an affectionate person, it was on occasion and usually not in front of strangers. Something must have happened. Her concern must have shown. When he pulled away, he sighed.

"Don't look at me like that. It's just been a long damn day."

Madi cut him some slack. She didn't push.

They went back into the kitchen while she made Des a sandwich. Or started to. There was no way to hide how tired she was and no way to avoid the obvious—she needed to rest. So when Julian took over the food preparations she caved.

"I'm going to go shower in the empty guest suite and, to be honest, probably lie down and watch some TV. My feet are killing me, my ankles are killing me and I'd really like to forget everything awful that has happened if only for a little while." She turned to Julian. "You have full rein of the inn." Then to Des, she added, "Let me know if anything happens, okay?"

They both nodded and went back to their conversation. They had switched to Julian's military experience. It was a subject she'd like to learn more about but just didn't have the stamina for currently. She wobbled out of the kitchen.

Because that was how tired she was. Usually she could walk like a normal human being. Right now?

Penguin.

Through and through.

Just as she imagined herself waddling across the North Pole, Madi wondered how Julian saw her. And not just physically.

That flutter that had finally landed earlier took flight again.

A normal woman would have her mind on more pressing issues and yet…

Julian was there.

In her thoughts, swooping in without any rhyme or reason.

She might not be a normal woman, but it certainly didn't help that Julian wasn't your average man.

BLOOD SWIRLED AROUND the drain. It was an unsettling contrast against the clean white tile of the shower. Julian watched it for a while. The cut along his thigh looked back at him, angry. The edge of Madi's bed had been even angrier.

Julian was used to physical exertion but he'd never encountered such an infuriating bed in his life. He and Des had hit their legs against the frame several times before they'd even managed to wrestle the mattress off. Julian had seen Madi's legs before. They weren't covered in bruises and cuts, which only meant the innkeeper had some kind of secret for navigating the awkward piece of devil furniture.

But before he could complain too much about it, the dark stain had reminded him that there were much worse fates. They were quiet as they hauled the mattress out of the room and to the garage.

"I'd say we take it to the dump but it's pretty clear Detective Miller has an ax to grind," Julian had said after they pushed it up against one of the walls. "I don't want to give him any more ammo."

Des had nodded. Julian could see the same anger in his eyes that had been in Madi's.

"You're right about that," he had said, curt. Julian was about to get back to clearing out Madi's room but Des had more to say. Like his sister, Des's expression had become impassive, guarded. "I don't think Madi understands how…bad this situation is. I don't blame her for that. I know she's trying to keep it all together, trying to keep her stress levels down for the baby, but I don't think she's really thought about how it all looks."

"She didn't do it," Julian had to reiterate.

"But someone sure went through the trouble to make it look like she did, didn't they?" It had been a constant thought in the back of Julian's head. He nodded. "If you hadn't provided an alibi, things would have been astronomically worse. And if Miller hadn't been around when the unknown blonde woman was attacking the coroner's van?" Des had lowered his voice. "A murderer is out there and somehow they're involving Madi in their sick games. We have to keep her safe, Julian."

Julian hadn't even hesitated.

"We will."

It wasn't until just after nine that Des agreed to go home. Julian had gotten a little sleep that morning but he was pretty sure Des hadn't had a wink since Loraine had been found. He'd given Julian his number, told him to protect his sister again and driven off, leaving Julian to lock up. He had gone over every inch of the house—every door, every window—before finally going to the guest suite Madi was using.

There he'd found her, curled up on her side on the bed

and fast asleep. Julian almost hated to turn the shower on in the next room. Then again, he was drenched in sweat and a bit of blood. Neither of which he thought she would appreciate. He was determined not to leave her side until the real killer was caught. He'd even left the door open to the bathroom, just enough to see Madi's sleeping face. It was comforting. More than it should have been.

He had realized that *complicated* didn't begin to explain his feelings for the woman. She had ended things before they had ever gotten started. She hadn't wanted to continue to see him. And now that she was pregnant with his child? From the vibes he was getting, that hadn't changed her mind.

So what would they be?

Ex-lovers with a baby?

Friends?

Where did that leave his new life? Would Madi move to his new job or would he move to Overlook? Would they co-parent from different states?

It all left a sour taste in his mouth.

Julian finished the shower after a few more passes over his cut, and dried off. He knotted the towel around his waist and wiped the condensation off the mirror.

One thing at a time, he thought.

He nodded to himself, rolled his shoulders back and looked into the mirror, fully expecting to see nothing but his tired eyes and stubble that needed to be shaved.

Instead what he saw made his blood run cold.

It was Madi. She was no longer in bed but standing beside it, facing the bedroom's main door. Both hands were clutched around her stomach. Even in profile Julian could see the sheer terror on her face.

Then she spoke.

It wasn't to him.

"Who are you?"

Chapter Ten

"You're going to tell me the truth or else," a man threatened. His voice was deep and raspy. Either from age or a hard-lived life. Julian couldn't get a visual on the man from his vantage point. All he could see was Madi slowly backing up.

"What truth?" Her words were hard but Julian could hear the undercurrent of fear.

He needed to take out the threat. He also needed to know if that threat had a gun pointed. Julian didn't want to rush out there only to have the unknown man fire off a few shots. There was a chance that he wouldn't be able to shield Madi in time. Or their unborn child.

Some risks were worth taking; that wasn't one of them.

"Loraine Wilson." His accent was odd. Off. If he was from the South, he was purposely hiding his drawl.

Julian quickly looked around the bathroom. He knew what it held—nothing that was equal to a gun. Julian grabbed his phone and fisted his hand. He'd just have to do it the old-fashioned way. Madi shook her head but stopped walking backward. To her absolute credit she kept her eyes everywhere but where he was.

"I didn't kill her," she said. "I don't know who did."

The man laughed.

It shot adrenaline through Julian's veins.

"Listen, if you want to make this hard from the start, I'm not one to argue, lady. Honestly? I like it when my prey has a little fight in them."

Julian flung the bathroom door open and threw his cell phone like a pro pitcher in dire need of a strikeout. The man, much too close to Madi, had not suspected anyone else was around. The surprise showed clear in his eyes right before the smartphone slammed into the side of his face. Something cracked. Julian didn't have time to figure out if it was his phone or the man's face. His focus had switched to the knife in the man's grip.

Rage pulsed through Julian.

Guns were easy. Knives took work. Knives combined with trying to get information? That ran right to torture.

Whoever he was, he would never be the same when Julian was through with him.

"Who the hell—" the man yelled, cradling his face with one hand and trying to get his balance with the other.

Julian wasn't about to answer any questions. He used his considerable height to his advantage. With two powerful strides forward, he closed the distance between them and threw his foot out in a high kick. The man hadn't expected that, either. The kick landed square against his gut. He gasped and doubled over. It was a miracle that the man was able to put his knee down to retain some balance.

It was also a miracle Julian's towel stayed on.

The man wheezed, trying to get his breath back. It was too much of a break in Julian's opinion. He pulled back his fist, ready to deliver what he hoped would be a knockout blow when the tables were horribly turned.

What Julian had in height, muscle and power, the man had in speed. He maneuvered the knife around so quickly that all Julian could do was stumble back. Madi's scream heralded a hot, searing pain across his left side. He didn't have time to assess the damage. The man changed his momentum until it was on a backward arc headed for Julian's right side.

This time Julian was prepared.

He caught the man's wrist as the cool blade of the knife bit into his skin. It drew blood but wasn't as deep as the other had been.

And Julian didn't intend to let it go any deeper.

With his left hand wrapped around the man's wrist, Julian brought his right fist low. It hit the man's ribs. Hard.

But this man must have seen his fair share of fights.

He was quick on the uptake again. With his free hand he delivered a quick jab to the first wound he'd inflicted.

Julian couldn't help the grunt of pain. Or the vulnerability it created. The men detangled from each other. Julian took a breath, knowing every second was precious in a fight meant to have only one ending, when the lighting in the room changed.

Darkness was followed by something weirdly shaped coming right at them. Julian backpedaled. His opponent did not. The bedside lamp hit his face so hard that Julian almost felt the pain.

The man didn't yell out. He didn't even groan.

He just dropped like a sack of potatoes.

Julian lunged for the knife as soon as the man's fingers went limp around it. It was covered in blood. *His* blood. Yet Julian didn't care. All his focus swept up to the pregnant woman breathing heavily at his side.

Madi's eyes were wide, her cheeks flushed.

"You hit him," Julian said, awe in his voice.

Madi looked between him and the man on the floor.

"I did."

"With a lamp."

She nodded.

"It was either that or a pillow, and I didn't think that would be as effective."

Despite himself, Julian chuckled. The movement hurt. He looked down at the first cut he'd been given. It was deep. Not life-threatening, but it would need stitches. He pressed his hand against it. Madi gasped.

"Oh, Julian, you're hurt!"

"I'm fine," he said, fending her off. He put the knife on the bed and backtracked to the bathroom, eyes never leaving the man on the floor. He swiped the fresh pair of boxers and jeans he'd laid out before his shower and stepped into them in record time. Blood ran down to stain them before he could cover his wound again. There was no time to worry about it. "Do you have something I can restrain him with?" he asked, coming back and kneeling down next to the unconscious man's side. "You got him good with the lamp but I don't want to take any chances."

Madi thought for a moment and then snapped her fingers.

"I have a pair of handcuffs in my room. They're pink and fluffy but they'll do the trick." That got Julian's attention. He quirked an eyebrow up. The color in her cheeks darkened. "They were a gag gift from one of my college girlfriends but they really do work."

She didn't say anything more and hurried out of the room. Julian leaned over the man and for the first time took a really good look at him.

He was clean-shaven, including the blond hair cut close to his scalp. Julian guessed he was around his age, maybe younger even. His relaxed face held a youthfulness, even if the rest of him looked on the worn side. Julian lifted up the bottom of his shirt, which had shifted open in the tussle. A tattoo of a scorpion was faded against his side. It looked familiar but Julian couldn't place it. Other than that there were no telling signs that pointed to who he was or why he was there.

Julian moved to the pockets of the man's slacks, marveling at how well dressed he was. It didn't fit with the way he had spoken. Or his knife. The man looked like he should be on Wall Street, not creeping around a bed-and-breakfast in Tennessee, threatening a pregnant innkeeper for information about a murder. Something was off. Something was *really* off.

There was nothing of importance in his right pocket. Lint and a stick of gum. No ID or cell phone. Julian moved to search the other.

That was when he heard it.

A creak. From the stairs. Short and whining but definitely there. Madi's room was down the hall, not on the first floor. There was no reason why she should have been there. Julian jumped up and hurried to the door. Adrenaline rushed back into his veins.

The second-floor landing was laid out with the stairs in the middle. A half wall surrounded them, keeping guests from falling on their way to the two guest suites. Julian was in the one closest to the opening of the stairs. Loraine and Nathan's room was to his right and behind the stairs. Madi's private quarters were in the corner, on the opposite side of him.

A more-than-troubling distance when that creak in the stairs turned into a mass of dark hair that in no way belonged to Madi. Julian silently cursed himself for leaving the knife on the bed but there was no time to retrieve it. Another stroke of bad luck in a long line of unfortunate events.

Madi walked out of her room holding fuzzy pink handcuffs, just as the new arrival made it out onto the landing. Like the unconscious man, this one also wore a nice shirt and slacks, as if he'd simply taken a wrong turn at a business convention and just so happened to find himself in a closed inn. Unlike the man Julian had fought before, this one didn't have a knife.

He had a gun.

SCREAMING WAS POINTLESS, and yet Madi did it anyway.

The man at the stairs didn't seem put off by the sound. In fact, he was smiling. Between that and the pistol in his hand, Madi felt like she had woken in a worse nightmare than before.

"Well, I can't say I've ever been greeted by *that* before." The man motioned to the handcuffs. "But I'm always up for new experiences."

Madi's blood ran cold. This time she couldn't play it cool. She couldn't keep eye contact, hoping to give Julian the element of surprise. This time she couldn't help but look for the dark-eyed man who had been her savior.

And there he was.

Standing in the doorway of the guest suite, staring right back at her.

"Madi, run!"

The man on the stairs followed her gaze just as Julian yelled. He cursed and turned his aim. Madi instantly thawed. A feeling of such possessive power overcame her, like it had with the lamp. With a wild war cry she threw the second thing that night.

The pink fuzzy handcuffs flew through the air. They hit the man's head, much like Julian's cell phone had. This one, however, was faster on the uptake. He managed to get a shot off before he stumbled.

Madi's heart almost stopped. Fear replaced any and all bravado she'd had. Julian had disappeared from view. Had he been hit?

"What the—"

The man moved around the half wall to get the same answer. Julian was polite enough to oblige.

He rammed into the intruder like a defensive back. The man shot again but the bullet whizzed over Julian and embedded itself into the doorjamb. This time Madi listened to Julian's original order.

She turned on her heel and retreated into her living space, holding her stomach as she went. She had been taught to stay and fight, but with her daughter along for the ride? Those stakes were too high.

Madi hurried around the room, searching it like she'd never once stepped foot inside. Adrenaline was making her movements jerky, her mind sluggish. She wanted to help but for the life of her couldn't think past the fuzzy pink handcuffs.

And she'd just thrown those.

A man groaned so loud Madi froze on spot. Another gunshot rang through her inn. Footsteps thundered across the hardwood. She clutched her stomach but it was Julian who ran into view.

"Bedroom," he yelled out, breathing labored.

Madi listened as Julian threw the door shut and locked it. He did the same in the bedroom the second he was through the door. Then he yanked over her dresser. It crashed to the floor and blocked most of the door.

"Any guns in here?" he asked, pulling her toward the window.

"No! The cops took my handgun!"

Julian cursed.

"We need to get out of here," he said, changing tactics. He nodded to the window. Madi understood. She just didn't like it. A crash vibrated through the floor. Madi unlocked the window and started to slide it up.

"There's nowhere to go, you hicks," the man yelled. The door handle shook. Then the door quaked. Next came a bullet. The mirror over the bed shattered but it did nothing to slow Julian's pace. He had Madi up and out of the window before half of the glass could even hit the floor. When he was at her side, he lowered his voice. It by no means undercut the severity of their situation. He grabbed her hand.

"I need you to guide us out of here, Madi."

They might have been standing on a roof at night, chased by a man with a gun, but feeling Julian's hand was like taking a deep, steadying breath.

She nodded.

"Let's go!"

Chapter Eleven

The roof was mostly flat outside Madi's bedroom and bathroom. It hung over the downstairs lounge before dropping off at the back patio. They could have run to the edge and jumped down right next to the back door but all she could think about was the drop. And how the gunman would have an easy sight line to their backs.

So she cut left and hurried along the second story until the flat roof ended and the one that pitched high over the kitchen rose above them.

"We could jump off here or climb over," Madi explained, already slightly out of breath. "There's another small overhang on the other side that has that big wooden trellis attached. I—I don't know if it can hold our weight, though. Just like I don't know if I can make the jump here."

The night sky was clear above them. It was the only reason the moon was giving off enough light that Madi could just make out Julian's expression. He was looking between her two options and, no doubt, playing through both scenarios in his head. Neither was ideal.

A gunshot tore through the quiet. Glass shattered. Madi squeezed Julian's hand like her life depended on it.

"Do you think you can climb this?"

"I've done it before, just not while I was pregnant," she admitted. "And not at night."

Clear as the day it wasn't. Julian's face hardened into worry. Their pursuer's voice, yelling something Madi couldn't make out, seemed to tip the scale of which option was more worth the risk. Julian let go of her hand and motioned to the field of shingles to their left.

"Ladies first."

Madi was proud of herself for several reasons as she placed her hands out and walk-climbed up the pitched roof. For one, after her shower she'd dressed in comfortable clothes instead of her pajamas, fully expecting to help the boys after she was rested. That meant she was rocking her most flexible pair of yoga pants and a loose blouse that didn't complain as she moved at the weird angle. She'd also fallen asleep with her tennis shoes on. Now they were a godsend, gripping the shingles with a proficiency her body naturally lacked thanks to the sheer awkwardness of almost being in her third trimester.

She was also pleased that despite the danger, her nerves had gone weirdly calm. She focused on her hand and foot placement. Focused on the sound of Julian's breathing and movement behind her.

They needed to get as far away from the man as they could.

The ridge above the kitchen wasn't the highest point of the inn but it was tall enough to be of concern. With extreme caution, Madi and Julian crept to the other side, where they needed to climb down to where the roof flattened and ended with the overhang. Madi had half a mind to suggest they just hide on the roof.

Maybe their mystery man would think navigating a roof at night would be way too stupid for a pregnant woman and injured man to attempt. Maybe he'd think they had jumped and were currently fleeing.

Maybe—

Another shot rang out somewhere over their heads. It caught Madi so off guard she fell on her side in the middle of trying to take it slow down the side of the peak. Julian scrambled after her, grabbing at her shirt. He caught a handful of the fabric but couldn't stop the two of them from sliding down. Her on her side, Julian on his stomach. A scream caught in Madi's throat, fearing the worst as they skidded downward, when her feet stopped on flat ground. They'd made it to the overhang.

Julian cursed something awful as he let her go and caught the roof with his hands. Together they fumbled into easier positions. Then Julian was pulling her up and hurrying to the edge.

"We have to hurry."

Madi couldn't agree more.

She followed him to the edge and tried really hard not to think about their combined weights. The trellis was made of sturdy wood entwined with vines. It covered the entire left side of the kitchen wall from the ground to a few inches above the roofline. Madi turned around and accepted Julian's help in getting her first foothold.

She tried thinking light thoughts as her shoe slid into the second one. Then her hand into another.

For a moment they both waited for the terrifying crack of their only lifeline breaking.

Thankfully, and much to their surprise, it never happened.

"Hurry," Madi exclaimed.

Julian did as he was told.

Together, they awkwardly climbed down. Madi did so with less speed and much less grace. Her stomach was too big. Every movement she had to angle away from the makeshift ladder. She missed the last few gaps altogether because of it. She let out a small scream. Two strong hands caught her back and side before any damage could be done.

Then it was just the two of them on the ground.

Julian's head swiveled. Madi didn't have the patience. She started to run around the corner of the house but those strong hands held her firm.

"We don't know if there's more of them," he whispered, pulling her closer to his chest. "The house isn't safe for you."

Madi didn't like how he put emphasis on *for you*.

"Well, you're not going in there, either, then," she said, trying to stay as quiet. "If it's not safe for me then it's not safe for you." Every time she thought they had a moment of safety, something would burst that bubble. Now being on the ground was no exception. A man's voice let out a string of expletives somewhere across the roofline.

Julian took that as a reason to get moving. He pulled her along with him around the back of the house. A scuffle sounded on the roof near where they had been, proving his move to be a good one. Whoever their pursuer was, he was nothing if not determined.

A truly terrifying trait given the context.

They crept along the side of the inn, keeping close to the house until the back patio was only a few feet away. Madi didn't need lamplight to see the blood glistening on both of Julian's sides. Nor the limp he'd adopted since their run across the roof.

Madi had fallen in love with Hidden Hills' off-the-beaten-path location, but at the moment, it felt like a point in the bad guys' column. How could they go up against a gun when Julian didn't even have shoes?

It wasn't a fair fight.

Madi fumbled for Julian's hand. She squeezed it as a thought zipped her spine straight.

What if they didn't need to fight at all?

"I know the forest like the back of my hand," Madi said with no segue. She looked over to the stone path that she'd walked less than two days ago with the guests and Jenna. "Get us to the tree line at the end of that path and I can make us disappear."

JULIAN STAYED AT Madi's back like the shield he was prepared to become if the gunman saw them make a break for the trees. She stumbled once but then, together, they fell into a groove.

They became a unit.

One that wasn't spotted.

Julian felt relief uncoil inside him less than a step inside the forest. He wanted to keep moving but Madi decreased her pace to an almost crawl.

"I—I need to slow down," she panted, hand rubbing her stomach. "It's not good to—to push myself unless I have to."

Julian fought the urge to run back to the inn, find their mystery man and beat him to a pulp. How dare he or *anyone* threaten the well-being of his child? How dare they put Madi in this position?

Julian couldn't stop his anger from rolling into even angrier words. Madi patted his hand, meeting his eyes with a small smile.

"I'm okay," she whispered. "Just not used to all of this exertion. Usually getting out of the recliner is a chore."

He nodded that he understood and let her lead.

During his earlier stay at Hidden Hills, Madi and he had explored several of the nearby trails, but the more they walked, the farther off those trails Madi took them. Julian marveled that the woman could even see where she was going, let alone guide them to a strategic location. Yet he wasn't about to doubt her sure-footed movements. Not when most of his attention was behind them.

The two men had surprised him well enough. Julian wasn't about to give a third the satisfaction.

Madi slowed as the ground started to slope downward. The trees thinned out. Julian's eyes made the adjustment for the change in the light. At least here he could see farther than a foot in front of him. The sound of running water became more pronounced until finally Madi stopped.

"Do you think he's following us?" Her question was so soft. Vulnerable. In the new light Julian could see her exhaustion in more detail. Her shoulders sagged; her back hunched slightly. Her lips were thinned and pulled down in a frown that was equal parts thought and worry.

"He may be trying," Julian said, "but I don't think he realized we ran off into the woods in the first place. And if he did, I don't think even I could have tracked us here. You did one hell of a job of getting us lost."

That frown rocked up into the smallest of smiles.

"The perk of growing up in a smaller than small town." She motioned behind her. "There's not much to do other than explore."

The water belonged to a small creek. They walked to its edge. Julian dipped his foot in. It was cold.

"If we follow this it will either take us to my closest neighbor—" she pointed to the west and then pointed to the east "—or the county road, where we may or may not be able to flag someone down."

"And how far are we talking to each location?"

Madi bit her lip. Julian pretended it didn't distract him just a bit.

"I'd say to the Jansens' place it's…maybe two miles? The county road maybe a bit less than that but the trek there is a little rockier than here."

Julian pulled his hand away from the bigger of the two wounds on his side and surveyed the cut, trying to think strategically about which direction to go. The bleeding had slowed. He made sure to keep his wince internal. Madi's eyes were already wide enough as she took in the wound.

"Here, try this." Madi grabbed the bottom of her shirt. She tore it but instead of it going along the bottom, it ripped up over her stomach. "Well, crap. I was trying to be cool. They always make it look so easy in movies." Julian chuckled. Madi moved closer. "Go ahead and tear off a piece if you can. The shirt's already ruined."

He did as he was told, grabbing one side and making a smaller, more precise tear. His knuckles brushed against the skin of her stomach in the process. She tensed. Julian took the piece of cloth and pressed it to his cut. He didn't move away. Neither did Madi.

Slowly she angled her chin up, meeting his eye.

"After I found out I was pregnant, a part of me didn't want you to answer when I called." Her voice was soft, low. "After what happened when I was a kid… Well, the unknown can be insanely terrifying for me. I was worried that if you answered and I told you, you wouldn't want to have anything to do with us, with me. But truthfully, I think I was more afraid that you would." She put her hand on his bare chest. The warmth in that touch reached every part of him. "No matter what happens later, I have to tell you—right *now*—I'm really glad you're here."

Madi pushed up on her tiptoes.

Her lips were soft. Oh so soft.

He could have stayed against them forever.

But then she ended the kiss as quickly as it had started.

She took a step back, giving him space, and let her hand fall from his chest.

Julian knew that now wasn't the time to talk about what

they meant to each other, what priorities the child between them would shift and change, and how their choices would affect their futures. He knew their current focus should be on getting out of the woods and away from the men who were after Madi. He couldn't afford being distracted. Not when Madi's and their daughter's lives were on the line. Yet looking at her staring back at him expectantly, lips as beautiful as the rest of her, Julian almost caved.

Almost.

"I think our best bet would be to go to the neighbors'," he said after clearing his throat. "They should at least have a phone or car we could use."

It might have been a trick of the light but Julian thought he saw a brief look of hurt pass across Madi's face. One second it was there; the next she was nodding.

"I'm right behind you."

Chapter Twelve

Two miles might as well have been ten. Madi's swollen ankles and general exhaustion sank in twenty minutes into their trek following the creek.

"I need to rest," she finally admitted. "And I need to do it now."

Julian didn't complain. He hovered around her with concern, his movements quick and rigid. Together they eased her to the ground between two trees while she tried not to focus on the pain radiating up her legs.

"These tennis shoes were made for walking but the pregnant belly, lack of sleep and ravenous hunger were not."

She tried her darnedest to give him a reassuring smile. It must have fallen flat instead. He crouched down next to her, hand already trying to steady her as she readjusted to get comfortable. Or at least to get to some semblance of it.

"I just need to rest," she said. "That's it."

"You need to not be in these woods in the first place," he growled back.

Madi put her hand over his. Julian's anger was touching.

"I won't argue with you there. I'd much rather be back in bed. Blissfully asleep until my bladder punched me awake." She sighed. "Which, if I were more hydrated, would be an issue." As it was, Madi was more concerned with keeping off her feet. Their jaunt through the woods hadn't been so daunting until the adrenaline had fully worn off. Thankfully that meant the mystery men weren't with them. In fact, Madi was positive they hadn't followed. The sounds that had filled the world around them for the last twenty minutes or so had belonged to insects, the wind and animals that were between curiosity and sleep.

"I should have grabbed my phone," he added, still grounded in his anger. "After I threw it back in the room. I should have grabbed it."

"Cell phone service out here is spotty at best. Even if you had, I don't think it would have helped."

"It wouldn't have hurt."

Madi shrugged. "Honestly, I'm still impressed you used it as a weapon. Wearing nothing but a towel. I mean, it's no set of fuzzy pink handcuffs, but it was still impressive."

"I may not know what's going on here, but if there's anything I've learned tonight it's that our kid is going to have one hell of a throwing arm." She couldn't see it, but Madi heard the faint smile in his voice.

It made her chest squeeze. She rubbed her stomach and smiled.

"There are worse things we could hand down."

Julian shifted but didn't stand. The cloth beneath his hand had changed colors completely now. In the dark it was easy to forget he was hurt. Who were these men? Who sent them? She was so focused on those questions, she'd forgotten to be vigilant about checking up on Julian. A flood of shame rushed through her. Julian might have been her savior but that didn't mean he was immune to danger.

"You need to get help," Madi decided. "Keep following the creek and you'll run straight into the Jansens' house. You won't be able to miss it. They're friendly enough, though I imagine Bill might have some questions before he extends any offers."

"I'm not leaving you, Madi."

"You're hurt. I'm only tired. There's a big difference there."

Julian shook his head.

"We got lucky tonight. I don't want to test how much luck we have left. Just because those men aren't here now doesn't mean they won't get here eventually," he said. "I'll be damned if I leave you to face them alone." He took a breath. When he spoke again there was a new emotion behind his words. One Madi hadn't yet heard from the man. "When the first man saw you while I was in the bathroom, did he look surprised at all?"

Madi felt her skin start to crawl again. The shower had woken her up. She'd assumed it was Julian. Her thoughts had tangled together, wondering what would happen when he was done—would she offer to let him sleep with her? The couch was so small that he'd never fit. Then another, hotter what-if had sprung up. It had been enough to get her out of bed and send her in search of water. Though she never made it past the getting-out-of-bed part. When the man had walked into view, he'd been smiling.

"No," she answered. "Not even a little."

"Which means those men came in with knives and guns, ready to *use* them, already knowing you were pregnant."

It was a sobering thought. Suddenly, Madi felt more tired.

"I can hide," she offered, still unmoved from her original plea. "Long enough for you to go get help and come back. I know these woods. I know what to listen for." Madi angled her face to see him better. The moonlight through the shadows of the trees illuminated only the tilt of his head and his brows drawn in together. "Julian, you're no good to me—to us—if you lose your health, and I'm here to tell you, I need to get off my feet for a good bit."

Julian wavered. She could feel it through his hand still on her arm, still trying to make sure she was steady sitting there. No part of him wanted to go, yet his mind was coming to the same conclusion hers had already. She wasn't going to be walking anytime soon, he was still bleeding, and if by some chance the men did find the two of them the outcome wouldn't be favorable. Definitely not for Julian. And if something happened to him? Madi would have no hope.

"I don't like this," Julian finally said, voice thrumming low.

"And I can't make the walk right now. This is our best option."

He cursed low but stood tall.

"We're going to make you a damned good hiding place first."

For a man who had once told her he'd grown up in a big city, Julian was decidedly handy when it came to camouflaging a rather large woman in the woods at night. Where there had been hesitation before, there was now dedication. He pulled her deeper into the trees and spent several minutes rearranging the foliage, creating a wall with part of a fallen tree and branches he'd collected. He pulled back and stalked around her. He made a few adjustments until he was satisfied.

"I don't like this," he repeated afterward. "But I think even if the sun comes up, you'd be hard to find here."

"I'd have to agree."

The truth was, Madi could barely see a thing around her. She felt like she was in a tree without the hassle of climbing it.

Julian lowered himself to a crouch. Madi wished she

could reach out and touch him. To give him another kiss. One that showed more than her appreciation. One that showed that her desires ran much deeper. But that would defeat the purpose. Julian wouldn't leave then, even when the blood running from his wounds would only continue to run.

Instead Madi took a deep breath.

"Be careful, Julian."

His words were grit in the dark.

"I'll be back before you know it."

THE JANSENS WEREN'T HOME, but that didn't stop Julian. He tried the front and back doors. Both were locked. Same for the first-floor windows. His patience didn't extend past that.

"I owe you one, Bill."

Julian shattered the window that took up the top half of the back door and tossed the rock he'd used into the bushes. He snaked his arm through and easily unlocked the dead bolt.

The Jansens' home was filled with cool air and silence. Julian would have preferred to find someone home, even if he'd have to explain himself in record time, but he was sure no one had stirred because of his break-in. At least now he could search for a landline without worry of being arrested.

He moved with purpose through the first floor, turning on lights as he went. He thrummed with the urgency of Madi out in those woods. He didn't need stealth right now. He needed speed. The living room, dining room and kitchen were well lived-in, but no phone or computer was in sight. Julian had never had a strong opinion about the current state of technology, but in that moment, he loathed cell phones.

Surely a house out in the middle of nowhere would invest in *one* landline?

He moved upstairs, all thoughts of being considerate thrown out the window. He knew he was trailing blood from his bare feet. He knew the doorknobs he touched were graced with a crimson coat. He knew that anyone from outside the situation would view him as a madman.

Just as Julian knew that every moment he was in the house, Madi was in the woods. There wasn't time to waste.

The two bedrooms upstairs weren't empty but they had no phones, either. Not even the room that seemed to be used as a library.

Julian couldn't help the frustration that kicked in at the sight of the empty desktop next to the window. Who were these people and how did they communicate with the outside world? Did they use powerful walkie-talkies to stay connected? Morse code? Signal fires?

He grabbed a loose piece of paper, intending to throw *something* to feel an ounce of control, when a light in the distance caught his eye.

Hope sprang eternal. On the opposite side of where he'd come out of the woods was a structure tucked back in the trees. It was small, but there was an undeniable glow at the windows.

That was all Julian needed.

He left the house and struck out across the clearing and into the trees. There was a dirt path leading to the small building but branches and roots littered the way. The path wasn't well-used; neither was the building.

The wood and siding were fading and chipped. A rusted-out wheelbarrow sat beneath a boarded-up window while an assortment of gardening tools cluttered the perimeter. The building was either a roomy shed or a small mother-in-law suite. Julian hoped for the latter. Surely it would have a phone. If it didn't, then he hoped the place was used for storage. Including an ATV or motorized bike of some sort. Anything to help Madi out of the woods without adding more stress to her body.

Julian moved closer to the main door but paused at the second window. It was only partially boarded up, light from inside pouring out.

Adrenaline shot into Julian's already-exhausted bloodstream.

"No," he whispered, hoping his eyes were playing tricks on him. Yet the longer he stared, nothing changed. "No, no, no."

He moved over a few feet and liberated a broken hoe from the discarded items spread out next to the building. The handle was snapped in half but he could still do some damage with it if needed.

Julian squared his shoulders and went to the door. He took a deep breath and tried the handle.

It was locked.

"I owe you again, Bill."

This time Julian didn't break a window.

Instead he kicked down the door.

Inside sure wasn't a mother-in-law suite.

The space was mostly open. A few boxes covered in dirt and dust took up places across the faded floor. Two folding chairs stood against the back wall, an old milk crate flipped over between them. The overhead light reached every part of the room, but there was a flashlight on one of the chairs. It was turned off but pointing at the only real thing of note in the building.

A man bound to a metal chair, surrounded by blood. He was hunched over, completely still.

Julian hurried over, keeping his sight line to the only open door, and immediately went for the man's neck.

Again he didn't stir but then, slowly, the beat of a pulse pressed against Julian's fingers.

It was a welcome feeling, though it didn't last long. Julian cussed and then said the second thing that came to mind.

"What's going *on* in this town?"

Chapter Thirteen

Madi was trying not to fall asleep, so she gave herself permission to think about the first time she and Julian had made love.

It was the last day of his stay at Hidden Hills and Madi had agreed, once again, to have drinks with him after dinner. They'd already spent the day before together, drinking sweet tea outside until the late hours of the night. They'd talked, laughed and explored the property. Neither had seemed keen on leaving the other's company.

Their time together went outside the bounds of her duties as an innkeeper but Madi couldn't get the man out of her thoughts.

She couldn't stop how she felt, either.

Being around Julian had infused her with a giddiness that made her feel carefree, wistful and capable of anything, all at once. A schoolgirl crush amplified by a shrinking timeline.

Then, right before dinner, Julian had shown up at her door. Dressed down, up or anything in between, Julian Mercer looked good. Madi's brain could no more deny that fact than her body could ignore it.

And that night, Madi had all but sighed as he stood in the doorway smiling.

"I was getting restless in my room, so thought I'd swing

by and see if you wanted to join me on a little walk before dinner."

It had been a smooth line in a smooth voice.

Madi had grinned wide.

"Already restless, huh? Don't worry, I can get you
checked out of here as early as you want tomorrow. I happen to know the owner."

She'd winked, trying her best at transferring that feeling of being carefree into flirting, but Julian's smile had
wavered somewhat.

"As much as I appreciate the connection, I believe feeling restless has more to do with wanting to spend time with
the owner, not leaving." Madi could still remember the
heat that had crawled up her neck. Not because his words
had caught her off guard, but because she'd felt the same.

"I've never made someone feel restless before," she had
responded, not trying to hide the blush that had conquered
her cheeks.

Julian had taken a small step forward. Madi hadn't
moved an inch.

"I think you're underestimating yourself."

He'd reached out and brushed his fingers across her
cheek. He'd gone through the motions of tucking a strand
of hair behind her ear. When his objective was complete
he was back on the other side of the door frame, holding
his arm out to her.

Madi's body had revved at the contact, just as her chest
had fluttered at the closeness. It had all made her terribly impulsive.

"I'd like to change if that's all right," she'd said. "Would
you like to come in and wait?"

"It wouldn't bother me in the slightest."

He'd followed her into the living area but stayed at the
couch. Madi's heart had raced as she'd gone through her

bedroom, looking for an outfit that would do her justice. She'd settled on a dress that wasn't formal, wasn't casual and made her legs look absolutely wonderful.

The only catch?

"Um, Julian?" The man was at the door in a second. "Could you pull this up for me? I can't reach the zipper."

Later, Madi would wonder if she'd unconsciously picked that dress so that Julian would need to help her with it. That he'd have to run his hand up her bare back. So she'd have to feel the heat of his skin so close to hers.

Sitting in the dark, back against a tree and hand protectively on her stomach, Madi still didn't know.

"There," Julian had said when the zipper had reached the top. Madi had turned around, ready to thank him, but any and all words had stalled on her tongue. Dark eyes had locked onto hers with a look that Madi didn't need help translating. "Perfect," he'd breathed. "Just perfect."

It had been a movie kiss. Unexpected, completely wanted. Hard, searching. Filled with heat that traveled with every swipe of their tongues and every gliding touch across their skin.

What had started as a mostly innocent task had boiled over into longing that had somehow formed between relative strangers in less than two days.

Every moment was so right. When Julian undid his handiwork and helped the dress hit the floor, hands and fingers skating along her skin. When Madi lifted his shirt to feel the hardness of his chest and abs without a barrier between them before moving down to ease the rest of his clothes off. When Julian looped his finger in her panties and pulled them down to join their other clothes on the floor. When he hoisted her naked body up into his arms and took her to the bed, not once breaking their kiss. When he pushed inside her and she yelled out in pleasure.

It all had felt right. From the top of her hair to the end of her toes, moving with and against Julian felt unbelievably amazing.

And then he'd stayed at the inn for a week. Madi had never been happier.

But then the real world had come knocking. Julian was supposed to leave for his interview. The one that would lead him to his new life. A life she wouldn't fit into. Hidden Hills, Overlook… They were her life. Julian deserved to have his own.

So Madi had called it off before it ever really started.

Look what good that had done.

Julian was tangled in the same dangerous web Madi had found herself caught in. He'd committed a crime to try to protect her and had gotten hurt. Never mind the "hey, I'm pregnant and she's yours," which must have thrown him for a loop.

Madi had always tried to be a good person, better with each passing day…and yet…bad seemed to follow her.

She sighed into the chill that had started to make her shiver. Her focus needed to be on the present, not the past. Not the future. Someone had killed one of her guests. A detective had been kidnapped, a coroner had been killed and two men had come for her with weapons ready.

Why?

It was a question that stayed with her as the darkness around her started to lighten. Minutes had become what felt like hours. Through the treetops, the sky glowed a soft orange and yellow, tinged with strips of pink. A sense of dread weighted Madi's heart at the sight. It was time to go.

Her feet and legs protested when she finally managed to stand. She braced herself as her head swam for a moment.

"This is going to be a long day," she muttered to the tree that had been her backboard. "I'm already starving."

Julian had been right. Her hiding place would have continued to do its job during the daytime. It felt like she was in some kind of wild jungle, trying to find a hidden waterfall or temple.

"And I have to pee something fierce," she continued, moving branches around her out of the way, careful not to lose her balance. "My luck, though? The cavalry would show up while I was in the middle of relieving my poor, abused bladder. Yep. That's definitely how good my luck has been lately. Miller would probably be the one to do it, too. Ugh, with a camera crew to boot. National, not just local."

The trees around her kept quiet as she mumbled out more complaints. Then, finally, she saw the water. It didn't help her bladder situation but it somehow made her feel more calm. She knew where she was and how to get to where she needed to be. Still, she stretched wide and was about to grumble some more in an attempt for catharsis when the sound of an engine echoed up the creek.

Madi slunk back against the closest tree.

The creek was too small for a boat and the creek bed was too narrow for a car. Her heartbeat sped up as she waited.

Then one heck of a sight came into view.

It was Julian.

On a riding lawn mower.

Madi stepped out of her hiding place. A feeling of such acute relief replaced every other thought in her head. Her hormones took the already-intense emotion and tripled it. When Julian cut the engine a few feet from her, Madi felt the tears in her eyes.

"Are you okay?" He jumped from the worn seat and was at her side in a flash. His hands wrapped around her arms. Always trying to steady her.

Madi nodded.

"I—I'm just glad you're okay. I was worried."

Julian's expression softened. But only for a moment. Madi realized then that there were two bandages over his knife wounds, both taped to his bare skin. He also had on work boots.

He caught her eye.

"I would have been here a lot sooner but... Well, let's just say you're not going to believe what happened. I barely do."

THE HOSPITAL'S FLUORESCENTS weren't helping his mood. Nor was the angry man in front of him. Julian rubbed at his temples. A tension headache was on the long list of things currently plaguing him. The top of that list was red faced and tapping his badge.

"I've been doing this job a long time," Detective Miller said. "A long time. Do you know how many ridiculous excuses and stories I've heard through the years?"

"I'm sure plenty," Julian answered, knowing it had been rhetorical. His patience with the lawman was thinning. "But that doesn't mean a thing when it comes to what happened last night. What's been happening the last two days. Someone tried to frame Madi. They tried to hurt her. And, for whatever reason, that extended to Detective Holloway."

Miller's lips thinned. The crease in his forehead deepened as he became even more unhappy, if such a thing were possible.

"The man you just happened to find," Miller stated. Again.

Julian took a deep breath. He reminded himself that picking up the smaller man and throwing him across the room would do nothing to help his case. It certainly wouldn't help Madi. She'd already been through enough without adding fuel to Miller's fire.

"Listen, I know you have issues with Madi and the rest of her family." Julian readjusted his tone. He wanted to get out of the lobby's corner where they'd been talking since the detective had arrived. Pushing the man's buttons by adopting an even angrier attitude, no matter how badly he wanted to, would only delay him reuniting with Madi. Not to mention giving an even bigger lead to her attackers. "If it was anyone else, you'd already be out there looking for the couple who shot your colleague in the hand and the men who had no problem trying to torture and kill a pregnant woman." The detective's jaw visibly hardened but he let Julian continue. "You were with us when the coroner's van was attacked. You saw the damage at the inn. Holloway told you himself that he'd never seen Madi or me before. Just because this isn't all adding up doesn't mean Madi is to blame. And you know it. So, please, let me take her to the ranch so she can get some rest. She and the baby need it."

Miller's stare was unwavering. To Julian's surprise, he didn't spout any hotheaded rebuttal. Instead he sucked on his teeth, then came to a decision. Julian just hoped it was the right one.

"You're tying your ship to hers. If she goes down, you will, too. I hope you realize that."

Julian nodded. Miller looked over as Detective Devereux walked in from the hallway. Desmond was at his side.

"Don't leave town," he said, giving his badge one more tap. "And, Mr. Mercer, just because Madeline isn't behind everything that's happening doesn't mean she isn't in the center of it. If I were you, I'd watch out."

Julian didn't respond. Not that Miller expected it. He

gave Desmond no more than a stiff nod of acknowledgment before leaving the hospital with his colleague. Julian met the Nash triplet with a less-than-enthused nod himself.

"I still think it's a huge conflict of interest having Miller run this case," he greeted. "He clearly is partial as hell when it comes to the lot of you."

"As much as I'd agree with you in any other instance, I will say that for once, Detective Miller's anger issues might work in our favor." Julian raised his eyebrow at that. Desmond explained, "He'll try his hardest to find a way to pin this on us. Now that this case has picked up attention and involved another officer, Miller will need hard evidence to make that happen."

"And since Madi isn't some deranged puppet master behind all this pulling the strings—"

"He'll find the real puppet masters," Desmond finished.

Julian saw the logic there, but that didn't mean he had to like it. He squared his shoulders. The need to protect Madi was ringing through him once again.

"Not unless I find them first."

It had been a long while since Madi had been in bed with Julian and yet, hours after she had thought about their first time, there they were…in bed together again.

This time there was a lot more between them. Not just physically. Lying on her side, facing him, Madi ran a hand over her stomach beneath the covers and met his eyes with a sigh.

"I'm fine," she reiterated. "We're both fine. The doctor checked us out. All he said was to get some rest and drink some water. And definitely don't go climbing over the roof again."

Madi gave a wry smile. He returned it, though there was still undeniable concern in his stare.

"When we get to more solid ground on this whole thing, I'd like to know more." His smile turned sweet, quiet but heartfelt. "About the pregnancy, about the baby. I have to admit, I don't know much about either in general."

Madi's heart squeezed. In a perfect world he would have gone along with her every step of the way after finding out they were pregnant. But she'd messed up that perfect world when she'd turned him away. Talking with him about the child they'd made was a painful reminder about what she'd rejected.

"I'd be happy to," she said honestly.

He nodded, his head against the pillow.

They were back at Des's house in Madi's old room. This time there was no wondering where Julian was or would be. After they'd eaten, Madi had made it clear she didn't want to be alone for the sleep they both needed to get. Julian had made it clear he was on the same page. He wasn't leaving Madi's side anytime soon.

"Is there anything I need to know now? Anything I should, uh, look out for?" Madi chuckled. It rubbed off on him. "What can I say? I'm so out of my element that I don't even know what to ask about specifically. Dilation? Sonogram? Applying for preschool early? Am I somewhere in the ballpark?"

Madi was beside herself with laughter.

"You're at least in the parking lot," she said when she could manage.

Julian grinned.

"Good."

"But all you need to know right now? Honestly, I'm about to pass out. I'm so tired. I mean, I'm always tired lately, but if I fall asleep in the middle of us talking, I'm sorry…and then *when*—not if—I wake up to pee for the billionth time, I apologize again." She reached out for his hand but hesitated. "She usually starts moving around when I first lie down. Want to see if you can feel her?"

Julian's entire demeanor changed. Madi worried she'd crossed some kind of line. But then, slowly, he reached out and met her hand in the middle. Madi shifted the blanket and guided him to her stomach. She lifted her shirt so he had the best chance of catching the little gymnast. His skin was, as always, so wonderfully warm.

It was comforting. So much so that she yawned.

"Don't worry if you can't feel her," she said, stifling a second one. "So far I'm the only one to catch her in the act."

Julian nodded stiffly. He was concentrating. It would have melted a part of Madi's heart had her eyelids not gotten so heavy.

He was just so warm.

Chapter Fourteen

Two days passed before Madi felt much more like herself. Not only had she slept through both nights, she'd taken several daytime naps. A feat that was harder than normal considering Julian hadn't left her side. Sure, he gave her space when they were in the house when she wanted it, but if she needed him he was there with seconds to spare.

His brow would pull in, he'd look at her stomach, and then he'd look into her eyes and she knew in her bones he was prepared for anything. Their close call at the inn had changed something between them. It was one thing to lie for her; it was another to see her and their child in danger.

Madi knew this because seeing him get stabbed, twice, had been so close to soul crushing that, even safe on the ranch, she worried about him, too. Especially since no one knew anything about those men, the couple who had taken Detective Holloway or who had killed Loraine.

The mysteries were slowly driving the Nash family crazy, Madi included. Now that she was back to normal she didn't like the idea of sitting on her hands any longer. A point she brought up at breakfast. Moments before it was shot down hard by Caleb and Des.

"This is the safest place you can be right now," Des said, frowning and shaking his head. "We can control what goes on here. Once you leave through the front gate it gets harder."

Caleb agreed, his cowboy hat bouncing as he nodded with enthusiasm.

"The department and Kilwin PD are more invested than ever in catching these people," he added. "They're following several leads. It's just taking some time. Don't make it more complicated for them by making yourself accidental bait."

Madi couldn't help it. She went for a section of her hair, ready to start an angry braid, but Julian caught her hand before she could clear the table. Neither Nash brother saw the action. Caleb and Des had never been the overbearing and aggressive type of brothers who hovered around the men she dated, but she had been surprised that neither had questioned Julian yet. Everyone was now on the same page about him being the father. She had expected the news to carry consequences for the burly man holding her hand against his thigh, trying to calm her down. Yet as far as she knew, none of the Nash brothers had flexed their sibling muscles at him.

Madi assumed their focus was elsewhere, and maybe at some point they'd start questioning his absence. Then again, she hadn't missed the embraces they'd each given Julian in the hospital after Madi and the baby had been cleared. They respected him.

"How about instead of town you can show me around the ranch?" he offered, speaking to her but addressing the table as a whole. "I've still only been here and the main house. I'd love to see the rest."

Des and Caleb shared a look. They didn't flat out say no but Madi recognized their "how do we say no without seeming like jerks" expressions. She'd been on the receiving end of them a few times during their angsty teenage years.

"May I point out that there's a patrol car at the gate, Deputy Hudson keeps driving through every few hours, *all* of the staff is on the lookout *and* my escort is an ex-marine who is built like a sexy, jacked-up house?" She held up her hand to keep them quiet so she could finish. "The same sexy, jacked-up house who went head-to-head with two armed men with nothing more than a cell phone and his fists. And, by the way, managed to get a big ole pregnant woman across a roof, down to the ground and to safety without a scratch. All while *he* was hurt."

Madi gave her brothers a pointed stare, nearly begging them to fight her. They shared another look. Julian squeezed her hand twice. She glanced over. His expression was blank. Or almost blank. Madi could have sworn there was a smile trying its darnedest to pull up those delicious lips.

Des was the first to concede. Caleb sighed for effect.

"Just don't do any of the trails," Des said. His face softened. "Please. You know how easy it is to be caught by surprise on one."

Madi's momentary frustration at her brothers disappeared. She looked between them and, as it happened sometimes, she saw the eight-year-old boys she'd sneaked off into the woods with for an innocent game of hide-and-seek. Another unspoken conversation occurred among the three of them. Madi couldn't explain it any more than she could ignore it.

"I won't take any unnecessary chances," she finally promised. "But I can't stay locked up in here forever, either."

"Okay," they said together.

"Make sure your phones are charged," Des added,

standing with his empty plate. He scooped up Julian's and Madi's before shoulder checking Caleb. He rolled his eyes and started collecting their empty cups and mugs.

Madi felt a twinge of excitement. She hadn't lied when she said Hidden Hills felt like home, but she couldn't deny she now felt ready to see how Julian liked the place where she'd grown up.

"I have to pee again but then I'll be ready to go," she said to him.

It earned a laugh. She beat him to the reason behind it. "And yes, I did have to go before I sat down for breakfast. Like I said, this girl loves Riverdancing on my bladder."

Julian gave her a little push up and then she was off. When she finished in the bathroom she pulled her phone off the charger with more pep in her step than she'd had in a while. Her phone had finally been returned the day before by Detective Devereux. They hadn't seen Miller since the hospital, which was A-OK with Madi.

The temperature outside wasn't too hot or too humid. Still, as soon as they got into his SUV Madi flipped on the AC.

"I thought we could park at the stables and walk around from there. I can show you the retreat, too. It's a quick walk from there."

Julian adjusted his shirt over the back of something in the waist of his jeans. He caught Madi's quizzical stare.

"Your brothers gave me a gun."

"They what?"

Julian shrugged.

"Honestly, I was expecting a stern talking-to so I'm okay with the gun." He smirked. "Still, it wasn't the weirdest thing that happened today."

Madi felt her eyebrow rise.

"What's weirder than my brothers slipping you a gun in the kitchen?"

He put the vehicle in Reverse and then pulled out onto the main road that ran through the ranch.

"I'd have to say it was being described as a, and I quote, 'sexy, jacked-up house.'" Madi's cheeks flamed to life. Julian laughed. "I mean, don't get me wrong, this sexy house is flattered. It just was a first for me."

Madi groaned.

"It's these darn hormones," she defended. "They killed the filter that usually keeps these things in my head!"

"But you still think I'm sexy, right?"

Julian actually winked.

It did a number on those same hormones that had already bypassed her personal filter. Heat of a different nature started to spread through her. When she answered, her voice had dipped lower. She motioned to her stomach.

"Clearly."

Julian didn't respond beyond the grin he was already wearing but when they parked outside the stables, the air around them had changed. Madi didn't know how to deal with it. She'd gone from offhandedly calling him sexy to wanting to take him to the back seat and show him just how bendy she still could be.

Hormones. It's the pregnancy hormones, she thought. *You also thought a bag of Cheetos was the best thing in the world last night.*

Yet Madi knew her lame excuse wasn't the entire truth.

She didn't think she had ever stopped wanting Julian.

He cut the engine, got out and walked around to her door. When he opened it, Madi felt like she was on fire. She bit her lip to stop herself from blurting something more dangerous than a weird compliment.

Julian reached out. She assumed it would be for her hand; instead, his knuckles brushed across her cheek.

"You are the sexiest of us all, Madi Nash."

His thumb hooked beneath the line of her jaw, sliding along it until he had her chin in his hand. She let him tilt her head up. He bent over to complete the advance.

Like she had done to him in the woods, Julian gave her a kiss that was soft and brief. Unlike their time in the woods, they weren't in immediate danger. They could do more if they wanted.

Did she—

Yes. Before she could even finish the thought she knew, without a doubt, she wanted to be taken by Julian. Again and again.

The real question was, did he want her? After all of this time? After everything that had already happened?

Someone cleared their throat. Julian was in front of her in a flash, eyes darting to the culprit.

"Ray!"

Ray Cutler gave an awkward little wave and smiled.

"Sorry, I didn't mean to interrupt." He pointed back to the stables behind him. The main doors were open, letting the breeze carry in front of the stalls. "I just got back from a ride with Clive."

Madi stumbled out of her seat and hoped her cheeks weren't as red as she assumed they were.

"That's awesome! I didn't know you knew how to ride."

Ray ran a hand through his hair and gave a hearty laugh.

"I'm not a pro or anything but I can get from point A to B without falling. Half the time at least." He walked over and outstretched his hand. Madi noted that along with a cowboy hat, he was wearing riding gloves and boots. It made him look at home. Madi was glad for it.

After the two mystery men had shown up at the inn,

they'd asked Ray to stay at the Wild Iris Retreat instead of returning to Hidden Hills. It looked like he was enjoying the ranch. It eased a little of the guilt that had been weighing on her since Loraine's body had been found.

Hidden Hills offered relaxation and beauty. Instead, both had been violently destroyed.

"I'm Ray," he introduced. Julian returned the shake.

"Julian."

"So I've heard." Ray stepped back and gave a sheepish look. "I may not be from around here but word travels fast. Your heroics this week have been sweeping through town. Here, too." He thumbed back to the barn, most likely referring to Clive, a family friend as well as the stable master. Also a lousy gossip if he was in a good mood.

"I wouldn't call what I did heroic," Julian responded. He gave Madi a quick look. "Just necessary."

That heat beneath Madi's skin burned even hotter. Apparently her hormones didn't care that Ray was there. Her body wanted Julian. Badly.

"Whatever you want to call it, it's a good thing you were around." Ray changed his attention to Madi. He cleared his throat before continuing. "I'm glad I ran into you. I wanted to apologize for telling the cops what I heard you say about Loraine. I knew it was just said in frustration and I didn't for a minute think you did it, but I didn't want to lie, either."

Madi waved her hand through the air, dismissing the thought.

"I wouldn't have wanted you to lie. You did the right thing. No worries here."

A small voice in the back of her head reminded Madi that the man next to her *had* lied. What would have happened if he hadn't?

"I'm just glad it didn't get you into any permanent trouble." He flashed another quick smile and then tipped his hat down. It looked like such a natural motion. One that the Nash men did like it was second nature. Either Ray had lived a life out on the land like they had on the ranch or he was a quick study. Whichever, the mantle of cowboy suited him. Though Madi's brothers would never let their prized hats get as dirty as the one Ray had on. A few black smudges showed along the side. Ray caught her eye. He chuckled. "Not all of us can be perfect, can we?"

A memory started to stir at his words. One that came with a gut punch of urgency. It must have shown on her face.

"You okay, Madi?" Julian asked, hand pressing on the small of her back. Ray's eyes had gone wide in alarm, as well. Madi tried to laugh off both of their concerns.

"Just a little spacey is all." She pointed to her stomach. "This one has a way of making me a bit ditzy from time to time. Nothing to worry about. Just lost my words."

Ray kept searching her expression with concern, but Madi was starting to get tired of all the men giving her that look. She mustered up the best customer service smile she could and let it shine wholly on the man.

"I'm glad you're enjoying yourself, Ray. Please let any of us know if you need anything and we'll make it happen."

It did the trick. He loosened and nodded to them both again, heading to his cabin after they said goodbye.

"A bit ditzy?" Julian repeated, voice low. "Are you sure you're okay?"

"Have you ever had a word on the tip of your tongue, but for the life of you, you can't remember it?" Julian nodded. "All of a sudden it's like I need to remember that word but can't."

Julian's hand moved across her back so slowly that goose bumps spread across her skin.

"Then why don't we get your mind on something else so your subconscious can figure it out?"

Madi raised her eyebrow at that.

"Are you saying that you want to distract me, Mr. Mercer?"

Julian was smirking.

"I sure would like to try."

Chapter Fifteen

Madi might have had some trouble getting up from the occasional chair or low surface, but by God, she shimmied out of her shirt and threw it across the room like she had superpowers. Julian barely had time to shut and lock the barn's second-floor loft door. Then all he could do was take a moment to stare. It caught the woman off guard; her face turned a darker shade of red.

"O-oh no," she stammered. "Is this not what you meant when you said distraction?"

Julian answered by pulling his own shirt off. He threw it away with a smirk.

"This is *exactly* what I meant."

This time he was the fast one, closing the distance between them with two long strides. It had been too long since he'd held her. Too long since he'd run his hands across her bare skin. Too long since he'd tasted her.

Now he was going to make up the time lost.

Madi moaned against his lips as they finally skipped past the sweet and went straight for the hard. Desire thronging through Julian. So powerful he wound his hand in her hair and held Madi fast against his lips. When she lashed her tongue out, deepening it, Julian lost it.

He needed her.

Now.

It was a feeling that was reciprocated.

As he went for the hook of her bra, Madi reached for the button on his jeans. Neither broke their kiss. Both were successful.

Madi spilled out of her bra just as she tugged down on his pants. Julian had to step back then. Madi groaned. Then she looked mad as a kicked hornet's nest.

"What are you—"

He held up a finger to stop her from complaining. With his pants unbuttoned, he scanned the space for anything remotely soft. While he had no problem making love to a pregnant Madi, he couldn't help but feel protective, too. The loft's floor was old wood, rough and not at all ideal for the moves they were about to be taking pleasure in.

Thankfully, he didn't have to look too long. A box not far from their discarded shirts was partially opened. Over one side was the corner of a flannel something. Julian hurried to it, mindful that his pants were a lot tighter than they had been minutes before, and clapped when he saw it was a blanket.

"Good thinking," Madi said at his shoulder. Julian made sure not to look at her yet. Not until the blanket was down. He wouldn't be able to stop himself again.

The material was soft and thick and perfect for the two of them. Once he laid it out and was satisfied it would keep her comfortable, Julian finally turned to face the mother of his child.

"You are beautiful."

Her face was flushed, her blue eyes were heavenly and her smile was a sweetness he was ready to taste again.

Or maybe it wasn't all sweet. The corner of Madi's lips moved up into a smirk that made his jeans even tighter.

"Take those clothes off and tell me that again."

Julian couldn't help the growl that vibrated out of his chest. He did as he was told.

"Yes ma'am."

"WELL, I HAVE to say, it was nice to yell for *good* reasons instead of bad ones."

Julian chucked.

"Let's just hope Clive was still out in the field with the horses," he said. "Otherwise I feel like your brothers are going to have another talk with me. This time not about guns."

He picked up her shirt off the ground and handed it over. They'd both reclaimed their pants but only after taking at least a half-hour sojourn. Neither had been ready to get up and start moving around. Not after the romp they'd just had. Madi was pretty sure she'd seen stars at one point, maybe the universe being created at another. A small part of her had worried that being pregnant would be a deal breaker for the man. Yet somehow it made everything more intimate. Right after they'd finished, Julian had held her against his chest, a hand protectively placed over her stomach. It had moved her mind and heart from lust to something deeper.

Something she didn't want to think about just yet.

While their time together had been mind-blowingly wonderful, Madi knew they had to go back to their current reality.

They had bigger problems to attend to first.

Still, she couldn't help but feel a bit lighter now. A bit more content, too. She slipped her shirt on and gave him a sly smile.

"What would my brothers even talk to you about? Tell you to keep away so I don't get pregnant?" She pointed to her bump. "Sorry, boys, but that ship has sailed."

Julian laughed and went about dressing. Madi took the time to finally look around the loft.

"You know, when we were kids this is where we used to hang out," she said, moving through the closest stacks of boxes and plastic storage tubs. "This was like our unofficial party place. We'd wait until our parents were asleep and then sneak out and meet our friends here. It's been a while since I've been here, though." The cheer in her words started to ebb. "Not since right after Dad died."

Madi scanned the labels, passing over holiday decorations, old school memorabilia and family heirlooms that had been moved from the original Nash family house after it had flooded yet hadn't made it to the new one. Madi knew what was in all of them. Most of all the boxes in the far corner. They didn't have labels on them. They never would.

Despite years of not visiting the space, her feet led her right up to them.

It was amazing what the sight of a few cardboard boxes could do to a person. Madi's skin crawled. Her stomach hardened. An old ache started to rip through her. It allowed a familiar guilt to follow. Especially when she noticed that two of the boxes were partially opened.

Had she been the only one to avoid this place?

What did that say about her?

Had she pretended to have moved on when she was really just a coward?

A warmth came up behind her. Julian placed his hand on her back. A small yet meaningful gesture that gave her the courage to show him something she should have already told him about.

"Though I *thoroughly* enjoyed what we just did, the real reason why I think I wanted to show you the barn was because of these," she started. "And to give you the rest of my story. Can you grab those two boxes? The ones that are opened?"

Julian didn't question the request and soon had two pieces of the Nash family history on the floor in front of them. She placed her hand on the closest one but didn't look inside yet.

"My dad was a good man, but like I said, he couldn't let go of what happened to us when we were kids. The stress… It killed him. It changed us as a family. Even before Dad died. What had happened just changed us. Caleb became focused, analytical. We couldn't get answers but maybe other people could. He started fighting for the underdogs. If we couldn't get closure, then he could help others get it. Desmond became driven, too. But his focus was more on the aftermath. What happens when those who are hurt are forced to keep going. He wanted to help people live life, even after they'd been dealt a bad hand. He went into the business world and used his wealth to create organizations aimed at helping people move on." Madi smiled, as she always did when she felt the pride of what her brothers had managed to do with their lives. "Declan even changed. He was older when it happened, and even though no one has *ever* even remotely suggested it was his fault that we were taken, it hit him pretty hard, too. Caleb was about closure, Desmond was about moving on, but Declan? He became dedicated to stopping anything before it happened. Protecting our hometown, the county. I couldn't tell you what he wanted to do before that day in the park but there was no doubt in anyone's mind after." Madi wavered. She was getting to her part. The one she had never admitted to anyone else. Julian placed a hand over hers.

"And what about you?" he had to ask. It was the only way to get her to finally say it.

"I became angry." She balled her fist and continued,

"At first, I didn't even notice it. No one did. But then in elementary school, when I was ten, Andrés Casas ran up behind me at recess and pulled one of my braids. I still don't remember exactly what happened next other than I snapped." Madi sighed in defeat, tears starting to well up in her eyes. "He had to be taken to the hospital and I just broke. I became more impulsive and mean. I had problems trusting people and then connecting. Honestly, I think it drove Dad harder to find the man who attacked us. Why he couldn't let it go or move on. He thought solving the case would fix me."

"PTSD doesn't have one easy fix."

Madi looked into his eyes, surprised.

"No, it doesn't," she said after a moment. "Thankfully, Mom could see I needed help and so she got it for me. For all of us. We went to therapy, participated in a lot of different methods for children who had been through trauma. And eventually, I felt better. I started socializing again, evened out, and then one day would go by and I wouldn't think about what had happened. Then another would go by and then another. I'd be lying if I said there weren't hard moments, but for the most part, I thought I'd moved on."

Madi smiled, knowing it didn't reach her eyes.

"I think—I think a part of me still has a hard time connecting," she said. "It's easier to have walls built up than to try your chances outside, you know?" She ran a hand over her stomach. "But I don't want to be like that anymore. *So...*"

Madi leaned over the top of the closest box and started to rummage through it. She spied what she was looking for near the bottom. Julian was nice enough to bend over and get it for her. When he straightened he gave her an expectant look.

"These boxes hold reminders of our family's tragedies,

from Dad's investigation to things that happened during the struggle after." She smiled again. This time she felt more of a warmth in it. She had finally gotten to her point, finally bared a part of herself to Julian that she had never shown anyone else. "But you can only box something up and hide it for so long, and I don't want to keep a big part of my life hidden anymore. Not from you."

Julian's face softened. He looked at the photo album in his hands. It held pictures from the bad years, as Madi thought of them. Yet growing older was a funny thing. Becoming a mother was another interesting twist. Both gave her a perspective she hadn't had before. One that made her appreciate the fact that, while she wished things could have been different sometimes, the life she had now was formed by those bad years.

Without them she wouldn't have met Julian.

She wouldn't be carrying their daughter.

As if on cue with her thoughts, Julian closed the space between them again with a soft kiss. Instead of pulling right away, he lingered.

"You are an extraordinary woman, Madeline Nash."

Madi felt her smile grow. Now it reached her eyes.

"You're not so bad yourself."

Madi decided it was time to take the photo album instead of pretending it didn't exist. They left the loft with Julian holding it fast against his side. A wave of emotions rolled over her at the sight. At everything that just happened between them.

Julian hadn't judged her for her past. For her anger. He'd understood it and accepted it.

What did that mean for them?

What happened next?

"Madi! Madi!"

The sound of yelling took every good and confused

thought about her and Julian's future and threw it skyward. She whirled around next to the SUV. Julian was already in front of her, a barrier to keep her safe.

Clive came rushing out of the barn, phone pressed to his ear. He skidded to a stop in front of them, out of breath.

"What's going on?" Julian asked.

Clive held up his finger and took in a few breaths. He must have run in hard from the fields. The man was only a few years older than Madi and in great shape. Whoever was on the phone at his ear was talking loudly but he didn't appear to be affected by it.

"Molly just—just heard that something big happened in Loraine's case," he managed. Clive's wife, Molly, helped run the retreat. She was as plugged into the community as the Nash matriarch. According to Molly, she didn't spread gossip. She spread the truth. "They found something in what was left after the coroner's van was destroyed in the fire."

The hair on the back of Madi's neck started to stand. Clive straightened and looked as severe as Julian did.

"The body Carl and Lee were transporting wasn't Loraine Wilson."

Chapter Sixteen

"Someone switched the bodies before transport," Madi said. Her brother Desmond shook his head.

"There was a deputy with the body while it was stored in the hospital's morgue. Nobody wanted to risk a chain-of-custody issue, especially with you as a suspect and all the possible conflicts of interest. He only left its side when Detective Holloway showed up. Not to mention there are several cameras throughout the hospital that show no one tampering with the body. Definitely not switching it for another." Desmond sighed. "Caleb sneaked off and called me after he finished going through the footage himself."

"Did Detective Holloway have anything to add?" Julian asked. They were back in Desmond's kitchen. Desmond had been quick to confirm Clive's information when they'd come back. Small towns really did have an efficient rumor mill. "Maybe they stopped at a gas station?"

Desmond shook his head again. He'd relinquished his cowboy hat as they started to discuss the newest confusing piece of evidence. Now he ran his hand through his hair in exasperation.

"They never stopped until they were run off the road."

"By the man and the woman," Madi spelled out. Desmond nodded.

"'An eye for an eye' is what Caleb said she told Holloway. Because there aren't already enough stereotypical bad guys in the world without adding clichés."

Madi's eyebrows drew together in thought. Julian wished he had answers for her. For all of them. The other body found in the coroner's van had been confirmed as Carl's. Past that, Julian had nearly forgotten about the van attack, especially after the men had visited the inn. Now they were losing answers and gaining more questions.

"So what you're saying is the woman found at the inn *wasn't* Loraine to start with?" he asked to get them back on track.

Desmond sighed.

"That's the thought," he said. "They found a metal plate in the body with a registration number. It was linked back to a woman named Kathy Smart. Last I heard they were tracking down as much information on her as possible. I think she lives in Manhattan but Caleb didn't know more yet." He lowered his voice a little. "We're not supposed to know any of this, but considering that this case has done nothing but affect our family, he wanted us to know. We can't tell anyone else."

Julian agreed.

"Does Kathy Smart ring any bells for you?" he asked Madi. Maybe she had been a former guest?

The beautiful blonde shook her head. Her hair was already in two braids over her shoulders.

"I know it would be presumptuous of me to think that I know everyone in Overlook but, honestly, I know most," Desmond said. "I've never heard of a Kathy Smart, either."

"So what was she doing at a bed-and-breakfast all the way in Tennessee?" Julian supplied.

Madi readjusted herself in her chair, fingers splayed across her belly.

"I'll raise you one better," she said. "If the body I found is Kathy Smart, then where is Loraine?"

A moment of silence settled in the kitchen. There were so many questions going around that Julian hadn't yet gotten to that one.

"I'm assuming Nathan Wilson is being brought back in for questioning?" he asked. "Don't they usually look at the spouse first when a disappearance or homicide happens?"

Madi nodded.

"Unless there's someone else who jumps out at them first," she said dryly. "Wait, were they able to tell time of death?"

Another question Julian hadn't thought to ask yet.

"The coroner originally guessed two to three hours. I don't think that's changed, either."

"So whoever Kathy was, she was most likely killed in Overlook," Julian postulated.

Desmond nodded.

"With Dad's shotgun no less."

Madi's body tensed. Julian opened his mouth to ask what was wrong when Desmond's phone started to ring in his pocket. He pulled it out and frowned at the caller ID.

"This is work. I took the week off but apparently Jared doesn't understand what that means."

He excused himself and went outside to talk—a habit that all the Nash family seemed to share. They liked being out in the air, day or night.

"What is it?" Julian asked once the back door was closed. Madi's brow was still crinkled. She was staring at the tabletop but Julian could see the gears moving as she thought through what was bothering her.

"Dad's gun." Madi groaned. "Oh crap."

"What about it?"

She hung her head and sighed.

"You know how I said pregnancy brain was real and sometimes it makes my memory into scrambled eggs?"

Julian snorted at that. "I recall."

Madi pushed her chair back and struggled to stand. She moved closer to him until her round belly touched him.

"After I found the shotgun all I could think about was the last time we argued about it."

"We?"

She lowered her voice.

"Us Nash siblings are pretty close. Like, that's our *thing*. But there are a few fights we've never resolved. One of them was Dad's gun. See, it's kind of a family heirloom, passed down to my father from his, who also got it from *his* father. Originally it was supposed to go to Declan, but after Dad died, he decided he didn't want it for whatever reason. So it was supposed to go to the next eldest Nash kid." She pressed her thumb to her chest. "Which is me, *but* Caleb and Desmond freaked out. Said I was a girl and I couldn't have it—you know, typical sibling rivalry stuff—and that just made me so grumpy! Ma said until we could stop fighting about it she would keep it in her attic. After it was found at my place I told them that's where it was supposed to be and they came and looked around." She covered her mouth. Her eyes widened. She spoke around her hand. "But that's not the last place it was."

Julian felt his eyebrow rise.

"You moved it," he guessed.

Madi nodded, guilt written all over her face.

"I moved it last year and totally spaced about it." She groaned again. "Oh God, how do I keep looking more and more guilty? If I was me I would arrest me, too!"

Julian grabbed her shoulders and chuckled.

"You just had a lot more than most thrown at you in a

very short amount of time. Pregnancy brain or not, I don't think anyone would blame you for forgetting a few things."

"Miller would blame me. He'd do it in a second. It proves I was the *only* person who knew where it was. But also, what if there's evidence there that could answer something?"

Julian sobered. She was right.

"Then let's go check it out and see," he said, rubbing her arms to try to calm her. "There's probably nothing, but at least we can put it out of our minds. Okay?"

Madi took a deep breath.

"Okay."

"Good. Now, where exactly did you hide it?"

Julian watched with equal parts amusement and concern as Madi's face turned a lovely shade of red.

"It's on the ranch but in a very, very petty place. Let's just say I'm not proud."

THEY DROVE TO the opposite side of the ranch, following a dirt road that was well-worn but still gave them a bumpy ride until it dead-ended next to a sign that read Juniper Shoulder.

"This starts a stretch of woods that has two trails you can follow to the mountain or to the creek. We had to mark it before the retreat opened." Madi placed her hand on the top of the sign after they got out of the SUV. "But before the retreat and even before what happened when we were eight, Juniper Shoulder was one of our favorite spots to play." She waved him to follow. Julian met her pace and then slowed to keep it.

"We promised no trails," he reminded her, eyes already roaming their surroundings. The gun the Nash brothers had given him was back in his waistband but he still wasn't enthused about not having a complete sight line around them.

"We're not going that far in. We might have been adventurous when we were kids but we never went too far in."

True to her word, less than five minutes passed and they veered off the trail's path. A hundred or so feet later and Julian was looking at a wooden sign nailed to a tree. There was unintelligible writing across it. Madi translated.

"'No Girls Allowed.'"

Julian cracked a smile.

Madi crossed her arms over her chest.

"We might be a set of triplets but Des and Caleb still teamed up on me sometimes like jerks." He followed her around the tree and a few more feet. Madi stopped and pointed. Julian couldn't help but laugh.

"A tree house. You hid the gun from them in your childhood tree house."

She moved her index finger side to side.

"I hid the gun in the tree house I wasn't allowed in," she corrected. "In my mind, at the time, it was the equivalent of giving them the middle finger for bucking tradition just because I was a girl." She let out a long breath. It deflated her. "They would have told me if they'd found it and moved it."

"Which begs the question, how did the killer know where it was?"

The tree house was impressive. Held up and built around three trees close together, it had obviously been made by someone who knew what they were doing. Julian didn't ask but he assumed that Madi's father had been the one behind it. Even after all these years the stairs that led up to the small structure were still solid. Julian led the way up with Madi close behind.

"After the attack we stopped coming out here. It just

wasn't fun anymore," she explained. "The last time we were out here all together was right after Dad passed. There's a trunk inside where we used to keep our toys. I added a combo lock when I put the shotgun there. One with an important but totally unguessable combo." Julian wasn't going to ask but Madi shared the information anyways. "It's Kurt Russell's birthday."

Julian laughed as he pushed open the door, still wildly impressed by the craftsmanship of the house. It wasn't huge but it was big enough that playing inside must have been fun.

Madi started to tell him about how the roof was put on but Julian had stopped in his tracks just inside the door.

"Don't touch anything," he ordered. It was a little too harsh but it did the trick. He felt Madi tense behind him. "Go back down and, Madi, *don't touch anything*. Not even the trees."

Madi didn't question him. A part of Julian felt guilty at his commanding tone but he was doing it for her own good. Once she was back on solid ground, he stepped deeper into the room.

It was the size of a shed, smaller than the Jansens' but still wide and tall enough that Julian and Madi could have walked around without bumping into each other or the ceiling. Like she said, there was a trunk against the opposite wall. A broken combo lock was on the floor next to it.

Between it and him was what made him order Madi back.

Across the floor and sprayed across the wall was dried blood…and other bits.

Julian cursed low and long.

He pulled his phone out and took several pictures before carefully backing out of the small house. He ran a hand across his jaw, then cursed again as he stopped in front of Madi. Her face had gone pale. She clutched at her stomach.

"We're going to have to call Detective Miller, aren't we?" she said, close to a whisper. Dread underlined each word. Julian felt it in his chest, too.

He nodded and showed her the pictures.

"I think it's a safe bet that Kathy Smart was killed in there."

Madi crumpled against him. Julian kept her up with his arms, pulling her into an embrace he knew would do little to help the situation.

"Julian, I'm the only one who knew the gun was here," she cried. Her body stiffened. She raised her head. "I know everything keeps pointing to me but I swear I didn't kill her. I swear it!"

Julian leaned forward and pressed a kiss into her forehead.

"I know you didn't do it," he assured her. "But you weren't the only one who knew where the gun was. Someone else had to have known. And if you didn't tell anyone where you put it, then—"

"Then someone must have followed me."

Julian tried not to let his body tense. He nodded, gaze sweeping the trees around them.

"But why?" she asked into his chest.

More than anything, Julian wished he could give her an answer. He wished he could make it all better. Assuage her worries and take her to bed and give her some pleasure in place of the pain that seemed to keep finding its way to her.

But instead, he was about to invite more worry and pain.

"We have to call Miller. The longer we don't, the worse it's going to look."

Madi nodded against him.

"I know," she whispered, her voice so small. "I'll do it."

Yet she didn't pull away.

And he didn't let her go.

As far as Julian was concerned, for a few minutes they were the only two people in the world.

Chapter Seventeen

Madi flipped through the photo album with every intention of ignoring the lump of guilt growing in her stomach. She should have remembered the tree house.

"So you've always been a braid kind of girl," Julian commented from the driver's seat. To his credit, whether or not he was pretending that everything was okay until Detective Miller arrived, he was paying rapt attention to every photo she flipped through.

The one beneath her fingers now had Declan, Caleb and Madi on horseback. Desmond was a speck in the distance on his own horse. They had no idea that a few weeks later all of their smiles would be strained or lost. Most of the pictures were like that. Which was why they'd found themselves in a box in the loft.

"I definitely get it from my mama," Madi said, mindful to keep her voice light. There was already a long list of things to be depressed about. "I can count on my hands how many times I've seen her hair down."

Julian smiled.

"Bethany, my little sister, asked me to learn how to do a French braid so I could do her hair when we were teens." Madi gave him a questioning look. He chuckled. "I'm the more coordinated of the two of us. She's book smart like no one's business, but when she has to use her hands for something she's just about the clumsiest person I've ever seen." He held up his index finger and lifted his shirt. He pointed to a small scar on his side. It was thin and faded. Madi had already noticed it, along with several others. She'd never prodded for explanations, just like he'd never asked about the one across her cheek.

"When we were in high school there was this huge party going on at Stacy DeLuca's house," he continued. "I wanted to go because of Stacy's friend Krista, and then Bethany told me it would be social suicide if she didn't go. Problem was, our parents had already said no. But, like in all teen movies—"

"You sneaked out," Madi guessed with a laugh.

"We tried to sneak out." He rolled his eyes. Madi could almost picture teen rebel Julian. "Our bedrooms were on the second floor and the stairs and front door were impossible to get past without waking our parents. So we opted for the bedroom window. There was a big oak tree near it and, honestly, I can still remember how easy it was to jump on it and climb down. But not Bethany. She decides that she's going to freak out halfway down. I mean screeching like you couldn't believe." Julian laughed. "Now, I'm a big guy. Even as a teen I seemed like I was a foot taller than everyone, but Bethany is this little doll-looking human and weirdly fast. It was like trying to get a cat out of a tree." He ran his fingernail along the scar. "And this is what it looks like when a teenage cat decides to not take your hand and falls halfway down the tree but not before scrambling to grab on to something." He shook his head. "She even ripped my shirt."

"I'm assuming she was okay?"

He rolled his eyes again.

"Yeah, yeah. She was fine," he answered. "We were as

good as busted, though. Didn't make the party and became prisoners in our home for two months."

Madi laughed.

"I would have liked to see young rebel Julian Mercer."

He chuckled and lowered his shirt. His bandages from their attacker's knife looked out of place against the toned skin of his stomach. It made Madi's mood plummet.

"You know, I don't know much about your life but I feel like you've been forced into a crash course about mine."

Julian's expression softened.

"You know plenty. You know me. There's always time to learn the rest." He placed his hand over hers. Madi felt a part of her melting at the contact. "Now, show me another picture of Madi before she dyed her hair."

That surprised a laugh out of her.

"Hey, being a triplet can make it hard to feel like an individual. I did what needed to be done." She winked. "And don't act like you aren't a fan of my magical golden hair."

Julian laughed and then was back to focusing on the photo album. They went past more pictures of family before they got into the ones that Madi hadn't seen in a long time.

She said as much as they stopped on a picture that had a group of kids in it.

"This was actually toward the end of my anger issues." She ran her finger across the plastic sleeve over the six kids. They were standing around a long-burned-out fire pit. Madi stood in the middle with her arms crossed. Despite her defensive stance, she was smiling. "It was like a support group for kids who had been through trauma. Once a week for, I think, two months? I can't remember exactly. Caleb and Des didn't go because I think they wanted to see how I would do without them." She hoped she looked apologetic. "I was not the nicest kid in the beginning but I turned it around toward the end." She pointed to the girl at her elbow. "I still talk to Gina occasionally, but that's it."

Madi was about to point out the two kids in the group who had absolutely hated her when a truck appeared on the road behind them. She put the photo album down and tried to steady her nerves. Speaking of people who hated her...

Detective Miller hopped out of his truck with a scowl. He adjusted his belt and turned that scowl toward the trees. His badge shone in the daylight. The butt of his gun from its holster did, too.

"Detective Devereux isn't with him," she said. "He definitely won't be impartial without someone to balance him out."

"Oh, don't you worry," Julian said, opening his door. "I'll balance him out if I have to."

Miller's mood soured the closer they got to him. Madi hadn't seen him since the hospital. He hadn't talked to her then. That had been Devereux. Madi's stomach knotted again. Miller wasn't going to give her any benefit of the doubt.

"This better be good," he greeted. "While y'all have been relaxing out here we've been trying to do work."

Julian played it cool. Cooler than Madi. His body language was relaxed, no aggressive tension. No combative stance. Madi, on the other hand, balled her hands at her sides and clenched her teeth.

"This is something you need to see," Julian explained. "Which is why we immediately called you."

Miller snorted.

"I'm sure only after you called everyone on the ranch."

"You can check our phones," Madi butted in. "You were the only person we called."

That seemed to get a bit more of his attention. Still, he continued to wear the scowl like it was a summer hat. He moved his hand back so it was near his gun and nodded toward the woods.

"Then lead the way."

Julian waited for Madi to strike out first before putting himself between her and Miller. The detective seemed so small compared to him. It made Madi feel better. Yet that momentary relief ended before they ever made it to the tree house, especially since she'd finished recounting the triplet feud about the shotgun.

And that she had hidden it.

And forgotten to tell anyone.

Miller had stopped walking when she was through. He looked like a dog with a bone. His eyes brightened and then immediately narrowed.

"Are you kidding me?" he said, dangerously near a shout. "You just happened to forget key information about *the murder weapon*?" He shook his head. "Do you Nashes think you're above the law? That it can't touch you because you've been through some bad stuff in your lives?"

Madi's nerves hardened. Then they were glowing hot.

"This has *nothing* to do with what happened when we were kids," she yelled, not bothering in the least to keep calm. "I'm sorry that after finding a body and immediately being fingered as the murderer, a detail slipped my mind." She pointed to her stomach. "You try creating a kid, running a business, having to take crap from a lawman who clearly wants you to fry and then trying to keep everything in line. Two weeks ago I spent an hour trying to find my damn keys *that were in my hand*!"

"Don't compare this to losing your keys!"

"And don't forget I didn't have to tell you I'd remembered this at all," she shot back. "But here we are, shouting so close to the front of a crime scene you still haven't seen because you're too busy yelling at me!"

That shut him up. Miller's nostrils flared. He looked between Madi and Julian with what she guessed was barely contained rage. Julian was no longer carrying himself with a cool relaxation, either. He was mad, too. The three of them certainly were quite the trio. They didn't speak until the tree house was in front of them.

"Don't you two move," Miller finally bit out.

"Wouldn't dream of it."

Madi wanted to say more but Julian took her hand. It defused her next outburst before it could come out. They watched in silence as Miller disappeared inside the tree house.

"You didn't do it, Madi," Julian said. "I'm not going to let anyone say otherwise."

There was a severity to his words. A strength that was as intimidating as it was comforting.

Madi tried to hang on to that feeling as Miller finally came back out.

For the first time since she'd known the man, Madi couldn't read his expression. He descended the stairs without saying a word. Julian dropped her hand.

"Madi wouldn't have needed to break that combo lock that was on the trunk," he pointed out. "Whoever did that is the person you're looking for. She also didn't go inside today. Only I did."

Miller didn't respond.

At least not in words.

When he was right in front of them his eyes went over their shoulders and widened. Julian was quick to turn, body tensing and ready to deal with whatever came their way, but Madi was slower.

She watched in shock as Detective Miller pulled his gun out and smacked it against Julian's head. It was the perfect blow. Just as the man in the woods had done to her when she was eight.

Julian hit the ground hard.

He didn't move.

A scream of anger escaped Madi before she realized that the gun was now pointed at her.

"You're going to listen to me right now or all *three* of you die."

EVERYTHING WAS WET.

His hair. His skin. His clothes. The ground.

It was raining.

Julian's face was pressing into dirt that had become mud. It oozed across his cheek and stung his eye. Not that the mild annoyance was more concerning than the throb of pain at the back of his head. He'd been knocked out.

"Madi!" Julian tried to bring his hands up to help him push off the ground but came up short. They were bound.

They were *handcuffed*.

Julian let out a guttural sound. It was primal. It was protective.

"Madi," he yelled again.

He rolled onto his back and sat up. It wasn't a downpour but the drops were thick and heavy. They pelted the ground with force. Julian could no more see tracks across the ground as he could see the two people who might have made them.

Miller.

Julian rocked back enough to get momentum, then jumped up to his feet. It was a trick he'd made a point to learn since his buddies from his unit had said Lumberjack was too big to be that fluid. Now the trick got him to his feet and moving. He ran full tilt up the tree house stairs, heart in his throat, before kicking the door down. It didn't take much but Julian felt like he could tear down steel if it meant getting to Madi.

The dried blood was still splattered across the room but the combo lock was gone. So were Madi and Miller.

He was both relieved and pissed as hell.

If Miller had taken Madi then it meant she could be still alive.

Julian turned on his heel, words vile and anger filled spilling out of his mouth like the rain off his shirt. He ran back to the trail and out through the woods.

His SUV was gone. So was Miller's truck.

Julian kept on running.

Chapter Eighteen

The rain didn't let up. It made Julian's several-mile trek even more of a pain. At one point he had to stop, lie on his back, move his wrists under the back of his legs, around his feet, and stand so that his cuffed hands were in front of him. It was still constricting but made for much easier movement. He needed to be ready for anything.

Even though he hadn't been earlier.

Focus, he thought bitterly. *You have to find them.*

The pain in Julian's head and the burn in his legs and lungs were at an all-time high by the time the Wild Iris Retreat's cabins came into view. At least, he assumed that was what the cluster of small buildings were. He hadn't been given a proper tour yet and the rain was making it difficult to see or read any signage. He'd barely seen the lights on in one of the cabins until he was almost up to the front porch.

He ran up the stairs three at a time. A plaque next to the door declared the building was Cabin 3. It wasn't until Ray flung open the door after he pounded against it that Julian realized the guest had been thrown right back into the thick of things. Madi might have worried what that would mean for the future of Hidden Hills but Julian was worried only for her and their child. If that meant throwing Ray into the middle of a gunfight as his backup, Julian would do it in a heartbeat.

"My God, what's going on?" Ray asked, eyes zipping to the cuffs and then back up.

"Madi was taken by Detective Miller," Julian said, jumping in. "He knocked me out and restrained me. I woke up and they were gone. So were my phone, gun and vehicle."

Ray's eyes widened in acute surprise. He motioned Julian inside, shaking his head in disbelief.

"The detective heading up the case about Loraine? Why would he do that?"

Julian growled.

"A question I plan to ask him myself the next time I see him. Until then I need to call the department."

Ray grimaced. He hesitated and then held up his phone and shook it.

"I don't know how long you were out, but you must have missed the big show." He pointed to the window. "The storm got really rough there for a second. I'm guessing it damaged the cell tower that serves this area. No calls are coming in or going out. I'm surprised we even have power after all of that."

Julian cocked his head to the side. That was a small hitch in his plan. He wiped at the water falling from his hair into his eyes. The handcuffs clinked together at the movement.

"I need you to drive me to the department. I need to talk to the sheriff immediately. He has to know that Miller has gone rogue."

Ray grimaced again.

"My car is still at Hidden Hills."

Julian gave the man a flat stare.

"What?"

Ray shrugged, apologetic.

"Since the investigation at the inn, I was shuttled here. I haven't really missed having a car since I just stay on the ranch. I was told I could wait to get it on my way out of town if I wanted."

Well, that was more than a hitch in his plan than Julian wanted.

Ray held up his hand.

"But what I can do is get us into the retreat's main office. I don't think Nina or the other manager is there right now. It should have a landline, though!"

A loud clap of thunder backed up his offer. It sent a powerful feeling of foreboding into his bones. He hoped wherever Madi was, she was inside. She had joked about them having bad luck and now Julian was tempted to agree. Clear skies sure would have helped tip the scale somewhat back into their favor. Or at least make finding her easier.

Case in point, Julian was having a hard time just keeping the rain out of his eyes while inside. Running through the rain might have been thematic but it wasn't at all practical.

Ray seemed to agree. He eyed the growing puddle beneath Julian and pointed to the opposite side of the cabin.

"Let me grab us some towels first. They won't fix the downpour out there but maybe they'll help some."

Julian would have turned him down but his run was catching up to him. He was hurting, but even harder to ignore was how thirsty he was.

"I need some water."

The cabin only had three rooms. The living space, the bedroom and the attached bathroom. All small but functional. A tiny kitchenette was tucked in the corner of the living area with a little refrigerator and a sink. Julian was at the sink, head bent under the faucet, in seconds. Once the water hit his lips, he could have sung.

He had never tasted anything sweeter.

Julian drank like a man who had just crawled out of the desert and angled his head to get a better fix on the water. It put the miniature dining table directly in his sight line. A quaint round table with two wooden chairs tucked beneath with a vase and flowers on its top.

And next to it, a leather-bound book.

Julian cut the water off and stood.

Not a book. A photo album. One he'd seen before.

He went to the table and assured himself he was mistaken. Surely it wasn't the one he was thinking of and instead was a guest book, or maybe Ray had bought it as a souvenir.

Julian's adrenaline surged. He flipped the book open.

Three children standing arm in arm smiled up at him. The little girl in the middle had one braid thrown over each shoulder. There was no scar on her cheek yet.

"I'm sorry I don't have anything more helpful than towels," Ray said from the other room. "But I feel like we can better help her if we're not drenched to the bone."

Julian closed the album and moved back to the sink. He gave Ray a curt nod as the other man appeared with two towels. One look at Julian and his eyebrows drew in together.

"Are you okay? The detective didn't shoot or cut you, did he?"

Julian shook his head, careful to keep his expression as neutral as possible. Even if he was two seconds away from grabbing the man and trying to shake information out of him.

Why did Ray have the photo album they'd gotten from

the loft? The one that had been in Julian's SUV when they'd gone into the woods?

"Just a solid hit to the head. Nothing I can't power through."

Ray's eyebrow arched. A ripple of hesitation moved across his expression. Julian's almost-spent leg muscles tensed further. The cabin's charming facade crumbled. Now it was a possible staging area for a fight. One in which Julian already had a disadvantage with his hands restrained. Fighting in nothing but a towel hadn't been ideal; fighting with both hands bound was a stone's throw away from very, very bad luck.

"Well, we better get going, then," Ray said after a moment. "Let me just grab my key to the lobby."

Julian was curious about the game Ray was obviously playing. What was his plan? Play nice until they got to the phone? Or was the man waiting for an opening to take on Julian?

"I'm ready when you are," Julian said, changing his stance to provide more stability. Ray bent over a pair of jeans that was tossed over the couch's arm.

"You said no one knows?" Ray asked, rooting around the pockets for his keys. Julian noted that they were dark on the bottom of the legs. Wet. "I mean, about you and Madi going out to the trail in the first place?"

Julian clenched his jaw. If he hadn't seen the photo album his internal alarm bells would have been ringing at that. He hadn't said anything about a trail.

And Ray was taking awfully long looking for his keys.

"As far as I know."

Julian tightened his grip on the towel, wishing he had full use of his hands. It would have to do.

Up until now Julian had never really tried to get a read on Ray. There hadn't been a need. He was pleasant enough, quiet. Average, according to Madi's observation. Julian had agreed. But now he realized that Ray could have crafted this persona by design, and Julian wasn't wearing rose-colored glasses anymore. Now Julian saw a man who could get lost in a crowd with ease. A man who showed interest and skill in the outdoors.

A man who was still wearing his riding gloves and favoring his left hand.

Julian went through everything he knew about the case so far. His thoughts flew past Ray and to the death of the coroner. Detective Holloway's description of the man and woman who had taken him was generic. He'd claimed the man had black hair. Ray didn't, but Julian wasn't ruling him out on hair color alone. Not when Holloway had said he'd shot the man in the hand.

"It might be easier to find the keys if you took off the gloves."

It was clear Ray was now stalling. Still, he kept fishing for them, finally making it to the back pockets. Julian glanced around the other surfaces in the room. He wasn't surprised when he spotted the keys next to the door. Ray was definitely stalling. Julian leaned into it.

"You know, I wanted to apologize for everything you've been through while here in town," he started. "A murder wasn't exactly what Madi had in mind for her guests' experience."

"It wasn't her fault," Ray brushed off. He moved to the last pocket.

"I'm surprised I didn't run into you before today, though. I had to spend a long time at the department giving Madi's alibi. If you don't mind me asking, what was yours?"

Ray stopped. He slid his hand out of the pocket and stood to his full height. Another surge of adrenaline shot through Julian's system. His heart was hammering away, as if competing with the storm outside. For a moment the two of them just stared.

Then the sound of a cell phone ringing filled the room.

Julian wondered what else the man had lied about just as Ray's pleasant persona faded into a smirk.

"We both know that neither one of us had an alibi."

Ray reached around for something in the back of his waistband. Julian wasn't going to wait to see what that was. He ran the distance between them and lowered his shoulder before impact.

He'd been here before. The last two fights he'd encountered were a surprise. This one had the bonus disadvantage of his hands being bound. Julian didn't need to survive this fight. He needed to stop it before it started.

Something clattered to the ground as Julian slammed Ray against the front door. It was a harder hit than Julian had bargained for. Even though the door hadn't been properly shut when they'd first come in, it crashed open with such force that something cracked. The momentum carried them across the small porch and right to the top of the stairs.

Ray groaned as his back took the brunt of their fall. Julian rolled off the man but didn't stand. Julian moved into a crouch and grabbed the collar of Ray's shirt. He fisted the cloth and pulled the man up enough that if he had to, he could slam his head back onto the porch.

"Where is she?" Julian yelled. "Where's Madi?"

Ray coughed, squeezing his eyes shut and trying to catch his breath. Julian wasn't about to show the man sympathy. He shook him.

"Where is Madi?"

"I—I—" Ray tried. He opened his eyes. They were

angry. "I'm big—big picture. I've never been good at the details."

Julian felt the tension beneath his knuckles just before Ray struck. He might have been a smaller man than Julian but the movement was surprisingly effective. His head hit Julian's nose so hard that he knew it was busted before he ever saw the blood or felt the pain.

"Son of a—"

Julian recoiled but refused to let the head butt send him to the ground. He rocked on his heels, tensed his leg muscles and managed to spring up instead. It gave Ray the opening to roll over and get to his feet.

"You messed this up," he growled. "You—"

Julian intertwined his fingers and struck out, envisioning his joined hands as a sledgehammer. Ray yelled out. He danced backward and right off of the porch. Once again he hit the ground, this time on his side. He devolved into another fit of coughing. Julian jumped the stairs and landed next to him, adrenaline coursing through him with purpose. His head, nose and shoulder throbbed in pain. The rain drenched their clothes.

Though it was Julian's heart that was the loudest.

"Where is she?" he yelled. "I won't ask again."

Ray struggled to get up. Julian wasn't going to let him. Not without answers.

"Let him go!"

Julian never even heard her walk up. He turned around. A woman with dark blond hair had a gun pointed at him. Just far enough away that he'd be a goner if he lunged for it.

Had she been in the cabin the entire time?

"Move away from him," she added. "Or you're dead."

"How many of you are there?" Julian asked in anger. He did as she said but stepped behind Ray so his back wasn't to the man. "Every time I turn around there's someone else with a gun and a snappy line."

The woman smirked.

"I'm sorry we're inconvenient, but at least now you know how it feels."

She motioned to the cabin.

"Now, go inside. Slowly," she ordered, voice clear through the downpour. "Or a snappy line will be the last thing you hear."

Bad luck really did seem to be the theme of the day. Julian weighed his options again. Fight and flight both resulted in the high possibility of being shot…which he was hoping to avoid.

He couldn't help Madi if he was hurt. Or worse.

Julian raised his hands slowly and nodded. The woman moved aside, careful to keep the gun's aim true. Ray continued to cough and sputter. A few profanities found their way out into the rain before Julian could clear the cabin's front door.

He clocked all of the exits he could see and guessed at the ones he couldn't. He noted the lamp, a horse statue on the entryway table and the cabinet drawer where he would guess the cutlery was stashed. The couch was between it and him. He could use it for cover if needed.

"Don't get any ideas," the woman called from behind.

Too bad that was exactly what he was doing.

"Who are you?" he asked, eyes falling back to the small horse statue. It looked like it was made of metal and had a substantial amount of heft to it. It was no cell phone or pair of handcuffs, but he'd be able to use it if needed. "Where's Madi?"

The woman's laugh was biting. Julian stopped next to the entryway table and turned. Standing in the doorway with the light against her face and the rain at her back, she was a confusing sight.

Mostly because she was Loraine. Even beneath her blond wig, Julian recognized the face from the picture he'd been shown at the sheriff's department.

"I don't know, but I suspect I will soon enough," she said, smiling through dark red lips.

Ray walked up behind her, slightly hunched over. He held his chest, scowling.

"Careful," he warned.

Loraine snorted.

"He saw the photo album. He knows who I am. I don't think he's going to be quiet about either. Are you, Mr. Mercer?"

Julian kept his mouth shut.

He wasn't confident he could dodge any bullet at this range. Maybe he could take one in the shoulder before he got the gun away from her.

Loraine cocked her head to the side.

"What? Not going to talk now?" She shrugged. "It doesn't matter. The *real* question I want to ask is what's going to make all the difference."

She took a small step forward. It brought her within striking distance. Julian's muscles started to coil, readying. Loraine, however, knew just what to ask to make them freeze.

"How much do you *really* love Madi?"

Chapter Nineteen

Madi heard the rain start but she never saw a drop of it. Instead she'd been held in what she could only assume was an abandoned building in the woods. She'd been tossed into the van outside the Juniper trail and blindfolded. Just as her brothers had been all those years ago. This time she was conscious for the abduction and told not to make a sound. She hadn't. Instead she'd done her best to pay attention.

The ride hadn't lasted more than ten minutes, which meant they were still in Overlook.

Good news, all things considered.

It meant Julian and her brothers stood a chance at finding her.

A vise squeezed in her chest at the image of Julian on the ground. He had been so still.

"Stop moving," Miller snapped, tearing her thoughts away from the man she'd been forced to leave behind. "You're driving me crazy."

Madi rolled her eyes. If she could have reached her hair, she would have already braided it several times over. The only thing keeping her from devolving into a puddle of fear and memories of being eight and terrified was her daughter. Madi couldn't protect her or herself if her head wasn't clear. She had to keep as much control as she could. Even if, in the back of her mind, she was doing nothing but reassuring herself that she wasn't that scared child anymore. She was a mom. She was strong.

She had to be strong.

A task made more difficult by the man next to her. For the last half hour the detective had been in fine form. She'd never heard a grown man growl as much as he did. It was like being held captive with a grumpy bulldog.

Which wasn't a shock, given his temperament and general dislike of her, but what *was* a shock was Miller being a victim alongside her. She hadn't seen that coming. After he'd knocked Julian out, it had taken her longer than it should have to notice the men coming out of the tree house, guns drawn. She'd been so angry at the detective for attacking the father of her child.

"They said they'd kill us all if I didn't take care of him," Miller had said right after Julian hit the ground. "I'm a fast shot but I can't get them both before they shoot back."

Miller had been ordered to drop his gun and handcuff Julian before they'd been taken. They moved so fast that Madi hadn't had time to process until they were driving away. After the ride, she and Miller had been dumped in a windowless room, covered in dust, mold and dirt. The only piece of furniture was a weathered wooden bench set up in the middle. One that had become the bane of her existence.

They'd already tried to lift the bulky thing but it was too long and way too heavy. It didn't help matters that their wrists were zip-tied around the middle plank of the seat, palms up. It was an awkward position that neither could get any good leverage with, no matter how much begrudging teamwork they'd tried.

"I'm uncomfortable," Madi countered. "You try being tied to a bench with no backrest and a belly that makes sitting normally uncomfortable and try not to fidget."

Miller let out a loud, gruff sigh.

"There you go with that pregnant stuff again," he said. "We get it. You have a baby in you which makes your problems ten times worse than everyone else's."

Madi sucked in the bad words that immediately sprang to the tip of her tongue. When he wasn't mean, he was sarcastic. Neither was a good look on the man. A point Madi would have loved to make. Yet the truth was that fighting with Miller wasn't going to get her out of the situation. It could only stand to make it worse.

"*They* don't care that I'm pregnant," she said instead. A shiver ran down her back. Her anger at the detective deflated. "Why did they even take us? Both of us, I mean. It doesn't make sense." It was a concern they'd already passed around after realizing that breaking out of their restraints wasn't going to happen. Still, Madi thought it warranted saying again. "You're the law. Taking you only makes everything harder on them, just like when Detective Holloway was missing. Who would voluntarily take that kind of heat?"

Miller sucked on his teeth for a moment. His eyes stayed on the door.

"If these are the men who attacked you and Julian at Hidden Hills—"

"Which they are," she interjected. For the second time since they'd been in the room. "It's hard to forget the faces of the men who threaten to torture you and shoot at you."

"Then I'm assuming their jobs have changed."

"Their jobs?" Madi repeated.

Miller, ever a man to play it close to the vest, seemed to flounder between divulging the information he had and keeping quiet. Madi was ready to give him an aggressive piece of her mind if he didn't spill. Thankfully, he must have decided it was time for everyone to be on the same page.

"Julian said there was a scorpion tattoo on the man who

stabbed him," he started with notable reluctance. "There's a gang in Kilwin that has cropped up in recent years that have done a good deal of outsourcing certain jobs so they don't get them linked back to the gang. The group of men they outsource to are rumored to have scorpion tattoos hidden on their bodies. The mayor has been in talks with the chief about making a task force that will be dedicated to tracking them down and putting them behind bars for good, but after the latest budget cuts, it's been tabled until further notice." He took a moment to swear. "I think the men who came at you at Hidden Hills are a part of that group. I think they were hired to get the truth out of you about Loraine's murder."

"But Loraine isn't dead."

"Exactly. Which may be why their tactics have changed."

"They think I know where the real Loraine is," she realized.

Miller nodded.

"That would be my guess."

Madi took a second to chew on that. Her stomach was starting to knot up again. So far she had surprised herself with how calm she was being. The situation was way worse than when she was in the woods, hiding from danger. Now she was in the belly of the beast, waiting for the unknown. A violent unknown, if the other day was any indication.

For the umpteenth time since they'd been tied to the bench, Madi tried to touch her stomach. It was a feeble attempt to protect her child. The plastic of the zip ties bit into her wrists, making her raw skin burn even more. A feeling of defeat spread through her like wildfire. Its flames were fueled by the weight of the lie she'd been holding up. The same one that had tied Julian into the dangerous web she'd found herself in. Even though he had been the one to tell it first, Madi couldn't help but wonder what would have happened had she not gone along with it. If she had told the truth at the department in the first place, would he be okay now? And furthermore, would her child be in this much danger?

Madi did her best approximation of squaring her shoulders. She decided it was time to control what she could.

"I lied about my alibi," she finally said. "Julian showed up when I was being taken into custody for the first time, not before. I was alone in my suite when I found that woman in my bed. Julian only said what he did to protect me when everything started pointing my way." It was her turn to sigh. "But Miller, I didn't kill that woman and I don't know anything about what's happening. That's the honest-to-God truth."

It felt like a weight had been lifted from Madi's chest. It was one less thing to worry about. One less puzzle piece to hold.

Madi waited for the hammer to drop from the detective. For him to gloat about having grounds for arrest. That justice would finally find its way to the Nash family and he'd be the one to do it.

"I believe you."

Madi felt her eyes widen. They shared a look before his eyes dropped to her stomach. Then he was focused back on the door across from them.

"Really?"

"You're legitimately scared for your baby. There's no way in Hades you'd willingly put yourself in the middle of all of this." He shrugged. "Everyone lies at one point or another but there are some things you just can't hide. You wanting to keep that little one safe is ingrained like a reflex. But don't get me wrong, I still think you're more than capable of killing. I just figure you'd at least wait until the kid was born before you did it."

Madi snorted.

"Thanks. I think."

"Don't thank me." He tugged on his own restraints. His skin was past raw. Blood was drying around the plastic. He'd put up much more of a fight than she had. "If they are trying to get information out of us, *not* having that information isn't going to make our lives easier. It just means they're going to try even harder to break us."

Those knots in Madi's stomach multiplied. He was right. She'd told the man with the knife at Hidden Hills that she didn't know anything. That hadn't deterred him. Neither had her pregnancy.

"Julian and my brothers will find us," she rallied.

It was more for her than it was for him.

"I have no doubt that they'll try," he said. "So the new name of the game until someone comes to get us is stalling. If we can't get out then we'll have to buy time for someone to get in. Got it?"

Madi nodded.

"Stalling it is."

They lapsed into silence. It was surreal in a way. There she was, hitched to a bench, next to the only man her father had ever suspected in the triplets' abduction. The same man who had made clear, publicly, that he hated the Nash family and the love that the community had for them. Madi had seen that hate reflected in her father's eyes when talking about Miller. It made a lasting impression on Madi.

She hated the man next to her because of it.

Yet maybe *hate* was too strong a word. He'd been cleared of having any involvement in the abduction and had made a nice career in law enforcement in Kilwin. Most of all, he'd come up with a plan that had spared Julian's life.

Maybe Christian Miller wasn't as bad as her father had believed.

Or maybe Madi's pregnancy hormones were playing tricks on her and Miller was in on the whole thing.

Madi took a deep breath.

Speculating had gotten them nowhere.

The silence stretched for several more minutes before a new sound sliced it clean through.

"Footsteps," Madi whispered. "Someone's coming."

"Remember, stall."

A dead bolt could be heard retracting as the door was unlocked. Madi didn't know which hired baddie she hoped to see once the door was pushed open. The man who had seemed delighted to torture her or the man who hadn't been stingy with ammo when it came to shooting at her.

However, neither man came inside.

"You have *got* to be kidding me," Madi breathed out.

Miller wasn't far behind in his reaction. He swore like the devil.

Nathan Wilson didn't seem at all offended. He smiled delightedly.

"Oh, believe me, the feeling is mutual," he greeted. "I'd much rather pack my bags and get out of this hick town, but you know, I'd like my wife to be with me for that. And now look at where we are."

He made a grand gesture at the room around them. He looked as out of place as Madi felt, wearing a linen suit and brown dress shoes. He just didn't fit in Overlook, a fact that was even more apparent as he gave them a slow once-over. Nathan looked like he was on the way to see the horse races or attend a fund-raiser at the yacht club. Not popping in on two restrained people in some dilapidated and dusty room.

He dropped his hands to his sides and stopped a few feet from them. His gaze went to their wrists before meeting Miller's eyes.

"I'm really sorry you got caught up in this, Detective. Truly. I tried to help you, but this one here, well, she had her own help. Help I didn't bargain for."

"Help me?" Miller asked, back as straight as he could manage given the ties at his wrists. "How were you helping me?"

Nathan fingered a button on his blazer. It was a casual gesture that made the confusing situation even more bizarre.

"I was making sure she didn't get away with it. The murder." He shared a quick look with Madi. She made sure not to avert her gaze. She might not have understood everything going on but she wasn't going to give him the satisfaction of enjoying her fear. "I've done my research on the Nash family," he continued. "I know all about the unsolved case of the Nash children taken at a park. Held for days, only managing to escape by helping one another. A touching yet scary case for a small town, I'm sure. Especially since there have been no leads or suspects. At least, not since you were accused of being connected to the whole thing. Sure, you were absolved of it but that doesn't change what happened. A good cop and citizen had his name dragged through the mud because the accuser came from a family that everyone loved. That's what *you* said in countless interviews and public statements. Behind closed doors, too, as far as I can tell." Nathan shook his head. "I wasn't going to let Loraine's killer go just because her last name is Nash. Even if it meant conducting my own investigation."

"I don't think you can call what you've been doing an investigation," Miller said. "We don't kidnap and threaten people. We don't attack them. What you're doing isn't taking justice into your own hands. You're abusing it because you're frustrated."

Nathan laughed.

"Frustrated? You think I'm frustrated?" He shook his head. "All I am is a husband trying to find his wife since it's clear no one else is doing anything about it. As far as I can tell it's the law enforcement who are the last to know anything around here. Why would I sit around twiddling my thumbs when I could simply reach into my substantially deep pockets and get you the real culprit? The real murderer."

Madi felt her cheeks heat up in anger.

"But I didn't kill anyone," she replied, trying to keep her voice even. A muscle in Nathan's jaw twitched. Madi wasn't the only one trying to keep control of their anger. "You do know that, right? That it wasn't Loraine's body that was found?"

"She's still missing," he shot back. "And there's nothing you can say that can convince me you're not involved."

"So you've been following me?" Madi had to ask, stalling but still trying to find answers. For instance, how in the world his men had managed to ambush them at the tree house. All without being seen. "If you have, then you have to realize I've done nothing that warrants your belief that I'm involved with what's happening."

Nathan actually scoffed.

"I would have been had you not run away to the only place in this godforsaken town that could keep you hidden and safe," he said, annoyance obvious. "Which is why I ordered my men to keep an eye on the one man other than myself who would do anything and everything to see you taken from that safe place." Nathan shared a look with Miller. He actually smiled before turning back to Madi. "When it was clear he was going down Winding Road with purpose, I told them it was time to try to take you two in. My men, they've done their homework about the ranch.

The layout. They knew when Detective Miller turned off the main road and turned again. There were only a handful of places he could go, all away from any of the houses. The perfect spot to ambush you all. So they waited long enough so as to not raise suspicion before they had to and then simply drove up and parked their vehicle next to yours like guests ready to do some hiking. I'm not surprised Mr. Mercer didn't hear them following. Then again, I hire the best of the best." He grinned and motioned between Madi and Miller. "I'm told they were ready to take you then, but when your little fight broke out? Well, they used it to help even the odds in their favor. You were all so busy being angry you never even suspected two men were moving around you and into position inside the tree house." He laughed. It was unkind.

"And now you're here to interrogate us," Miller spelled out. It was clear he wasn't happy at having been followed. "To force a confession under duress."

Nathan took a step forward. There was a harsh glint in his eye that promised he was a man of his word.

"Don't worry, Detective. Remember, I'm on your side," he said. "The only thing you're guilty of is not getting a confession. So I'll get one for you."

The way his smile twisted, coupled with his certainty, left nothing but dread in Madi's stomach. How could she confess to something she didn't do? And even if she did confess, what would happen next?

She wasn't the only one who was wondering the same thing.

"Then what happens next?" Miller asked. "Let's say she tells you what you want to hear—what then? Do you let me take her to the station?"

That wasn't at all what Nathan had planned. Madi saw that as clear as day before he ever shook his head.

"I'm sorry but no, Detective." Nathan got so close Madi could smell his cologne. "We both know we're past that. No, what's going to happen is this." He pointed to Madi. "You're going to tell me what's going on and where my wife is. Then I'm going to go get her." He bent down so his eyes were even with Madi's. "And when Loraine is finally by my side, I'm going to be as surprised as everyone else in this town that Madeline Nash met her end in the same woods that scarred her when she was a child." Madi kept perfectly still as Nathan reached out and traced the scar on her cheek. "And at the hands of the same man her father suspected all those years ago."

He dropped his hand.

"If you're going to kill us anyway, why would we give you anything?" Miller asked. His voice was hard.

Nathan straightened his back, standing to his full height. He smoothed his blazer down and picked invisible lint off the sleeve. It was a more menacing sight than if he'd brandished a weapon and waved it in Madi's face. When he was done, he was smiling for all he was worth.

It terrified her.

"There is nothing either one of you could do to stop the outcome," he said. "Wouldn't you feel better finally doing the right thing before that happens?"

The name of the game was stalling. Madi knew that. Yet all words died on her tongue. She wanted to cradle her stomach; she wanted to tear through Nathan for being so callous. For being so wrong.

Miller didn't respond, either.

Nathan eventually shrugged.

"We'll do this the hard way, then."

For all his pomp and circumstance, Nathan simply left the room. The door shut behind him with a weight Madi felt in her bones. Only after the sound of the dead bolt locking did Miller speak.

"We're most likely in the old storage building at the park. The one that's been closed for years. If they stage it just right it'll look like I brought you here to kill you."

"Julian and my brothers will think I tried to stop you out of self-defense," she offered.

"And that me snapping is what made you do it. All of this starting with me knocking Julian out." Miller sighed. "He's put us all right where he wants us."

Madi's vision started to blur. The tears were fast, but they weren't sad.

No. They were angry.

She wasn't going to let that happen.

Chapter Twenty

He was wet, bloodied, handcuffed and mad as hell. Quite the sight, Julian was sure, as he ran into the Nash family's main house. Madi had once said it was the heart of the ranch. He didn't see how that was true since she wasn't there, but thankfully, one of her brothers was.

Desmond jumped up from the dining room table, which had papers stretched out across its surface, and took in Julian with blue eyes that only reminded Julian of what he'd lost.

"Julian! What's going on?"

His body protested the walk from the doorway to the table. After Loraine had posed her question, Ray had taken the gun from her. Julian didn't know if he meant to use it or just hold it for the woman so she could ramp up into a speech. Regardless, he hadn't stayed around to find out. Julian had charged them as soon as the gun's barrel was down and, once again, had thrown Ray's footing off. He'd used the opening to run as fast as he could into the rain, his mind made up.

He needed backup.

Ray and Loraine hadn't followed. Julian had made the run from the retreat to the main house with determined power in every movement of his muscles, yet the last few steps exhausted him even more.

"Tell your brothers to get here. *Now*." Julian dropped the soaked pillowcase and plastic bag on the ground. He crouched down and retrieved Madi's photo album. It wasn't wet, a small victory in what now felt like a long war.

Desmond eyed it with confusion but already had his phone out. There was no hesitation in him dialing. Ray had lied about no calls going out. Not that Julian was surprised.

He'd lied about a lot.

"Where's Madi?" Desmond asked. Judging by his expression, Julian knew the man realized it was nothing good. Still, they were working against time. Brevity was the key to getting her back.

"Detective Miller took her," he rushed. "And Loraine and Ray are hell-bent on getting her, too."

Desmond's eyes widened. Anger, worry and pain raced across his face.

Julian knew all three well by now.

TOO MUCH TIME had passed. From the moment he was knocked out until the moment after he'd caught up the Nash brothers and Caleb's partner, Detective Santiago, Julian was able to track the time they had lost. The period between the last time he saw the beautiful woman and the present.

Almost two hours, give or take.

Those were too many minutes. Too many seconds.

Julian, now free of his cuffs and wearing a change of clothes, felt each one of them like the stab of a knife.

They only continued to go by as the detectives and sheriff got on their phones and made several calls. It wasn't until Declan came back in, sheriff's badge pinned prominently to his belt, that the rest filed back into the dining room. There was tense authority behind the man's words as he addressed them all.

"There's an all-points bulletin out on Miller. The same for Loraine and Ray since Ray's cabin didn't have any clues as to where they might be. Officers, deputies, even reserve deputies are all out in force looking for everyone. If they're anywhere in the county, we can find them. Just in case, other departments and stations have been notified."

"And what about Miller? What did the chief say about his detective kidnapping a pregnant woman?" Desmond asked, hot under the collar. "Isn't that a conflict of interest to still have them involved?"

Declan took his cowboy hat off and rubbed the back of his neck.

"This entire thing is a conflict of interest for everyone involved. We're a small county, it happens," he said. "But we need the numbers and, truth be told, I trust the chief. I've never trusted Miller." He cursed. "I should have fought more to have him taken off the case. If he's working with Loraine and Ray, then that means he was involved with the people who shot Holloway."

"Not to mention his potential involvement in our kidnapping when we were kids," Caleb pointed out.

Declan nodded grimly.

"There is that."

Julian didn't feel the same certainty.

"Miller could have killed me," Julian said. "In fact, that would have been the smarter play. I'd seen him. Why not kill me? He had to have known I'd come to you all."

"Maybe he didn't want the mess or the hassle?" Detective Santiago offered. "It's one thing to be a kidnapper—it's another to be a cold-blooded murderer." The Nash brothers turned to her at that. "Sorry," she muttered. "But you know what I mean."

Julian rubbed at the raw skin around his wrists where the handcuffs had been.

"But what about the cars?" he added. "When I came to, both his truck and my SUV were gone. Who drove them? Miller and Madi? I can't imagine he would allow Madi behind the wheel of a car. She would try to escape."

"Loraine and Ray," Caleb said.

That didn't feel right. It hadn't since Julian had first thought about it.

"When I asked Loraine where Madi was she said she didn't know. Yet. Ray also seemed genuinely surprised to see me. Even more so when I said Miller had taken Madi. There's a lot of things you can fake, but true surprise is hard to hide."

"What are you saying?" Caleb asked. "That Loraine and Ray weren't behind Madi being taken by Miller? Or that Miller didn't take her?"

Julian stood. He'd already downed several bottles of water. Still, he knew the next day he'd be as sore as sore could be.

"I'm saying there are too many pieces. Madi is framed for Loraine's murder. Then the body is torched and the coroner killed. Then we have two men who attack us and want the truth about Loraine from Madi. Then we find out that the body wasn't even Loraine at all but Kathy Smart. Fast-forward a few days and suddenly Miller decides to take her after we found the place that Kathy was most likely killed? Then I run into Ray, who has this album? And Loraine doesn't know where Madi is?"

Julian leaned across the table to the photo album. He tapped his index finger on the cover.

"Why did they bother taking this from my car? When did they even do it? While we were in the woods or after Miller ambushed me? Out of everything *this* confuses me the most," he admitted. "Madi said this was boxed away because the memories were too hard. Why on earth would you chance connecting yourself to a kidnapping for some-one else's photo album?"

"You wouldn't," Desmond finally said. "Not unless it was important."

He moved toward the album and took the chair in front of it. Wordlessly he opened it and began to examine each picture. His brothers weren't as worried about it. Declan shook his head.

"I can only work with the facts I have on hand," he said. "And those are that Miller knocked you out and Madi is gone. Then Loraine and Ray attacked you and disappeared. We need more information." He turned to Caleb and De-tective Santiago. "Jazz, I need you to go talk to Nathan Wilson again. I know he alibied out for Kathy Smart's mur-der but since we've seen Loraine alive, maybe he'll have more to say. Caleb, I need you to find out everything you can on Ray, starting with another thorough pass over the cabin." Both nodded. "As for me, I'm going to dig deep into Detective Miller. Des, stay with Julian and work the photo album angle."

The sheriff put his hat back on. Everyone agreed on their jobs. Everyone but Julian. He followed the sheriff out to the front porch.

"Declan," he called. "I want to help. I can't do that with a photo album from the past."

Declan's expression softened. He clapped a hand on Julian's shoulder.

"You ran about ten miles today in a storm, hurt and bound, just to sound the alarm. In the last week alone you have fought off attackers while trying your damnedest to keep Madi safe."

"And Miller got her anyway," Julian said.

Declan shook his head.

"He was supposed to be a good guy," he replied. "They're

the worst kind of bad. The ones we never see coming." He dropped his hand and adjusted his hat. The rain had stopped but his hat was still dark from it. "Let the people who live here scour the county while you help Desmond. If we come at this thing from enough angles we'll eventually find Madi in the middle."

Julian didn't want to, but he nodded in agreement. The sheriff didn't waste any more time. He took off along with the detectives. Julian went back into the house and pulled a chair up next to Desmond.

"How much did Madi tell you about her past?" he asked without looking up from the page of pictures he was currently on. "About our past?"

"Everything."

"Even Andrés Casas?"

Julian nodded.

"The boy she hurt at recess," he supplied. That garnered a look from Desmond.

"The boy she hurt at recess," he repeated as confirmation. "As far as I know she's never told anyone that story before. At least no one outside therapy and those group functions we all went to." He gave Julian a small smile. "She must really care about you to open up like that." Julian couldn't deny that made him feel good, but he knew there was no time for it. Desmond looked back to the photo album but continued.

"You know, I've always told her that there's no shame in what she did to Andrés. She was a kid who had been through a trauma and hadn't had the right tools to process it yet. That's why Ma was so excited for Madi when she went to that camp thing with children who had been through traumas. She wanted Madi to see that she wasn't alone." He stopped on the page with the group shot of the children, Madi in the front, arms crossed and smiling.

"She said she turned around toward the end of it."

Desmond nodded.

"Yeah. The first few meetings weren't that great. A few kids tried to make friends with her and she roasted them. Ma got a call about it. Then they sat down and after that Madi got better."

"Roasted?"

Desmond tapped the face of a boy and girl a few kids down from Madi.

"I'm not proud of it but Caleb and I overheard Ma and Madi talking about it. Apparently they were making fun of some of the kids and she went off on them. I mean, she said some really nasty stuff." Desmond shrugged. "I'm sure I would have done the same, to be honest."

They lapsed into silence as Desmond went through the rest of the album. Julian looked over his shoulder, trying to see if an objective pair of eyes could see something family couldn't.

Neither had any success.

"These are mostly just us as kids," Desmond said, pushing the album away in frustration. "I don't know why they would take it. Unless it was by accident? It's just such a personal thing to take. I mean, I'm surprised Madi even took it out of the loft and *she's* in it."

Julian straightened in his chair.

"That's it," he said, a thought hitting him like a lightning bolt.

"What?"

He grabbed the album and started to flip through it in earnest.

"What is it?" Desmond asked again.

Julian didn't want to get either of their hopes up until he was sure.

"It's just a thought," he said, skimming each page

quickly. When he came to the end of the album his adrenaline spiked. "These pictures should only mean something to the people in them." He flipped to the middle and slid the album to Desmond. "I know it's a stretch but what if Loraine or Ray or both are in one?"

Desmond looked down at the group picture. He shook his head but didn't say no.

"Wouldn't Madi have recognized them or their names? They were guests at her inn. She talked to them at length."

"Why else would they grab the album? They look about the same age. Honestly, how hard is it to look completely different from when you were ten? I've seen people from high school who have had to remind me who they are, and that was a lot more recent than elementary school." Julian stood and reached across the table to Desmond's phone. He handed it to the man. "It may be one heck of a stretch but why don't we start with the two kids that you say hated Madi?"

Desmond took the phone.

"I'll call Caleb," he decided. "I mean, what have we got to lose?"

Julian knew it didn't need to be said out loud but he couldn't help it.

"If we can't find her? Everything."

Chapter Twenty-One

Only one man came into the room. It did little to calm Madi's nerves.

"Nice to see you again, Blondie."

He wore a smirk that was nowhere near charming. It was the man with the gun. The one who had chased them across the roof, shooting. Now that she could focus her attention on him and not escaping, Madi noted that his eyes were an alarming shade of green. Like they were radioactive. It was hard to look away from them. Green Eyes seemed amused as he dragged a metal chair through the doorway and across the room. He set it down in front of Madi with a widening grin and unbuttoned the bottom of his blazer.

"Last time we didn't get a chance to talk," he said, taking a seat. He was so close their knees nearly touched. "Let's do something about that now."

Madi shared a quick look with the detective. She felt more fear than she wanted to admit.

"Who are you?" Madi asked, careful to add a tremble to her voice. She and Miller hadn't gotten out of their restraints, but they had managed to make a plan. One that relied on her acting skills. She just wanted to get as many answers as she could first.

Stalling *was* the name of the game after all.

"I'm asking the questions," he skirted. "Starting with your involvement with Loraine Wilson's disappearance."

Well, that hadn't worked, Madi thought with disdain.

"My involvement with Loraine starts and stops with her being a guest at my inn. I didn't even make the reservation with her. I talked to Nathan's assistant. I don't know what happened to Loraine."

"You called and had her phone before she disappeared," he countered. "There was a dead woman in your bed who looked just like Loraine."

Madi had a hard time keeping her anger in check. Her frustration.

"I don't know how, but someone made that call from my phone. Not me. I was just as surprised as anyone to find that woman. I have no clue what's going on. Honestly, I thought it was you and your friend who were behind it after you came to the inn."

The man shook his head.

"If we wanted to kill someone, it wouldn't be as messy as all of this." He motioned around the room. "I'm just here for answers, and I don't believe for a second you don't have them. All fingers point to you on this one, Madeline Nash." Green Eyes reached into the inner pocket of his blazer. "Speaking of fingers."

He pulled out a handful of what looked like paper straws. Why paper straws, she wondered.

"She doesn't know anything," Miller ground out, pulling up against his restraints. "You can't make her talk about what she doesn't know."

That was when Madi realized the man was holding bamboo skewers. They were short but their pointed ends were enough to make fear roar through her.

"They say torture doesn't work," the man said, nonchalantly rolling the sticks between his hands. "But I don't think of what I do as torture. That's such an ugly word. What *I* do I view as more of an incentive plan. I ask a question and then give you a really good incentive to give an answer."

He put the skewers on the bench next to her but kept one in his hand. Madi tried to move as far away from him and it as she could but her hands could only go so far. He grabbed the fingers of her left hand, flattening the back of her hand completely against the bench. In his other hand he held the one skewer.

"So let's get to the incentive," he said. "To keep this wooden skewer from going under your fingernail I want you to tell me what you did to Loraine and where she is now."

Miller started to really struggle against his restraints. Madi didn't hear what he was saying. Her vision blurred. Fear and panic were slowly consuming her. Being threatened by a gun was terrifying, but unless you'd been shot before, it was hard to imagine the pain of being on the receiving end of bullet. But something going under her fingernail? Something being pushed into her skin? That was a pain she could already feel. It turned her blood cold and at the same time made her sweat.

It also made stalling harder.

She opened her mouth but didn't know what to say.

Then Miller spoke. He didn't look at Madi as he did so.

"We can take you to Loraine. But you'll need both of us to get to her."

The man twirled the skewer in his hand. He narrowed his gaze on the detective before moving it to Madi. She nodded to confirm the lie.

"Is she alive?" he asked.

"She is," Miller said before Madi could make a sound. "She's just hard to get to unless you know exactly where she is. That's why we didn't say anything. You don't stand a chance to find her without us."

"Without you two," Green Eyes deadpanned. "You're not working together. You hate each other."

"It's the perfect cover," Madi interjected. "Who would ever suspect?"

He kept twirling that skewer around. Every movement terrified her.

Finally he stopped.

"Fine. I'll bite." He let go of her hand and put the skewers back into his inner blazer pocket. He went to the door and stopped. As if it was a playful afterthought he looked over his shoulder. He was nothing but smug. "I should warn you, if you're lying, the incentives only become more enticing. So is there anything you'd like to add?"

Despite her fear, Madi surprised herself.

"If Nathan hadn't outsourced his dirty work we would have all been fine."

Green Eyes continued to stare.

Madi worried she'd lipped off to the wrong person. However, he finally snorted.

"It's always the damaged ones who cause all the trouble," he said. He left, shutting the door tight behind him.

Then they were alone with their lie.

DOROTHY NASH HANDED her revolver to Julian in secret.

"I follow the law," she said in an almost whisper. "My husband was law, my children are law and I respect it. I also know that look in your eye and know that we both understand sometimes laws can be broken for the greater good." She placed her hand on his and dropped her voice even lower. Desmond was out on the porch talking to someone on the phone. Through the open kitchen window Julian couldn't hear exactly what he was saying but his body language was loud enough that he got the gist.

New information had come through the wire and it wasn't good.

"Madi and I have butted heads time and time again but it's only because we're both stubborn, stubborn women," she continued. "That baby of hers, of *yours*, will no doubt be the same way. So it's best if you know now that there isn't anything my stubbornness wouldn't do for them. You get both of our babies home, okay? Whatever it takes. And here…"

Julian checked the gun and put it into the waistband of his jeans while she hurried out of the room. When she got back there was a Stetson in her hands.

"If it rains again this will help keep it out of your eyes." Julian gave her a small smile and bent down so she could place the cowboy hat atop his head. It was a surprisingly good fit. "Not bad, Mr. Mercer," Dorothy said with approval. "You look just like a local."

"Thank you, Mrs. Nash. I mean it."

"You're family now," she said with a dismissive wave of her hand. "And call me Dorothy."

Julian thanked her again. She embraced him in a hard hug.

"I've already told the boys but I'm going to tell you, too. The moment you hear anything, you let me know. I'll be at Desmond's with Nina, Molly and Clive. Everyone else who works on the ranch has been ordered to stay home until those awful people are caught."

"Will do."

Dorothy's body language was rigid, worry slowly crushing her. Julian felt the same weight against him. Since pitching their theory about the photo album to Declan, twenty minutes had passed. Waiting had been one of the hardest things Julian had ever had to do. If Dorothy hadn't come in for an update at the same time Desmond had gotten the call, Julian would have pressed his ear against Desmond's phone if he'd had to just to hear what was going on.

Julian hurried outside, checking to make sure the gun was secure again, and stopped next to Desmond with his heart in his throat. The Nash triplet kept his expression blank. He held up his finger.

"Fine," he said to the person on the other line. "Yeah. I get it… All right. Bye."

Desmond was angry. That much was clear. But he wasn't devastated. It was the only thing that kept Julian's mouth shut until the man explained himself.

"I can't believe it but you might have been right about Loraine and Ray being those kids in the picture," he started. "At least, they weren't always who they say they were."

"Let me guess, their real names aren't Loraine and Ray?"

"They are," Desmond corrected. "But they weren't always. Loraine apparently had her name changed five years ago, according to Nathan's assistant. Though she didn't know what the previous name was. Jazz is looking into that now. As for Ray, nothing on him has been found. Nothing. Zilch. He didn't start popping up until three years ago when he got a job on a construction crew. Caleb talked to his boss briefly. He said all he knew about Ray was he had a serious girlfriend and a nasty scar covered with a tattoo. Caleb is trying to track the girlfriend down now. That's all they've got so far but they're still digging." He sighed. "If they are in one of those pictures in the photo album, we don't have any proof. None of those kids look like them. We might still be grasping at straws here."

It was Julian's turn to hold up his finger to ask for pa-

tience. He turned on his heel and went to the dining room.
There he grabbed the photo album. He flipped through it
as he ran back to the porch.

"Since these pictures are older I'm not surprised that
their quality isn't the greatest. That, plus the fact that it's
hard to take a picture of a bunch of kids, made me think
that this was an error made by human or camera." Julian
found the group picture and pointed to a boy near Madi. He
moved his finger to focus on the boy's right forearm. His
entire arm was partially blurry. He'd moved as the picture
was taken. However, there was a dark patch across it that
disappeared around the elbow. "But now that you said it,
don't you think that could be a nasty scar?"

Desmond bent over the picture.

"Caleb said the scar was on his arm but didn't specify
where."

Julian felt another surge of adrenaline waiting in the
wings, prickling against his skin and mind. Ready to
pounce when the next puzzle piece finally fitted. An excitement he seemed to be sharing with Desmond. His eyes
widened.

"We need another picture of him. I know Madi put most
of her stuff from back then in the loft but Ma had us sneak
some of her old things into the Hidden Hills attic when
she moved out there. Maybe there are more pictures there
or something else we can use?"

"Or there could be more in the loft," Julian had to point
out. "Madi didn't look through any of the boxes after she
found this."

"We need more time!"

Desmond ran a hand over the back of his neck, stressed.
Julian had to agree.

"Why don't you go look through the loft boxes and I'll
go to Hidden Hills and look there? There's not much we

can do around here other than wait. We might just find something now that we know what to look for."

It didn't take long for Desmond to make up his mind. They floored it to the barn. Desmond hopped out and motioned to the driver's seat.

"There's a key to the inn on the key ring. The one next to the truck key," he said. "Call me if you find anything."

They didn't waste any more time talking. Julian took off toward the inn. Every inch he sped across—every foot, every mile—he thought of no one but Madi and his unborn child.

When he saw Madi again he swore he'd never leave her side.

Hidden Hills had been crawling with lawmen the last two times he'd come to the end of the road. Julian half expected the same this time around. Instead there were only two cars. One was Madi's. They'd been driving his SUV around when needed. The same SUV he hadn't expected to see again. At least not parked outside Hidden Hills.

Yet there it was.

Julian hit the brakes.

He came to Hidden Hills looking for a clue that could lead to Madi. What better one to find than the vehicle that had disappeared along with her?

"Well, isn't this fun?"

Green Eyes was not amused, despite his word choice. Madi was right there with him. Miller, too. The three of them were in varying states of agitation standing in the entryway of Hidden Hills.

"Should I worry about more pink handcuffs?" he added, eyeing the stairs.

"Not unless that's your thing," Madi shot back. Her fear

of torture had taken a momentary back seat. She hated being afraid in her own home.

Miller bumped her shoulder. The well-dressed man snorted.

"My *thing* is making difficult people tell me what I want to know." He dragged his eyes back to hers and smiled sweetly. "And making them pay when they lie to me. Are you going to be one of those people, Blondie?"

"I already told you, I need a key from upstairs before we do anything else." It was a lie. One she and Miller had cobbled together in the minute or so they'd been alone on the bench. Their goal was to create as many possibilities of escape, while also rolling the dice that they'd run into someone who could help them.

Madi had refused to lie about the ranch, as Miller had originally wanted. The man may have had bamboo skewers but that didn't mean he wasn't also carrying a gun. She wasn't going to chance Nathan and his men happening upon her family or the workers on the ranch who might as well have been family.

Now, though, Madi felt like the circle around them was tightening. No one was at the inn and Madi didn't know how to keep Green Eyes's attention without being subjected to torture.

And she had to pee again, if she was being honest.

"Hey, Cap, how does it look up there?" Green Eyes yelled up the stairs. His partner, who had surprisingly kept his distance from them, appeared on the steps. He wasn't as well dressed as his counterpart. Instead he had on a graphic tee of a band Madi hadn't heard of along with a pair of gray cargo pants. Those pockets looked weighted. Madi was afraid to know what he was carrying in them.

"I checked everywhere. No one's up there," Cap said,

annoyed. "I'll take her up and you and the badge can make sure no one sneaks up on us here."

Madi's stomach twisted at the suggestion. Green Eyes might have been terrifying but there was something about Cap that made her skin crawl.

"Oh, so *he's* the boss," Miller said at her side. He chuckled. "I was trying to figure out the dynamic but I get it now."

Cap snickered; his partner did not.

"Laugh it up, old man. I wonder if you'll still be this funny when I start carving into you for lying. You do anything and I'll gut her." Madi yelped as Green Eyes grabbed the back of her shirt and pushed her to the stairs. "I'll take them both up. Cap, you keep watch."

Miller fell in line with a grunt. Madi's mind was racing. While there was a key to her post office box in a desk upstairs, it wasn't going to magically make Nathan's men let her and Miller go. She didn't know how long it would even help them stall. What lie could she tell to save them?

There was another key to where Loraine really was in the PO box?

Madi wouldn't have believed it. She doubted the man at her side would, either.

"It's in my room," she said when he paused at the second-floor landing. The three of them shuffled into her living suite. The door leading into her bedroom was splintered. No thanks to the man next to her.

"You aren't leaving through the window this time," he warned once they were inside.

Madi's legs started to shake. Her bluff was failing. She shared a look with Miller. He knew it was about to get bad, too. He cut his eyes around the room and then back to the man. Green Eyes was watching them both with a grin.

"What seems to be the problem?" He crossed his arms

and stopped in front of them. He was so cocky. So smug. He was a man who was used to getting what he wanted. By force. No matter if his prey was innocent or not.

No matter if they were carrying a child or not.

The walk-in closet door was open behind him. The key she had alluded to was in her jewelry box inside.

Yet by the look in his eye, Madi already knew how that would play out. There was no lie she could tell to convince him to continue the wild-goose chase. He'd hurt her. He'd hurt Miller. Then Cap would join in.

They wouldn't stand a chance.

Julian.

She missed out on her chance to get to know him the last several months because she'd been afraid to let anyone in. Now? Now it was a regret that rivaled her fear of the unknown.

Not only did Madi want to continue to get to know him, she wanted the chance to love him, too. She wanted him to know her and to be loved by him. She wanted their family to grow.

And she wasn't going to let Green Eyes take that away from her without a fight.

"There's no problem," Madi answered. She slowly slid her right foot back to give her better balance. She could feel Miller's eyes on her. Madi hoped his hands being bound wouldn't throw off his survival instincts. "Because I just realized something you probably didn't think to hide."

The man's eyebrow quirked up.

"Oh yeah, what's that?"

Madi's muscles started to vibrate in anticipation. She glanced at Miller. She'd spent most of her life hating him, yet now she felt a kinship. An understanding. Whether or not he knew exactly what she was doing, he gave a small nod.

Madi stilled her nerves. She thought of Julian when she answered.

"I don't think you have a gun."

Miller threw his entire weight into the man. It pushed them both back into the closet. Madi followed, landing a kick to Green Eyes as they hit her hanging clothes.

"Cap," he yelled out. Miller's hands might have been bound but he did fast work of getting the man to the floor. Madi hovered, waiting for an opening. She didn't want to hit Miller and she certainly didn't want the man to get a hit in on her or her stomach.

"Cap!"

"Madi—" Miller grunted, swinging down at the man. "Go—go lock the door!"

Madi turned on her heel and ran for the suite's main door. There were bullet holes in it. The lock was busted. She hadn't noticed that detail before.

Footsteps thundered up the steps.

Madi felt an overwhelming sense of déjà vu as Cap appeared at the top of the stairs with a gun in hand. He pointed it without hesitation. Madi tried to shield her stomach as a gunshot exploded through the house.

She squeezed her eyes shut. Waiting for the pain.

Instead all she felt was the rapid beating of her heart.

Then she heard a thud.

"Madi?" Miller asked, running in behind her. It forced her to open her eyes.

Cap was on the floor. His eyes were open but blood was already pooling around him. Miller bumped up against her shoulder.

"Get back," Miller whispered, easing in front of her. "We don't know who it is."

"Julian?" Madi called, ignoring the detective.

Who else would have shot the bad guy?

Red hair ascended the stairs. A red-painted smile followed. Loraine gave her a wink.

"Don't worry," she cooed. "No one is going to hurt you but me."

Chapter Twenty-Two

Loraine swung the gun around and pulled the trigger. Miller made an awful noise. He stumbled backward into Madi. She barely managed to keep standing as his weight hit her side.

"Miller!"

"Get out of here," he yelled.

Loraine laughed. Madi grabbed the man's arm and pulled.

"Come on," she said hurriedly.

Miller didn't fight her but he did struggle. Together they barely made it back into her bedroom.

"He might have a phone," Madi realized, looking at Green Eyes in the closet. He was motionless against the floor.

Miller didn't respond. Madi went from pulling him along to pushing him. It wasn't gentle by any means but she wanted a door between them and Loraine. The closet was their best bet. Especially if it meant they could get the man's cell phone.

"Oh, Madi. Going in there isn't going to stop me," Loraine called from the bedroom doorway. She was taking her sweet time.

Miller hit the ground and crawled out of the way so Madi could close the door behind him. An antique glider her mother had given her when she'd found out Madi was pregnant sat in the corner. Madi dragged it in front of the door, heart beating a million miles per second.

It blocked the door but it wouldn't hold for long.

Madi knelt down and went through her would-be torturer's pockets. Desperate for a phone. All she found instead were the skewers and a knife she would have preferred to never think about again. However, it was their only weapon.

"You've got to be kidding me," she cried.

"Get away from the door," Miller said before his words devolved into coughing.

Madi joined him against the wall directly to the left of the door. Miller's gunshot wound was gut-wrenching. He'd been hit in chest. Blood had already soaked his shirt. Madi grabbed one of her T-shirts hanging above him and knelt next to him. It was an awkward movement with her belly. She tipped over to the ground and decided sitting was the only option if she wanted to help the detective.

"Put pressure on this," she ordered, handing him the shirt. "I need to be ready if she comes in."

"Oh, Madi, what are you really going to do?" Loraine asked through the door. Madi tightened her grip around the knife's handle. "I know you, baby girl, you're not that kind of gal. You let your words do the cutting, right? The rest of us are the ones who use the blades."

"I don't know what you're talking about, Loraine," Madi volleyed back. "I don't even know why you're here."

The door shook but never opened. Madi put both of her hands around the knife's handle. She was shaking.

"I really am going to have to thank Dr. Pulaski," Loraine said through the door. "When she said she could really make me look unrecognizable she wasn't kidding."

Madi shared a confused look with Miller. His face had become pale.

Loraine laughed.

"I guess you're confused, huh?" she continued. "Don't worry, that was the point. I would have been upset if you'd figured out who I was."

Madi shook her head, as if that would knock loose some answers.

"Who are you?"

Loraine's cackle was so loud it was like she was inches from them and not on the other side of the wall.

"Does Tabitha Walker ring a bell or did I fail to leave an impression?"

Madi felt like her world flipped upside down. She lowered the knife, eyes as wide as they would go.

"Who?" Miller whispered.

Madi shook her head, refusing to believe it.

"Answer him, Madi," Tabitha called out. "Tell him who I am!"

Madi's mouth had gone dry. When she spoke it was like sandpaper.

"A girl who hated me more than you ever did."

Tabitha laughed again.

"That's right! You aren't the only one, Detective Miller, who has dibs on cursing Madi Nash's name! That's actually why I had to shoot you. See, I need you to die so I can put it on Madi and then I need Madi to die so I can put it on my husband, who I will then take out in self-defense. My God, what a wild cycle this has become!"

Madi felt like she was going to be sick. Even more so when the door shook violently. "But I'd like to see your face for some of this, Madi! Open the door or I'll have to go get Cooper to help me."

"Oh no, no, no." Madi put a hand over her mouth. She squeezed her eyes shut. "No, no, no."

"What?" Miller asked. It sounded like he tried to move closer. He sucked in a breath. She met his stare.

"She's just realized how royally screwed she is," Tabitha answered. "I'll be right back! Time to tell Cooper the inn is secure enough and it's to come up! Don't go anywhere!"

"Why are you screwed? Who are these people?" Miller prodded.

Madi cradled her stomach. She took a deep, wavering breath.

"Tabitha Walker and Cooper Tosh. I went to a therapy camp of sorts when I was younger for kids who had been through traumas. They were in my group." She shook her head, remembering how the two had rubbed her the wrong way even as a child. "They were mean, vindictive. Used their anger to hurt anyone and everyone they could. One day they did awful things to one of the boys in the same group and I—well, I humiliated them in front of everyone. Used *my* anger as an excuse to cause more pain. After it happened, I turned over a new leaf, but they were pulled from the group before the next session. But that was so long ago. I actually hadn't even thought of them until earlier today." Madi laughed. It was a hollow sound even to her ears. "How's that for a coincidence?"

Miller tried to sit up straighter. The shirt he was using for pressure was completely drenched.

"You need to get out of here," he said. "Make it to the window and repeat what you and Julian did the other night along the roof."

"I'm not leaving you," Madi decided. "By taking that bullet you saved me and I'm not—"

"And by leaving me you can save your daughter."

Madi opened her mouth only to close it again. Miller's

expression softened. He was right. It wasn't just her she was trying to save.

She had to think of her child.

Miller must have seen the decision in her expression. He smiled.

"Godspeed, Madeline Nash."

Madi took the knife, moved the chair and threw open the closet door. She ran across the room without hesitation. Then it was another bout of déjà vu. A gunshot went off somewhere in the house behind her. Madi didn't wait to see who caused or received it. She needed to get back to the trellis and head for the woods. Julian would find her. She just knew it.

Madi used the palms of her hands to push the window up. The knife's blade tapped against the glass. It made the urgency of her escape grow.

Loraine had gone from stuck-up stranger with a mean streak to a vengeful specter from her past. Neither had cared about the child in Madi's stomach.

"I was about to worry that you weren't going to try to run. Though, I assure you, I'm not like my husband's lackeys," came a voice behind her. Tabitha had never gone to get Cooper at all. "I'm not about to go racing across the roof when a well-placed bullet can save me the work." Madi stopped midmovement. Slowly she turned, knife out in front of her. "I have work to do," Tabitha continued, standing in the doorway of the bedroom. She still had her gun. "And I'll be damned if I'm going to let you make it any harder than you already have."

Tabitha's voice was unforgiving. So was her expression. It twisted with anger.

"I don't understand," Madi admitted. "Why did you come here? What's your endgame? Why now? Have you really hated me this long?"

Tabitha shook her gun at the knife and then motioned to the bed. Madi suddenly felt exhausted. She dropped her weapon and perched on the edge of her bed. Now she was directly across from the woman. It seemed to satisfy her.

"You're putting yourself right back into the center of attention again," she started. "I'm not surprised. Thinking you're the cause of all of this *and* the endgame. Just like when we were kids, here you are clawing for attention. Making everything about you. You think your words back then could cause all of this?" She took a small step forward, nostrils flared and lips thinned. "Despite popular opinion, you aren't that good."

"Then why?" Madi asked, frustration nearly boiling over. So many questions, still not enough answers. "What are you really doing here? And how does Cooper fit into it? How does your husband? Why kill Kathy Smart?"

The corner of Tabitha's mouth twitched. Madi could only assume she was gearing up for another show of cruel disregard for basic decency.

"It's quite simple, really. Even after your boy toy showed up and ruined our original plan." She moved to the end of the bed. Madi wondered if she was like a Bond villain. Would the need to share her diabolical plan outweigh the need to keep her plan in forward motion?

Tabitha licked her lips. She smiled.

"Love," she said simply.

That caught Madi off guard.

"Love? You have a funny way of showing it for your husband."

Tabitha's smile vanished.

"Cooper is the one I love. The only thing I love about my husband is his money," she said. "Which is why I needed to die before I disappeared. You can't suspect a dead person of taking your money, now can you?"

"That's why you killed Kathy Smart. You needed everyone to think you were dead so you used that poor woman's body," Madi realized. "Then—what?—you decided to set me up for it and leave when I was convicted for it?"

Tabitha shook the gun, anger lighting up her features again.

"Don't make it sound that simple," she yelled. "We thought of everything. Everything! For years we looked for the perfect plan to make our escape so we could live out our days with the money I'd been collecting in secret. All that we needed was a fall guy. One we could set up perfectly. It wasn't until a lovely man approached us in a bar that I realized we could get what we wanted *and* knock down Overlook's beloved Madi Nash. You owning an isolated bed-and-breakfast? Well, that just made everything easier. Cooper even spent time up here months ago, watching, to confirm you were basically all alone. He became so good at sneaking around that he took it to the ranch and managed to stumble onto your tree house! He only got better, too. When we actually started to execute our plan, it was flawless! Taking your phone to call mine while you were distracted before you even went up to your room and then putting the body and shotgun in their places? All while you were in the bath? Perfect."

"But things got messy when Julian showed up, didn't they?" Another piece of the puzzle fell into place. "And let me guess, you didn't know about Kathy Smart's metal plate with a registration number. You didn't count on your husband hiring people to find out the truth, either, did you?"

Tabitha snarled.

"It doesn't matter what happened. We keep adapting." Tabitha nodded to the closet. "This crime scene will confuse everyone so much they won't think about me until we're long gone. Sure, it's not as ideal as the original plan of playing dead, but like I said, we keep adapting."

The sound of something heavy hitting the ground below them vibrated the house. Tabitha's eyes widened but she didn't say anything. Instead she pulled the gun up to aim at Madi's head, and for the first time since they'd started talking, Tabitha looked down at Madi's stomach. Her expression didn't soften. There was no remorse in her eyes when she returned her gaze.

"Please, Tabitha. Please don't do this," Madi pleaded. "You and Cooper, just go. Right now. Let me call in that Miller has been shot and the response will create an opening for the two of you to get out of town. You don't have to do this."

"I'd do anything to ensure our future. Anything."

Madi had never known fear so acute. It consumed her. She hunched over, absurdly hoping she could protect her child somehow. Pain squeezed her heart. She closed her eyes.

"Funny, I was thinking the same thing."

Madi's head flew up, her heart already singing.

Julian stood behind Tabitha. He had a gun to her head.

"If you hurt her, your guy, the one I just hurt very badly downstairs, dies," he said, voice so low and dangerous that goose bumps erupted across Madi's skin. "Give me the gun and he lives. Simple as that."

Tabitha opened her mouth to say something. She thought better of it. Julian slowly circled her, gun revolving around her head, until he was the one looking her in the eye.

"I should warn you. It will take a lot more than some bullets to keep me from protecting them."

Madi couldn't see Tabitha's face anymore but she heard the defeat in the sigh that followed. She threw her gun onto the bed. Madi scooped it up.

"Now, make sure Cooper doesn't die," Tabitha spit.

"I already did. I'm guessing most, if not all, of the law enforcement from Wildman County are almost here."

Julian ordered her to the closet, where he used Madi's belts to restrain her and Green Eyes. Sirens blared in the distance. Madi dropped down to Miller's side. He was unconscious but alive. She put pressure against his wound but looked up at Julian, standing sentry in the doorway.

Without the threat of a gun pointed at her, Madi took in new, terrifying details. He was bruised and bloodied, his clothes ripped and stained. However, the most alarming detail was the bullet wound in his side.

"Julian, you've been shot!"

The man, the beautiful father of her child, simply smiled.

"I wasn't lying. Nothing was going to keep me from you two. Not even bullets."

Chapter Twenty-Three

Chance Montgomery picked up the cowboy hat off the hospital nightstand and gave it an appraising look.

"Not bad," he said. "Not my particular style, but have you seen me?" He grinned. "You can't copy something *this* good."

Julian laughed. It hurt, but nowhere near as bad as it had before surgery. Now it was more of a soreness. A bullet to the side could have been a lot worse. Thankfully, Cooper Tosh had been a poor shot.

"Yeah, yeah, we get it. You're God's gift to mankind. Now, why don't you help me carry my stuff out of here?"

Chance laughed and put Julian's bag across his shoulder. Julian grabbed the cards that had been set up on the table in his room and both of them looped a vase of flowers under each arm. By the time they made it down to Chance's truck, they looked like they'd robbed a florist.

"I guess the town of Overlook has decided they believe you and Madi are the good guys." Chance threw the bag in the back and put his flowers on the seat between them. It was a crowded but colorful space in the small cab.

"Yep. Turns out Tabitha's love for Cooper wasn't just a dramatic declaration. She cut a deal and told the cops everything in an attempt to reduce his sentence. She owned up to killing the coroner, shooting Holloway and shooting Cooper's girlfriend, Kathy Smart." Julian shrugged.

"You don't think she did those things?"

"I think she did them, I just think she didn't do them alone. But I get it," Julian admitted. "She's trying to protect someone she loves. I know the feeling." Julian cut a look over to Chance. After he'd gotten out of surgery Chance had been in his hospital room along with Madi. She'd called the cowboy in and given him the lowdown on everything that had happened. Chance had been in town every day since, trying to help where he could.

He was a great friend. Which was why Julian had to apologize.

"When the cops checked my alibi and called you, you backed me up. I shouldn't have put you in that situation. Not after everything you've done for me. I'm sorry, Chance. I really am."

The Alabama cowboy took his hand off the steering wheel to wave off the concern.

"I trust you, even the lies you tell," he said. "You believed in Madi and I believed in you. That's no biggie in my book."

"Still, thank you for it."

"No problem."

They drove straight to the ranch and up to the main house. A thrill of nerves went through Julian. Neither man got out of the truck.

"Whatever happened to Nathan, by the way?" Chance finally asked. "I meant to ask but time kept flying by at the bed-and-breakfast with those Nash brothers. They're good at fixing bullet holes and broken things, but, man, when we got to talking about football, it was like the rest of the world went away."

Julian laughed at that. The Nash brothers hadn't been

the only ones pitching in to help with the damage that had been done to Hidden Hills and the ranch. Overlook wasn't just a town, it was a community. One that was quick to act. Madi's bed had already been replaced with a new mattress before Julian was even out of surgery.

"Last I heard he was still paying a fortune for a lawyer who wasn't doing a great job. I don't think anyone can save him from prison. He hired hit men to torture a pregnant woman and a lawman. Not to mention everything Tabitha added to it. Telling the FBI about all of his seedy business dealings definitely didn't do him any favors."

"And to think, he had no clue his wife had only married him to steal his money, fake her own death and run off with her boyfriend." Chance shook his head. "If Tabitha had just tried to run off without all the killing she might have made it. Instead she managed to go up against two separate parties all looking and fighting for the truth."

"Yep," Julian agreed. "My favorite part of this whole mess, and please note my sarcasm as I say *favorite*, has to be what went down with the photo album."

"What do you mean? When you found the group picture of the kids?"

Julian shook his head, still having a hard time believing what he said next.

"Right after Miller showed up at the trail and the three of us went to the tree house, Nathan's lackeys parked and went into the woods after us for the ambush. While we were in the woods Ray, aka Cooper, broke into my SUV and grabbed the photo album."

"How did he know you had it? Was he following you two?"

"Bingo. After he ran into us at the stable he apparently decided to keep an eye on us and use the excuse that he was just on the ranch as a guest if caught. That's what Tabitha said at least."

"So when he saw you with the photo album he decided he needed to take it just in case?"

"Tabitha told him to. She remembered them all taking pictures during camp when they were kids," Julian said. Then he shook his head a little, still in a weird kind of awe with how everything had panned out. "So, while Nathan's hired helpers followed Miller to get to Madi and had us in the woods, Tabitha had her partner in crime follow the photo album. How Cooper didn't see Nathan's men and vice versa is still mind-blowing. It's almost like some kind of slapstick comedy where the audience sees all the near misses but the characters never realize just how close everything came to intersecting."

Chance shook his head. He let out a long whistle.

"This was all just one heck of a mess, if you ask me."

"You got that right, brother." Julian looked at his watch. They still had a little time. "All right, we need to get these inside and then get going. You still up for it?"

Chance laughed. It was from the belly.

"Am *I* up for it? The question is, are you?"

Julian gave his friend a big smile.

"I've never been ready for anything more than I am now."

MADI RAN A hand over her stomach. It wouldn't be long before Addison would make her appearance. Madi's early worries of being a mother felt like a memory from long ago. Now all she wanted to do was hold her daughter and tell her how much she had been loved before she had ever even taken a breath.

A knock sounded on the door. Madi started to duck into the bathroom when a man's voice floated through.

"It's Miller," he called. "I was wondering if I could have a quick moment."

Madi's already-fluttering nerves slowed again.

"Come in!"

Christian Miller was in his Sunday best. He'd even donned a weathered cowboy hat. He took it off when he saw her and placed it against his chest.

"You look nice," he greeted, shutting the door behind them. Madi smiled.

"You don't look so bad, either. Especially for a man who needed two surgeries and should really be following the doctor's orders to stay off your feet."

Miller shrugged.

"What can I say, I'm a stubborn old man." He winced as he moved but Madi decided not to push it. Miller had tried and succeeded to protect her when it counted. He deserved to not be pestered. Plus, whatever had gotten him up the stairs must have been important. His demeanor shifted from pleasant to serious in a heartbeat.

"I know this probably isn't the best time to tell you this, but, well, I think you deserve to know."

"Know what?"

He took an uncertain step forward and dived in.

"Why your father thought I was involved with your abduction all those years ago." Madi hadn't expected that. "You see, when your dad started suspecting that the attacker had connections to the police force, he questioned everyone in the department at length. When he got to me, I lied about where I was and he knew it." A look of clear shame came across his expression. "When I was young I wasn't a good man. Not when it came to my wife. The day you were attacked and taken I'd been with a woman who wasn't my wife. I didn't want anyone to find out. Your dad saw that dishonesty and never let up. It turned every-

one's attention on me until, finally, I admitted the truth."
He let out a long breath and gave her a small smile filled
with regret. "I never blamed your dad for questioning me.
I blamed him for putting me in the spotlight. Even though
it was my own fault."

"I—I never knew that."

"Because when your dad realized the truth he promised not to tell. But you know how secrets in this town
work. Some found out, including my wife." He sighed
again. Then he was back to standing tall. "I just wanted
to let you know that your dad was a good man. It was me
who messed up and it's been me I've been mad at all these
years. I never really hated you or your family. Just my idiot
younger self. I'm sorry for how I've acted. I really am."

Madi closed the distance between them and hugged the
man, careful to be gentle.

"Thank you, Detective," she said at his shoulder. "That
means a lot."

Miller returned the hug and then stepped back. He put
his cowboy hat back on and cleared his throat.

"Well, now that that's out of the way, I think I'll go
find my seat. I'm sure Declan will be here any second
now to get you."

He gave her one more smile and left Madi alone again.
She didn't know if it was the pregnancy hormones or what,
but her eyes started to mist over. When Declan arrived
no more than a minute later, his eyes widened in worry.

"I'm okay," she said hurriedly, swatting away his concern. "I'm just—well, I'm just so *happy* and it feels weird."

Declan chuckled.

"That's good, right?"

Madi nodded and took his outstretched arm.

"It's great," she said. "And I have a feeling it's only
going to get better."

Declan smiled. While she had a special bond with her triplet brothers, she couldn't deny that the sibling love she felt for her older brother was fierce. He squeezed her hand as if to say it was mutual.

They walked down to the back door that led to Hidden Hills' patio. The blinds were all drawn but Madi could hear the music perfectly when her song started.

"In a different situation, I would point out that this is all happening so fast," Declan said, hand resting on the doorknob. "But somehow it doesn't feel right to say it here. Not with the two of you." Those nerves started to dance across Madi's chest and stomach. "He really loves you and you really love him, don't you?"

Madi nodded.

"I do."

Declan laughed.

"Then wait a few minutes and say that again."

He opened the door and all Madi saw was the man she loved standing at the end of a path of petals, dressed in a suit and smiling at her. Their friends and family stood on either side of the path, but Madi saw only Julian.

The memory of his proposal would forever be branded on her heart.

"You told me that your dad used to say that there's never enough time to do everything, so focus on the one thing you can do," Julian had said from his hospital bed. He'd pulled a ring from beneath his pillow. Madi would later find out he'd asked his mother to bring his grandmother's ring with her when she came to see them. Julian had held the ring up with a smile that she knew would never fade. "And I told you that I thought it was great advice. I still believe that. So I'm going to follow it and do the only thing in this world I think is worth doing." He'd used his other hand to tuck a strand of her hair behind her ear.

"And that is?" she'd asked, nearly breathless.

Julian's smile had only grown.

"Love you," he'd said simply. "You and our family. Forever and always."

Madi had smiled for all she was worth. Just as she was now beneath the wedding arch. That smile was reflected in Julian.

"You may kiss the bride," the preacher exclaimed.

Julian did just that.

"The only thing worth doing," he whispered when the kiss ended.

Madi kept on smiling. She agreed.

"The only thing worth doing."

* * * * *

COLTON 911: COWBOY'S RESCUE

MARIE FERRARELLA

To
Patience Bloom
For Always Being
My Guardian Angel

Prologue

The truth shall set Elliott free.

Maggie Reeves, formerly Maggie Corgan, had always been cursed with an insatiable curiosity. The slightest hint of a mystery could set her off. Which was why she was out here, in the middle of Live Oak Ranch—a ranch that belonged to her ex-husband's family, a local ranching dynasty—following a map that she had propped up beside her on the passenger seat, when she should have been back in town, getting ready for her sister's wedding.

Granted, the wedding was tomorrow and logically, there was plenty of time for her to get ready, even if she moved in slow motion. That was the argument Maggie had used on herself to assuage her conscience when she couldn't seem to tamp down her curiosity.

The wind was picking up. She pushed her blond hair out of her eyes and focused again on the road ahead. So many questions filled her head, it was hard keeping them straight.

Why would her ex-husband's late father leave her anything in his will? Yet according to her attorney, Adam Corgan had addressed the envelope to her, saying it was to be sent to her upon his death. When Maggie opened it, she had no idea what to expect, but it certainly wasn't a map of his property highlighting "the tallest live oak" with an X.

There was a note included with the map. She had read and reread the note a dozen times. As written, it was simplicity itself.

She just didn't understand it.

The truth shall set Elliott free.

What was that supposed to *mean*? What truth?

She knew who Elliott was. *Everyone* knew who Elliott was. Elliott Corgan was Adam's disgraced older brother. He had suddenly disappeared years ago, his location a secret that his family guarded closely. No one within the family spoke about him, but over the years, there had been rumors.

It was the stuff that local legends were made of, some of it possibly true, some of it obviously not. It all depended on what a person believed and who was telling the story at the time.

After her divorce, Maggie didn't give Elliott Corgan any thought at all.

Until the letter had arrived.

But just what was this "truth" and how would finding it—whatever "it" was—set Elliott free?

Free in the biblical sense or actually free? And free from what? Why would the man she had never met need to be set free? She didn't understand any of it.

An even-bigger mystery, in her opinion, was why had her ex-father-in-law sent this to her after his death? They hadn't been particularly close when she was married to James. They certainly were less than that once she had divorced his son.

And yet, Adam Corgan had left specific instructions that this be sent to her after he died.

Why?

"One mystery at a time, Mags," she murmured, glancing over toward the map again.

According to the directions, the tree that Adam wanted her to closely examine was located smack in the middle of some pretty rough terrain. Her vehicle was not equipped with four-wheel drive. There were times she felt it barely had front-wheel drive. The only way she was going to be able to reach the tree was to walk the rest of the way across the field.

Maggie sighed. She supposed that was why she had worn boots, in case this sort of thing came up. If she had any real sense in her head, she would just turn around and go back. But unfortunately, her curiosity trumped sense each and every time.

She got out of the car. The wind was really picking up, she caught herself thinking as she leaned into the passenger side and pulled out the map. Folding it so that it was more compact and manageable, Maggie began to make her way toward the tree.

She assumed that "setting Everett free" was probably going to require some digging. Well, she could do that when she returned after the wedding. For now, all she wanted to do was find the right spot.

Once she satisfied her curiosity—or at least as much of it as she was able to satisfy—she'd come back later on in the week. At that point she would do whatever needed to be done in order to discover this so-called "truth" that Adam Corgan had entrusted her with finding from beyond the grave.

"All very creepy if you ask me," Maggie stated out loud, even though there wasn't a soul around for what seemed like miles.

"Speaking of creepy," Maggie murmured, reacting to

the wind, which was making a really mournful, increasingly loud noise now.

Feeling uneasy, she looked around several times to assure herself that it *was* the wind and not someone, or worse, some*thing* that was howling like that. It almost sounded like a wounded animal.

But it wasn't.

Finding out that it *was* the wind that was making such a racket and blowing so hard didn't really comfort her as much as it should have.

By the time she came close to her destination, Maggie realized that the world around her, which had been fairly bright earlier, had suddenly turned dark and foreboding, as if a giant switch had been flipped.

Maggie stopped trudging over the rocky terrain about a foot shy of the tree her ex-father-in-law had marked and looked up at the sky.

The Texas sun had totally disappeared and the sky was beyond gray, almost black. The wind continued to pick up and was now making a really fierce noise.

That was when she suddenly remembered hearing something about a hurricane prediction. She had initially discounted it because half the time the weather bureau was completely wrong in its forecasts. Another 25 percent of the time, it was still off its mark by more than half.

"Why, of all possible times, did they have to pick *this* time to be right?" Maggie cried out in total exasperation.

The hurricane was no longer just a prediction. It was here. And getting worse.

Maggie quickly scanned the area. There was absolutely no place for her to hide. No place for her to take shelter from the coming storm.

And the hurricane, Maggie realized as she looked to her left, was coming straight at her.

Chapter One

When it was raging at its worst, Hurricane Brooke was gauged at having winds that were blowing through Whisperwood and its surrounding area at over 125 miles an hour, making it almost a category four hurricane. Taking the Texas town totally by surprise, the death toll quickly mounted and was currently up to thirty-eight and rising with dozens more still missing and unaccounted for.

A lot of Whisperwood's residents sought refuge in their basements, but others weren't so lucky. They were out in the open when the storm struck and scrambled for shelter anywhere they could, praying that shelter would hold.

Jonah Colton and three of his brothers had returned to the town where they were born a few days before the hurricane struck. At the time, they were all looking forward to seeing their brother Donovan become the first of their family to get married. As it turned out, three of the brothers belonged to Cowboy Heroes, a search and rescue team that scoured the countryside on horseback, rescuing people. They never dreamed they would have to put their skills to use in their own hometown, but things didn't always go according to plan.

And this was one of those times.

The moment the winds died down, before the hurricane was even officially declared to be over, Jonah, Dallas, Nolan and Forrest, a former police detective forced into retirement after sustaining a leg injury, were out, putting their acquired skills to good use, searching for and rescuing survivors.

Some of the houses in the area lucked out and were barely touched, but they quickly saw that others had been completely demolished. In some cases, the people who had lived in those houses were now buried beneath them in the rubble. Those were the people that Jonah and his brothers focused on helping first, bringing them to the church's recreational center, where survivors were being temporarily housed.

"You do a head count?" Jonah asked Forrest.

The latter, eight years Jonah's junior, had recently been forced to resign from the Austin Police Department when a bullet to his leg had left him incapacitated. Thanks to adhering to a diligent regiment of physical therapy, Forrest was now able to get around again, although he did have a pronounced limp. Unable to just do nothing, he had joined the volunteer search and rescue teams in order to feel useful. When the hurricane struck, he immediately volunteered to help find victims of the storm.

Jonah knew better than to insult his younger brother by treating him any differently than he would the other members of the team.

They had been at this now for over twelve hours without a break. Most of the people they had helped dig out had just sustained injuries, some more serious than others. But some of those they dug out would not be recovering. Those bodies were wrapped up as carefully as possible and placed out of sight until they could be taken to the morgue. Ironically, the morgue had been untouched by the hurricane.

Inside the rec center when Jonah had asked him the question about a head count, Forrest knew that his brother was referring to the members of their family. He was relieved to answer in the affirmative.

"Dallas found Mom and Dad. They're okay," he said, realizing that was the first thing that any of them would have asked. "So are Donovan and Bellamy," he told Jonah. "Nolan's supposed to be bringing them here," he added, looking around the rec center.

The recreation center was quickly filling up with people and cots at this point, but it was the largest common area available in Whisperwood. This was where town meetings were held, although the meetings had never drawn half this many people.

"There's no way we are going to be able to put up even *half* the town in here. There's got to be at least 5,500 people living in and around Whisperwood," Dallas Colton guessed as he walked into the center.

"We're sending the overflow to Kain's Garage and the General Store. They've got large storm cellars," Jonah told the others. "Hopefully, the storm's not going to be doubling back. Otherwise," he speculated as he looked from one brother to another, "the damage is going to be even worse than it is now."

"This really isn't so bad," Dallas commented, reviewing what he had seen in the last twelve hours. "Compared to other hurricanes."

Forrest frowned. "Try telling that to the families of the people who lost their lives in this," he said grimly.

Rehashing the situation served no purpose now. "You're right," Jonah agreed. "Help now, talk later," he told his brothers.

At that moment, Jonah spotted Donovan heading toward them, his hand firmly holding on to his fiancée's.

Donovan appeared exhausted and he looked as if he could definitely use a change of clothes. His were wet and streaked with mud. Beside him, Bellamy appeared almost numb.

"Are you two all right?" Jonah asked, concerned that the woman next to his brother looked as if she was about to have a complete breakdown.

"I am, but—" Donovan began, but he never got a chance to finish.

Because at that moment, Bellamy grabbed Jonah's arm, clutching it as if she was holding on to a lifeline. The zombie look on her face vanished, replaced by an animated expression that looked as if it was actually bordering on hysteria.

"You've got to find her," Bellamy begged him with feeling.

"Her?" Jonah repeated, unsure of who the woman was referring to.

"Magnolia—Maggie—my sister," Bellamy almost shouted before she was able to get herself under control. "Please," she pleaded, still clutching his hand and squeezing it hard for emphasis. "She's out there somewhere, maybe hurt, or—"

Bellamy couldn't bring herself to utter the condemning word. It was just too frightening to give voice to. Instead, she repeated herself. "You have to find her and bring her back."

After years of being estranged, Bellamy and her younger sister, Maggie, had finally cleared up the misunderstanding, centered around their parents, that had kept them apart all this time. Bellamy had thought that Maggie had turned her back on the family to marry well and run off, when the exact opposite turned out to be true. When they finally sat down to talk, the truth came out.

Issues had been resolved to the point that Bellamy had asked Maggie to be her co–maid of honor, along with her best friend Rae Lemmon. Maggie had happily agreed.

And now this happened.

"You *have* to bring her back," Bellamy insisted. "I can't lose her!"

"Where did you last see her?" Jonah asked, trying to retrace Maggie's steps.

Bellamy closed her eyes, trying to clear her head and summon the memory. It didn't come at first.

"At the house." Her eyes flew open. "The last time I saw her was at the house," she exclaimed.

"But she's not there." Donovan spoke up. "We went there are soon as we could," he explained to his brothers.

"Something awful's happened to her, I just know it," Bellamy declared, struggling to keep her tears back. "You have to—"

Still clutching his arm tightly, Bellamy was beginning to make his hand seriously numb. Even so, Jonah smiled reassuringly at his future sister-in-law.

"We will. We'll find her, Bellamy. I promise," he added. "But if I'm going to do that, I'm going to need the use of my arm," he told her, looking pointedly down at her hand.

Bellamy followed his gaze, totally oblivious to the fact that she was holding on to him so tightly.

"Oh," she cried, as surprised as he was that she was gripping his arm so hard. Belatedly, like a person waking up from a dream, she released her hold on him. Collecting herself, she asked, "You'll let me know the second you've found her? One way or the other, you'll let me know," she begged.

"If they get the phone lines working, I promise I'll

let you know as soon as I find her," Jonah told Donovan's fiancée.

"As soon as *we* find her," Dallas corrected. "We're in this together, remember?" he reminded Jonah. "Don't worry," he told Bellamy. "Four sets of eyes are better than one." And then he turned toward Jonah again because there was no denying that Jonah was the team leader. "Just in case your superhero radar is off," he said, attempting to add just a little levity to what was a very dire situation.

"Spread out, guys," Jonah ordered, ignoring Dallas for the time being. "Before we go running off, beating the bushes for any sign of Maggie, let's find out if anyone here saw her or talked to her before this storm decided to redecorate the landscape. Plenty of people here to talk to," he added, gesturing around at the people who occupied the rec center. Still more were filing in by the hour.

JONAH FELT HE was getting nowhere. Questioning resident after shaken resident, he was forced to detach himself, putting up a wall between himself and those who were so very desperate to share their story with someone. He hated being so impersonal but needed to keep a clear head if he wanted to be able to find Maggie.

And he did.

Not just to keep his promise to Bellamy, but because he felt a special connection when it came to the woman he'd been tasked with finding. He remembered Maggie Reeves all too well from school, even though he was five years older than she was. He'd been a gawky kid back then, skinny as a rail until he'd started working on his parents' ranch in his teens. He'd filled out then, but Maggie, Maggie had been born beautiful and only grew more so as time went by. He remembered that she'd even won the coveted title of Miss Austin in a beauty pageant. There had been other accolades along the way. But that was before she had gotten married.

The marriage didn't last, but he could have predicted that if anyone had asked. James Corgan might have been wealthy, but he was an amoral alley cat. All the money in the world couldn't change that, Jonah thought as he continued questioning survivors. He never understood what Maggie had seen in James, but whatever it was, her vision cleared up soon enough and she had divorced him.

And now Maggie was out there somewhere, hopefully alive—

"Hey, Jonah, I found somebody who saw Maggie maybe an hour before the storm hit," Forrest called out.

Jonah looked up to see his brother trying hard not to limp as he made his way over. The former detective had Rae Lemmon with him. Adrenaline raced through Jonah as he instantly crossed to the duo, meeting them more than halfway.

"You know where she went?" Jonah asked the young woman with Forrest.

"I think so. Maggie talked to me just before she left." The petite brunette nodded, as if that added weight to what she was about to say. "She told me she was going to Live Oak Ranch."

Jonah looked at Rae, puzzled. "Doesn't that belong to her ex's family?" he asked the woman. Maybe Rae had gotten her facts confused. "Why would she be going there?"

Rae raised her slim shoulders in a helpless shrug. "I don't know. Maggie said she was going there because she needed to uncover a secret."

"A secret?" Jonah echoed, in the dark as much as ever. He glanced at Forrest, who just shook his head. He obviously didn't have a clue, either. "What secret?" Jonah asked the paralegal.

"I don't know," Rae repeated helplessly. "She wouldn't tell me anything. Maggie said she'd know more once she got there." And then Rae remembered something. "She did say she had a map."

"A map." Jonah was beginning to feel like a parrot, just repeating things that made no sense. He felt as if he'd been swallowed up by the hurricane and was now being tossed around without rhyme or reason. "Why would she need a map?" he asked. "Maggie lived on Live Oak Ranch when she was married to James, didn't she?"

"Yes," Rae answered. "But she took the map with her because she said she needed to pinpoint the biggest tree on the ranch." Rae shrugged again, feeling frustrated and helpless. She pressed her lips together, silently upbraiding herself that she hadn't made Maggie tell her more. "She really wasn't very clear, and I have to admit that I wasn't paying much attention to what she was saying. I was too busy going over last-minute details for the wedding," Rae confessed.

Rae flushed. The excuse sounded so weak now that she said it out loud.

"Not that it looks like that's going to happen now, at least not on schedule," she added in a small voice. Her tone shifted as she returned to the more important subject under discussion. She needed to tell Jonah anything that sounded even remotely relevant. The smallest thing could be instrumental in locating Maggie. "But I know Maggie—she gets something in her head, she doesn't let it go. I'm positive that she was there somewhere on the ranch when the storm hit."

"And you're sure about this?" Jonah pressed.

He was still somewhat skeptical about this information. After all, it had been a significant amount of time since Maggie had gotten divorced and she and her husband had gone their separate ways. From what he had heard, hers wasn't one of those divorces where the couple remained friends even after their marriage was dissolved. Maggie gave every indication that she didn't want to have anything to do with her ex.

So why would she suddenly go wandering around his family's ranch?

It didn't make any sense to him.

But sense or not, it was the only lead he had about Maggie's last whereabouts, so unless he found out something that was more immediate, he was going to act on this.

And he made up his mind that he was going to act on it alone.

"Absolutely sure," Rae told him solemnly. There was a slight hitch in her voice. "You're going to find her, right?"

"Right," Jonah replied without a moment's hesitation. "I'll find her." And he fully intended to do just that, even if it was the last thing he ever did.

More reports of missing residents were coming in even as Jonah stood there, listening to Rae. The volunteer search and rescue organization he and his brothers belonged to was already stretched to the limit, not to mention exhausted. He wasn't about to ask any of them for help, but he didn't plan on stopping until he located Maggie. The thought of her out there, stranded, possibly in danger and clinging to life, wasn't something he could live with if things took a turn for the worse.

Even if he hadn't already given his word to Bellamy and to Rae, he had made up his mind to do everything in his power to find Maggie.

By the sound of it, the wind was picking up again.

Jonah looked out the rec center windows and saw the trees bending like flexible dancers before the oncoming winds.

Were they in for a second wave? It didn't matter, he thought. He knew he needed to get out there now, before traveling on horseback became hazardous and maybe even impossible.

"Thank you, Rae," he told the distraught woman. "You've been a great help."

She began to say something more, but he didn't have any time to waste. Jonah searched the area for someone he could charge with looking after Rae for now.

"Forrest," he called to his brother. The latter turned toward him after a moment, eyeing Jonah quizzically. "Look after Rae, will you?" he requested. "She seems like she could use a friendly shoulder to lean on."

Forrest didn't look happy about the reassignment. "What about going to look for Maggie Reeves?" his brother asked.

"I got this," Jonah said, shrugging off the implied offer to help. "You take care of Ms. Lemmon and anyone else who might need you."

Forrest's face darkened as he took offense. "I was shot in the leg, Jonah, not the head. I'm perfectly capable of going out there with you to look for Bellamy's sister. Don't treat me like I'm an invalid," he warned his brother.

Jonah backtracked. "I know you're not an invalid," he said gruffly. He wasn't accustomed to trying to tread lightly around any of his brothers and doing so was tricky. "After you make sure Rae's taken care of, go out with the others and search for survivors. And I'll do the same," he declared authoritatively.

With that, Jonah headed out the door. He zipped up his rain slicker. Not that the outer garment would give him much protection if the storm got worse again. He supposed he was doing this more out of habit than anything else. If he followed a ritual, covering all the steps, maybe that would help him find Maggie.

No stone unturned, he thought.

Jonah hurried across the street toward what was left of the town's stable. He and his brothers had housed their horses here to keep them from being left out in the open once the storm hit.

Once inside, he made his way over to his horse, a sleek palomino. Aside from the horses, there was no one around.

"How are you doing, Cody?" Jonah asked, taking time to interact with his mount before going out. He and Cody had been "partnered" for three years now. "Okay, boy, ready to play hero and earn your feed? I know, I know," he said as he put the saddle on his horse and tightened the cinches, "I don't want to go out, either. But there's a crazy woman out there who needs us because she doesn't have enough sense to come in out of the rain—or take shelter when a hurricane is predicted to come rolling through," he said, talking to the palomino as if he was a person. Taking the horse's reins in his hand, he swung into the saddle.

"Let's go do this. The sooner we find her, the sooner we can come back."

Cody whinnied as if he understood. Jonah never doubted that he did.

Chapter Two

"I don't like this any better than you do," Jonah told Cody as he urged his horse on through the increasingly inclement weather.

He had been talking in a calm, steady voice ever since he and his horse had left the stable in Whisperwood. He wasn't sure if he was talking for Cody's benefit or his own, but it helped in both cases.

The farther away from Whisperwood he went, the more Jonah found that he had to steadily raise his voice, because not only had the wind picked up, but so had the threat of rain.

Actually, it wasn't a threat any longer. Rain had turned into a reality, falling with a vengeance. It would recede, only to return, coming down harder than it had before.

If this kept up, the chances of floods throughout the already-beaten-down area was a given. Jonah drew in his shoulders, trying vainly to stay dry. His rain slicker and Stetson were fighting a losing battle, but it wasn't in him just to give up. There was a woman out there who needed to be rescued.

"C'mon, where are you?" Jonah called out impatiently in his frustration.

He did his best to scan as much of the surrounding area as possible. According to his calculations, he had ridden onto the Corgan ranch about fifteen, eighteen minutes ago. Because of the rain that was still coming down, his visibility was limited. He hadn't been able to make out anything except for an occasional tree here and there. Certainly not a person.

In any event, Maggie wasn't near any of the trees he had made out.

"Maybe she's not here at all," he said to Cody. "And we're just wasting our time—not to mention that we're seriously running the risk of drowning out here if it gets any worse." Cody whinnied, as if agreeing with him. Despite the situation he found himself in, Jonah grinned. "I know, I know, we're the ones who don't have enough sense to come in out of the rain, not her. But legend has it Maggie's as stubborn as hell and if she said she was coming out here to find answers, this is where she probably is—but where?" he asked, frustrated.

Lowering his head, Jonah shoved his hat farther down on it, hoping to keep the wind from blowing it off.

"You see her, Cody?" he asked the palomino. "Because I sure as hell don't."

With one hand holding on to his hat, the other one wrapped around Cody's reins, Jonah raised up from his saddle, standing as best he could in his stirrups. He was blinking furiously to keep the rain out of his eyes as he scanned the area again, searching for a familiar shape, or some indication that Maggie was indeed out here, or at least had passed this way.

As he surveyed the area, Jonah realized that his horse had ridden in very close to this humongous oak tree. The tall, wide branches were offering him some degree of shelter from the rain—just in time, it seemed. The rain was coming down harder and harder now.

Some sort of natural reflex had Jonah glancing up

over his head. It was not unheard-of for animals to go climbing up into the first available tree they could find. It was a self-preservation instinct to keep them from being swept away in a storm or a flood. The animals that he knew reacted this way were mountain lions—and bears.

The last thing he wanted was to be under a tree when a mountain lion or bear decided it wanted a snack more than it wanted to stay dry.

But when Jonah looked up, it wasn't a mountain lion or a bear that he saw.

Maggie!

Thank God.

"A little old to be climbing trees, aren't you?" Jonah asked her, amused despite the less than ideal conditions they found themselves in.

Startled, Maggie had been so intent on holding on, she hadn't even realized that he was there.

"Oh lord," she cried, "you are the answer to a prayer!"

It had taken her more than a couple of moments to convince herself that she wasn't hallucinating. After all, she had lost track of how long she had spent up here in this tree. She could hardly believe that she was finally going to be rescued. And if that wasn't enough, this knight in shining armor was nothing short of gorgeous.

Part of Maggie wasn't fully convinced that she *wasn't* imagining all this. That she really *would* be rescued. Her arms had all but gone numb from hanging on to the branch she had climbed up on eons ago. At this point, she couldn't remember *not* being up here.

Jonah slowly angled Cody, as well as himself, right beneath the woman he had come to rescue. He wrapped the horse's reins around his saddle horn, then tightened his thighs about Cody's flanks so that he could hold his position as steadily as possible.

Having taken all the precautions he could, Jonah raised his arms. "Climb down," he instructed the woman perched above him. "Don't worry. If you slip, I'll catch you."

Maggie looked down uncertainly. She really had her doubts about his assurance. "That's a pretty tall order," she called back.

Jonah could appreciate why she was so uneasy. There were several feet of space separating her from his out-stretched arms.

He reassessed the situation. "Are you going to make me climb up there and get you?"

It was more of a challenge than a question. Or maybe she was just interpreting it that way. Maggie didn't know. But she had never been the type of woman who would willingly cleave to the "damsel in distress" image. She wasn't the type to be rescued, either. She preferred doing the rescuing, the way she had tried to come through for her parents.

"Just hang on to your patience," she told him, slowly shifting her weight so that she could start to make her way down.

It took a second for her to release her grip on the branch, but she knew that it was either this or just stay-ing where she was, clinging to a branch like some help-less female while this tall, dark and gorgeous specimen of a man played superhero. While that did intrigue her, it just wasn't her way.

Holding her breath, Maggie inched her way down.

The branch swayed and groaned with every move she made—or maybe that was the wind that was groaning. She didn't know. The only thing she *did* know was that she had to move slowly because there was no way in hell that she was going to come tumbling down out of this tree and wind up on the ground right in front of Mr. Magnificent's horse.

Watching her progress, Jonah grew steadily more uneasy. He continued to hold his arms up and opened. The wind yanked at his Stetson, then ripped it right off his head.

"Damn," he muttered.

Maggie thought the remark was meant for her, but the next second she saw the cowboy's dark Stetson fly by her and then it disappeared into the darkened distance.

"I owe you a hat," she told her rescuer, raising her voice so that he could hear her above the howling of the wind.

"Just get down here," Jonah ordered, reaching up even higher. "We'll settle up later." His shoulders were beginning to ache. "You sure you don't want me climbing up there to get you?" he offered, watching Maggie's painfully slow descent.

"I'm sure!" she snapped, irritated that it was taking her so incredibly long to reach him.

It certainly hadn't felt as if it had taken her this long to climb *up* into the tree. But then, at the time, she'd been propelled by a dire sense of urgency. Maggie had been convinced that the floodwaters would just keep rising to the point that she would be in danger of being swept away.

Mercifully, they had receded and even though the rain kept falling, it didn't do so with anywhere near the intensity that the weather bureau had initially promised.

If it had, all of Texas would have been submerged by now, Maggie thought, inching her way down. And then she managed to reach the man who had come to her rescue.

"Sorry," Maggie apologized just as she finally reached Jonah's arms. "I really didn't mean to yell at you."

"Did you yell?" he asked, feigning ignorance. "I didn't notice."

Having succeeded in lowering her into the saddle, Jonah shifted so that he could position himself right behind Maggie.

Seated snugly, he closed his arms around her as he took hold of the reins again.

"Are you hurt?" he asked.

"Other than feeling stupid and having my pride wounded because I had to be rescued out of a tree? No," Maggie answered.

Taking a moment longer to remain under the tree and somewhat out of the direct path of the storm, Jonah considered her answer.

"Could have been worse," he told her.

Maggie found that she had to rouse herself in order to keep focused. Right now, she was losing herself in the warm feeling generated by having this hero's arms wrapped around her.

"How?" she asked, her voice sounding almost hoarse. She coughed, clearing her throat.

"You could have not known how to climb a tree," Jonah answered. He began to urge Cody to start heading away from the tree. The rain was just not letting up. "It looks like the floodwaters rushed through here before they receded back to a decent level."

"They did," she told him. "That's why I was up in the tree. I lost track of time," she ruefully admitted. "Do you have any idea how long I was up there?" Maggie asked.

"A long time," Jonah deadpanned. "Your sister and Donovan just had their first baby a week ago. It was a boy," he told her with a totally straight face, although she couldn't turn around to see it. "They named him Jonah, after me."

That was when Maggie laughed. "You know, you had me going there for a second," she told him.

"Oh?" he asked innocently. He kept his head down, talking close to her ear so that she could hear him. "What gave me away?"

"Because after what we've just been through," she told him, almost shouting so that he could hear her and not have the wind whip her words away, "Bellamy wouldn't have gotten married without me there. Really," she asked more seriously, "how long have I been out here?"

He thought back to what Rae Lemmon had said to him. "By my best estimation, probably close to twenty-four hours."

That made sense, Maggie thought. "That would explain why I feel like I'm starving," she said. And then she ventured another look up at the sky. She almost wished she hadn't. "It looks like it's going to rain harder," she reported in dismay.

Without his hat to shield him, Jonah quickly glanced up and then looked down again. "That would be my guess," he concurred.

She looked straight ahead and had no idea where they were going. She could hardly make out anything. The rain was obliterating everything around them.

"Are we going to get back to town in time?" she asked him anxiously.

That was easy enough for him to answer. "Nope, afraid not," Jonah replied simply.

That startled Maggie enough for her to attempt to twist around to get a better look at him. She nearly wound up sliding off the horse.

Jonah immediately tightened his arms around her

again. "Didn't anyone ever teach you not to make any sudden moves when you're riding double in the middle of a storm?"

"Never had a need for anyone to point that out before," Maggie answered, feeling exasperated again. "If we're not headed to town, then where are we going?"

"Well, we definitely need shelter so we're going to the closest place I know of—if it's still standing," he qualified. He hadn't checked on it since Hurricane Brooke had paid the area this unexpected visit.

He could feel Maggie growing antsy. "My place," he told her. "It's a one-room cabin, but right now, it's probably our best bet if we want to wait out this newest wave of Hurricane Brooke," he said.

As he answered her question, Jonah shifted ever so slightly so that he could pull the ends of his slicker apart. The second he did that, Jonah carefully tucked the two sides around the woman sitting directly in front of him.

"It's not much," he granted, "but at least it'll give you some protection against this rain."

"I'm already soaked," she told him. "But thank you," she added in a politer tone. Then, turning her face toward him—carefully this time so she wouldn't slid off—Maggie added, "And thank you for coming out to look for me."

"Hey, no big deal." Jonah shrugged off her thanks. "As it turns out, I just happened to be in the neighborhood," he cracked.

Maggie knew the man behind her had said something, but because the wind had increased, whipping his voice away, she hadn't been able to hear him. "What?" she practically yelled.

Jonah started to repeat what he'd said, then gave up. Instead, he just shrugged. "Never mind."

He didn't think she heard that, either. Right now, it felt as if the wind was scattering his words to the four corners of the earth before they could be heard.

Leaning in over the woman he was holding tightly against his chest, afraid she would slide off if he loosened his grip even just a little bit, Jonah raised his voice and yelled, "We'll talk later."

She nodded, not bothering to try to answer him.

Maggie kept her face forward, searching the area for a sign of something that resembled a building or anywhere that they could take shelter until this latest onslaught of rain finally passed. There was nothing.

She had never felt this dismally wet and cold—and hungry—before.

Finally, just as she was about to give up all hope, she thought she could make out what looked to be a small cabin up ahead. For a second she fought the impulse to turn around and ask her white knight if what she saw was indeed his cabin. But considering the fact that her words would probably be lost before he even had a chance to hear them, Maggie decided that it would be in her best interest to just be patient and see if this was the actual final destination.

At this point, Maggie was grateful for any place that could keep them even moderately dry. She wasn't picky.

When they came to a stop, Maggie saw that they were right in front of the cabin. Up close, it looked less rustic and more modern, but as long as it kept them dry, that was all that mattered.

Maggie could feel her white knight dismounting. She was right—this *was* their destination. At least until the storm had passed.

Holding on to Cody's reins, Jonah faced her, waiting. "Need any help dismounting?" he offered.

She looked at him as if she debated whether or not to be offended.

"I'm Texas born and bred, so no," she replied. The next second, she got off the horse as gracefully as possible. But when her feet hit the ground, she found that her legs were a lot less sturdy than she'd thought. The honest truth was they were downright wobbly, and she almost sank straight down to the ground.

And she would have if he hadn't caught both her arms in an attempt to steady her.

"Careful," Jonah cautioned.

Embarrassed, Maggie murmured a stricken, "Sorry about that."

"Nothing to be sorry about. You spent a day up a tree. You're lucky you still remember how to walk," Jonah told her.

She took one tentative step only to find that her legs still insisted on buckling rather than supporting her.

"Not so sure I do," she admitted.

There was a part of him that couldn't believe he was actually holding Maggie Reeves like this, the way he had once dreamed of doing. Usually, dreams had a way of not measuring up to long-cherished expectations. However, in this case, holding Maggie Reeves against him was everything he had thought it would be—and more.

Her heart was doing a glorious, uninhibited dance in her chest and just for one wild moment, Maggie thought that Jonah was going to kiss her.

She could feel her breath all but backing up in her throat, held perfectly still by sheer anticipation. She wasn't sure but she thought she might have even leaned in a little to offer him a better target.

And then nature interfered.

Again.

"The wind's picking up again," Jonah told her, pulling his head back. "We'd better get inside before it gets any worse."

Maggie nodded, knowing that he was right and that in all likelihood, the weather had just stopped her from making a huge mistake.

She told herself that she was relieved but wasn't altogether sure if she was.

Chapter Three

In contrast with the chaos that was going on directly outside, the moment that Maggie walked into the cabin, she was struck by its strong, clean lines. There were no unnecessary extras visible anywhere, nothing personal that pointed to the man who lived here whenever he was in town. It could have been a rustic hotel room waiting for someone to come and inhabit it. And at least for now, it had been spared by both the hurricane and the ensuing flood that had come in its wake.

If there was any detraction at all, it was that very little light came into the cabin.

"I don't suppose the lights are working," Maggie said. To test her theory, she hit the switch by the door. Nothing happened when she did. "Apparently not," Maggie said with a resigned sigh.

Jonah looked up at the living area's vaulted ceiling. "At least the roof is intact and not leaking," he told her.

"There is that," she agreed with a smile as she glanced up.

Jonah made his way over to the gray flagstone fireplace. "I'll get a fire going. That should warm us up a little." He turned toward Maggie. His eyes slid up and down the woman and for the first time since he'd finally managed to locate her, he realized that she was drenched and dripping. "Why don't you go look in the bedroom closet and see if you can find something to change into?"

Almost self-consciously, Maggie glanced down at herself. There was a pool of water forming on the wooden floor just around her feet. She looked up again.

"What about you?" she asked.

"I'll change my clothes, too. But first I have to go back out and put Cody up for the time being." He could see she was about to ask him where he planned to put the horse. There was no barn on the premises. "The shed behind the house is still up."

"That's a piece of luck," she remarked.

"Yeah," he agreed with a laugh. "Otherwise, I'd have to bring Cody in here with us." He saw the surprised look on Maggie's face. The way he saw it, he wasn't suggesting anything *that* unusual. "I can't take a chance on losing our only means of transportation. Otherwise, we'll be stranded."

Made sense, she thought. "Need any help?"

Jonah sat back on his heels and watched as the bits of paper he had tucked in between the firewood began to burn. The flames spread, greedily consuming the wood that was all around them.

"No," Jonah answered, rising once he was sure that the fire in the hearth wasn't going to go out. "I got this covered. You just do what you need to do to get dry. The bedroom's back there," he added, pointing toward the rear of the cabin.

Not that it would have taken her an inordinate amount of time to find the room. The cabin consisted of the living area with a kitchenette on one side and a bedroom along with a three-quarter bath tucked directly behind the back of the fireplace.

Maggie looked after him uncertainly. "You sure you

don't mind my rummaging through your closet?" she asked just as he crossed back to the front door.

Jonah smiled, surprised that she was standing on ceremony, given the unusual situation they found themselves in. "There're no skeletons in there if that's what you're worried about."

Maggie flushed slightly. "It's not that. I just thought that…"

Feeling awkward—after all, she didn't know the man *that* well—her voice trailed off, letting him fill in the blanks for himself.

"And you won't find anything in there to embarrass you—or me," he assured her. Turning up the collar of the all-but-useless rain slicker, he put his hand on the doorknob, turning it. "I'll be back as soon as I can," Jonah promised.

The next second, he pulled open the door and stepped out into the gusting rain.

Maggie hurried over to the front window to watch Jonah for as long as she could before he disappeared around the side of the cabin. From what she could see, it didn't look as if the hurricane was going to double back. With any luck, she thought, crossing her fingers, Brooke was done with them.

Now if the rain would just let up…

Backing away from the window, Maggie glanced down at the wooden floor she had just traversed. Her entire path was marked by drops of water.

"Time to stop leaving puddles," she murmured. "Guess I'll go see what he *does* have in his closet."

She'd thought that maybe Jonah would have some items of clothing that an old girlfriend had left behind—or perhaps even a current one. The way she saw it, it was more than possible. A man who looked like Jonah Colton couldn't be going through life unattached for long, she reasoned. He was the kind of man that women literally threw themselves at.

But all she could find in the lone closet as well as in the tall chest of drawers were his clothes. Debating, Maggie finally decided to borrow one of his flannel shirts, but there was no way in the world that she was going to put on a pair of his jeans. Jonah Colton had a good eight inches or more on her, not to mention about eighty or so pounds—if not more. Any of his jeans that she would have put on would have come parachuting down.

She listened for a moment to make sure Jonah hadn't come back, but only silence met her ears. Moving quickly she stripped off her utterly soaked shirt and put on one of the button-down work shirts from the closet.

Just as she thought, it fit her like a tent. She tied the ends together to make it nominally shorter.

Even so, it was way too big for her. It felt roomy enough for two of her to fit into the shirt.

Maggie had just finished assessing herself in front of the freestanding large mirror when she heard the front door open and then close again. Holding her breath, she hurried out to make sure that the person she heard was Jonah and not someone who had stumbled upon the cabin while looking for some shelter from the storm.

She released her breath when she saw it was Jonah.

"Is your horse all tucked away and dry for the time being?" Maggie asked as she joined Jonah in the main room.

"For now." His eyes swept over her. He did his best not to laugh. "I see you found something to wear—sort of," he tagged on, his eyes sweeping over her. "And you kept on your jeans," he realized. "Why?" Jonah asked, tossing off the rain slicker and heading for his bedroom.

"Well, decency is the first reason that comes to mind," she answered. "You and I aren't anywhere near the same size and while I can get away with sporting a pup tent as a shirt, there's no way I could wear a pair of your jeans without constantly worrying that I was about to wind up executing a pratfall."

"Point taken," he answered, his voice floating in from the back where he had disappeared. "Wow," he cried, "it feels good to peel off these wet clothes." He seemed only half-aware that she was there.

He might only be half-aware of her but that definitely was not her problem, Maggie thought. To say the least, she was exceedingly aware of *his* presence. So much so that she was trying hard *not* to envision the way he looked right now, standing in his bedroom, bare chested and who knew what else was bare—trying to decide what to put on to replace his wet clothes.

"You know," he said as he came out, startling her, "I do have a belt that I can lend you. It would help to keep my jeans up for you," he offered.

She couldn't help staring at his waist. Flat and muscular, her guess was that his belt would still be way too big to her.

"You might not have noticed," she told him, "but I'm a lot smaller than you are."

"Oh, I noticed, all right," he assured her.

Jonah had become keenly aware of every single inch of Maggie years ago, long before this hurricane had hit. He'd noticed her when he had still been an ugly duckling and she had been a swan. And she was right. Her waist was way smaller than his. He thought of a solution.

"I have a length of rope you could use around here somewhere," he said, looking about the living area.

"That's okay," she told him, waving away his suggestion. "They're practically dry."

"Liar," he teased. But he wasn't about to push this. Jonah rolled up his sleeves one at a time. "You said you were hungry."

Her eyes were drawn to his muscular forearms, and she remembered the way his arms had felt around her. Belatedly, she realized that he was probably waiting for her to answer.

"Starved," she told him, still looking down at his forearms.

He rummaged through the pantry that was right next to his refrigerator. "I'm afraid all I can offer you is either a box of sugarcoated cornflakes, or half a loaf of bread. Anything else—if I had it—would require a stove and electricity to make it edible."

Turning toward her, he held out the box of cornflakes in one hand and the loaf of bread in the other.

"Both," she said without any hesitation. "I don't remember the last time I ate." Her stomach rumbled as if on cue. She flushed as she glanced down, self-consciously. "But obviously my stomach does."

"We've all been there," he said, glossing over her rumbling stomach to help her cover up her embarrassment. "Have at it," he told her, handing her the box of breakfast cereal and the partial loaf of bread.

Maggie accepted both. If this was all he had on hand, he obviously didn't believe in stuffing himself. "I see that gluttony isn't one of your vices."

Jonah laughed, appreciating that she had retained her sense of humor despite the situation she had endured.

"No, but curiosity is." And then Jonah became serious as he asked, "What the hell were you doing out there with a hurricane about to hit the area? You were taking an awful chance with your life."

Rather than make up an elaborate excuse, Maggie leveled with him. "To be honest, I forgot all about the hurricane. Besides, the weather bureau is usually wrong with its forecasts more than half the time, anyway."

He watched her go at the cornflakes as if they were going out of style. She wasn't kidding about being hungry.

"You forget about Bellamy and Donovan's wedding, too?"

"No, I didn't," she answered, a little indignant that he would think she was such a scatterbrain. "I just thought I'd have enough time to get to Live Oak Ranch and then get back. When I left for the ranch, the wedding was a day away."

He supposed she had a point. But he had another question. "And just what was so important at the ranch that you had to go right then?"

Maggie waited until she'd had consumed another handful of cornflakes before answering. "The answer to a riddle."

Jonah frowned. She wasn't being clear, he thought. Was that on purpose, or was she just as in the dark about her so-called "mission" as it sounded?

"What kind of a riddle?" he asked.

Rather than just give him another vague answer, Maggie leaned forward and pulled out the map she had hastily tucked into her back pocket just before the threat of being swept away by the rushing waters had her climbing up into the tree.

Then she told him the whole story, such as it was. "A couple of days ago, I got a letter from my attorney informing me that my former late father-in-law, Adam Corgan, had left instructions in his will to send this map and the note he wrote to me after he was dead."

Well, he could see why that had aroused her curiosity. It would have aroused his, as well.

"May I?" Jonah asked, nodding at the map and note in her hand.

Maggie held out the papers for him to take. "Sure, go right ahead."

Jonah read the note twice and was no more enlightened than he had been a minute ago.

"'The truth shall set Elliott Corgan free.'" He read out loud, then looked up at Maggie. His brow was furrowed. "What's that supposed to mean?"

Maggie shook her head. "I have no idea. I found the tree," she told him, indicating the map. "That was the one I was clinging to when you rescued me earlier today," she explained. "But I didn't find anything there that made what was in the note any clearer. To be totally honest, I have no idea why Mr. Corgan would have wanted me to have this, or what he was cryptically trying to tell me. None of it made any sense to me."

"It's suspicious, all right," Jonah agreed, frowning as he glanced at the note again. Something was off here, he thought. He could feel it in the pit of his stomach, like something solid that just sat there. "Maybe the police chief has some idea what your late father-in-law was trying to say," he suggested.

"Late *ex*-father-in-law," Maggie corrected. She wasn't related to any of those people anymore. Emotionally, she never had been.

The corners of his mouth curved slightly. "No love lost I take it."

"Adam was okay, I suppose," she told him charitably. "But James…" she said, referring to her ex-husband. "Well, that's another story."

"That makes this note you were sent even more suspicious," he said, waving the map and note.

She laughed dryly. "You won't get an argument from me."

He'd been watching her as Maggie made short work of the bread and cereal he'd given her. "Sorry I can't offer you anything more than just that bread and stale cereal," he apologized again.

"Right now, this is a feast," she assured him—and then suddenly she realized what she was doing. "And I'm hogging it all," Maggie said. She tilted the open box toward him. "Here, have some of your own cereal. There's not much left."

He held up his hand to keep her from pushing the box toward him. "That's okay, you eat it. I can wait until we get back to town."

Town. That sounded a million miles away, Maggie thought wistfully. "Is that going to be anytime soon?" she asked. "My sister must be worried sick about me."

Jonah laughed dryly. "Your sister is the reason I was out here looking for you in the first place. She was pretty scared now that you mention it. She was afraid that you might have drowned—or been blown away."

Maggie raised her chin defensively. "She should have known I can take care of myself," she said, doing her best not to let guilt overwhelm her. Her lips formed a pout. "You win a couple of beauty contests and everyone thinks you have cotton for brains and can't find your way out of a paper bag."

"I did find you up a tree," Jonah pointed out, trying not to smile.

"Right," she agreed. Then she said deliberately, "I

was in a tree, I wasn't floating facedown in some storm-filled ditch."

"Well, if it means anything," Jonah told her quietly, "I never thought you had cotton for brains."

The unexpected affirmative comment caused Maggie to smile. "It means something," she replied. And then she stopped suddenly, cocking her head toward the window. "Hey, listen," she said, alert. "Hear that?"

Jonah did as she instructed. But, he thought, he obviously didn't hear what she did.

"Hear what?" he asked Maggie. "I don't hear anything."

"Exactly," she exclaimed, her eyes shining as she abandoned the empty cereal box on the scarred table and hurried toward the front window. She looked out, scanning the sky. "The storm's over," Maggie announced like a town crier. "Or at least it's stopped for now." She turned around to face him. "I think we should take advantage of the lull and get back to town before the weather decides to change its mind again."

"Best idea I've heard today," Jonah told her, although there was a part of him that would have liked to have lingered in the cabin a bit longer.

Maggie was already at the door. "What are we waiting for?" she asked. She couldn't wait to get back to civilization.

"I need to put out the fire," Jonah told her. When she looked at him, her brow wrinkled in confusion, it occurred to him that she might have misunderstood what he was saying. "In the fireplace," he added. And then he proceeded to do just that.

"Oh." Maggie felt like an idiot. She thought he was referring to something she'd felt going on between them. "Of course," she murmured belatedly.

"You wait here while I saddle Cody up," Jonah told her. He could see that she wasn't the type who liked being left behind. "I'll hurry," he promised, closing the door behind him before Maggie had a chance to protest.

Or before he had a chance to act on the feelings that were bubbling up inside him.

Chapter Four

Bellamy was helping a family of three settle into their temporary quarters because the hurricane had rendered part of their house unlivable when she happened to look in the general direction of the side entrance. She dropped the blanket she was holding and completely lost track of everything else.

"Oh my lord, he found her!" Bellamy cried. "He found her!"

Before any of the family she was helping could ask her who she was talking about, Bellamy was racing across the rec center, trying not to bump into any of the people or the cots that had been hastily arranged throughout the large room.

Bellamy descended on her sister with an enthusiasm that came straight out of their childhood. Reaching Maggie, she threw her arms around her, hugging the somewhat-bedraggled younger woman for all that she was worth.

Donovan reached Jonah and Maggie while Bellamy was laughing and crying, all at the same time.

"It's you, it's really you!" she exclaimed, beside herself with joy. Part of her had been terrified that she'd lost Maggie to the hurricane.

"Yup, it's me," Maggie managed to get out.

Bellamy was squeezing her so hard it was difficult for Maggie to draw a breath, much less actually be able to say something intelligible.

"You have no idea how scared I was that I'd lost you," Bellamy cried. "And we'd just finally resolved all those things between us and had gotten back together." Still hugging Maggie, she looked over her sister's shoulder at Jonah, who was standing right behind Maggie. "Thank you!" she cried, tears sliding down her face as her eyes met Jonah's. "I don't know how to ever repay you for this."

"It's just all in a day's work," Jonah assured his future sister-in-law.

He hadn't searched for Maggie in order to be thanked or praised, he'd done it because for him there was no other choice. If he hadn't found Maggie, he would have still been out there, searching for her.

"Bell," Maggie all but squeaked. "I can't breathe," she protested because her sister was hugging her even harder.

"Oh, I'm sorry," Bellamy apologized self-consciously. She released Maggie and took a step back. "I was just so sure that I'd lost yo—" Bellamy stopped talking as she took a better look at her sister. "What are you wearing?" she cried in amazement as she looked at the work shirt that was hanging off her sister's upper torso, all but going down to her knees.

In the excitement, Maggie had temporarily forgotten all about the shirt she'd put on. Collecting herself, she glanced down. She could see why Bellamy had reacted the way that she had.

"Oh, this. It belongs to Jonah." Because that all but *begged* for a further explanation, she told her sister and Bellamy's fiancé, "My blouse was completely soaked so

Jonah offered me one of his shirts so I could have something dry to wear."

Bellamy looked quizzically at her sister's savior. "You carry spare shirts with you?" she questioned, somewhat confused.

"No," Maggie interrupted, "I got the shirt from his closet when we stopped at his cabin."

This wasn't making anything clearer. If anything, it was making things even more obscure. Bellamy exchanged looks with her fiancé.

"You stopped at Jonah's cabin?" she asked Maggie, trying to get things perfectly clear in her mind.

Jonah could see this conversation was going somewhere that seemed destined to make Maggie uncomfortable. Rather than get more tangled up in an explanation, he waved his hand dismissively at all of it.

"Long story," he told Bellamy and his brother. "Maggie'll tell you all about it once things settle down a little around here." To him it was more important to see to the survivors than explain why Maggie'd had a wardrobe change.

The recreation center was completely packed now and the people who had either lost their houses to the hurricane or had their houses so severely damaged that they were deemed unlivable would have to stay here until other, more permanent arrangements could be made. But the lucky ones would be going home soon, Jonah thought.

However, that didn't mean that his job, as well as that of the other members of the team tasked with rescue efforts for the town, was over. Far from it. There was still a great deal to do.

But he wanted to do one more thing before turning his attention back to rescuing the residents of Whisperwood. Jonah wanted to get a second opinion on this so-called riddle that had all but sent Maggie to her death.

"Has anyone seen the police chief around recently?" he asked his brother and Bellamy.

"Chief Thompson?" Donovan asked, surprised that Jonah was looking for the man. "I just saw him. He brought a stranded couple to the rec center in the last hour." Donovan looked around the area. "There he is," he declared, spotting the chief halfway across the rec center. He pointed toward the man for Jonah's benefit.

Chief Archer Thompson picked that moment to look in their direction. Seeing that Donovan was pointing at him, the chief headed toward the group to see what he wanted.

Tall, lean, with an authoritative air about him and very few gray hairs despite being in his midsixties, the chief smiled warmly at Maggie as he approached the small group.

"I see you found Maggie," he said to Jonah. "Nice work. Are you all right?" the chief asked the young woman, politely making no reference to her unorthodox oversize attire.

Maggie nodded, appreciating the man's concern. "I am now."

Since she was back, safe and sound, the chief allowed himself to comment on her initial disappearance. "Fool notion, going out like that in a storm," he admonished her. "Didn't you listen to the weather report?"

"In my defense," Maggie told the police chief, "there was no storm when I left—and the weather bureau only gets things right a fraction of the time."

"Yes," he agreed. "But it *was* the day before your sister's wedding." He would have thought she would be busy helping her sister with the details for the wedding. "If you don't mind my asking, why were you out, running around the countryside like that?"

Jonah decided to step in. "That's what I wanted to talk to you about," he told the chief. He took out the map and the note that Maggie had given him. Glancing at Maggie to see if she had any objections about sharing this information with the chief—she apparently didn't—he handed both over to Thompson. "Maggie was looking into this."

Jonah saw the chief raise an eyebrow and in the interest of brevity, he explained, "Adam Corgan left instructions in his will for the map and note to be sent to Maggie upon his death. We'd like to know what you make of it?"

All the chief needed was one glance at the map to tell him that he was looking at the Live Oak Ranch. The accompanying note, though, proved to be more of a mystery.

"'The truth shall set Elliot free.'" Thompson read, then looked up at Maggie and Jonah. "What truth?"

"To be honest, that was what we were hoping you might be able to tell us," Maggie confessed.

Thompson frowned, looking at the note again. It was just as obscure on the third reading as it had been on the first two.

"Well," he said slowly, "this obviously has something to do with Adam's older brother, Elliot."

"The one who up and disappeared years ago? Wasn't he rumored to be that serial killer?" Donovan asked. Everyone but the chief looked at him in surprise. For the most part, Donovan had just been listening to what the others were saying, but this had made him think back to the stories he'd heard shared from decades ago. "The one who killed those six young women? That was, what, forty years ago, wasn't it?"

Thompson suppressed a sigh. This had been hushed up by Corgan's family but after all this time, the chief saw no reason to keep it silent any longer.

"Exactly right," the chief said grimly.

Maggie felt totally bewildered. "He was a serial killer?" she cried.

"I'm afraid so. The Corgan family paid good money to have this covered up. But with Adam dead, this was bound to come out," the chief said.

Maggie looked at the note again. "What do you think it means?" she asked the chief.

The look on the chief's face grew grimmer. "It means that you should stay away from anything that has to do with this case." He glanced from Maggie to Jonah. Neither one looked as if they were in the least bit intimidated. "I'm serious, you two. I don't know what Adam had to have been thinking when he wrote this or why he would have wanted to pull you into this family mess after all this time. But I guess now we'll never know, since Adam's not going to be answering anyone's questions anymore."

"But maybe Elliot could," Jonah suddenly said, speaking up. If anyone should know what was behind this riddle, it would be the man the riddle specified by name. "Do you know where he is, Chief?"

"Yes," Thompson replied, making the decision to end his own silence. "He's in Randolph State Prison in Austin. Has been for forty years."

"Then he was convicted of killing all those women?" Jonah asked.

Stunned because she'd never known any of this when she was married to James, Maggie asked, "How was this not public news?"

"I told you. The family paid to keep this quiet," the chief said.

"That money they paid, did that include you?" Jonah asked.

"I had other reasons," Thompson answered without elaborating any further. He was long passed the point of getting annoyed by careless questions. "What's important is that Elliott was found guilty by a jury of his peers and he's been incarcerated for the last forty years," Thompson said quietly. "The bastard got what he deserved," the chief added with genuine feeling and finality. "I was serious before," he said to Maggie and Jonah. "I want you to stay away from this. There is no 'truth' to set Elliot free. He killed all those poor young women who, as far as was known, never did anything to him except to have the misfortune of crossing his path. The man needs to go on paying for his crimes."

As if on cue, the shortwave radio Thompson kept attached to his belt began to crackle, calling for his immediate attention.

He held up his hand to stop any further discussion. "I've got to take this," the chief said, addressing the small group.

So saying, Thompson removed the radio from his belt and walked away so he could speak to the person who was calling in private.

Maggie frowned, looking at the chief's back as the man walked away from them. "He's not telling us something."

"I'm sure Thompson's not telling us a lot of things," Jonah commented. He looked at the situation from the point of view of the job he'd been tasked with. "The man's got a lot on his mind right now, including roughly four dozen missing town residents—" He glanced down at Maggie. "One less of course, now that you're here."

"No." Maggie shook her head. "I meant he's not telling us everything about Elliot Corgan," she insisted. "Did you notice the look that came over his face when he said the man's name? I thought his jaw was clenched so hard it was going to snap."

"Well, he probably was one of the police officers on the case at the time," Jonah guessed. "The chief had to have had firsthand knowledge of all those killings and how they affected the victims' families. This note from beyond the grave from the guy's brother just brings it all back for him," Jonah speculated. "Combine that with what he's doing now and none of it can be easy for him."

Maggie hardly heard him. Instead, she suddenly recalled something. "Donovan said something about six victims."

Jonah looked at her, wondering where she was going with this. "So?"

"What if there were more than just six victims?" Maggie asked him. "All this was kept hushed up, right. Well, what if Elliott hadn't been forthcoming about the number of women he killed? What if this so-called 'truth' that Adam referred to in his note refers to more bodies?"

"How would finding them set Elliott free?" Jonah asked.

"I haven't figured that part out yet," she admitted.

"The chief told us to stay away from this," Jonah reminded Maggie. He looked at her face. He imagined that she had the same look when she went off to seek this so-called "truth" that Adam had urged her to unearth. "But you're not going to listen to him, are you?"

She turned toward Jonah. "I can't shake the feeling that I got that note for a reason. That this 'truth' I'm supposed to find has something to do with finding out if there's more to Elliott's killing spree than the chief knew about. If there are more bodies out there, their families deserve to know about it. They deserve closure instead of thinking the women just ran off."

"I agree," he told her. "But, again, how would that set Elliot free?"

She shrugged. "I don't know. It could be that Adam wasn't firing with all four cylinders," she guessed. "Maybe in Adam's mind, finding more bodies will somehow absolve Elliot of those murders. Maybe he *didn't* kill those women."

Jonah was studying her as Maggie talked about this. "You sound like this has really gotten to you," he observed.

She flushed a little, but she wasn't about to apologize or make excuses. "I guess it has."

Jonah hazarded a guess. "Is it because this is your ex-husband's family?"

She laughed dismissively. "If anything, that would be enough of a reason to make me keep my distance from trying to find an answer to this riddle. No, I'd have to say that this intrigues me," she confessed. "I hate unsolved mysteries and here's one right in my own backyard."

He nodded slowly, taking this all in. "So you're planning on looking into this even though the chief told you not to."

She didn't see it as being defiant. She looked at it from another point of view.

"You said yourself the chief's got his hands full. He can't be everywhere, which means he definitely can't take the time to look into this now and like I said, I feel like I owe it to the victims' families to find some answers."

He'd seen that stubborn expression on her face before,

although only from a distance. This was the first time that he'd been so close to it. The woman was gorgeous when she had her mind made up.

"So you're going to go ahead with this investigation no matter what I say," Jonah concluded.

Maggie raised her eyes to his and asked, "What do you think?"

"Honestly?" he asked. Maggie nodded. "I think you're going to need a keeper."

She took offense at his words. "Look, you rescued me, and I know I owe you a great deal, Jonah. Maybe even my life, but that doesn't give you the right to order me around."

He cocked his head, confused at her interpretation. "I didn't say that."

Was he trying to backtrack? "You said I need a keeper," she reminded him.

"Yes, I did," he agreed. "The last time I looked, what a keeper does is keep track of whatever or whoever he's 'keeping.' In my book, that means that if you decide to play detective—"

"When," Maggie corrected.

Jonah continued as if she hadn't interrupted him, "You can't go running off on your own. You'll need backup."

Maggie had to admit—albeit silently—that she liked the idea that Jonah would be there with her to help if she needed it—which she willingly admitted that she very well might. The man was the very definition of capability—not to mention exceedingly easy on the eyes. If Jonah could find her in the aftermath of a hurricane and with floodwaters threatening to rise again, she had a feeling he would be invaluable in her search to discover if there were any more victims and why their bodies had never been recovered.

A lot of questions and no direct path to an answer, Maggie thought.

"Are you suggesting we form a partnership?" she asked Jonah.

Jonah didn't answer her immediately. Maggie was an ex-model and beauty contest winner who now taught etiquette and deportment lessons in her apartment, while he was part of Cowboy Heroes, a search and rescue team that did a great deal of their rescuing on the back of a horse. He was also a trained EMT.

They were as diverse and different in their approach to life as night and day, and the only thing they really had in common was that his brother was marrying her sister. But for whatever reason, Maggie was leaving herself open to accepting his help. There was *no* way he was going to tell her no. Somehow, he just had to get Maggie to hold off until he could be there for her. He did have people to rescue.

"In a manner of speaking," he finally said. And then he decided to be direct with her. "Listen, those other victims—if they do exist—aren't going anywhere and Adam Corgan sure as hell isn't, either. Why don't you give me a couple of days, maybe help me to coordinate rescue efforts for the town, and after that, I'm all yours?"

All hers.

The man had no idea how tempting that sounded, Maggie thought.

Before her imagination could take off, she roused herself and asked, "You want me to help you?"

"Not just me," he corrected. "You'll be helping the town."

Maggie smiled. He'd said just the right thing to get her attention. She had always wanted to give back to the community, to be seen as something more than just a pretty face. Mannequins had pretty faces, and no one thought highly of them—or at all, she thought. This, at least, was something meaningful and productive. Jonah was right. Adam and his riddle could certainly wait a few more days.

"Sure," she told Jonah. "Count me in. I'd be more than happy to help with the rescue efforts," she said with a warm grin, "seeing as how I have firsthand experience with what it feels like to be rescued."

"Then, if you're feeling up to it," he qualified, "let's get started."

"Absolutely," she responded, following him out the door. "Let's."

Chapter Five

Jonah slanted a look toward Maggie. She was holding up a lot better than he had thought she would, considering the fact that this morning he'd found her stuck up in a tree. Anyone else would have easily milked that experience and placed themselves out of commission for at least a couple of days, if not more.

But she hadn't. Maggie had insisted on coming out with him to help with the search and rescue efforts.

There was no doubt about it. Maggie Reeves was one tough lady. Somehow, although she wasn't trained for it, she'd managed to keep up with him all day. She spent most of that time helping him find survivors, digging them out whenever that was necessary. Overall, what the survivors they found needed most was to be comforted and that, he quickly realized, seemed to be Maggie's specialty. She was kind and comforting, able to quiet children when they cried, and on occasion, she could even make them laugh.

All in all, she was a great asset.

It was getting dark when he finally came up to her and said they were calling it a day for now.

"Are you sure?" she asked, even though she felt more drained and exhausted than she ever had before in her life. "There're more people out there," she protested. Not to mention that there was still a little bit of daylight left.

"Yes," he agreed, "and there are also more people than just the two of us to help find them." Jonah smiled at her and without thinking, he wrapped one arm about her shoulders, gently guiding her away from the pile of sticks and plaster that just a short while ago represented someone's house. "You did good today. Better than good," he amended. "But I definitely think that it's time you went home. C'mon," Jonah gently urged, "I'll take you." When he saw Maggie open her mouth, he knew what was coming. Jonah was quick to put a stop to any protest. "Don't argue. I'm the leader."

Maggie laughed softly, shaking her head in surprise. "I thought this was a partnership."

"It is," he assured her. "But I'm still the leader. That means you have to listen to me. Let's go," he prodded politely, leaving no room for argument.

Because he had stabled Cody earlier in the day, Jonah was driving his pickup truck now. After getting in, he fastened his seat belt and waited for Maggie to get in on the passenger side. He knew where she lived, but he waited for her to give him her address.

Over the years, for one reason or another, he had inadvertently found out a great many things about Maggie. He had taken an interest in her life. However, he knew how that would sound to someone else—or to Maggie herself if she knew. The last thing he wanted was for her to think he was stalking her, even though in this instance the only reason he knew where she lived was because Donovan had mentioned it to him when his brother and Bellamy had been putting their wedding together.

"Okay, direct me," he told her, waiting. "Where do I go?"

The second Maggie sank down in her seat, she felt instantly exhausted. Rousing herself, she mumbled the address to Jonah. She lived in an apartment located within a collection of buildings that had been whimsically named Whisperwood Towers.

"Whisperwood Towers, here we come," Jonah announced, turning the key in his ignition. His pickup truck rumbled to life.

As he drove to the Towers, he spared a glance in Maggie's direction. Her head was definitely beginning to droop.

"Why don't you get some shut-eye?" he suggested. "You've earned it. I'll wake you up when we get there."

"I'm fine," she told Jonah even as her eyelids were shutting on her.

A few minutes later, Jonah smiled to himself as he listened to her even breathing. "Yup, I can see that," he murmured quietly, amused.

But Jonah's amusement vanished as he approached the site of Whisperwood Towers—or where the apartment buildings were supposed to be.

The structures were no longer standing tall and erect. The Towers had received the brunt of the hurricane's assault as Brooke passed through the town. In more than three-quarters of the buildings, there was rubble where the walls had once been.

"Damn," Jonah swore under his breath. Adjusting the rearview mirror, he carefully tried to pick his way back out. Without meaning to, he rolled over something large in the road.

The sudden thrusting movement had Maggie waking up with a start.

The first thing she noticed was that the pickup was moving backward. She looked at Jonah. "Why are you heading away from the apartment buildings?" she asked. And then, only because there was a full moon out, she saw the reason why he had suddenly reversed his direction. Her eyes widened in shock. "Omigod, is that…?"

Jonah really wished he could tell Maggie that she was looking at something else, but he wasn't about to insult her with a lie. Maggie could see for herself the remnants of Whisperwood Towers—the place that she had been calling home even before her divorce had been finalized.

"I'm afraid so," Jonah said, answering her unfinished question.

Stunned, Maggie felt her throat closing. Everything she had ever called her own was in that demolished apartment. She could only stare at what was left of the towers and say the words that so many others had either thought or said out loud in the last couple of days. "I have no place to stay."

Jonah never hesitated. "Yes, you do," Jonah informed her, his tone leaving no room for Maggie to mount an argument. "You're staying with me."

Still staring at the Towers remains, which were now growing smaller and smaller as Jonah drove them away from the scene, Maggie needed more than a second to absorb his words.

When she did, Maggie shook her head. "That's very generous of you, but I can't take you up on your offer," she protested.

He hadn't expected this to be easy. He had a feeling that it was her damn pride that was making her say that. "Why not?"

Maggie's mind jumped to the first logical excuse that came to her. "Well, because there's only one bedroom in your place," she pointed out.

He wasn't about to let her refuse. "I know you're a

gorgeous ex-beauty queen, but I promise I'll find a way to restrain myself," Jonah told her. And then, more seriously, he said, "We're two adults, Maggie, who are in the same dire situation everyone else around here seems to find themselves in. I'll take the couch and you can have the bed. There's a lock on the bedroom door. You can use it if it'll make you feel any better," he added.

"I trust you," she told him, ashamed that she had instantly thought of Jonah behaving just like James would have in the same circumstances.

Jonah wasn't anything like James. To begin with, James would never have been out there, trying to find survivors and rescuing them. James had never done a selfless thing in his life.

"Good," Jonah replied, doing his best to keep a straight face as he told her, "and I trust you."

"Me?" Maggie questioned incredulously.

"Sure. Why, you never heard of a woman having her way with a man?" he asked her, struggling to maintain his straight face.

Gripping the steering wheel, Jonah stared straight ahead. The full moon and his headlights provided the only illumination for the pitch-black road in front of them. Lucky for him he could find his way to his family's ranch even if he were blindfolded.

Jonah had sounded so serious when he asked the question, Maggie had to laugh. After everything she had gone through today, she'd thought that she would never be able to laugh again.

It really felt good to laugh. She silently blessed Jonah for that.

"I promise I won't have my way with you," Maggie told him when she finally stopped laughing.

Humor curved his lips. "Just so you know, I won't

hold you to that," he told her with a wink. And then he grew serious again. "I'm really sorry about your place, Maggie."

A sigh escaped her lips before she could suppress it. "Yeah, me, too."

"I've got an idea. Why don't we swing by come morning and take a look at the damage?" Jonah suggested. "Maybe it's not as bad as it looks right now in the dark."

She knew that Jonah was just saying that for her benefit. He was only trying to make her feel better.

"Maybe," Maggie murmured only out of a sense of obligation. She pressed her lips together. "I guess that was pretty egotistical of me, thinking that my place could have been spared after so many other places in town weren't."

"Not egotistical," Jonah said, correcting her. He had another word for it. "Human. Everybody undoubtedly hoped that their home had been spared because a few of the other homes and places of business had been." He really felt for her and tried to comfort her the way she had offered comfort to the rescued survivors today. "There's no rhyme or reason to what a hurricane does, why one building is either totally wrecked or pulled off its foundation and the one right next to it is totally bypassed and spared. It just happens," he concluded with resignation. "You can't drive yourself crazy wondering why. There's no real answer to that question."

She didn't know about that. "If I'd been home instead of out there, trying to unravel Adam's damn puzzle—"

She didn't have to finish. He knew what she was thinking. And he didn't want her dwelling on it.

He pointed out why. "You might have been like Dorothy in *The Wizard of Oz* and gotten transported to another place."

Maggie could feel the tension beginning to leave her shoulders. She laughed. "That is really sugarcoating it," she told him.

"Hey," Jonah said, pretending to balk at her assessment of what he had said. "It's been a long day. Humor me."

She knew Jonah wasn't actually asking her to humor him, he was attempting to humor *her.* Or to at least soften the blow of what had just happened to her place and not allow her mind to dwell on a far more serious, unsettling scenario.

Maggie changed the subject. "You know, you don't have anything to eat at your place," she reminded Jonah. "I cleaned out your cereal."

"But we still have what's left of the bread," he teased her. Because he didn't want her contemplating going to bed hungry, he quickly rectified the image that she might be contemplating. "Don't worry, there's food. I asked one of the guys on the team to swing by the General Store—one of the places that hadn't been demolished by the hurricane—and pick up a few things. He brought them over to my place."

He smiled at her, trying to keep the situation light. "It was either that or come home after a grueling long day and start gnawing on the wood. I hear splinters are really bad for your digestion."

"You're trying to make me feel better about eating all your cereal, aren't you?" Maggie asked, smiling at him.

"Trying my damnedest. How'm I doing?"

Maggie deadpanned. "That depends on what that friend of yours managed to pick up at the General Store."

"Well, we're here," Jonah declared, pulling his truck up right in front of the cabin. "Why don't we go in and find out?"

After the chaos and destruction she had witnessed today, his cabin seemed even more like a haven to her than it had previously.

The Colton family's ranch was comprised of a thousand acres. Jonah's cabin was nestled in one corner of it, removed yet still very much a part of the whole general property.

This time, when Jonah walked in and threw the switch that was right by the front door, light permeated the interior of the cabin.

"What happened?" Maggie asked, looking around in surprise. "Was the power suddenly restored while we were driving over here?"

"Our power was," Jonah explained. "My family keeps a generator on the property. It had to be started up, but once it is, we're no longer at the mercy of the downed power lines throughout the surrounding area. This is no doubt thanks to the generator."

She turned toward the kitchenette. "If you've got a working generator, does that mean that the stove works, too?"

"Absolutely," he answered.

"And the refrigerator?" she asked, not wanting to take anything for granted.

"And the refrigerator," he echoed with a grin.

"Oh good. So let's see what your friend wound up getting for you."

Pulling open the refrigerator door, Maggie quickly took inventory of what was on the shelves. There was a carton of eggs, another loaf of bread and a package of bacon.

Maggie felt as if she'd just crossed into paradise.

"I see your friend is a great believer in breakfast being

the most important meal of the day," she commented with a laugh.

She moved the newly purchased items around to see if they were blocking her view of anything else more substantial in the refrigerator.

They weren't.

Jonah had a feeling she had been hoping for more than just breakfast food.

"That's probably all that Jack could get for now," he said, referring to his friend by name. "The General Store is probably rationing their supplies, allowing customers to only buy a certain amount of items to insure that nobody goes hungry. Things'll get better once deliveries start being made again."

"I'm not complaining," Maggie assured him. "I like eggs better than I like cereal and I plowed through half a box of that today." She grinned ruefully. "I guess you can tell people I ate you out of house and home."

His eyes swept over her. "Not with that figure," he told her. "Nobody would ever believe me."

Maggie smiled at the compliment. It made her feel less grungy.

"Thanks. I needed that." She stifled an involuntary yawn, then looked at him ruefully. "I'm sorry. I guess I really am exhausted."

Jonah nodded understandingly. "Look, I'll just use the facilities and then you can have the bedroom so you can get to bed."

She had thought about that and had no intention of displacing him. "That's all right, Jonah. You don't have to be noble and give up your bedroom for me. I'm perfectly capable of taking the couch. Hey, I fell asleep in your car," she reminded him. "I can certainly sleep on the couch."

"This isn't up for debate," Jonah told her. "You'll sleep on the bed. Just give me a second," he said as he disappeared into the bedroom.

If he'd been alone, after the day he had put in, he would have taken a shower. But in the interest of letting Maggie get to bed, he skipped his shower and grabbed a change of clothes for tomorrow.

Coming back out, Jonah called, "It's all yours, Maggie."

When she made no response, he came into the main part of the cabin and looked at the couch. "Maggie?"

Coming closer, he saw the reason why she hadn't answered him. Maggie was totally out.

Jonah shook his head. "You had to have your way, didn't you? You are a damn stubborn woman, Maggie Reeves. But news flash, I can be stubborn, too," he said to the woman who was curled up on his couch, her head cradled in the crook of her arm.

He almost hated to disturb her, but he knew that she'd feel better in the morning if she didn't spend the night in such an awkward position.

Bending over, he slid his arm under her body and moving very slowly, he raised Maggie up from the sofa. Looking down at her face to see if he'd woken her up, he was satisfied that she was still asleep.

"Guess you were more tired than I thought," Jonah murmured.

Shifting her slowly, he began to head for the back of his cabin and his bedroom.

Maggie had nestled her face against his chest, and she made a noise now that sounded a little like a contented cat snuggling up for a nap. Jonah stopped walking for a moment, thinking that perhaps the motion might wake her up. But when she went on sleeping, he resumed making his way to his bedroom.

"Here you are, ma'am," he said quietly, reaching his bed. "Not exactly a palatial suite, but it's comfortable and you're welcome to use it for as long as you're here." Saying that, Jonah gently laid Maggie down on his bed.

He paused only long enough to remove Maggie's shoes and then to lightly cover her body with the ends of the bedspread that his mother had given him and insisted that he put to use.

Maggie Reeves, in his bed. Who would have ever thought it, he wondered, quietly looking at her sleeping face for a long moment.

"Sleep tight, Maggie," he whispered. "You've earned it."

And with that, Jonah tiptoed out of the bedroom and closed the door behind him.

Chapter Six

The disorientation was immediate.

When Maggie opened her eyes the following morning, she had no idea where she was.

And then she remembered. The thought hit her like the sudden flash of a lightning bolt.

All her things were gone, destroyed because the building she had lived in had committed the sin of being in the path of a hurricane with the improbable gentle name of Brooke.

Throwing off the comforter that Maggie couldn't remember covering herself with, she sat up, blinking and trying to focus on her surroundings.

Daylight was creeping into the bedroom, making its way along the wooden floor. That told her that it had to be morning.

But how did she get here?

The last thing she remembered was leaning back against the sofa's cushion. She must have fallen asleep, Maggie thought. But that still didn't explain how she had gotten into this bed.

Wanting answers, Maggie slid off the bed. The second her feet hit the floor, she realized that she was barefoot. But she'd had on boots when she fell asleep, she was sure of it.

A quick search around the perimeter of the bed reunited Maggie with her boots. Try as she might, she couldn't remember taking them off. And if *Jonah* had removed them without waking her, then she must have *really* been out of it.

Her eyes suddenly widened as another thought occurred to her. Had he removed anything else from her person?

A quick check of what she was wearing—and if it had been disturbed in any way—told her that if Jonah *had* undressed her, he'd put everything back just the way he'd found it. That seemed highly unlikely.

Jonah wouldn't have tried to undress her, Maggie silently insisted. He'd taken the boots off—and left them off—purely for her comfort. But he'd obviously left everything else just the way he had found it. She had known Jonah Colton for most of her life—not intimately, but well enough to know that his character, as well as that of his brothers and parents, was exemplary.

Still, a tiny kernel of doubt nagged at her.

Well, there was only one way to find out, she told herself. She was just going to have to ask him.

Maggie headed toward the bedroom door and went to open it—just as Jonah presented himself on the other side of the door, about to knock. As a result, his raised hand came very close to making contact with her forehead.

It was hard to say which of them was more startled by the other's sudden appearance. They both jumped back before they could bump into one another.

"Sorry," Jonah apologized, dropping his hand to his side. "I was just coming to tell you that breakfast is ready."

Maggie didn't care about breakfast. She needed something cleared up first. "What was I doing in your bed?"

The question caught him off guard. "Sleeping would be my best guess."

Was he being flippant? "No, I mean how did I get there?"

He didn't understand why she looked so annoyed. "You fell asleep on the sofa, but you didn't look all that comfortable, so I carried you into the bedroom and put you in my bed," he concluded, thinking that would satisfy her.

"Anything else?" Maggie asked.

Jonah thought for a second, trying to recall if he had left anything out. "Well, I took your boots off because I thought your feet might start to hurt if you spent the night in them."

Maggie blew out a breath. Was he stalling? "What else?"

He looked at her as if he didn't understand what she was trying to get him to say. "I pulled the comforter over on you."

Maggie waited. When he didn't say anything further, she asked, "And that's all?"

Was there some ritual she had expected him to follow? "Why? What else was I supposed to do?"

Maybe she'd spent too many years with James and it had made her suspicious of all men. "Nothing," she answered, then hesitated. "But—"

He took that as her final answer. "Well then, I lived up to your expectations, didn't I?" Jonah concluded. "C'mon," he urged, "your breakfast is getting cold." Turning on his heel, he led the way back into the kitchenette. "I made coffee," he added, then warned her, "but there's no cream or sugar."

She usually liked to have both, but this wasn't the time to be choosy. "That's all right. I'll adjust," she said.

Biting her lower lip as she sat down at the small table and looked at the plate he'd prepared, she felt a little uncomfortable about the conversation that had transpired between them. The man had gone out of his way to be nice and she was interrogating him.

"I didn't mean to sound as if I was accusing you of something just now—" she began.

Another man might have enjoyed having her squirm through an apology, but that sort of behavior had never been Jonah's style. Thinking to spare her, he was quick to gloss over the incident.

"That's okay—I understand. You woke up in a different place than where you remembered falling asleep. The truth of it is we don't know each other all that well anymore." As he picked up his fork, he shrugged away the need for her apology. "You're a beautiful woman who's probably dealt with more than your share of overbearing Neanderthals who felt they were entitled to share more than just your company. It's only natural for you to have your imagination run away with you." Pausing before he began to eat, he looked into her eyes. "But I'm not a Neanderthal," he told her simply, "even though I was ready to climb into that tree to get you."

That completely broke the tension that was building between them. Relieved, Maggie laughed.

"So we're good?" he asked, taking a cue from her laughter.

"We're good," Maggie answered. "And so is breakfast," she added, looking down at her plate. She had almost finished half of it without even realizing it. "I never pictured you as being able to cook."

He didn't think that was much of a mystery. "Hey, considering the kind of life I lead, it was either learn how to cook or get really, really skinny. I decided to learn how to cook."

She nodded, trying not to be obvious about looking at him. "Good choice." She paused as she put another forkful into her mouth. It wound its way through her system, then down into her stomach. Maggie thought of what he had just told her. "So this is what you do for a living? You go around on your white horse, rescuing people?"

"Cody's a palomino," he corrected her. "And don't forget the search part," he said, amusement curving his mouth. There was also another part of his job. "I'm also trained in emergency medicine, but to answer your question in a nutshell—"

"Too late," she teased.

He didn't miss a beat. "Yes, this is pretty much what I do for a living. The organization's branch office is located in Austin. It's where I live," Jonah added.

That would explain why she hadn't seen that much of him these last few years, she thought.

"Well, lucky for me, you decided to come down for the wedding," Maggie told him.

He didn't want to take any undue credit. "Once the hurricane hit, headquarters would have sent my team out here to look for survivors one way or another."

Maggie shrugged away his attempt at modesty. "You look at it from your point of view, I'll look at it from mine."

Finished, she began to rise to bring both her plate and his to the sink.

"I'll do that," Jonah told her, quickly getting up from his chair.

She wasn't about to relinquish the plates, pulling them out of his reach "You cooked, I'll clean up. I like pulling my weight."

Jonah raised his hands up to indicate that he was withdrawing his claim to the dishes. "I didn't mean to imply that you didn't," he said. Smiling, he reminded her, "I saw you in action yesterday, remember?"

Maggie wasn't following him. "What does that mean?" she asked him.

He didn't want her getting all defensive on him again. They needed to progress past that point.

"It means that I know you can pull your own weight. Look, why don't we just agree that we're in this together?" he suggested. "That way you can stop circling around me, waiting for me to do or say something to challenge you. This isn't a contest, or a competition," he told her pointedly. "If you like, I can make you a temporary search and rescue team member. Will that make you feel better about this whole thing?"

People had a tendency, because of her looks, not to take her seriously. That Jonah just took her seriously without having her argue him into it felt as if she had just taken a huge step forward.

"I'd like that a lot," she replied. "What do I have to do?"

"Just what you've been doing since yesterday," he told her.

Maggie looked at him, waiting for more. When Jonah didn't say anything further, she asked, "And that's it?"

He smiled at her. "Trust me, that's more than enough," he assured her. "Okay, let's hit the road."

She was more than eager to go.

THE REST OF the day was more or less a replay of the kind of work he and Maggie had undertaken the previous day.

Because Jonah was worried about how wandering around the rubble that had once been her apartment might affect Maggie, he made the decision that he and Maggie would concentrate their search and rescue efforts to another portion of Whisperwood.

For the most part, they helped coordinate the different rescue groups, deciding where each of the groups could be best utilized, depending on the nature of their skills.

However, Jonah knew that he couldn't put off having Maggie deal with whatever destruction had befallen her apartment indefinitely. So sometime in the midafternoon, he and Maggie made their way back to Whisperwood Towers. Or at least what was left of it.

Jonah could almost *feel* Maggie stiffening as she sat next to him in the truck. They were drawing closer to the site of what had once been the Towers.

Maggie shivered. "It looks worse in daylight," she said, the words coming out in a hushed whisper.

The building that she had lived in had been comprised of three floors. Her apartment had been located on the second floor. All three floors had come down, the first two floors crushed beneath the third.

"It looks like a deflated accordion," Maggie added under her breath, walking through the rubble. "I don't think there's anything from my apartment that I can even find. At least not in one piece." Blinking, she struggled to keep her tears from spilling. She refused to cry. Deep down inside she knew if she started to, she wasn't going to be able to stop. Turning toward Jonah, she said, "It's all gone."

"Maybe not," he told her, doing his best to bolster her spirit. "You'd be surprised what can turn up during the cleanup efforts."

"Don't," she said, a warning note entering her voice. "Don't pretend like you can hold out hope for me when there isn't any."

"I'm not pretending," Jonah insisted. "I've been at this a lot longer than you have and I've seen miracles, large and small, happen all the time, especially when you least expect it." He could see that Maggie refused to buy into his optimism. "I'll be sure to tell the cleanup team to sift through this area carefully rather than just bulldoze through it." But she remained impassive. "You might be surprised."

"Uh-huh, sure," Maggie answered, staring down at what might or might not have been part of her apartment. There was just too much rubble to be able to tell.

Jonah knew she didn't believe him, and in her place, he probably wouldn't have, either. But as he had told Maggie, he had seen things that she hadn't, so he was in a better position to hold on to hope, however slim the thread was.

"Do me a favor, Maggie," he requested.

The eyes that looked up at him were watery. He could see she was doing her best not to let what she saw get to her, but it seemed to be a battle that was destined to be lost—and soon.

"What?" Maggie asked, doing her best to regain her composure.

"Reserve judgment until all this is over," Jonah said.

"Fine," she sighed, forcing herself to think of something else. Anything but her apartment and the possessions that were in it. "Consider it reserved." Wanting desperately to change the subject and focus on something else, she turned the conversation around back to Jonah. "I've been meaning to ask, why aren't there any personal touches in your cabin?"

"It's very simple. Because I don't live there anymore," he answered. "I haven't really lived in the cabin for a few years. But whenever I'm home, I use it as a base."

"So where do you live?" Maggie asked. "I mean on a permanent basis."

He thought he'd already answered that. Maybe she hadn't understood. Given what she was going through, he couldn't fault her. "I live in Austin."

"Any particular reason?" she asked, curious. She knew why she had left—she was looking to help her family. But she had returned once she'd decided to divorce James and now she felt safe here as well as happy. She didn't understand why he would choose to leave Whisperwood when his whole family was here.

"I wanted to make a name for myself someplace where the name Colton doesn't instantly bring my father and his ranch to mind."

She thought of her own situation until recently. "Is there bad blood between you?" she questioned. She hadn't heard anything, but that didn't mean that all was rosy within the confines of the Colton family.

He was quick to set her straight. "Not at all, I just don't believe in hanging on to anyone's coattails." He smiled at her. "I prefer my own coattails."

"I guess I can understand that," she admitted.

For her, family had always been the source of pain and misunderstanding. She had married James with the best of intentions. Yes, in the beginning, she had been in love with him—James had been her high school sweetheart—but her marriage had quickly soured when she discovered that he was cheating on her. She'd married him because she loved him and because she wanted to use his money to help her parents, who had incurred a great deal of medical debt since they'd been involved in a car accident. Her love for James might have died, but her resolve to help her parents did not.

However, she wasn't able to get the money quickly

enough. Both of her parents had died before she was able to pay off their debts. Not wanting to have anything to do with James's money once she was finally awarded it, she wound up using it to buy her sister the house where they had grown up.

Stunned, Bellamy was forced to reassess her feelings about and toward Maggie. She realized that when Maggie had gotten married and moved away, she was really doing it in order to help the family, not to escape dealing with the problems that nursing two invalids created. Once she realized that, all of Bellamy's bitterness vanished.

"Although," Maggie went on to tell Jonah, recalling her own situation, "sometimes it's nice to have family coattails to hang on to. You don't realize that until you suddenly find that there aren't any coattails for you to reach out for. That all you're grasping is air."

She really sounded as if she was in a bad way, Jonah thought. He hated to see her like this, hated what she had to be going through. He didn't want to pry, not yet, so he dealt with the situation another way.

"Why don't we knock off early?" he suggested. "Give you a chance to breathe, clear your head, forget about all this?" He gestured toward the rubble around them.

"It'll still be there to deal with tomorrow," Maggie said.

Then she understood what he was saying, Jonah thought. "Exactly. Tomorrow might be better."

But Maggie shook her head. "No, what I mean is we might as well make more headway today. That'll be that much less we all have to deal with tomorrow. And," she concluded, "we'll be one step closer to getting back on our feet."

Jonah studied her for a long moment, replaying her last words in his head. He had to admit that he was impressed. "Like I said yesterday, you are one tough cookie, Maggie Reeves."

"I don't know about tough," she told him. "But I'll tell you this much." She squared her shoulders. "I certainly have no intentions of crumbling."

Jonah nodded, smiling at her. "Good for you. Okay, Maggie, let's get back to this while we still have some daylight."

He would get no argument from her.

Chapter Seven

A week went by and in the midst of all this chaos, Jonah found that he and Maggie had managed to forge a routine of sorts. Each morning they got up, had breakfast and then they joined the search and rescue efforts, trying to locate the residents who were still missing. They would spend the entire day digging, clearing and searching. At the end of the day, they would return to Jonah's cabin, almost too tired to chew.

To show their gratitude to the Cowboy Heroes, the owners of the General Store threw open their doors and generously provided provisions for all the volunteers involved in the search and rescue.

They also fed the volunteers who were clearing away the remnants of the houses that had been mostly blown down. The damage that had been sustained was just too great to repair. What was left in those cases had to be cleared away to allow new homes to rise out of the ashes, like the legendary phoenix.

Jonah noticed that Maggie was barely putting one foot in front of the other as they walked into his cabin at the end of another overly long day.

"Tired?" Jonah asked her.

She looked at him, wondering if he was trying to be funny. "I'd have to have a pulse to be tired. I think I'm beyond that," Maggie confessed. She sighed. It was an effort to form words. "And I am *so* beyond tired," she added with as much feeling as she could muster.

Because of the nature of what he did, Jonah was used to working like this. "You sit. I'll make dinner," he told her, gesturing toward the chair.

"That's not fair," she protested even as she practically fell into the chair, the absolute picture of exhaustion. "You made dinner last night. And the night before that. And the night before that."

She didn't think it was right that he had to do it again, although she couldn't summon the energy to get back up on her feet.

"You know," Jonah said, raising his voice as he took out a steak he intended to split between the two of them, "any other woman would be happy with this arrangement and accept it as her due without drawing this much attention to it."

"Well, I'm not any other woman," Maggie told him, meaning that, despite her exhaustion, she didn't think that this was her due or that taking advantage of him was fair.

Jonah laughed softly to himself. "You can say that again," he murmured under his breath.

He hadn't meant for her to hear that and she hadn't, at least not completely. But she'd caught enough to make her turn around to face him.

"How's that again?" Maggie asked.

Jonah debated saying something vague in reply, or simply telling her that he hadn't said anything. But instead, he turned up the heat under the frying pan, put the meat in the pan and said, "I certainly never thought that you were like any of the other girls when we were in school."

She stared at him, slightly bewildered. "You were

five years ahead of me in school. I doubt you even noticed me."

The steak was sizzling and Jonah flipped it onto its other side. Was she actually serious? "*Everyone* noticed you," he told her simply. "Even before you hit high school, you were always too beautiful not to notice." He smiled, remembering the effect she'd had on him. "You were like an exquisite diamond in the middle of a basket filled with coals."

He'd said too much, Jonah thought. How had they even gotten to this subject? He had to learn not to say the first thing that came into his head.

He turned his attention back to the steak. Jonah knew that they both liked their steak rare, so frying it took next to no time at all. Done, he flipped the steak onto a plate, then cut it in half. He slid each piece onto a separate plate.

"Here," he said, placing the piece he had just cut in front of her and taking the remaining piece for himself. "Eat. If you're going to keep on arguing with me," he told Maggie, "you're going to need to keep up your strength."

She waited until she took the first bite. Damn, but that was good, she thought. "I wasn't arguing."

Jonah inclined his head, humoring her. "My mistake," he conceded.

She was tired, Maggie thought. Maybe she was being too touchy. "Telling a woman she's beautiful is never a mistake—unless you were just feeding her a line," Maggie said, just in case that was what he was doing.

"No line," Jonah assured her. "If you own a mirror, you'd know that." His eyes met hers. "You've always known that," he added. No one could be that oblivious to her looks.

When his eyes met hers, Maggie stopped eating. She was also fairly certain that for a minute, she'd stopped breathing, too. And just possibly, the world around them had stopped spinning.

The man sitting across from her was having a devastating effect on her.

"If *you* thought that," she said, "why didn't you ever say anything?"

He found that really amusing. "There was always such a crowd around you, I doubt you would have heard me," he replied.

Maggie frowned. "There was no crowd, Jonah."

He begged to differ. "You were one of the *really* popular girls. You were voted both the junior *and* the senior prom queen." And then he mentioned the biggest obstacle that kept him from making his feelings known. "Not to mention the fact that James Corgan was always there, ready to beat off any guy who came within two feet of you."

Maggie flushed when he mentioned her ex-husband. Having the man as part of her life wasn't something she liked being reminded of. But she couldn't dispute what Jonah was saying, either.

"He was my boyfriend at the time," she said, her eyes offering a silent apology for that part of her life and what had happened during that period.

"My point exactly," Jonah agreed. "I wasn't about to push my way in between the two of you. Not when you looked as if you had stars in your eyes whenever you looked at him."

Right now, it took everything for her not to shiver at the memory. "Maybe I didn't have stars in my eyes so much as I had sand in them," she corrected. When he looked at her, puzzled, Maggie explained, "I had sand in my eyes and I wasn't seeing clearly—or thinking clearly for that matter, either." Uncomfortable, she blocked out those memories. "Please, let's not talk about the past, Jonah."

He was more than happy to oblige.

"Fine with me," Jonah said. "If you don't mind, I'm going to grab a quick shower. I won't be too long," he promised. "And then you can have the bed."

Maggie gestured toward the back of the cabin. "It's your cabin," she reminded him.

"And you're my guest," Jonah countered. "That means I put your wishes ahead of mine."

Because of her marriage to James, she wasn't used to being treated with this much deference. "By all means," she told Jonah. "You take a shower."

"Five minutes," he promised, holding up all five fingers to underscore what he was saying as he crossed the room.

"Splurge," Maggie ordered. "Make it ten."

And then she found herself alone.

Maggie tried her best to keep her mind—and her hands—occupied as she waited for Jonah to come out again. But the moment he had closed the bedroom door behind him, tired as she was, her mind went into overtime, going to places that it had absolutely no business going.

Trying to rein in her thoughts, she reminded herself that even though circumstances had thrown them together again, circumstances would definitely pull them apart once this unusual epoch finally passed. Hadn't he told her that his life was in Austin, while hers, now that everything had been resolved, was finally back here.

Still, she just couldn't stop thinking about him or envisioning the way the water was probably lovingly cascading over and down that incredibly muscular body of his.

She forced herself to do something to occupy her mind.

Rinsing the dishes, she curled her hands into her palms, trying very hard not to picture him like that. So of course she did.

"All yours."

Stifling a squeal, Maggie swung around to see that Jonah was walking back into the living quarters, his hair still wet from the shower he'd taken.

Her hand covering her pounding heart, she told him, "You scared me."

"Sorry," he apologized, crossing to her. "I didn't mean to do that. I just thought that you'd want to get to bed as soon as possible so I came out the second I was finished taking my shower."

She felt her skin warming as his words evoked yet another image in her mind's eye.

Maggie pressed her lips together. "That's very thoughtful of you."

Trying to pass by him in what was rather a narrow space, she breathed in the scent of the soap Jonah had used. It was something manly and arousing—just like he was.

She tried to find her voice again. "But you didn't have to hurry on my account."

"Okay," Jonah replied, the words hanging between them as they stood so close to one another they were breathing in each other's air. Jonah could feel his pulse speeding up, rushing through his body as very strong desires swept through him, urging him to take her into his arms. "Next time I won't," he told her in a quiet voice.

His eyes, Maggie was sure, were saying other things to her, things that had nothing to do with a shower. A warm shiver inched up her spine.

She didn't know why she was feeling so vulnerable right now, or what had triggered this reaction from her.

Yes, they were both working side by side, but they were doing it as part of a whole.

However, at the end of the day they left together, and when they "came home," they occupied the same small space together.

Standing next to him now, she found herself almost willing Jonah to kiss her. She didn't think of it beyond that, didn't dwell on any of the consequences. All she knew was that, with her whole heart and soul, she really, really wanted Jonah to kiss her.

And then what? the voice in her head asked. Once the kiss happened, she would be opening up a whole can of worms, a can of worms she might not be capable of dealing with.

It was better not to go there and wonder than to kiss him and be disappointed. Although something told her that she wouldn't be disappointed.

Maggie was about to briskly tell him good-night when she felt the back of Jonah's long, tapering fingers brush along her cheek as he moved back a stray lock of her hair, lightly tucking it behind her ear,

Jonah was struggling to contain himself. Struggling not to give in to the urgent desire that was rushing through him as powerful as the river after the flood hit. He found himself being taken captive.

He desperately wanted to taste those lips of hers, to satisfy his mounting curiosity. But that in turn might ruin everything. They were getting along right now. If he gave in to the passions that were all but pounding urgent fists against the walls of his weakening restraint, he just might wind up regretting it.

Especially if he saw Maggie looking at him with disappointment in her eyes. Right now, they were friends, working together in total harmony. If he gave in to himself, all that could be lost.

He didn't want to chance it.

"You'd better get to bed," Jonah whispered, moving back. "We've got another long day ahead of us tomorrow."

She knew that, but wasn't he forgetting about something?

"What about the investigation?" Maggie asked, forcing the words out of her mouth. He'd told her that they would get back to it, but several days had passed and they still hadn't.

"Investigation?" he repeated, his mind still focused on how very tempting her lips looked and how much he wanted to kiss her.

"Into seeing if there were any more victims buried around that big oak," she explained patiently. Why else had her ex-father-in-law sent her that cryptic note if it wasn't to try to find other bodies?

The serial killer had left his victims buried in shallow graves, with barely just enough dirt thrown over their bodies. Other bodies would have surfaced by now—if he had buried them that way. But what if he hadn't? What if Elliott had decided to change his MO? Or what if there had been a copycat killer? Someone who had wanted to put his own signature on his victims?

What if *that* killer was the *real* killer and Elliott wasn't guilty at all?

Maggie wanted answers.

"You said that once the search and rescue had gotten underway, we'd go back to Live Oak Ranch together, to search around that tree that Adam marked off on his map," she reminded Jonah.

He nodded. "I remember."

He should have known that Maggie wouldn't forget about that. She had already proven to him that she was far too tenacious to allow the matter to drop no matter how busy she got. Or what the chief had said to both of them to get them to drop the investigation. It was obviously front and center on her mind.

"So when can we go?" she asked Jonah, her eagerness at war with the very tired look on her face.

"Tell you what," Jonah suggested. "We get everyone organized and going at the next search site tomorrow, and then the two of us can take a trip over to the Corgan ranch."

"To follow the map?" Maggie asked.

He knew better than to laugh at the eagerness he detected in her voice.

"To follow the map," he told her. "Maybe between the two of us, we can find whatever it was that Adam was trying to direct your attention toward." He thought back to the cryptic note she had shown him. The one her late ex-father-in-law had left her along with the map. "It would have been nice if he hadn't resorted to riddles and just told you outright what it was he wanted you to find out there and just where you were going be able to find it."

She agreed that would have made it so much easier, but at least they did have something to go on.

"Look, I'm surprised that James's father even tried to reach out to me. I don't think, in all the time that I was married to James, that his father and I had any sort of a conversation that lasted for more than a couple of minutes and was about anything that went deeper than just speculating about the weather."

"And then he suddenly decides to put *this* on your shoulders?" He shook his head. It just didn't make any sense. "That is definitely a mystery," he agreed. Pointing toward the door right behind her, he ordered, "Go. Get to bed."

Maggie laughed, taking no offense. Every bone in her body wanted to do as Jonah instructed. "You are going to make one hell of a father someday," she told him.

He grinned at the thought. "I certainly hope so," he freely admitted.

Exhausted though she was, his response caught her off guard. "You want kids?"

"Absolutely," he said without any hesitation. "Two of each." And then he reconsidered his answer. "No, make that four of each."

"Four of each," she repeated, overwhelmed by the thought of that many offspring. "You trying to lose your wife in the crowd?"

"No way. My parents had five of us and nobody ever got lost in that crowd," Jonah told her in complete sincerity.

To each his own, Maggie thought. His family apparently had much better luck with kids. Hers, it seemed, hadn't. Relations had broken down between her and her parents as well as between her and her sister. That had been a painful thing for her to endure. She didn't know if she was up to rolling the dice on having kids and risking that sort of rejection, not again.

"Okay," she declared as if that closed the subject they were discussing, however peripherally. "I'll see you in the morning."

"Right," Jonah agreed genially. "You'd better go get some sleep before we wind up finding something else to talk about."

She nodded, retreating and going into the bedroom. Maggie had a feeling that if she didn't, Jonah would be proven right. The man was easy to talk to and they *would* continue to find things to talk about. If that happened, before they knew it, it would be morning.

Being groggy and going out to be part of the search and rescue team was nothing if not completely counterproductive. In that state, someone would probably wind up having to rescue *them*.

Squaring her shoulders, Maggie told him, "Good night."

Jonah echoed the words back to her, the sound of his voice wrapping itself around Maggie, whispering a promise that was guaranteed to keep her warm until morning.

Maybe longer.

Chapter Eight

Jonah, Maggie happily discovered, was a man of his word. The moment he had finished overseeing the coordination of the day's rescue efforts and made sure that there were no new, unexpected emergencies festering in the wings, about to spring up, he turned toward her and said, "How do you feel about taking a ride out to Live Oak Ranch?"

Maggie had thought it was going to take him a lot longer before he said they could go. His question had caught her completely by surprise.

"Now?" she asked.

"Yes, unless you'd rather stay here and continue helping plow through all this dirt and rubble," Jonah answered, gesturing around the chaotic area. They had made a great deal of headway, but they weren't out of the woods yet. Not by a long shot.

"No, no," she quickly assured him.

She knew that it was work that needed to be done and she was more than willing to help. But Maggie also had this deep sense of urgency that was all but twisting her insides into a knot, an urgency that made her feel she was on the brink of solving a puzzle that was bigger than she was given to believe.

"Now is good," she told Jonah. Then she amended, "Now is perfect."

"Then 'now' it is," he responded, amused by her excitement as he led her over to his truck.

Trying to contain herself, Maggie climbed into the pickup truck. The moment she did, Jonah started the truck and they were on their way.

They traveled for over ten minutes and, at first, Maggie didn't say anything because she thought that maybe she had somehow gotten turned around during the search and rescue excursion this morning. She wasn't one of those people who was blessed with a powerful sense of direction that allowed her to find her way around even if she was moving in utter darkness.

But after another few minutes had gone by, Maggie became increasingly convinced that she *wasn't* mistaken. Jonah was driving them back into town, the completely opposite direction from Live Oak Ranch.

This wasn't making any sense to her. She shifted in the front seat to look at him.

"I thought you said we were going to Live Oak Ranch," she said.

Jonah continued driving, keeping his eyes on the road. "We are."

"No, we're not," she argued. "You're driving back into Whisperwood," she pointed out. Didn't Jonah see that?

"I know," he answered, his voice calm. "That's where the horses are."

"The horses?" she questioned, feeling increasingly lost. Had she missed something?

"Sure," Jonah answered as if the reply was as plain as the nose on her face. "If we're heading back to look around that tree you were clinging to when I happened by to rescue you," he reminded her, still teasing her about the incident, "that's some pretty rough terrain. We'll make a lot better time getting there if we go on horseback."

She blew out a breath. "Said the man who was practically born on the back of a horse."

He laughed at the "voice-over" Maggie had just used to illustrate her objection to his idea. He wasn't buying it. "This is Texas," Jonah reminded her. "Everyone was born on the back of a horse."

Obviously, he didn't see the problem. "Not everyone," she argued.

The road ahead was mercifully unobstructed so he could afford to look at her for a moment. Maggie had caught him completely by surprise. "You can't ride a horse?"

She didn't like the way that sounded. As if she was deficient in some way.

"I can get on a horse without falling off," Maggie said defensively. Then she added, "Although it is kind of tricky." She cleared her throat, looking straight ahead. "Most of the time I find another way to get from place to place—like using a four-wheel drive vehicle."

"Horses are better when it comes to getting around on terrain that's inhospitable." In his opinion, that only made sense. And then a question occurred to him. "How did you manage to get up to that part of the ranch the day of the hurricane?"

She shrugged. "I drove as far as I could and then when the going got really rough, I went the rest of the way on foot." At the time, it hadn't seemed like such a big deal.

Jonah's brow furrowed as he thought over what she had just told him. He reviewed the scene in his mind when he'd gone out to search for her. "I didn't see a car when I got there."

Maggie frowned. "That's because it was probably

swept away in the flash flood," she admitted ruefully. "I haven't seen it since that day." She turned her head toward him, the expression on her face daring him to lecture her.

Jonah thought it best to focus on the positive aspects. "Well, the threat of the flood is over and the waters have all been receding. If nothing unexpected happens, water levels should be back to normal within the week. Who knows?" he speculated. "Maybe your car'll turn up."

"Maybe," Maggie echoed, although she really wasn't holding out any hope that she was going to find it "washed up" somewhere. "But if it does show up, most likely it won't be in any condition to be driven." It would probably be far too waterlogged for that.

"And *that* is the reason why we're going to go there on horseback," he told her.

Which brought up more questions for her. "We're going to be riding out on Cody?" she asked, remembering her rescue and how Jonah had brought her to his cabin with the two of them riding on his horse.

"*I'm* riding Cody," he corrected. "You'll be on Strawberry." Before she could ask, he told her, "That's one of the extra mounts the team brought with us. We use Strawberry and the others interchangeably when our own horses need to be switched out."

"Strawberry?" Maggie repeated, the name giving her hope. "Is she gentle?"

"She has a good disposition," Jonah assured her, adding, "Don't worry, I wouldn't put you on the back of a bucking bronco even if you told me you were an accomplished rider."

That should have comforted her, Maggie thought, but it really didn't. She saw the stable just ahead and instantly felt a knot forming in her stomach.

Pulling up the hand brake as he parked his truck, Jonah leaned in toward Maggie and told her confidently, "Don't worry, you can do this."

Maggie had never liked being thought of as inept, but she wasn't the type to make a show of false bravado, either.

"Right. Easy for you to say," she murmured, getting out.

"And easy for you to do," he assured her, sensing that what Maggie needed was to have someone display unwavering confidence in her. He joined her outside the truck. "Cody and I will be right beside you."

"Doing what?" Maggie asked. "Laughing?"

"I'm not planning on laughing," Jonah told her so seriously that she believed him.

"Okay," she answered haltingly as she followed Jonah into the stable. "I'll try hard not to give you anything to laugh at."

"Sounds like a plan," he replied good-naturedly. "Tell you what, in the interest of time, I'll skip teaching you the proper way to saddle a horse and just go ahead and saddle both horses for us—this time."

She didn't understand. That sounded rather ominous to her. "*This* time?" Maggie questioned.

"Yes," he replied simply, taking his saddle and placing it on Cody. Maggie all but shrank against the stall's walls. "The next time we go out, I'll expect you to follow my directions—unless you already know how to properly saddle a horse?" He left his question up in the air, waiting for her to address it one way or another.

Lying would only get her into trouble. Besides, she had found that she didn't like being on the receiving end of lies, so the idea of lying herself was rather off-putting to her.

Which meant that Maggie had no choice but to tell him the truth. "The few times I attempted to ride a horse, someone else saddled the horse for me."

Jonah nodded. "I thought as much," he said, but there was no note of superiority in his voice, no condescension, either. As far as he was concerned, Jonah was just telling her his assumptions on the matter.

Maggie moved to one side, allowing Jonah to have unobstructed access to the horse he'd told her she would be riding. This way, he could saddle the mare for her quickly.

Jonah's movements were smooth, she observed, almost as if he didn't even have to think about them. He just went ahead and did what needed to be done. He had probably been doing this all his life, Maggie mused.

Jonah saddled both horses in less time than it would have taken her to saddle just the one. But then, given what he did for a living, that only seemed natural.

Finished, Jonah held on to Strawberry's reins as he turned toward Maggie.

"Okay," he announced, "your horse is all ready to go."

Maggie wasn't aware of running the tip of her tongue along her very dry lips, but Jonah was. He could almost *feel* himself being drawn in as he watched her. Not only that, but he found himself fighting a very strong urge to sample those very same lips.

"That makes one of us," she murmured moving a little closer.

"C'mon," Jonah urged. "I'll give you a boost up," he offered. "Hold on to the reins." He handed them over to her. Their hands brushed and it occurred to him that her fingertips were absolutely icy. She was really nervous about doing this, he realized. "Put one foot into the stirrup and then swing the other leg over the back of the horse," he coached. "I'll be right here."

She followed instructions, almost freezing in midmotion. She felt his hand lightly making contact with her posterior, just enough to get her to complete the mount without an incident—or falling.

"Getting on the horse isn't the problem," she told him once she was finally seated in the saddle. "*Staying* on the horse, however, might be."

He wanted to get moving, but not at the cost of having something happen to Maggie. She badly needed to build up her confidence.

"Then we'll take it slow," he promised her.

Watching Jonah swing effortlessly into his own saddle, Maggie couldn't help thinking that he was the very picture of ease as he sat astride Cody.

"Keep a light—but firm—hold on the reins and press your knees against Strawberry's thighs," he instructed. "Remember," he reminded her seriously, "you're the one in charge."

"In charge. Right," Maggie laughed dryly at the idea. "I'm not sure that Strawberry's aware that she got that memo."

"Then *make* her aware of it. Don't worry," Jonah said as if he could read Maggie's thoughts. "Strawberry expects to be directed around."

Maggie sincerely had her doubts about that. "You sure about that?" she questioned. She wasn't the type to impose her will on others, that included horses.

"I'm sure," he answered. "But that doesn't mean that she's not going to try to test you." He thought of another way for her to approach the problem. "Think of Strawberry as if she was a kid. Kids expect to be told what to do, but that doesn't stop them from trying to test the boundary lines that have been drawn around them."

The analogy amused Maggie. He might actually have something there. "Like I said, you're going to make a good father someday."

Holding her breath, Maggie tested what he'd told her to do and pressed her knees against the mare's flanks. In response, the animal sped up a little.

"Hey, it worked," Maggie cried in surprise.

"Told you." Jonah grinned, pleased. "Just keep telling yourself that you're the one in charge. If you believe it," he stressed, "Strawberry will believe it."

Maggie still had her doubts about that, but she was a little more willing to give it a try—especially with Jonah riding beside her. She had absolutely no doubts that if something were to go wrong, he would jump in and rescue her. After all, it was in his nature. He had already done it once. Rescuing her from a runaway horse had to be a lot easier than finding and rescuing her from the ravages of a hurricane.

"You look more confident," Jonah observed several minutes later as they made their way toward the tree that Adam Corgan had singled out on the map he had sent along with his posthumous note.

"That's all your doing," Maggie responded. She wasn't about to accept any compliments that she felt she hadn't really earned.

"No, it's not," he countered. "I could talk myself blue in the face, telling you what to do and how to do it. But you're the one who took that advice and put it to use. So, the way I see it, the credit belongs strictly to you." He gave her a penetrating look. "So just accept it."

The smile that formed slowly on her lips made Maggie beam. The expression turned a beautiful woman into something even more. It made her into someone who could create an ache inside him.

Rousing himself, Jonah shifted his attention back to the reason why they were out here in the first place, searching for clues about someone who possibly didn't even exist.

"You think this is a fool's errand, don't you?" she asked him, her question breaking into his thoughts.

Jonah framed his reply cautiously. "I'd say it's too soon to tell."

"But if you had to make a guess?" Maggie pressed.

"Before I did that," he qualified, "I'd want the answer to other questions." He saw her raise an eyebrow. "Like why now? Why send you on this scavenger hunt without even telling you what it is you're looking for? Why is the only thing that the dearly departed *did* specify is that whatever you find—*if* you find it—will provide a 'truth' that will make his brother, a convicted six-time serial killer, 'free'?" he asked. The missive in the note didn't make any sense to him. "Is 'free' just meant in the poetic sense, or is there actually something there that would tell us that Elliott Corgan is really not guilty of all those murders? *Those* are the questions I want the answers to," he told her.

Maggie sighed, trying not to allow a wave of hopelessness to slip in. "Those are a lot of questions," she finally agreed.

Maybe he shouldn't have laid it out like that, Jonah thought. But now that he had, he asked Maggie, "Got any answers?"

She shook her head. "I don't even have one."

He had another, possibly easier question for her to answer.

"When you were up that tree, did you happen to see anything from that vantage point?" he asked. There was a possibility that perhaps Maggie saw something that she didn't even realize she was seeing.

"The only thing I saw were rising waters," she answered.

Until Jonah had come riding up like a real live hero, she had started to seriously worry that maybe she *wasn't* going to make it back for her sister's wedding. The thought of the water rising so high that it would eventually engulf her had become an increasingly serious concern for her.

"But you didn't see anything else?" he asked.

"To be honest," she admitted, "nothing else was on my mind except getting back to town for my sister's wedding. When I saw you riding up on Cody like some white knight out of a story about King Arthur and his Round Table, my heart stopped. I could have sworn you had a gleaming white light shining all around you like some huge halo."

He grinned at her narrative. "That would be my saving-a-damsel-in-distress aura," Jonah told her—and then laughed. "I'm just really glad I was able to find you."

"That makes two of us," she told him in all honesty. The next moment, she realized that they had ridden up to the tree in question.

Cody was trained to remain where he was once Jonah dropped his reins and they touched the ground. Swinging off the horse now, he turned toward Maggie. "I'll help you down," he offered.

If she had any confidence in her abilities to sit astride a horse, she might have told him that she was perfectly capable of getting down herself. But she hadn't built up that sort of confidence. Luckily, her common sense wasn't in short supply.

Meeting his offer to help with a simple, "Thank you," she gratefully allowed him to put his hands on her waist in order to help her dismount. She was itching to begin the search.

Chapter Nine

Taking hold of her waist, Jonah eased Maggie off her horse. She slid down, her body not even a whisper away from his.

By the time her feet touched the ground, all sorts of alarms had begun going off in every inch of her throbbing body.

And by the expression on Jonah's ruggedly handsome face, she could tell that she wasn't the only one whose body temperature had risen from a normal 98.6 degrees to a temperature that was just too high to be measured by a regular thermometer.

Maggie was even more unclear about what happened next. For the life of her, she wasn't sure exactly *who* made the first move.

Maybe it was simultaneous, born and executed in the heat of the moment.

She didn't know—she didn't care. All she was aware of was the intense yearning that washed over her. She was aware of that and of the overwhelming kiss that all but exploded between them.

He kissed her.

She kissed him.

They kissed each other.

Exactly who instigated that first kiss was utterly

moot—except for the all-consuming effect that occurred in the wake of lips meeting lips.

Maggie gave in to the feeling instantly, as if she had been waiting all of her life for this one moment, this one occurrence.

Maybe, looking back, she had been. James had *never* kissed her like this.

Rising up on her toes, Maggie immediately lost herself in this kiss. She was aware of everything going on within the small, tight sphere that only the two of them occupied. The rest of the world wasn't there. All that mattered was that he was.

Jonah hadn't meant for this to happen, although he would have called himself a liar if he hadn't admitted to thinking about this.

Longing for this.

Ever since he had arrived back in Whisperwood and saw Maggie from across the room, talking to his brother Donovan and her sister, desire had slowly taken root within him. Once rooted, it continued to flower and spread with a vengeance despite his efforts to keep it all under control.

But the moment her body had made contact with his, it was as if a blazing lightning bolt had flashed through him, disarming him even as it temporarily disengaged his common sense.

Jonah cupped the back of her head as his lips came down on hers, claiming her. Branding her.

Branding him.

He felt far more alive than he had in years.

His heart was pounding so fast, sending adrenaline racing throughout his entire body, as if there was a need to alert every single fiber of his being that there was something magnificent going on.

Something to celebrate.

Jonah slanted his mouth over Maggie's again and again, the kiss growing deeper and more consuming each time until they were both utterly submerged in it.

Maggie could feel him wanting her. They were out here, all alone in the world except for the horses. There was no one to see them.

The conditions were far from ideal, but right now, she didn't care.

She—

Moving backward to get a better footing, Maggie felt her heel hitting something and she stumbled. Startled, she gasped, her lips breaking away from Jonah's.

His arms quickly closed around her. If they hadn't, she would have fallen backward and wound up on the ground.

"Maggie?" Surprise underscored her name, and Jonah looked at her, confused.

With the moment abruptly stolen from them, Maggie looked down to see what she had stumbled on. She thought she saw something white-ish poking up out of the ground. Her brow furrowed as she tried to look closer.

What *was* that?

She was certain that the last time she had been at this location, that white thing had *not* been here, or at least not sticking out. The floods and winds had played havoc with the dirt and leaves that had been clustered at the foot of the tree, gathering at that spot since forever. The hurricane was responsible for clearing it all away and exposing whatever that was underneath.

At a loss as to what was going on, Jonah continued holding on to her. He searched her face. "Are you okay?" he asked.

"I will be once—"

She didn't get to finish her sentence and maybe that

was just as well because she had almost said something about her racing heart. Instead, she looked down again, staring at what she'd thought was a white stick.

That was when she realized that it wasn't a stick at all.

A scream rose in her throat, but she managed to stifle it. However, her eyes, flying open so wide they made him think of proverbial saucers, gave her away.

Grabbing his arm, she pointed to what was protruding out of the earth. In a hushed whisper, she asked, "What *is* that, Jonah?"

For the first time, he looked down at the ground. What she was pointing out didn't make any sense to him. Jonah dropped to his knees beside the newly uncovered article to get a closer, better look at it.

Gathering her courage, Maggie knelt down beside him.

"Omigod, is that—" She had to swallow in order to produce enough saliva to allow her to say the word and not have it stick inside her mouth. "Is that a bone?"

Taking his handkerchief out, Jonah cleared away the remaining dirt that was clinging to it. "It's a bone all right."

"Is it human?" she whispered.

"It certainly could be." Before he could say anything further, he saw that Maggie had started digging in the dirt that was just beneath where they had found the bone. He caught her hand, momentarily stilling it. "Maggie, maybe you should wait for the police chief."

But she shook her head, rejecting that idea. "This might not be what we think it is and then we've gotten him out here for nothing. He's got enough to deal with with the flood and everything else. We need to be sure this is an actual human body before we drag him out here."

"You're right," he agreed. "But only dig just enough so that we can be sure it *is* a human body. The second we are, we'll stop digging." It wasn't a suggestion.

"Stop talking and start digging," she insisted, sinking her hands into the muck and moving as much as she could each time.

IT DIDN'T TAKE long for them to find the rest of it. The rest of the body. The bone that Maggie had accidentally stumbled across had somehow been separated from the rest of the skeleton. That was the result of either some scavenging animal searching for food, or maybe even the hurricane itself.

When they had cleared away the dirt and debris, Maggie stared in horror at what had been uncovered. It was the fully mummified skeletal remains of what appeared to be a woman, due to the larger, rounded pelvis region.

And then it suddenly dawned on her. "This is it," Maggie cried, looking up at Jonah. "This is what Adam Corgan wanted me to find."

It didn't make any sense to him. "How is finding this woman supposed to set Elliott Corgan free?" Jonah questioned. He looked back at the skeleton. "And who is she?"

Maggie struggled not to think of the skeleton as the remains of what had once been a living, breathing human being, but just as the embodiment of a puzzle. She looked down at the mummified body. There were no clues, no indication who she had once been. Nothing to identify the woman.

"I have no idea who that is," she confessed.

"Well, maybe the chief might be able to tell us," Jonah speculated. "Thompson's been part of this town it seems like forever. According to my parents, he was definitely on the police force when all this went down." Getting up, he offered his hand to Maggie and helped her to her feet. "He must have heard about a missing girl, one who hadn't been accounted for when those other bodies—seven in all—started turning up in shallow graves."

She still seemed a little uncertain about bringing this to the chief's attention. "He told us not to get involved," she reminded Jonah.

"Well, we obviously are," he said, gesturing toward the preserved remains. "And he's got more important things on his mind than to take us to task for not listening to his advice." Jonah looked back at the body. "For one thing, he's now got an unidentified mummified body to deal with."

"So are we going to ride back into town to tell him?" she asked Jonah.

He didn't think that was a good idea. "I don't think we should leave the body. You never know, another animal might make off with part of it. Besides, we don't even know if the chief is in town. He might be anywhere." Jonah took out his cell phone from his back pocket and held it up. "I've got a signal! The lines have finally been restored," he told her. He looked at his phone to double-check. There were bars. "We'll call Thompson and tell him what we've found."

Maggie looked down at the mummified body again. "He's going to be thrilled," she murmured.

"Thrilled or not," Jonah said, "the chief needs to be told."

The cell phone on the other end of the number that Jonah had keyed in rang a total of nine times. On the tenth ring, he knew his call was about to go to voice mail. Just then a gruff voice picked up and answered, warning him, "This had better be an emergency and it had better be good."

Jonah looked down at the mummified remains wrapped in plastic. "Well, it definitely qualifies as an emergency. As for the other part, it all depends on your definition of 'good.'"

"Is that you, Jonah?" Chief Thompson questioned, although he was fairly certain that it was.

In his haste to get the chief down here, Jonah realized that he hadn't identified himself. The lines might be up, but obviously caller ID wasn't functioning yet.

"Yes, it is," Jonah said.

A trace of annoyance came through. "Jonah, what the hell are you going on about?"

"Well, Chief, I'm out here with Maggie Reeves," Jonah began.

"Where's 'here'?" the chief asked.

"Live Oak Ranch," Jonah said quickly. He didn't wait for the chief to say anything further but dived straight into the heart of the reason he was calling. "And we're looking at what appears to be the mummified remains of possibly a young woman. There's nothing near the body to tell us who she is."

There was a long pause on the other end and Jonah thought he might have lost the connection. But then the chief's booming voice came on, calling him on the carpet. "I thought I told you two to stay clear of all this."

"You did say that, Chief," Jonah agreed, steering the conversation in another direction. "And we really weren't looking for them. Maggie and I just happened to find the remains totally by accident," Jonah said, his eyes slanting toward Maggie. He wanted to protect her from the chief's anger.

"Uh-huh." Anyone could tell that the chief didn't believe him, Jonah thought. "Just where are you on the ranch?"

"We're right on the site of the ranch's biggest oak tree, the one the Corgans claimed is the oldest tree in the whole state. Are you familiar with it?" Jonah asked Thompson.

"I'm familiar with it," the chief replied. His voice was strangely devoid of all emotion and sounded as if he was half-dead inside.

"Well, we found the body right near the tree," Jonah told him. "I guess the hurricane must have blown away all the dirt that killer used to bury the body in his attempt to hide it from anyone's view," he added, trying to get some sort of a response from the chief.

Thompson sighed. "All right, since you found this body, I want you to stay right there with it," the chief instructed. "I'm coming out with my forensic team to see if the killer left any evidence."

"I don't think they're going to have much luck, not after the hurricane went barreling through here," Jonah told him.

"We'll see," the chief said, his tone still unreadable.

Sensing that the chief was about to hang up, Jonah had one last thing to ask him. "Hey, Chief, do you have any idea who this last girl might have been?"

"Yeah," Thompson answered grimly. "I do have an idea."

When the chief didn't say anything beyond that, Jonah pressed the man, "Well? Who was it?"

Jonah thought he heard the chief make some sort of noise, but he wasn't certain. "I'll talk to you when I get there," Thompson said almost curtly just before he terminated the call.

"What did he say?" Maggie asked the second Jonah put his phone away. "The chief's got a booming voice, but I couldn't make out everything. He's coming, right?"

"Yes, he's coming," Jonah told her. "And he's bringing his forensic team with him."

Maggie nodded, pleased. "Well, that's good." She thought of the last thing that she'd heard Jonah say to the chief. "Did he say he knew who this was, or that he at least suspected who it might be?"

Jonah shook his head. "No, he cut me off when I asked."

Maggie frowned. "That's not like Chief Thompson," Maggie noted. "If anything, he's usually very outgoing and friendly."

Jonah shrugged. "Well, I guess this hurricane has been hard on everyone," he told her. "It's been making people behave in ways that they didn't think they ever would."

She looked at him. Was Jonah talking about the chief, or was he possibly referring to himself? Specifically, was he referring to what had happened between them seconds before she'd accidentally uncovered that mummified skeleton?

Maggie felt her cheeks growing warm. If she hadn't taken that step back and tripped on it, who knew what might have happened?

She had felt him responding to her. It wasn't all in her head. He'd wanted her as much as she had wanted him. Both of them had been lost in the heat of the moment and they could have easily taken it to the next level and gone further.

The idea of making love right on top of a hidden skeleton was appalling to her now that she knew the body had been there, but at the time, they hadn't known anything except the hunger that was so obviously consuming both of them.

She shivered, thinking how grateful she was that fate had intervened when it did. What if they had gone along with their erupting passions, if they had made love right then and there? Once they discovered that they had come together right on top of the wrapped-up remains of a murder victim—because it was obvious that was what she must be—what might have been the beginning of something beautiful would have been forever tainted. They would never be able to look at one another without remembering that they had made love on top of a murdered woman's hidden grave.

Jonah watched Maggie's expression change. She was obviously thinking about the dead woman again. And judging by her face, Maggie's thoughts were unsettling.

"Are you okay?" he asked her gently, still watching her for any indication that she wasn't telling him everything.

"You mean other than feeling sick to my stomach because we just found the remains of a mummified murder victim?" Maggie asked.

"You're right." He understood what Maggie was implying. "That was a stupid question I just asked. As soon as the chief gets here with his team, I'll take you home."

"The hell you will," she said with such effusive spirit that it surprised him. "I'm not going anywhere. I want to find out who she is."

Jonah sighed. He shouldn't have been surprised. The Maggie Reeves he had come to know these last few days wasn't about to retreat and go home if her questions weren't answered.

Chapter Ten

They didn't have that long to wait, which was good, because every extra moment she had to occupy in the same vicinity as the wrapped-up, mummified skeleton was beyond unsettling for Maggie. Her heart leaped when she heard the sound of the chief's all-terrain vehicle coming closer and approaching the area where they were.

It had taken less than an hour for the chief to come, but it felt a great deal longer than that.

The chief's vehicle was followed by the van containing three members of the crime scene investigative team.

Jonah caught a glimpse of Maggie's face. It didn't take a genius to guess what was behind the look she was wearing.

"They would have made better time getting here if they had come on horseback," he told her, knowing that Maggie had to have felt that the chief and his team using vehicles to get here supported her own desire to do the same.

"I guess we'll never find out," she replied tersely. "The point is, they're finally here."

The next moment, there was no longer time for any sort of a debate on the subject. The chief had gotten out of his Jeep and was heading straight for them. The man looked as if he was loaded for bear. She really wasn't in any sort of a mood for a lecture.

Looking at the chief, she could have sworn that she almost saw steam coming out of Thompson's ears. The scowl on the man's face would have stopped a hardened criminal in his tracks.

"I thought I told you two to keep clear of this investigation." Thompson all but growled the words at the duo. The chief was as close to being furious as Maggie had ever seen the man. He appeared weary, but his eyes were flashing. "You need to leave this kind of thing to the professionals. Colton, you of all people should understand that. I would have expected this kind of Nancy Drew behavior from Maggie here, but you, you really should have known better," he told Jonah, vainly trying to keep his voice down.

Maggie didn't feel right about having someone else take the blame for something that she had instigated. She remained silent for as long as she could, but inevitably, she lost the fight.

Surprising both the chief and Jonah, she stepped in between the two men.

"Don't go yelling at Jonah, Chief," she warned sharply. "It wasn't his fault. I was the one who wanted to come out here again and take a second look around. Jonah just came with me to make sure that I was safe and didn't get into any trouble."

"Maggie," Jonah began, trying to pull her aside before she got carried away.

But Maggie had gotten all wound up. She had no intention of standing by meekly as Thompson gave Jonah a dressing-down for something that she was responsible for getting underway.

Putting her hand up to indicate that she hadn't finished talking yet, Maggie informed the chief, "And it's a lucky thing that I did, because if we *hadn't* come back up here, then who knows *when* this body would have been found?" she asked. "The poor thing might have gone another thirty, forty years before she was finally discovered."

Thompson appeared to be doing a slow boil. "Are you finished?" he asked in his deep, authoritative voice.

Maggie felt a little intimidated, but did her damnedest not to show it.

"Yes, I am. For now," she added as an afterthought in case anything else occurred to her in the next few minutes.

Both she and Jonah expected the chief to explode, but instead, all he did was nod curtly. "All right then, the forensic team will get on with its work and you two are free to go." Thompson waved toward the path he assumed they had taken to get here. "As a matter of fact, I think you should," he snapped.

Thompson turned away from them and returned to the body that had been carefully lifted from its grave, a grave that appeared to have been dug far deeper than the graves of the other women who had been killed.

Maggie regretted having become so combative with Thompson. There was something about the set of his shoulders that suggested to her a man in pain. The image tugged at her heart. She knew that his body language had nothing to do with the fact that she'd yelled at him. But there was something else going on here. Something that was deeply affecting the chief.

"Maggie, let's go," Jonah urged as he reached for her arm.

But Maggie drew her arm away before he could take

hold of it. Instead, she moved a little closer to the chief, peering at his face.

"You know who that is, don't you, Chief?" she asked quietly.

"Yes, I do." The chief's voice was solemn, heavy. He didn't look at Maggie. Instead, he continued staring at the mummified remains lying on the ground not too far away. Maggie thought she saw tears gathering in the chief's eyes. "I wasn't sure until just now, but yes, I know who that is."

He picked up his head and looked at the two people who had discovered the body. "That's my little sister, Emmeline." His voice tightened as he told them, "See that bracelet on her left wrist?"

Maggie had noticed the bracelet when she and Jonah had cleared debris away from the body. Small, thin and delicate, the bracelet had what looked like tiny roses embossed along the length of it.

"Yes," she answered, waiting for the chief to continue.

"I gave that to Emmeline for her birthday." He laughed shortly at the memory. "She was always losing things. She lost the bracelet the very first week after I gave it to her." He pressed his lips together to regain control over his voice. "She had all her friends looking for it. She was so relieved when it finally turned up." He blew out a breath, the memory weighing heavily on his chest. "Emmeline was afraid of losing it again so she had the two ends welded together so that it couldn't come loose again. That way, she said, she'd always have it and it would remind her of me."

Thompson took in another long breath, as if that somehow helped to clear his mind. "I always knew that Elliott Corgan must have killed her, although he denied it when I questioned him." The chief's jaw hardened as he all but spit the words out. "Corgan said he wasn't the kind of man who would take credit for another man's work."

"Maybe he didn't do it," Jonah ventured, thinking that maybe the killer had been honest for once in his life.

Thompson gave him an incredulous look. "Why would you say something like that?" he demanded. "This is Corgan land. Elliott's younger brother all but drew Maggie a map where she could find Emmeline's grave. We've got Elliott serving life in prison for killing six other women. It's not exactly a giant leap from there to the conclusion that he killed my sister."

Jonah wasn't completely convinced, although it pained him to argue with the chief, a man he both respected and liked. "But didn't you say that all the other women were buried in shallow graves?" he asked Thompson.

"Yes," the chief answered impatiently. "It's a matter of record."

"But your sister's grave was dug much deeper and her body was painstakingly well preserved," Maggie pointed out, picking up the thread of Jonah's argument. "If the same man who killed all those other women killed your sister, why go through all that extra trouble? Why did he single this particular victim out and give her this special treatment?"

Thompson lost his temper. "How the hell am I supposed to know what went on in that degenerate's head?" the chief demanded. "There could have been all sorts of reasons why he did things differently when it came to—" his voice faltered before he pushed on "—Emma's murder. The man's a deranged, insane serial killer."

Thompson threw up his hands. "Maybe he just wanted to mix things up. Or maybe he wanted us to waste our time, talking this to death and taking it apart while he has himself a good laugh over it. I don't know," the chief

stressed angrily, shouting at them. And then, realizing
that he had crossed a line, Thompson took a moment to
compose himself. "Look, I want you two to leave this
alone. Do I make myself clear?" the chief demanded,
looking from one to the other.

"Perfectly," Maggie replied a bit guardedly.

Her heart went out to the man, but at the same time,
she felt that he was making a mistake, barring them from
looking into this. For one thing, it was clear that her late
father-in-law obviously wanted her to get to the bottom
of all this. Why, of course, was a completely different
matter.

"Yes, sir," Jonah was saying. He took hold of Maggie's arm with the intent of leading her back to where
their horses were waiting. "Loud and clear," he told the
other man.

"Uh-huh," Thompson replied. It was clear by his tone
that he was far from convinced that the two of them
would take his words to heart this time.

Disappointed by the turn of events, Maggie wasn't
aware that they had to return to town via horseback until
she was practically standing right next to her mount. She
was far from happy.

"We're going to be riding back?" she questioned.

"That's usually how it works," Jonah told her, amused.
"We ride out on horseback. We have to return on horse-
back. It's either that, or we have to walk beside the horses.
Take your pick," he teased.

Maggie didn't seem happy. "I'll ride. But I have a feeling I'm going to be really sore by tomorrow morning."

"Only one way around that," he told her.

Was he going to share some magical rubbing oint-
ment with her?

"Oh?" Maggie said, waiting for him to tell her about some secret cure he'd discovered.

"Just keep riding until it becomes second nature to you," he said. "You'll stop hurting then. Practice makes perfect."

She should have known he'd say something like that, Maggie thought. "Thanks, but if you don't mind, I'll just keep on using my car to get around."

Maggie stood beside her horse, not relishing the idea of getting back into the saddle. She was feeling rather drained by their discovery.

About to swing into his own saddle, Jonah stopped when he noticed the pensive expression on Maggie's face. "Want a boost?" he guessed.

What she wanted was to be driven back, but the chief and his team were all busy and would be for a couple of hours to come.

"Sure, why not?" she said.

The words were no sooner out of her mouth than Jonah was right there at her back, boosting her up into her saddle. She swallowed her surprised gasp as she felt Jonah's hands quickly guiding her up.

"All ready to go?" he asked her, swinging up into his own saddle.

Maggie turned back for one last look. The forensic team was scattered, spread out on several sides of the tree and adjacent ground. They were sketching, taking pictures and in general documenting the entire scene where the chief's sister had been found.

She sighed, turning back again. "Well, since the chief obviously doesn't want us around, sure, let's go."

"You know," Maggie said, once they had gotten clear of the chief and his men and were riding toward Whisperwood, "I used to think of Chief Thompson as a nice, friendly man. Now he's acting as if we were a pair of bungling, annoying civilians who were trying to mess up his crime scene."

"You've got to see that this is personal for Thompson," Jonah told her.

"That's why he should welcome all the help he can get," she insisted.

But Jonah looked at it from the chief's point of view. "He doesn't see it as help. He sees it as interfering."

Maggie grew annoyed. Jonah should be taking her side in this, not the chief's.

"That's because he's being closed-minded," she insisted. She thought of how they had gotten here in the first place. "Besides, I have a unique perspective on this."

"What you have," Jonah told her calmly, "is a note from a dead man who might have had his own reasons for taunting the chief." He glanced at her, not wanting to set her off, but trying to make her see this logically. "By your own admission, you and Adam Corgan never had a close relationship."

"We didn't have much of one at all," Maggie corrected.

"Aha, that's my point exactly," he told her. He warmed to his subject. "Why reach out from beyond the grave? Why get you involved in this at all?" he asked, examining the details. "You broke your ties to the family when you divorced Adam's son. Adam had no reason to pull you back in."

"Which are all very good questions," Maggie responded. "And I want to find the answers to all of them." She began talking faster, trying to get him to agree. "My gut instincts tell me that the answers to all those questions can be found if we just continue to conduct our own investigation into this mystery. And since the chief doesn't want us doing that, we need to be doing this on our own—as a team."

That caught him off guard. How did they get from just riding out to the old ranch to here? "When did we become a team?" he asked her.

She looked at him in surprise. "You don't want to be a team?" Maggie asked.

"I didn't say that," he told her. She was putting words into his mouth, he thought. "I was just curious when this momentous pairing occurred."

She thought that was obvious. "I guess that happened the first time you took me along to help you conduct a search and rescue effort."

He supposed he could see her point. He wasn't about to argue with it, that was for sure. "If I had known that, I might have marked the occasion with a little speech," he told her.

Her mouth quirked a little in a grin. "I guess we all dodged a bullet there."

"So we're partners?" he asked, wanting to be sure exactly where they stood in this.

She nodded. "Partners. At least when it comes to this," she qualified. Thinking back to the kiss they'd shared, she felt it necessary to add, "Just don't get any funny ideas."

"Well, these are very serious times, thanks to the hurricane—and the murders," he replied. "I'd say that we have to take our laughter where we find it," he told her significantly.

Maggie shifted on her horse. She wasn't comfortable, not on horseback or with the subject matter. Both made her feel vulnerable.

"So, where to now?" she asked when she realized that

she wasn't sure if they really *were* headed for town or some other destination.

"Still a lot of search and rescue work to be done, not to mention that there's still a lot of debris to be cleared away." Jonah realized that he was just taking for granted that she was up for this. "Look, if you're tired, or just want to recharge, I can drop you off at the cabin and take the horse back to the stable. Your call."

That was the last thing she wanted. "If it's all the same to you, I'd rather not be alone with my thoughts right now."

There was sympathy in his voice when he asked, "Finding that mummified body really got to you, didn't it?"

She laughed dryly and nodded. "I could have lived my whole life without seeing that."

That hadn't been his idea. "You're the one who wanted to go there and look around," he reminded her.

"I know, I know," she was quick to acknowledge. "I can't help it if I'm curious. It's a congenital defect," she told him.

She said it with such a straight face, he wondered if she actually believed what she was saying was true.

"Maybe I'm here to save you from yourself," Jonah said.

"And maybe I'm here to get you to use your special skill set of finding things to see if we can find just what Adam meant by that message he left and, more importantly, that you use those skills to help find out if the chief's sister was really killed by the same serial killer who's currently behind bars."

"We'll see," was all that Jonah was willing to say on the subject for now.

He felt it was safer that way.

Chapter Eleven

As far as hurricanes went, the lifespan of this particular one had been mercifully short. However the short amount of time did not minimize the damage that Hurricane Brooke did both physically and emotionally to the people of Whisperwood who had found themselves on the receiving end of the hurricane's sweeping effects. Added to that were the people who had not suffered losses, losing neither their homes nor any of the people they loved, but were still affected. Those were the people who were suffering from the acute effects of survivor guilt. Those were the people who were haunted by one question. Why were they spared when those around them were not?

Jonah found himself at a loss when he tried to comfort one of these guilt-ridden survivors to absolutely no avail.

Maggie felt sorry for both Jonah and the woman he'd been vainly trying to comfort. With her heart going out to Jonah, she quietly inserted herself into the scene, much to his obvious surprise and relief.

Taking his place, Maggie looked at the woman who had broken down in uncontrollable sobs when Jonah had asked her how she was doing.

Instead of shrinking back from Kayla, a young woman who she knew by sight but had never gotten close to beyond that, Maggie tried to put herself in the thirty-four-year-old woman's place.

Mentally she asked herself how *she* would react in a situation like this. It gave her a great deal of empathy for the anguish that Kayla was suffering.

"Why?" Kayla asked her, her voice cracking. "Why am I still here and not Jacob? He was the better person, not me."

"Instead of trying to find the response to something that you have no real way of ever knowing the answer to, why don't you make up your mind that you are going to be the best version of yourself that you can possibly be?" Maggie gently told the woman.

Kayla's sobs slowly subsided. She raised her red-rimmed eyes and looked into Maggie's. She struggled a couple of minutes, attempting to catch her breath. "I don't under—understand," she cried.

"Try to help the people around you. Comfort them, offer to listen. Right now, people are more vulnerable than they have *ever* been in their lives. They need to feel that they can make it through this, that there *is* a light at the end of the tunnel even if they can't see it yet. Help them to think positive. You'll wind up helping them as well as yourself," Maggie told the other woman. "That is why you were spared."

Kayla was still fighting back her sobs. "You really think so?"

Maggie never hesitated. "I really think so," she said, squeezing the shaking hands that had been clutching hers.

"All right, I'll try," the other woman said. There was still a hitch in her voice.

"That's all anyone can ever ask," Maggie said, giving Kayla a long, warm embrace. The other woman seemed to take heart from that.

"THAT WAS PRETTY GOOD," Jonah said to Maggie several minutes later when they finally walked away, leaving Kayla with one of the other survivors. "How did you come up with that on the spur of the moment?" he couldn't help asking.

"Easy," she answered. "I just put myself in her place and told her what I would have wanted someone to tell me." And then she elaborated. "That I was important in the scheme of things. That I didn't survive by accident but for a reason—so I could help others come to grips with their own losses. What?" Maggie asked when she saw the way that Jonah was looking at her.

"Nothing. I was just thinking how amazing you are—and how glad I am that I was able to find you before you wound up falling out of that tree and hurting yourself," he added.

She had no idea what possessed her to ask Jonah the next question, but before she could censor herself, the question just came tumbling out. "Is that the only reason you're glad you found me?"

Jonah turned his head toward her, and the way he looked at her sent a shiver running up and down her spine.

"I think you already know the answer to that," Jonah told her, his voice low, caressing.

The desire to kiss her was almost overpowering. But they were out where everyone could see them, and he didn't want anyone gossiping about Maggie. Besides, once things were back to normal and his brother was married, he would be on his way back to Austin. He didn't want to leave Maggie to deal with unwanted speculation on her own. It wouldn't be right.

"Why don't I drop you off at the cabin—" he began, only to have her cut in.

"Drop me off?" she repeated, confused. "Why? Where will you be?" she asked. Earlier he'd made it sound as if they would be working together for the rest of the day.

He hadn't even wanted to say this to Maggie. Jonah knew that the mere mention of her apartment would sadden her. But he wasn't about to lie to her, either.

"I'm just going to see how cleanup is going around the Towers. You've done enough for one day—more than enough," he emphasized, thinking of the body that had been uncovered. "Why don't you take it easy and I'll come to the cabin in a little while?"

She didn't like the idea of resting—or being alone with her thoughts. "I can help," Maggie insisted as she followed him to his truck.

"I know you can," he told her. "But you don't have to feel like you need to keep proving yourself to anyone over and over again. Trust me, I get it," he assured Maggie. "Now get some rest before you wear yourself completely out." He thought it might help if he filled her in about what was going on. "We've got a bulldozer coming in to clear away the larger debris so we can get started rebuilding that area. It looks like the Towers sustained the most amount of damage."

An ironic smile played on Maggie's lips. "It figures."

He could almost *see* what thoughts were going on in her head. "Take your own advice, Maggie, and stop over-thinking things."

"You sure you don't want me there?" she asked as he drove them to his cabin.

"I'm sure," Jonah said firmly.

Maggie shrugged, sinking back in the passenger seat and surrendering. "I guess you're right. Besides, the chances of my finding anything in that pile of rubble are pretty nonexistent anyway."

The wistful note in her voice caught his attention and Jonah looked at her. "Completely," he agreed, even though it pained him to do so. "Why, what is it that you'd try to look for?"

She felt almost silly talking about this, but she had been the one who had started this, so she answered his question. "I had this snow globe as a kid. My dad gave it to me for my birthday. I don't remember which one," she said honestly. "I was five, or maybe six. Anyway, the globe had a puppy in the center of a snowstorm—at least it was a snowstorm when I shook the globe," she amended. "I must have spent hours when I was a kid, just watching the snow coming down and engulfing that dog."

Realizing what she had to sound like, Maggie laughed at herself. "I guess I was easily entertained, but it's the one thing I remember my dad giving me. He wasn't very big on gifts," she confided.

"I can look for it," Jonah told her. "But to be honest—"

She nodded. "I know there's no way it could have survived that hurricane. At the very least, the globe probably shattered when the apartment came down," she said, ending his sentence for him.

He was pulling up in front of his cabin.

"Are you going to be okay here?" Jonah asked as she began to get out. He suddenly felt as if he was abandoning a waif, leaving her alone in the cabin.

She smiled at his concern. Jonah was a good man, she thought. He'd proven it over and over again.

Maggie tried to set his mind at ease. "As long as there's not another hurricane on its way, I'll be fine."

Still, he didn't like leaving her alone. But he liked dragging her over to the ruins of the Towers even less. He chose the lesser of the two evils.

"I'll be back as soon as I check in to see how everything's going," Jonah promised.

"Take your time," Maggie told him, one hand on the doorknob as she opened the cabin door. "You don't have to rush on my account."

But he did, Jonah thought as he pulled away from the cabin, watching Maggie grow smaller in his rearview mirror. He did have to rush on her account because he wanted to get back to her as soon as he possibly could. Despite her swaggering displays of independence, there was something about Maggie Reeves that brought out his protective nature.

She might come on like gangbusters, the way she had around the chief this morning, but she didn't fool him. He saw the vulnerable woman under all that and he had this overwhelming desire to keep her safe even though the immediate danger, according to the weather reports, had passed.

But he had been at this job long enough to know that there were all sorts of dangers to be afraid of, not just the ones that could be heard about on weather forecasts.

Maybe *he* was the one who was letting his imagination get carried away, Jonah told himself.

He pressed down harder on the gas pedal.

THE SECOND SHE closed the door behind her, she felt it. The cabin seemed eerily silent to her without Jonah there. She wasn't the sort of person who was afraid of the dark or who held her breath, waiting to hear something go "bump" in the night. Still, Maggie decided that having a light on while she made dinner out of whatever she could find in the refrigerator wasn't all that bad an idea, even though it wasn't dark outside yet.

If one light was good, several lights were even better, she decided, switching on the lamps and overhead lights in the kitchenette. For good measure, she put on the lights in the living room, as well.

Opening the refrigerator, she searched the crisper drawer and found that she had missed a quartered chicken the last time. She decided that she would use it to make fried chicken. It was simple, difficult to mess up and most importantly, she'd never met anyone who didn't like fried chicken.

Once she saw that Jonah had a little bit of flour and some oil in his pantry, she felt as if she had gotten a go-ahead sign and got started.

Maggie really had no idea if Jonah was going to be back soon the way he had promised, or if he would get caught up in something and be home a great deal later. Either way, she knew that fried chicken tasted good served hot or cold.

Maggie got started, taking her time with each step while humming fragments of a song under her breath. It was a familiar tune and the sound of it comforted her, although for the life of her, she couldn't remember more than five words from the lyrics.

Doing something as normal as making fried chicken helped to soothe her, as well.

She had just immersed the last piece of chicken in the flour mixture she'd created when she heard her cell phone begin to make a pulsing sound, demanding her attention. She paused to wipe her fingertips on a kitchen towel that had seen better days, then she pulled the phone out of her hip pocket. Maggie swiped across the screen even as her brain registered the fact that she didn't recognize the caller ID.

But then, maybe Jonah's phone had died and he had had to borrow someone else's phone to call her. Most likely he was calling to tell her that he was going to be late getting back. It was to be expected. Jonah felt he was indispensable and for the most part she had to admit that the man was right. Everyone turned to him for guidance.

Maggie caught herself smiling. If he was calling about that, then Jonah was also incredibly thoughtful.

But when she unlocked her phone, she saw that she wasn't getting an incoming call. Instead, it was a text message.

And the message wasn't from Jonah. It was coming from a blocked number.

Stop sticking your nose where it doesn't belong or you might not live to see another dawn.

Maggie stared at the screen, rereading the message. There was no mistaking the meaning of the text. It was definitely intended as a threat. But who would want to threaten her? And exactly *what* was this person referring to? What did he mean by "sticking her nose into" something? Was he talking about her finding that body on the Corgan ranch?

And *how* would this anonymous person even know anything about that? She and Jonah had only notified the chief this afternoon. Thompson had brought his forensic team with him when he arrived on the scene, but they were all part of the police department.

Was whoever had texted her this threat part of the police department, as well? Or had he hacked into the police department so he could keep tabs on what was going on?

Why would he want to?

Unless…

"Unless he's the killer," Maggie cried out loud.

"Unless who's the killer?" Jonah asked, picking that exact moment to walk into his cabin.

Maggie yelped and jumped. She'd been so caught up in trying to figure out who had sent her the threatening text, she hadn't heard Jonah pulling up in his truck.

Great work, Maggie, she berated herself. *Whoever wrote this text could have pulled up in a train and you wouldn't have heard him until he killed you.*

"And why do you have all the lights on?" Jonah asked just before he saw that the chicken pieces in the large frying pan were about to begin burning and smoking. Moving swiftly, he turned down the flame and pushed the pan onto another burner until it could cool off.

"Hey, is everything all right?" he questioned, crossing over to Maggie.

For the first time since he'd walked in, Jonah saw the frightened, distressed look on Maggie's face and the way she was clutching her phone.

"What happened here?" Jonah asked.

"Everything is fine," Maggie answered, her voice hardly louder than a squeak. There wasn't a shred of conviction in it.

"No, it's not," Jonah contradicted forcefully. He took hold of her shoulders and looked into her eyes. "Now tell me what's wrong."

Rather than say anything, she touched her screen to refresh the message, then handed her phone over to Jonah.

His expression hardened as he quickly scanned the message.

"Who sent you this?" he asked.

"I have no idea," she answered. "It came in as anonymous."

Maggie double-checked to make sure she hadn't

missed anything that might indicate who the sender was. She hadn't.

Jonah didn't like this, but he didn't want to say anything that might fuel her fears further. "It's probably just a crank call from some pathetic idiot who gets off thinking he's frightening people with vague threats." His eyes narrowed as he looked at Maggie more closely. "Is it working?" he asked.

"Well, I do feel better now that you're here," she told Jonah, taking back her phone and returning it into her pocket.

Jonah put his arm around her shoulders, giving her a quick hug. "Good, that means I've done my job. I'll see if I can find someone at the police department who can track down this coward for me and I'll tell him to back off if *he* knows what's good for *him*," Jonah said, paraphrasing the mysterious caller's initial threat.

"In the meantime," Maggie said, looking over at the frying pan and its semicharred contents, "I burned some chicken for you."

"Mmm, burned chicken. My favorite. How did you know?" he teased.

"Wild guess," she quipped. "No, really," she said, changing her tone. "You don't have to eat it. I'll make you something else."

"Hey, seriously, I really like burned fried food," he assured her. To prove it, he picked up a chicken thigh out of the pan and bit into it. "Hot!" he declared. "But delicious."

Chapter Twelve

Maggie looked at the burned fried chicken on the plate that Jonah had taken. She frowned. "You're just saying that," she told him.

"And meaning it," Jonah insisted. "Besides, this chicken is only moderately burned. The skin's just crispy, that's all." He took another healthy bite. The skin crackled as he sank his teeth into the piece. "Turns out that the meat inside is just fine."

"But—" Certain Jonah was just pretending to enjoy the chicken, Maggie began to take the chicken away.

Jonah was not about to relinquish his plate. "Stop arguing with me and let me enjoy my chicken in peace," he told her.

Maggie gave up trying to change his mind. Truthfully, she felt rather relieved that he could actually eat what she'd prepared. The anonymous text she'd gotten had put her in a very strange mood, making her doubt herself and everything else. Having the chicken pieces start smoking and burning only seemed to amplify that feeling.

She had taken a few pieces for herself, but right now, all she was doing was pushing the pieces around on the plate.

About to do justice to his second piece, Jonah saw that Maggie wasn't eating. "Why aren't you having any?" he urged. "I'm betting that you probably haven't had anything to eat since this morning."

She didn't feel up to having Jonah analyze her, so she lied. "I did," Maggie said defensively.

He'd been with her for most of the day. He had a feeling that she hadn't had anything in the short time they had been apart while she'd been making dinner. Still, he was willing to play along and asked, "Okay, what did you have?"

"Food," Maggie answered grudgingly.

Now he knew she was lying, but he wasn't about to come right out and say that. Instead, he asked good-naturedly, "Anything more specific than that?"

"Good food," she answered.

Maggie was prepared to go down fighting, he thought, and it amused him. Jonah started to laugh and wound up laughing so hard that he came close to choking.

Maggie realized that he wasn't kidding. She jumped to her feet and began pounding Jonah on his back. He sucked in his breath. Whatever had gotten caught in his throat had been dislodged.

Holding his hand up, his eyes almost watery, Jonah gasped, "Uncle. I give up." He sucked in more air. "You know, you're a great deal stronger than you look," he told her.

Maggie was still looking at him closely. "Are you all right?" she asked. "You had me worried there for a minute."

He waved away her concern. "Just a little food that went down the wrong way."

She knew that her flippant comment was what had set him off. "I'm sorry," she apologized.

She was kidding, right? "You have nothing to be sorry for. After the kind of day I put in, between finding that body and then digging through more rubble, it felt good to be able to laugh at something." Jonah looked at her for a long moment, his expression growing somber. "There hasn't been all that much to laugh about lately."

Maggie immediately thought of the strange text she had received warning her to back off.

"No, there hasn't been," she agreed. "But we need to hold on to a good thought so that we can move forward. Even when I was up that tree when the floods hit, clinging to that branch for all I was worth, I never thought that was going to be the end for me."

He hadn't even considered that part. He had just assumed that she had been afraid. "Just what did you think?" he asked Maggie.

She smiled at him now. "That's easy. I thought that someone would come along to save me, and look—" she gestured toward him "—you did."

That surprised him. "You thought *I'd* come and save you?" he questioned.

"Well, not you specifically," she admitted. "But *someone.*"

His eyes washed over Maggie and he felt those same stirrings again. There was no doubt about it. He was attracted to Maggie.

Jonah smiled at her. "I guess I'm glad it was me."

"Yeah, me, too," Maggie replied. She saw that Jonah had finished the chicken he had put on his plate. "Can I get you something else?" she asked, about to take the plate from him to throw out the pile of bones.

Something about the way Maggie had asked the question increased those stirrings he was feeling. Attempting to get them under control wasn't working.

"As a matter of fact, there is something else," Jonah answered in a low voice.

"What?"

She'd breathed the word rather than just said it out-right. It hung between them like an unspoken, tempting invitation.

Jonah was aware of rising to his feet, his hands on her shoulders, bringing her up with him. The next moment, he leaned in and his lips met hers.

The kiss ignited a host of other things, feelings that had not really faded away but had been hiding just be-neath the surface, ready to leap up and seize the moment.

For just a second, his body was sealed to hers. The close proximity woke up every single inch of her.

She wove her arms around his neck, losing herself not just in the kiss but in the man, as well. She could feel her pulse racing, feel herself yearning for more. But that would only be opening up the door for things that might be glorious in the moment, but that undoubtedly came with consequences. Consequences she didn't think she could handle on top of everything else.

With effort, Maggie forced herself to draw her head back. Trying to lighten the moment, she pretended to con-tinue a conversation that hadn't actually gotten underway.

"So you were saying that you'd like some dessert?" she asked.

Understanding why she was doing this, Jonah picked up on her cue. "Yes, but I don't think that there's any available."

"Why don't I just take a look?" Maggie suggested, stepping away. She discreetly took a few deep breaths in an effort to still her erratic pulse as she crossed to the refrigerator. Opening the freezer, she looked in. There wasn't much there. "How do you feel about refrozen ice cream?"

"How's that again?" he asked.

She pulled out a half-filled container of chocolate ice cream. "Refrozen ice cream," she repeated. "It looks like it melted a bit when we lost power, then refroze again when the power came on." She turned the carton around, looking at it from all sides. "I don't think it's bad. At worst, it just probably doesn't taste as good as it should."

Because he was still trying to play along, Jonah turned over the idea of having the ice cream in his mind. "Well, I'm willing to give it a try if you are," he told her.

Maggie hadn't even realized that he had come up behind her just now. She sucked in her breath in surprise as she turned around.

Trying to appear nonchalant, she managed to sound cheerful. "Sure, why not?"

Taking a large spoon, she began scooping out the contents. There was just enough left in the container to provide two decent-sized servings. Maggie divided the chocolate ice cream equally between two bowls and handed one to Jonah.

"Too bad you don't have any whipped cream," she commented, looking down into the bowl.

"I take it that chocolate ice cream isn't your favorite?" Jonah guessed.

Maggie examined the contents again. She wasn't aware of wrinkling her nose just then, but Jonah had taken notice of it.

"It's too chocolaty," she said as they sat down on the couch.

He thought the way she'd wrinkled her nose made her look adorable, but he didn't want to embarrass her, so he kept that to himself.

"Really?" Jonah asked, rather surprised at her answer. "It's my favorite."

"I like mint chip best," Maggie confided.

"That has chocolate in it," Jonah pointed out.

"Yes, but it's not overpowering. It's not *chocolate*," she said, all but shouting out the word to make her point. Looking at her bowl again, she made up her mind. "You know what? You can have mine," she told him, holding out the bowl to him.

"You really don't want it?" Jonah questioned. He was almost finished with the ice cream in his own bowl. Without thinking about it, he had all but inhaled the contents quickly.

"I've had enough," Maggie assured him. "Here. Really," she said, urging him to take the bowl. She glanced at his empty bowl. "I can see that you really do like it."

He placed his empty bowl on the coffee table but instead of taking the one she was offering, Jonah told her, "I do." There was just the slightest dab of chocolate ice cream on the corner of her mouth. "Um, you have a little bit of chocolate right there."

"Where?" she asked, reflexively running her tongue along the upper part of her lip with hopes of clearing away the offending trace. "Here?"

But she hadn't come close to it. "No, right there," he told her.

The next moment, giving in to his urge, Jonah leaned in and removed the tiny dab of ice cream with his own lips. Chocolate ice cream had never tasted this good.

He heard Maggie sighing in contentment against his mouth. That only fanned the flames that had instantly sprung up on contact.

He kissed her again, this time with even more feeling and enthusiasm.

Not wanting to make Maggie feel as if he was attempting to overwhelm her, Jonah forced himself to slowly pull back.

He smiled at Maggie. "No doubt about it," he said. "I really do love chocolate ice cream."

This was her chance to draw away and call it a day. To step back from temptation before she got in over her head and did something she might regret.

To—

Oh, the hell with it, Maggie thought, mentally throwing up her hands and giving in. Who was she kidding? They were clearly drawn to one another, why was she trying to resist so hard? The truth of it was she couldn't remember ever being so attracted to a man the way she was to Jonah. Not even to her ex-husband.

Yes, she knew that she didn't have a prayer of this actually going anywhere once this unique scenario was resolved. But they were both here now and maybe, just for a little while, they could enjoy one another without any strings attached.

"You know," she said with a contented sigh, "I think I'm beginning to really change my mind about chocolate ice cream."

"Oh?" he asked, rubbing his finger along her bottom lip, "How so?"

"I'm finding that I'm developing a really strong taste for it," she murmured just as their lips came together again.

All systems were go, but still, Jonah didn't want to take anything for granted. What if he was misreading her signals?

"You're sure about this?" he asked her, giving her a chance to pull away.

She was grateful to him for asking, but at the same time, she didn't want to waste time debating with him.

"I'm sure," she responded. "Now stop talking and let

me sample some more of the ice cream that you've managed to get on your mouth."

There was almost a twinkle in her eye, which aroused him.

Everything about her aroused him. There was no use fighting it.

"With pleasure," he told her.

For a moment, as he settled her back into his arms, she thought that Jonah would just take her right then and there, making the most of the moment and her willingness. It was what she was used to, thanks to her ex.

But Jonah surprised her.

He didn't just race to the finish line with her. Instead, he went about making love with her slowly. He began by nibbling on her lips, then moving on to sample other parts of her, gliding his lips along her throat, her shoulders, the soft inviting slope that led down between her breasts.

He made love to her slowly, lyrically, leaving no part of her untouched, unworshipped. He used his lips, his teeth, his hands. Every part of him made love to her.

Maggie tried to keep up, but then she would find herself slipping into the wild, wonderful haven that Jonah was creating for her.

Over and over again, her breath caught in her throat and she would lose her train of thought, lose herself in the wild, wonderful moment that was encompassing her.

He made her forget who she was. *Where* she was. All that existed was this all-consuming fire that he was stoking.

Pulling her blouse from her shoulders and then undoing her bra, letting it slowly sink away from her breasts, Jonah covered her with a fine web of openmouthed kisses, moving slowly along her throbbing skin.

Jonah was vaguely aware that she was trying to open

his belt, fumbling with the clasp. He paused for the slightest moment to undo it for her.

He felt her smile against his skin as he went to kiss her again.

"Always the gentleman," she murmured.

"I do my best," Jonah answered just before he brought his mouth back down to her lips, then to the hollow of her throat.

He reveled in the way her breath was growing louder as well as shorter and shorter in response to what he was doing.

Maggie felt as if her whole body was on fire. She never knew that lovemaking could be this wild, exhilarating experience that had her craving more and more even as it made her want to live in the moment, savoring every second of what was happening.

She was amazed that this experience was so different from what she had experienced before. After all, she'd been married, and James Corgan hadn't exactly been a virgin when he'd taken her. But his expertise for the most part lay in his satisfying himself, not in making love *with* her or *to* her. Compared to Jonah, her ex had been an inept boy. He hadn't been anywhere near the experienced man that Jonah was right at this moment.

Jonah, she realized, seemed dedicated to pleasing her, thereby pleasing himself.

Completely captivated by him, at first Maggie didn't realize that Jonah was carrying her into the bedroom, not until he'd crossed the threshold and was about to place her down on the bed.

This was the way she wanted it to happen, Maggie thought. Not like some tawdry affair, but on a bed like two lovers who had all the time in the world.

The moment she felt the bed against her back, she

began to tug on the remainder of his clothing, eager to feel his skin against hers when he drew close to her again. Her fingers flew, as did his, and within moments, they were both as naked as their desire for one another rendered them.

As he began to kiss her over and over again, Maggie firmly wrapped her legs around his torso, holding him to her, urging him to finally consummate their union once and for all.

But still he continued to take his time with her, despite the fact that he could feel an urgency racing through him. He could feel his eagerness growing by quantum leaps until he just couldn't hold himself in check any longer.

Rolling Maggie onto her back, he drew his body slowly up along hers. He wanted to look into her eyes when they took the final step. But as he balanced himself directly over her, he saw that her eyes were closed.

"Open your eyes, Maggie," he whispered. When they continued to remain closed, he said, "Look at me."

For the first time, just before they became one, she opened her eyes. Her heart was hammering wildly against her chest. She saw Jonah smile down at her and she felt something stirring in response. She had never felt so close to anyone as she felt to Jonah.

And then his knee was nudging her legs apart. Not urgently, as if it was his right, but gently. Her heart melted.

She opened for him and drew in her breath as she felt him entering her. The movement was gentle, not anything like the way James had done it, as if it was his right and she was his property.

The same heart that had melted was swelling now. At this moment—just for this one singular moment—she fell in love with Jonah as he began to move slowly, then more urgently within her.

She met him movement for movement, glorying in their union and eagerly racing toward fulfillment, that wonderful race to the top of the mountain, followed by that breathtaking leap that eventually sent them spiraling downward.

She dug her fingers into his shoulders as they took the leap together.

Chapter Thirteen

Though he tried to hold on to it as long as he could, Jonah found that the euphoria between them receded all too soon. As he listened to her breathing become steadier, quieter, Jonah leaned in and pressed a kiss to the top of her head.

Maggie stirred and stretched against him, then turned to look up at him quizzically.

She appeared just as stunned as he felt. Smiling, he gently swept her hair out of her face. "That was a surprise," he told her.

Maggie drew herself up on her elbow and gazed at him, bemused. "Did you expect me to start throwing things at you?"

"No, of course not," he responded, searching his brain for the right way to put his thoughts into words. "I just didn't expect…" His voice trailed off and then he finally said, "for all this to happen."

"And now you're regretting it?" she guessed, bracing herself for the disappointment she knew would come if he hinted at that.

Jonah's dark eyebrows drew together in utter confusion that she should think something like that.

"Oh hell no," he told Maggie. "I just didn't want you

to feel overwhelmed—" That didn't come out right. "I mean—"

She smiled at him. He was concerned that he had imposed his will on her, she realized. The man was incredibly sweet.

"I know what you mean," she said, stopping him. "And trust me, Jonah, if I didn't want this to happen, it wouldn't have. I know how to take care of myself, and you," she emphasized with a grin, "don't strike me as being a Neanderthal."

"I'm not," he agreed with feeling.

Her eyes smiled before her mouth even began to curve. "I know."

"So you're okay with what happened?" Jonah asked, searching her face and wanting to be totally sure that they really were on the same page.

"I'm better than okay," Maggie assured him, snuggling up in the crook of his arm.

Jonah grinned. "Well, in that case…" His voice trailed off provocatively.

She raised herself up on her elbow again, tantalized by what she heard in his voice. "Just what did you have in mind?"

The expression in his eyes was positively nothing short of wicked. "Guess," he challenged.

Her pulse sped up again, going into double time. "You'll have to give me a hint," she teased.

Jonah leaned in and kissed her, a wave of unbridled passion beginning to churn within him in a matter of seconds. It was hard to hold himself in check.

She was practically breathless when he drew his lips away. Taking a second to collect herself, Maggie whispered, "I'm going to need more of a hint than that."

He pulled her to him, her back sliding along the sheets.

"More of a hint coming up," he told her just before he sealed his mouth over hers again.

HOW COULD IT be dawn already?

Maggie opened her eyes warily, hoping she was imagining things. But she wasn't. Daylight was skimming along the floor in the cabin bedroom. She felt as if she had gotten less than three hours sleep.

Trying to be quiet, Maggie slipped out of bed, her whole body still humming from the activities of just a few hours ago. Quickly collecting her clothes, she got dressed in the living area. Her plan was to make coffee, maybe even breakfast if Jonah had enough eggs left in the refrigerator.

After that, she'd see where the day took them.

She had just managed to crack four eggs and deposit them into the frying pan when Jonah tiptoed up behind her, slipping his arms around her waist and giving her a quick hug.

Kissing her neck, he told her, "I would have made breakfast."

She tried not to shiver as the kiss zipped along her sensitive skin.

"It's my turn," she reminded him.

He laughed, releasing her. "I would have thought after last night, you would be too tired to get up and cook."

She gave him a side glance. His shirt was hanging open with a tempting view of his muscular chest. Maggie ordered herself to focus.

"The same would go for you, wouldn't it?" she asked, scrambling the eggs.

Stepping back, Jonah started to put out the utensils to set the table. "I'm used to getting by on very little sleep and putting in a long day."

"So you're telling me that you do this sort of thing all the time?" she asked, tongue in cheek.

"Yes—no," he quickly corrected, realizing what she was saying. "I mean—"

Delighted, Maggie laughed. He looked adorable when he was flustered. "I'd quit while I was ahead if I were you, Jonah," she advised. The toast popped just then. She nodded toward the toaster. "Why don't you make yourself useful and butter the toast?" she suggested with a straight face.

Jonah nodded. "I should butter the toast," he agreed. Dropping the four slices onto a plate, he took out the butter and began to spread it generously across each of the four surfaces.

Maggie laughed. Good-looking, good-natured and a fantastic lover, the man really was a rare combination. She told herself not to think any further than today.

"You realize I'm giving you a hard time, don't you?" she asked.

"I'm tough," he declared, deliberately keeping a serious face. "I can take it."

"Oh, but you do have a very soft center," she said wistfully, allowing herself to drift back to last night just for a moment.

"I'd rather we keep that just between us," he told her.

She wondered if that gave her an exclusive edge. She decided not to explore that thought too closely. "Consider it done," she replied.

Dividing the scrambled eggs between the two plates, she placed two pieces of the toast he'd buttered on each plate and then handed him one plate while she took the other.

"I've been thinking," Maggie said, taking her seat opposite him.

"When?" Jonah asked in all innocence. They'd made love almost all night and then when he woke up, he'd found her in the kitchen, busy with breakfast. The woman was a whirlwind. "When did you have time to think?"

Maggie grinned, knowing exactly what Jonah was referring to.

"I multitask," she told him. With a wink she added, "I can do at least two things at once."

She was telling him that her mind was whirling even as they were making love last night. "I don't know if I should be impressed or insulted," he told her.

"Flattered," she corrected. "You should be flattered because you're an inspiration and you were the one who got all my juices flowing."

Well, put that way, he couldn't be insulted that her mind was elsewhere. "And exactly what is it that you were thinking about?"

Maggie smiled like a woman who knew she was about to drop a bombshell. And then she did. "I think we should go and pay Elliott Corgan a visit."

Jonah's fork froze just as he brought it up to his mouth. He looked at her as if she had slipped a gear. "You want to go and visit the serial killer?"

Maggie nodded. Swallowing what she had put in her mouth, she said, "One and the same."

"But the man's in prison," Jonah protested. Had she forgotten that?

"I know. But I think we need to talk to him," she insisted. Now that she knew all about the "family secret," she had questions she wanted to ask James's uncle. "He might be the only one who could tell us what happened to the chief's sister."

"Thompson said he talked to Elliott and the man denied killing her," Jonah reminded her, finishing his eggs.

"And serial killers are always so truthful," she responded sarcastically.

Jonah frowned. She had a point. "You're serious about wanting to talk to Elliott?" he questioned.

Finished with her own meal, she wiped her mouth, then dropped her napkin onto the plate. "Absolutely."

He could see that she was serious, but that still didn't make this doable. "And we're just going to waltz up to that prison in Austin and ask to see Elliott Corgan," he asked incredulously.

"No," she said simply, "we can drive. Waltzing will take too much time."

"Very funny," he responded, then rephrased his question. "And we just walk into Randolph State Prison and ask to see him, out of the blue. What makes you think we can pull that off? Or that we can even get him to talk to us?"

Though she had only come up with this while making breakfast, she had given it a lot of thought.

"Well, technically, I am family, so to speak. I'm his nephew's former wife. More importantly," she stressed, "the man's a serial killer. Once they're caught, they revel in attention, in showing everyone how much more clever they are than everyone else."

He could almost see her mind figuring out the details. He was in awe of the way it worked.

"We can tell Elliott that we're true crime documentarians and that we're interested in bringing his story to the small screen. Once he knows that, we probably won't be able to get him to *stop* talking," she said confidently.

He still wasn't sold on the idea. "Thompson told us to stay clear of this. Again," Jonah reminded her.

She sighed. "I know, but you can't tell me that he doesn't want to know who's responsible for his sister's death."

"I'm sure he does," Jonah conceded, "but Thompson's perfectly capable of going to question Elliot himself if he wanted to do that."

"He already did," she reminded Jonah. "That's how the chief knows that Elliot denied having anything to do with Emmeline's death," she said, paraphrasing what Jonah had just said earlier.

Jonah saw the look on Maggie's face. She was determined to do this, he thought. "But you don't believe him," he guessed.

"Let's just say I need to be convinced of Elliott's innocence in this case. After all, he *is* the likely killer," she pointed out.

Jonah felt as if they were going around in circles. "Again, if there is something to pursue, Thompson's the one who should do it."

She agreed, but there was a glaring problem with that. "He's a police chief. His hands are tied by rules and regulations."

Jonah eyed her, rather bemused. "And ours aren't?"

Maggie smiled at him. "Let's just say that for us, the rules and regulations are bendable." Picking up the empty plates, she piled the utensils on top and took everything to the sink. "You don't have to say anything," she told him. "I can do all the talking. You can just be there as my backup. Or my cameraman," she said, really beginning to get enthusiastic about the idea.

"Don't get carried away," he warned. He knew someone who had tried to make a film on the premises and had gotten stymied. "There are all sorts of forms to fill out if you want to bring a camera onto prison grounds. That'll take time to get clearance and I can see by the look on your face that you're dying to just jump in and do this thing."

"Okay, no camera," she told him, perfectly willing to adjust her plan to fit the situation. "You can just be there to take notes."

He made a calculated guess. "So you'll be the producer."

"Hey, it's my idea, right?" Maggie reminded him with a grin.

"And if I said that it's not a good idea?" Jonah challenged.

She wasn't about to force him to go with her. "All right, you don't have to come. I'll go by myself," she told Jonah.

If she thought he was about to go along with that, she didn't know him at all. He had absolutely no intention of letting Maggie go into the prison by herself. "The hell you will."

Inwardly, she breathed a sigh of relief, then smiled at him. "The offer's still open to be my sidekick," she told Jonah.

"You are incorrigible, you know that, don't you?" he said, shaking his head.

"Oh, I might have heard that before," Maggie conceded.

He laughed dryly. "With good reason, I'm sure." He saw that Maggie had opened her mouth, a clear sign that she was about to share a story with him, most likely about the last time she had been called incorrigible.

"Wait," he spoke up before she could get started, "I don't want to know."

There was humor in her eyes. "Your loss," Maggie said glibly.

"That is a matter of opinion," Jonah countered with feeling. He thought for a moment, doing some mental juggling. "I'm going to have to go by the latest rescue site to find out if I can be spared today," he told her.

This was turning out to involve a lot of logistics, she thought. "I said I can go alone," Maggie reminded him.

Jonah had made up his mind. There was no way he wanted her to see that killer without protection. "The hell you can."

She looked at him for a long moment. For once, Jonah couldn't begin to guess what Maggie was thinking.

"You realize that you can't order me around, don't you?" she asked.

"I saved your life," Jonah reminded her. "In some cultures, that means your life belongs to me. If it belongs to me, I get to have a say about where it goes or doesn't go."

Her eyes narrowed as she tried to discern whether he was joking not. "Are you serious?"

"No," he admitted. "But it was worth a shot. However, if you insist on doing something stupid and try to take off without me, I'm within my rights to handcuff you to my bed until you start thinking clearly."

"You wouldn't dare," she told him, unconsciously sticking out her chin.

"I wouldn't go betting anything on that if I were you, Maggie," he told her, his tone so serious that she wasn't sure if he was putting her on or not. "I'm just asking for a couple of hours. You can come with me," he added.

She sighed. "I guess I can do that," she responded.

Admittedly, she wasn't all that happy about this delay, necessary though it was from his viewpoint. Now that she had come up with a plan, she wanted to be out there, implementing it. If pressed, she couldn't exactly explain why, but she had this sense of urgency vibrating within her, as if she felt that she only had a limited amount of time to get to the truth before it would be lost to her forever.

Maggie supposed that the hurricane was partially responsible for creating that feeling. Having watched the giant funnel rip through buildings that had seemed so solid looking one minute, only to become a pile of rubble and wood the next made her feel that everything could come apart with a second's notice, burying vital answers forever.

"All right, you have a deal. Just let me finish washing the dishes and I'll go with you. But you have to promise me that barring another hurricane—or flash flood—we are going to go to Austin to see Elliott Corgan—"

"Your former uncle-in-law," he acknowledged.

"Well, I didn't know that at the time," Maggie confessed. "I never met the man and no one in the family ever told me about him."

"Small wonder. If you'd known, you might have opted out of the wedding," Jonah guessed.

She would have liked to have agreed with him, but she couldn't, not without lying about it.

"Actually," Maggie admitted, "I couldn't. I had obligations and the only way I knew how to meet them was to marry James."

"You married him for his money?" he asked her. That didn't sound like her, but then, how much did he really know about Maggie?

"No, I married him because I loved him, but I'd be lying if I said that the money was of absolutely no consequence to me. I needed the money to help my parents the only way I knew how," she admitted. "They were drowning in medical bills and needed help. By marrying James, I could provide that help. Unfortunately," she said sadly, "I wasn't able to do it before they died."

"That must have been really disappointing for you," he said.

"It was." She roused herself. There was no point in dwelling on the past. "So I used the money to buy Bellamy our old family home. I didn't want to have anything to do with the money," she said passionately. "Having it made me feel cheap."

"*Cheap* is the last word I would associate with you," Jonah told her as he locked the door to his cabin.

She really was something else, he couldn't help thinking. The more he knew about her, the more he found to like.

Chapter Fourteen

Jonah felt torn.

Because of the amount of damage created by the hurricane and the subsequent flooding, he felt it was his duty to remain in Whisperwood so he could help with the cleanup efforts. At this point, it was no longer a search and rescue operation. Whoever might still be buried beneath all the debris was most likely dead.

But just because there were no more rescues to head up, that didn't mean that there wasn't work to be done. The nature of this work involved digging up whatever bodies might still be buried under all that havoc caused by the storm, plus clearing everything else away so that the rebuilding could begin.

But although his sense of duty urged him to stay and work alongside his team, a far greater sense of loyalty had him wanting to accompany Maggie to the Austin state prison. He knew she couldn't be talked out of trying to get to the bottom of the riddle that her late former father-in-law had sent to her via his lawyer. She was stubborn that way.

There were others on the team who could take his place and do the work that was needed, but as far as he was concerned, there was no one available to go with Maggie, so his choice was clear.

The way he saw it, he didn't *have* a choice. He had to go with Maggie. Not just to be beside her when she walked through the prison gates, but also because of the anonymous text threat she'd received.

Jonah supposed that the latter could just be a stupid prank, but his gut told him it wasn't. It was something he had to take seriously. Otherwise, if he just ignored it, he had a feeling that he would regret it.

And worse than that, Maggie might just wind up regretting it. That sealed the argument for him.

So, less than an hour after they had left his cabin, he and Maggie were on the road, driving toward Randolph State Prison in Austin.

But he had to admit that he still felt uneasy about the venture.

"You sure you want to do this?" Jonah asked her when they were about twenty minutes into their trip to the prison. "It's not too late just to turn around and go back."

"It's not exactly a destination I'd pick out for a fun road trip, but yes," Maggie answered, "I'm sure—because there is no other way around this. No stone unturned, right?"

He didn't quite see it that way. "You know, there's no shame in just abandoning this whole thing. It's not up to you to find the answers," he pointed out.

A smile slowly curved her mouth. "You don't know me very well, otherwise you wouldn't say that. I don't abandon things," she told him with pride. "I see them through."

He blew out an impatient breath. "I'll make sure they put that on your tombstone."

If he was being sarcastic, she wasn't buying into it.

"There are worse things to have on a tombstone," she told him glibly.

Jonah gave up trying to convince her to let him turn the truck back. He knew if he did, she would only set out for the prison on her own the first chance she got. While he liked the fact that Maggie was brave and determined, there was such a thing as being *too* brave and *too* determined. In his opinion, that was only asking for trouble and they already had enough of that, thanks to the hurricane.

He went on to a more immediate problem. "Okay, we're almost there. You still want to go through with this supposed documentary filmmakers ruse?"

"Sure," she answered. She saw the doubtful look on Jonah's face. "It beats pretending that we're some kind of ghoulish groupies or fans. I hear that a lot of mass murderers have them." Even as she said it, Maggie couldn't help shivering at the improbable thought. "I will never be able to understand people like that."

"That's because you're normal," Jonah told her simply. He took in a long breath. They were approaching the massive prison gates. Even in broad daylight, the prison looked foreboding. "Okay, time to take out our IDs," he prompted. "Remember, these prison guards are always on the lookout for any kind of suspicious behavior. Randolph State Prison hasn't had a successful prison break in the last forty years."

"I hope that doesn't mean they're overdue for one," Maggie murmured, feeling progressively less secure the closer they came to the gates.

"Positive thoughts, remember?" Jonah found it ironic that he was reminding Maggie of the basic philosophy that she espoused.

"Right," Maggie mumbled under her breath, taking out

her wallet. She passed it over to Jonah just as he pulled his truck up next to the guard.

"Well, that wasn't the least bit intimidating," Maggie commented as they were waved on through the gates several long minutes later.

"Actually," Jonah told her as they drove through the parking lot, searching for a space, "as far as these sorts of things go, this was rather laid-back and routine," he told her.

"Laid-back, huh?" she questioned. "Remind me to live an exemplary life once we get out of here," Maggie cracked.

"Remember, you were the one who wanted to come here," he told her.

"I know, I know," Maggie answered. "You're right. And I don't regret this," she wanted him to know. "I'm just going to need a long hot shower once we get back home," she said.

Home. She had just referred to his cabin as home, Jonah thought. He wondered if she even realized that, or if she'd thought of it as a mistake the second the words were out of her mouth?

He eyed her, but there was no change in Maggie's expression and he wasn't going to be the one who brought it to her attention.

For all he knew, she'd meant it. Maybe she had actually started to think of his cabin as "home." Jonah turned the idea over in his head. He didn't know if he felt uncomfortable about that—or if he was actually rather pleased.

And then, suddenly, there was no longer any time left to contemplate anything. They had left the truck behind them and were now about to walk through the prison doors.

Showtime.

"I think that by the time we leave here, our IDs are going to be worn-out," Maggie commented as they followed a prison guard to a general gathering area where prisoners were allowed to meet with family members and friends. By her count, they had produced their IDs four times since approaching the prison gates—and then had to surrender them as well as their cell phones at the last station.

"That's probably the general idea," Jonah replied. He saw her looking at him in confusion, so he explained. "Fake IDs don't stand up to all that handling, at least the poor ones don't," he amended.

Maggie shrugged, at a loss. "I know you know what you're talking about, but I'm not really sure I understand that," she confessed.

Just then, before Jonah could explain it to her more clearly, Maggie grabbed his hand, holding on to him very tightly.

Her eyes were riveted on the scrawny, mangy-looking man with the unruly gray hair. He was wearing an orange jumpsuit and being escorted in by not just one guard, but two, one positioned on either side of him.

Elliott Corgan was just a shade smaller than his two uniformed bookends, not to mention a good deal older. But neither time, nor size could subdue the very menacing shadow that the man cast just by his mere presence in a room, no matter how large that room was.

The sharp, almost-black eyes moved around the area, taking in everything at once.

Even now, as old as he was, Maggie had the feeling that Elliott Corgan was not a man she could safely turn her back on.

When one of the guards pointed toward Jonah and her, Maggie could feel her throat closing up a little. And when

Elliott stared in her direction, his small, marble-like eyes honing in on her even at that distance, for just a moment, Maggie thought she was going to be sick.

Sheer will had her keeping her breakfast down. Maggie refused to give Corgan the satisfaction of knowing he had intimidated her.

Noting her pallor, Jonah leaned in and whispered, "We can still leave."

But she was adamant. "No, we've come this far, I'm not about to turn tail and run now," she told him fiercely. A little more fiercely than she was actually feeling at the moment.

Drawing her shoulders back, Maggie released her death grip on his hand and made her way toward an empty table.

Jonah was right beside her, intent on being her bodyguard. He didn't like the way that Elliott Corgan was looking at her, as if he was sizing her up, no doubt just the way the man had sized up his victims all those years ago.

This was a bad idea.

Elliott put his hand on the back of the chair, claiming it. He sat down opposite them.

Prison hadn't broken him, Jonah thought. Instead, Corgan held himself erect like a man who was confident in the fact that he was feared and thus respected in the warped world where he resided.

The intense dark eyes passed quickly over him, but it was Maggie who seemed to interest Corgan.

Corgan devoured her with his eyes.

Maggie had to struggle in order not to shiver or to allow the revulsion she felt toward the prisoner to show through. If Corgan saw contempt in her eyes, she knew he wouldn't be inclined to cooperate.

He still might not be, she thought. But she had to try.

Corgan was first to speak. "Who are you?"

Lies were best if they were kept simple—she had heard that somewhere. So she gave the convicted serial killer their real names.

"I'm Maggie Reeves." She nodded toward Jonah as she completed the introduction. "And this is Jonah Colton. We've come to get your side of the story and present it to our audience."

A flicker of interest rose in Elliott's dark eyes. He stared at her intently. "You two are saying that you're filmmakers?" he questioned.

Maggie raised her head, refusing to look away, refusing to be intimidated. She met his gaze head-on. "Yes," Maggie answered proudly.

Elliott smirked at the duo sitting before him. "You ain't no such thing," he snarled in a superior tone. "You're frauds and you're wasting my time," he told them, pushing the chair back as he began to rise.

"Seems to me that you've got nothing but time," Jonah told him. His gaze was unwavering even though being so close to Corgan literally turned his stomach. But this was important to Maggie so he pressed on. "Don't you want to know why we're really here?" he asked the man serving several life sentences.

Elliot sat down again. His eyes lingered on Maggie before he said to Jonah, "Okay, I'll bite. Who are you two and what the hell are you doing here?"

Maggie spoke up. "I already gave you our names," she told him, then added, "I used to be married to your nephew, James." She watched the serial killer as the information sank in.

The thin cheeks spread in a chilling, lecherous smile. "Well, come here, darlin', and let me give you a hug to welcome you into the family," Corgan told her, rising again. The chair scraped along the floor as he pushed it back.

He leaned over the table, his arms spread out toward Maggie.

The guard, who had remained in the doorway watching Corgan, was instantly alert and crossed the room to the prisoner.

"Hey, you know the rules. No contact," the guard barked at him.

The latter raised his hands in mock submission. "No contact," Corgan repeated in a scornful voice. Then he looked at his visitors. "They're afraid if I touch someone, they'll wind up dead," he chuckled, amused by his own joke. "You're not afraid of me, are you, darlin'?" Corgan asked, leering at Maggie.

"Why don't we get down to business?" Jonah said in a cold, stern voice.

"I'm always all about business." Corgan's thin lips pulled back in a sneer as he looked at Maggie again.

Maggie had planned to approach her questioning slowly, but obviously this wasn't a man who responded to subtlety. He had to be all but beaten over the head with questions.

So rather than find the right way to ask, she just forged ahead and asked her questions. "We found Emmeline Thompson's body the other day. She was buried beneath that really huge oak on your brother's ranch," she told Corgan, watching his face for any sort of a reaction.

Corgan's drawn face remained impassive. "Do tell." He leaned in over the table, stopped just short of making contact. "Why don't you refresh my memory, darlin'?"

"You should remember this one," Maggie all but spit out. "You mummified her and wrapped her up in plastic." To her horror, Corgan began to laugh. She exchanged looks with Jonah.

"What are you laughing at, you pervert?" Jonah demanded.

"Emmeline Thompson," Corgan repeated with a chilling smile. "I remember."

Maggie looked alert. "You remember killing her?" she cried.

"No, I remember really *wishing* I had done her." Corgan looked up, making eye contact with Maggie. "But I can't take the credit for that." He spread his hands out. "I'm innocent."

"You've never known an innocent day in your life," Jonah snarled at the man.

Corgan inclined his head, conceding the point. "Maybe so, but I'm innocent of killing the Thompson girl. Don't get me wrong, I'd love to add another kill to my list, but I can't because I didn't touch her." And then he looked at Maggie, his interest aroused. "Did you say she was mummified?"

Maggie found it extremely difficult not to shout at the lowlife scum sitting right in front of her. "You know she was."

Corgan shook his head. "Like I said, it wasn't me. But you saying that she was mummified, well, that gives me an idea about who actually did do the deed." He smiled mysteriously.

That was when the prison guard came up to the table again. "Time's up, Corgan," the burly man announced.

"Who was it?" Maggie asked as Corgan got up from the table. "Who killed Emmeline?" she asked him urgently.

Corgan was obviously enjoying this. "Well, if I'm right, that guy's still out there, probably killing more young women. Maybe even as we're all standing in here, talking about him."

"Who?" Maggie demanded, her voice rising. "Who is it?"

"Hey, I'm not going to tell you again, Corgan," the guard growled at him.

"Sorry, you heard the guard." Corgan was enjoying himself now. "I've gotta go," he told the two people questioning him with relish. "But y'all come back and visit me real soon now, you hear? Maybe I'll tell you who it is then," Corgan tossed over his shoulder, relishing this game that he was playing with them. "You know where to find me. I'm not going to be going anywhere for a long, long time."

Corgan paused one last second in the doorway, just leering at Maggie, before the guard roughly pulled him away.

Since their meeting had been abruptly terminated, Maggie and Jonah got up to leave. Another guard was there to make sure they didn't linger.

When they stopped to get their personal possessions from the guard in charge of holding on to them, Maggie turned toward Jonah and asked, "Think he's telling the truth? That he knows who's responsible for Emmeline's death?"

Reunited with his phone and his watch, Jonah put them into his pockets. "Ordinarily, I'd say no, that Corgan just said that to mess with your head. But there was a look that came into his eyes when you mentioned that the chief's sister was mummified and wrapped up in plastic."

"What kind of look?" Maggie asked, because she had totally missed it.

"Surprised. Like this was news to him. And then he brightened up," Jonah continued as they made their way down the corridor and to the first exit, "like he suddenly made a connection. The man just might be a consummate actor, and given that he got away with all those murders for so long, he could be, but my gut tells me that maybe, just maybe, we caught Corgan off his game for a second. He really looked surprised by the details of Emmeline's murder."

Passing through another doorway, they finally made their way outside. "So that means Corgan *does* know who did it."

Jonah nodded. "And if there's a chance that he does, our next step is to tell the chief."

"You're right," Maggie agreed.

He grinned. "Finally."

Chapter Fifteen

They were almost back in Whisperwood when Maggie's cell phone buzzed, announcing that she had received another text message.

Jonah glanced at her. "Maybe that's your sister with an update on the wedding," he said hopefully.

Hurricane Brooke had forced everyone's plans to be placed temporarily on hold and that included Donovan and Bellamy's wedding. But the rec center, which was where the reception was to be held, had miraculously avoided being on the receiving end of any damages, major or minor. With all the people who had initially been invited to the wedding slowly getting their lives back in order, things were looking up. It seemed to Jonah that all that needed to be done at this point was to decide on a new date and then proceed with the actual wedding.

With that thought foremost in her mind, Maggie pulled out her phone, entered her passcode and swiped open the message center.

When she didn't say anything, Jonah looked in her direction.

Maggie's expression was grim.

Red flags immediately went up. "I take it from the look on your face that the text you just got isn't from Bellamy."

"No," Maggie answered quietly, "it's not."

The next second, she pressed the home button, causing the message she'd just read to disappear.

"Who is it from?" Jonah asked, although as far as he was concerned, it was a rhetorical question. The tone of her voice had told him everything.

"I don't know." It was the truth. She didn't, and the fact that she didn't both exasperated and frightened her.

"You received another anonymous text?" Jonah asked, already making that assumption. He waited for Maggie to fill him in on the details.

Maggie shrugged, looking out the side window. "It doesn't matter."

"Yes, it does," Jonah insisted. He abruptly pulled his truck over to the side of the road, pulling up the handbrake. As the truck idled, he turned in his seat to look at Maggie. "It was from that same person again, wasn't it?"

She sighed, still staring out the window. "It looks that way."

"Let me see it," Jonah said, holding his hand out and waiting.

Although she was far from happy about it, Maggie surrendered her cell phone to him.

Jonah found himself looking down at a dark screen. Handing it back to her, he said, "Nice try, Maggie. Type in your passcode."

Reluctantly, she typed it in, then pulled up the last text message that had just come in from the anonymous sender. She gave the cell phone back to Jonah. He read aloud.

I warned you to back off if you want to live.

He looked at Maggie. "He gets right to the point, doesn't he?"

"Don't worry about it," she told Jonah, slipping her phone back into her pocket. "I said it's just a stupid prank."

"I *am* worried about it because it's not a stupid prank," Jonah insisted. "Once is a prank," he told her, "twice is a pattern. Best-case scenario, somebody wants to scare you off. Worst case—we don't want to think about worst case."

"You think this is somehow connected to Emmeline Thompson's death?" she asked him.

He didn't need to think about it to answer. "Well, it's a hell of a coincidence if it's not. You got the first text from this guy after you went 'exploring' in the middle of a hurricane—"

"The hurricane hadn't hit when I went out to the ranch," she reminded Jonah with a touch of defensiveness.

He gave her a look that clearly told her he thought she was splitting hairs.

"And this latest text came just after you went to visit Corgan in prison to question him about the body we found," Jonah said.

"You think we're being watched?" she asked, forcing herself to put her fear into words.

What he was worried about was that *she* was being watched, but he didn't want to state it that way because he didn't want to scare Maggie any more than he had to. He felt it was better to stick with the pronoun she had used.

"That would be my guess," he said. "Maybe the chief has an IT person who could backtrack this text message to a specific phone."

Maggie nodded, agreeing. "Then I guess we have two reasons to see the chief," she said. She pointed toward his idling engine. "You're wasting gas, you know. Let's go."

Amusement came into his eyes. "Yes, ma'am," Jonah responded easily.

Her eyebrows drew together over flashing blue eyes. "Call me 'ma'am' again and that'll be the last word you ever get to say."

This time Jonah laughed. "Information duly noted, Ms. Reeves." He pulled back onto the road. "Now let's go find the chief."

THEY LUCKED OUT and found Chief Thompson as the latter was heading back to his office. He gave the appearance of someone who had been out working all day. He also looked far from happy.

"What the hell's wrong with people?" he complained the moment they caught up with him and managed to get his attention.

"I've got a strong feeling that you're about to tell us," Jonah guessed.

Thompson didn't appear to even hear him. If he did, he didn't comment on Jonah's attempt to infuse humor into the serious situation.

"Don't get me wrong," Thompson said. "Most of these folks are out there helping one another and that's how it should be."

"But?" Jonah asked, waiting for the chief to get to the end of his thought and tell them what was bothering him.

"But then I find two of our younger citizens who should know better looting. Looting!" he repeated with disgust. "They were taking advantage of this catastrophe and making off with things other Whisperwood residents could put to use." His eyes blazed as he shook his head. "If I live to be a hundred, I will never understand that sort of behavior," he declared angrily.

"These sorts of disasters bring out the worst in some

people, but they also bring out the best in others and usually the latter outweighs the former," Maggie told the older man, hoping that might restore his usually even temperament. They needed him clearheaded.

"I know, I know," Thompson answered, still disgruntled. "It's just that the former leaves a really bad taste in my mouth."

The chief shook his head again, unlocking his door and walking into his unoccupied office. His other officers were out in the field, helping out and doing whatever needed to be done.

"Well, we have some news, Chief, that may or may not cheer you up," Jonah told Thompson, watching the older man's face.

Gripping the armrests, Thompson eased his large frame onto his office chair. The way he did it indicated that this was the first time he'd sat down all day. "I'm listening," he practically bit off.

Jonah looked at Maggie, indicating that, for better or for worse, this was her story to relate. So she took over. "Jonah and I drove over to Austin to see Elliott Corgan at Randolph State Prison this morning."

Thompson received the news with all the joy of being on the receiving end of a gut punch. He scowled at the two people before him.

"Damn it, I told you two to stay clear of this case! Why the hell didn't you listen?" he demanded.

"It's not his fault, Chief. I insisted on going and Jonah didn't want me to go alone," she said, looking toward Jonah before continuing. "I thought if I could confront Corgan, I could get him to tell me if he killed your sister."

"And what did he say?" the chief asked, his expression dark.

Maggie took a breath. "He said he didn't do it."

"Big surprise," Thompson commented sarcastically. "Of course he'd deny it. I already told you he denied it when I questioned him," the chief reminded the two people in his office.

"I know," Maggie replied. "But it was the way that he denied it. Like he really wished he could have been the one to have done the deed."

"Sick bastard," the chief muttered under his breath in total disgust.

"But that's not all," Jonah said, injecting his own take on the interview with the serial killer. "When Maggie described the way your sister was buried, that her body was mummified first, Corgan got this look on his face, like he suddenly had a revelation."

The chief seemed to come to attention, his whole body growing rigid. "What kind of a revelation?"

It was Maggie's turn to speak. "I think he might know who did kill your sister."

Thompson looked at her doubtfully. "You sure you're not just reading things into this?" he questioned, looking from Maggie to Jonah.

"Very sure," Maggie answered. "Elliott really enjoys being the center of attention. He likes having an audience and right now, he's drawing his story out, baiting us until he finally finds the right moment to reveal his information."

"And you think he's going to tell you who this other killer is?" the chief questioned.

"Yes," Jonah answered. There was no mistaking his confidence.

"Well then, let's go," Thompson urged, rising up from his chair.

"I think we should be the ones to go back and talk to him," Jonah told the chief. "He shut you out once," he reminded Thompson. "But I get the feeling that he likes bragging and preening in front of Maggie."

"Must me my fatal charm," Maggie said sarcastically. She wasn't happy about Corgan's attraction to her, but she was determined to use it to her advantage.

The chief didn't look overly happy about this revelation, even though he didn't contest it.

Resigned, he said, "Fine, then the two of you go back and see him tomorrow morning. It doesn't matter who gets the truth out of him as long as the truth does come out. But the minute you leave that cold-blooded scumbag, I want you to report everything he told you back to me. Am I making myself clear?" Thompson asked, his steely gaze shifting from Maggie to Jonah and then back again.

"Crystal," Maggie answered.

"Um, chief, there is just one more thing," Jonah said as Thompson was about to turn his back on them and get to the paperwork he absolutely dreaded.

Thompson's eyes rose to pin Jonah down. He leaned in closer. "Yes?"

"Maggie's been getting threatening texts on her phone lately," Jonah told the chief.

"Is this true?" Thompson asked her.

She really wished Jonah hadn't said anything, but she had no choice. She had to answer in the affirmative. "Yes. But there've only been two," she protested as if that made it all right.

Thompson's complexion flushed. "Why didn't you come to me with this, Maggie?"

She gestured toward his desk as if it was a symbol for the whole town and what he was carrying on his shoulders.

"Well, it's not as if you didn't already have your hands full," she pointed out.

The chief didn't bother dignifying her excuse with a comment. "Do you have any idea who might have sent them?" he asked her.

Maggie shook her head. "Not a clue."

"That's why we brought this to you," Jonah explained. He held his hand out for the phone. Maggie reluctantly surrendered it. "We thought maybe your IT person could track the texts back to their source."

"He could," the chief agreed, his mouth set grimly, "except for one small problem."

"And that is?" Jonah asked.

"Jim Ellis, my IT person, was one of Hurricane Brooke's casualties," he told them. "The first, actually," he confessed unhappily.

Maggie was the first one to react. "I'm so very sorry for your loss, Chief."

"Yeah, we all are," the chief told her. "Jim was one of those eager beavers who came in early, stayed late and never walked away until he had finished his job. He was really good at it, too."

"Did Jim have a family?" Maggie asked sympathetically.

"No, but he was hoping for one," he told her. "Jim was engaged," he explained, then added sadly, "I was the one who had to break the news to his fiancée." He looked at them with a very sober expression on his face. "There are times when I really hate this job."

And then he focused not on the news that they had brought him about his sister, but on Maggie's threatening texts.

"Let me see your phone," he said to her.

Maggie put in her passcode, then pulled up the two texts for the chief to look at.

"And you got these when?" he asked after reading each one.

"One came in just after we got back from finding your sister's body, the other one came today after we got back from seeing Corgan at the prison."

"Did you tell anyone about going to see Corgan?" he asked.

"No one," Jonah answered for her.

"Did you notice anyone following you?" he asked them.

"The aftermath of the hurricane has people milling around all over the place," Maggie told the chief. "I never took notice of anyone in particular, but that's not to say that someone *wasn't* deliberately following us," she said.

"We're kind of shorthanded right now, otherwise I'd assign someone to protect you around the clock," the chief said almost apologetically.

Jonah cleared his throat. "In case you didn't notice, Chief, I'm here. I can provide Maggie with all the protection and care she might need to keep her safe and sound from this maniac who's trying to scare her off by texting."

The chief looked at him skeptically, but when he spoke, he said, "Well then, I guess there's nothing to worry about, is there?"

"Are you being sarcastic?" Jonah asked him good-naturedly.

"No, but I am reminded of that old saying. You know the one I mean. It's the one about the best-laid plans of mice and men," the chief answered.

"Okay, you *are* being sarcastic," Jonah concluded. "Well, don't be. Search and rescue aren't the only things I'm trained in," he assured the chief.

Maggie raised her hand to draw attention to herself and away from a possible brewing dispute. "I'm right here and although I am touched that you're both concerned about keeping me safe. I am perfectly capable of doing that myself."

"No one's arguing with that," Jonah told her, "but there is that other old saying," he said, taking a page out of the chief's book, "about two heads being better than one. That goes for protectors, as well," he told Maggie in no uncertain terms.

She smiled at him. "Seeing as how it's me you're trying to keep safe, I'm not going to argue with that."

Jonah looked at her. He knew there was more coming. "But?"

"No 'but,'" she said innocently. "However, didn't you say if we got back early, you wanted to lend a hand in the cleanup efforts?"

He thought that in light of the text, things had changed. "I did, but—"

Maggie pretended not to hear his protest. "Well then, let's go, Colton," she ordered. "We're standing around, wasting daylight."

He nodded toward the chief, taking his leave. The chief waved them on.

"You ever give any thought to being a drill sergeant?" Jonah asked her as he held the chief's office door open for Maggie. "Because you really should. I think you'd be perfect for the job."

"Think so?" she asked. When he nodded, she said cheerfully, "Then maybe I *will* give it some thought."

Chapter Sixteen

Dinner that evening was courtesy of an extremely grateful woman named Molly McClure who wanted to express her thanks to the team that had rescued her ten-year-old son, Nathan, who was buried alive beneath a pile of rubble earlier that week. Because the general store was receiving regular deliveries now, Molly was able to go all out with her preparations. She wouldn't allow any of the team or the volunteers to leave until they had all had at least two servings of her fried chicken, mashed potatoes, corn and something that was supposed to pass for a green salad.

It was a treat for the team to gather together, talking and sharing stories—doing something other than digging through debris.

Consequently, by the time Jonah and Maggie walked into his cabin, it was a great deal later than they had anticipated. They were both quite tired.

Even so, Maggie turned toward Jonah and smiled. "That was rather nice. I guess you're kind of used to this, aren't you?"

Exhausted, Jonah dropped his large frame onto the sofa. "You mean eating?" he asked. "Yeah, I try to do it at least once a day."

"No, wise guy," Maggie laughed at him. "I mean being regaled as a hero."

Jonah frowned in response, shaking his head. "I'm not a hero," he denied with feeling. "None of us are. We're just doing what we would want someone else to do if they were in the right place at the right time. Help," he concluded simply, eschewing any sort of fanfare beyond that.

But Maggie was not about to allow Jonah to brush off everything he'd done for the town and its residents so lightly.

"Yes, you are," she insisted. "It takes a certain kind of person to risk their lives to save others like that."

"You did it," Jonah pointed out. "I saw you," he reminded her. "You've been in the thick of things more than a few times since I got you out of that tree," he added with a grin.

Maggie sighed. The tree again. "You're not going to let me forget that, are you?"

The expression on his face told her that she was right.

"It still has some mileage in it," Jonah said glibly. And then he grew a little more serious as he asked, "It doesn't really bother you, does it?"

"No," she admitted. "Not if it makes you smile like that." Although she really wished he didn't find so much amusement in his good deed.

"Know what else makes me smile?" Jonah asked, moving in closer to her.

Maggie looked up at him, a totally innocent expression on her face. "What?"

He didn't mind playing games when she turned out to be the prize. "You," he answered softly. The single word all but encompassed her.

"Oh?" Maggie questioned.

"Yeah, oh," Jonah echoed just as he leaned in to kiss her.

She felt herself melting even seconds before he made contact. He had the ability to really set her on fire with just one kiss.

"I thought you were tired," Maggie murmured against his lips.

His grin, beginning in his eyes, was positively wicked. "I guess I just got my second wind," Jonah said a beat before he took Maggie in his arms and kissed her again.

Maggie totally surrendered to the thrilling wave that came rushing over her.

She had every intention of making the most of this interlude while it lasted. She was more than aware that what was happening between the two of them had a limited life expectancy, because very soon, Jonah would be returning to Austin on a permanent basis. That was where his job was, while her place, she had come to accept, was here.

With Bell marrying Donovan, there would probably be children on the horizon, and while she was undecided about having children of her own, "Aunt" Maggie was more than willing to pitch in and help her sister when Bell's children made their appearance.

With the immediate future, not to mention everything else, so up in the air right now, all she wanted to do was live in the moment.

And right now, the moment was delicious, she thought, her body heating as Jonah kissed her over and over again while they slowly made their way into the bedroom to make love.

Everything else was put on hold.

"I CAN'T BELIEVE we're actually going to go back to that prison to see Elliott for a second time," Maggie said with a large sigh as she lay beside Jonah the following morning.

She had woken up before him and had been awake

for a few minutes now. But she hadn't said anything or even attempted to get up until she had felt him stirring next to her.

Jonah slipped his arm around her now, bringing Maggie closer. "If you'd rather not, I can go alone," he told her, kissing the side of her head.

"Thanks, but I started this. I'm not about to bow out just because the man makes my skin crawl." She shivered just thinking about Corgan. "How could people not have caught onto him right from the beginning? For heaven sakes, the man almost *looks* the part of a crazy serial killer."

The moment the words her out of her mouth, other thoughts occurred to her. She had married into the family not knowing about its dark secret.

"For that matter, how did my ex's family manage to keep this all—the dead bodies, Elliott's conviction—quiet for so long?"

"You forget, money can buy almost anything, including silence," Jonah told her. "It also has a long reach," he added, "which was one of the reasons that I moved to Austin."

That caught her attention. Jonah hadn't really talked about what had made him leave Whisperwood before.

Maggie drew herself up on her elbow to look at him. "You wanted to get away from your family?" she asked, curious.

"No, just from their name," he told her. As he spoke, he played with the ends of her hair, tantalizing them both. "I wanted to be my own man, to know that whatever I accomplished, it wasn't because of the Colton name, but because of the effort I put into whatever career path I chose to follow." He smiled then, laughing at his own naïveté. "I never thought that my becoming part of the

Cowboy Heroes would wind up bringing me right back to my hometown."

"Well, speaking for your hometown," she said, "I'm very glad that it did."

"Just speaking for the town?" he asked, arching a brow as he looked at her.

"And me," she added, knowing that was what he was going for. "That goes without saying."

The grin instantly reached his eyes. "Oh, say it," Jonah coaxed.

She ran the back of her hand along his cheek. "Okay. I'm very glad that you came back just in time," she told him.

"Otherwise," he said, enjoying himself, "you might still be up that tree."

"Don't push it, Colton," she warned. But there was a smile in her voice as she said it.

"Oh, but I like pushing you," he told her, stealing a quick kiss that threatened to blossom into something far more consuming.

But before she got too carried away—Jonah was quickly becoming her weakness—Maggie placed her hands against his chest to keep him from kissing her again. "We're going to wind up being late," she predicted.

"Corgan's not going anywhere. And we're not on the clock," he reminded her. "I think, all things considered, that he can wait an extra half hour or so for us, don't you think?"

Maggie gave up fighting Jonah as well as her own desires. "You're right," she agreed, happily surrendering to him—and herself.

INSTEAD OF THE predicted half hour, it was closer to two hours later when they finally drove up to Randolph State

Prison. Unlike the day before, this time the visitors' parking lot was fairly empty.

"See, I told you there was no reason to hurry," Jonah said to her. "Maybe if Corgan has to wait for a while, he'll be more inclined to talk so he doesn't wind up losing our attention." Jonah pulled up into the first row and parked his truck there. "Looks like we'll practically have the place to ourselves."

She looked around. There were about one quarter of the cars here today than were in the lot yesterday. "I'm not sure if I think that's a good thing or a scary one," she confessed.

"Nothing to be afraid of," Jonah reminded her. "I'm going to be right here with you." To illustrate his point, he took her hand.

Yes, he had a way of making her feel protected, but she couldn't get used to this, Maggie told herself. She was a realist. The town was already getting back on its feet, although it was rather wobbly. But the fact was that Whisperwood was starting to look better. Sure, there was still lots of work left to do, but reconstruction really wasn't part of Jonah's job. That meant that Jonah wasn't going to be around that much longer.

The thought left her cold.

As if to underscore that very point, Jonah let go of her hand. Without thinking, Maggie reached for it. He glanced in her direction and smiled. His fingers curled around hers.

Why did she find that so comforting? she asked herself. She'd always been able to stand on her own before, even when she was married to James. She could certainly do that again.

She just couldn't allow herself to grow dependent on Jonah, she thought fiercely.

But she continued to let him hold her hand as they made their way through the various gates and doors until they were finally in front of the prison guard who took their phones and their wallets from them, securing the items until they were ready to leave again.

"It's for your own safety," the guard recited mechanically. "You'll get your things back when you leave Randolph."

"That can't be soon enough for me," Maggie said to Jonah.

As before, a guard brought them to the large communal room. Jonah told a second guard the name of the prisoner they had come to see.

The second guard, a different man from the day before, frowned at them as if the request was personally putting him out.

"Take a seat," he all but snarled. "We'll bring the prisoner down to you."

As the guard left, Maggie looked around the communal room. There were only two other people there and they were already seated, each talking to the prisoner that they had come to visit.

"Looks like we have our pick of tables, too," she commented.

Jonah chose a table that was located in the very center of the room. It was visible from all angles.

"I guess this is a really slow day at Randolph," he said.

He waited for Maggie to sit down, then took the seat beside her.

Several minutes passed. Jonah looked at his watch. "I don't remember it taking them this long to bring Corgan down the last time."

"Maybe Elliott's stalling because he wants to make a grand entrance," Maggie guessed. "He's probably drawing this out for as long as he can because he knows that once he tells us who he thinks is responsible for Emmeline's murder, that's it. There's no more reason for us to come back again to talk to him. We'll have the information we need and we'll go from there—and he knows that."

Jonah looked at his watch again. "You're probably right," he replied, trying to contain his impatience.

But after another fifteen minutes had passed and Corgan still hadn't made an appearance, Jonah was on his feet, ready to find someone in authority to tell them what was going on.

"Something's wrong," he told Maggie. "Even if he was deliberately dragging his feet, Corgan should have been down here by now. Or at least the guard should have come back to tell us why Corgan was taking so long. Maybe Corgan isn't going to meet with you."

"Speak of the devil," Maggie said, tapping Jonah's shoulder. She pointed to the doorway. The guard who had gone to get the prisoner had returned.

"Looks like 'the devil's' alone," Jonah observed, annoyed. He crossed to the doorway with Maggie following closely behind him. "What's the matter?" Jonah asked the guard. "Why isn't Corgan with you?"

"If he's refusing to see us—" Maggie began, cutting in.

"He's refusing to see *everybody*," the guard informed her, a nasty edge to his voice.

Jonah was tired of playing games. "He can't do that," he protested.

"Yeah, he can," the guard contradicted, "if he's dead," he added.

"Dead?" Jonah repeated, stunned. The guard had clearly buried the headline. Deliberately?

"What do you mean, dead?" Maggie demanded, pushing herself in front of Jonah. "We just saw him yesterday," she declared.

"Well, yesterday, he was alive," the guard answered. "This morning it looks like he hung himself in his cell, using his bedsheet. And I'm the guy who found him," he added in disgust. "I had to get someone to help me cut him down. That's what took so long," he told Jonah, scowling as he obviously anticipated that was going to be Jonah's next question.

Jonah frowned. This didn't sound right to him. "Corgan hung himself just like that and nobody saw anything?" he asked the guard, annoyed by the vagueness of the whole situation. He was certain that someone was hiding something.

"What do you want from me?" the guard demanded. "This is prison, not a frat house. Nobody *ever* sees anything," the man snapped.

Though the guard's attitude annoyed him, what he'd just said really didn't surprise Jonah.

"I want to see the body," Jonah insisted.

"Sorry, buddy, you're gonna have to get your jollies somewhere else," the guard retorted.

"I am asking you officially," Jonah ground out between clenched teeth. "I'm Jonah Colton." For the first time in years, he stressed his last name. "And I'm part of Cowboy Heroes, the search and rescue team that just put in two weeks saving and digging Whisperwood out of the rubble that hurricane created. And this is Maggie Reeves," he said, gesturing toward Maggie. "That dead prisoner was her uncle." Jonah conveniently skipped over the part about Maggie no longer being married to Corgan's nephew. "Now, if you've got a drop of human decency in those veins of yours, you will take us to see the body," he told the guard.

The guard obviously didn't like being overridden. "How do I know you are who you say you are?" he challenged Jonah.

"You can check our IDs," Maggie told the guard. "They're being held by the guard up front." And then she changed directions. "Do you know if Elliott said anything to anyone before he died?"

"How the hell should I know that? I wasn't his nursemaid," the guard snapped. But then grudgingly, the guard relented. "Follow me. You can talk to the guard who helped me cut him down. It's the best I can do."

"This doesn't make any sense, you know," Maggie insisted as they followed the guard. "Elliott wouldn't commit suicide," she insisted.

The guard turned around to look at her. "Why? Because he was so happy here?" the guard asked sarcastically.

"No, because when we spoke to him yesterday, he gave every indication that he intended to live a long, long time, enjoying all the attention that his 'handiwork' had garnered him. That's not a man who was planning on hanging himself in the morning."

"Look," the guard told them angrily, "all I know is that if you go talk to the other guard, he's not going to tell you anything different than I did."

Suddenly, as he brought them out into the corridor leading to the prison's interior, a shrill alarm sounded, calling for all visitors to immediately evacuate the prison.

Chapter Seventeen

"What's going on?" Jonah demanded

No one was answering him. Exasperated, he caught hold of Warren, the guard who was, until a moment ago, bringing them back to Corgan's cell.

There were guards armed with rifles rushing past them, while civilians there to visit prisoners were being evacuated, herded in the opposite direction, toward the exit.

Everything suddenly appeared to be in a state of chaos.

"There's a riot in Cell block C," Warren shouted, responding to a message that had just come through on his cell phone. "You have to go back the way you came," he told Jonah.

If he had come out here on his own, then Jonah would have been perfectly willing to find his way out of the prison, no problem. But he wasn't alone. He had Maggie to think of and he wanted an armed escort to lead them out since he had no way to defend her or himself. He had surrendered his weapon along with his wallet and ID at the desk before they had passed through the last prison door.

"Look, man, you need to escort us out of here," Jonah insisted, raising his voice because the din coming from scrambling civilians and rioting prisoners was getting louder.

But the guard was just as adamant that they had to do as he said and part ways.

"Sorry, but we've all got our assigned duties in the event of a riot. Look," he said, leaning in so that his voice carried without the need to shout, "the prison is in the process of being locked down so my advice to you is to get the hell out of here. *Now*," he ordered. "Go that way," Warren said, pointing behind Jonah.

Annoyed, Jonah turned away from the guard and told Maggie, "We're on our own."

He found himself talking to no one.

"Maggie?" He repeated her name, looking around, but she was nowhere to be seen. A sense of growing panic instantly set in.

Where was she?

"Maggie!" he called out again. Receiving no answer, Jonah dashed after the guard and grabbed hold of Warren's wrist before the man was able to get away. "I can't find the woman who was just here with me."

Warren's ruddy complexion was even more flushed than usual as he tried to pull free. The look on his face made it clear this wasn't his problem.

"Looks like she's smarter than you are and took off. If I were you, I'd do the same," he told Jonah, and made another attempt to pull free.

But Jonah just tightened his grip on the man's wide wrist. He wanted answers and he wanted the guard's help. "She wouldn't just take off like that," he all but growled at the guard. "Something must have happened to her."

Annoyance creased the man's low forehead. "Well, good luck with that. I've got a lockdown to deal with," he said again, trying to yank his wrist free of Jonah's grip.

"No," Jonah told the guard, measuring out each word

evenly, "What you've got to deal with is helping me find her, you understand?"

"Look, jackass, I've—"

And then, whatever curse or choice words the guard had intended to utter never materialized. Instead, his small dark eyes widened in surprise as he pointed behind Jonah toward a scenario that was unfolding down the corridor.

When Jonah turned around, he saw that one of the inmates who had apparently managed to escape from Cell block C was holding a knife to Maggie's throat. He was dragging her back there with him.

"You do what I tell you to do, bitch, and maybe you'll live to see tomorrow." The escaped inmate, a man in his late thirties, was skinny and by the looks of him, he was obviously high on some kind of drug. All it took was one look at the man's eyes to see that he was completely out of it.

Jonah's first instinct was to run toward Maggie and somehow wrestle the knife away from the inmate. But he knew that there was no way he could launch any kind of a frontal attack on the prisoner without also endangering Maggie, maybe even getting her killed.

"Do what he says, Maggie," Jonah called out to her. "Don't fight him."

"Listen to your boyfriend, honey, and you and me are gonna have us a real a good time," the inmate promised, leering as he dragged Maggie with him down the corridor. Within moments, both the inmate and Maggie disappeared from view.

The second he lost sight of Maggie, Jonah turned back to the guard. "Where does that corridor lead?" he demanded.

"That one? That goes back to Cell block C," the guard told him.

A chill washed over Jonah. He couldn't allow that to happen. "Do any other corridors intersect it before it gets to Cell block C?" he asked.

"I don't know. Maybe," Warren answered with a careless shrug.

Jonah resisted the temptation of shaking the information out of the guard. Instead, he kept his temper in check and said, "'Maybe' isn't good enough." When the guard didn't volunteer anything further, Jonah's face darkened.

"I'm not a violent man, but if anything happens to that woman, I'm going to devote my life to making sure you live to regret it. Now does any other corridor intersect with the one that inmate just dragged that woman down?" Jonah repeated.

The guard actually appeared to think for a second, fully aware that Jonah was tightening his grip on his wrist with each passing moment. "Yeah, yeah it does," he finally cried.

"Show me!" Jonah ordered, pushing the guard out in front of him.

"Look, you're just making things worse for yourself," Maggie said to the inmate who had the knife to her throat and was dragging her backward with him. She'd almost stumbled twice. "If you let me go now, things will go easier on you." It took everything she had for her to remain calm.

"What do you think I am, stupid or something?" the inmate shouted at her. "I let you go, I've got no leverage. Holding on to you is the only choice I've got. Besides, you have any idea how long it's been since I had my hands on a woman? Too damn long, that's how long," he yelled, taking out his frustration on her and becoming almost hysterical before he managed to calm himself down.

"Why don't you take that knife away from my throat?" Maggie suggested, keeping her voice friendly. "If you accidentally cut me, I'll be bleeding all over you and what fun would that be?"

"If I cut you, there won't be no 'accidentally' about it," the inmate promised her. "And you think I don't know that if I take the knife away from your throat, you'll take off?"

"I won't take off," Maggie told him, adding, "You have my word."

"Your word," the inmate mocked. "Like that means anything anymore." He continued dragging her with him, one arm held tightly around her waist, the other hand holding the knife to her throat. "Besides," he said, pausing just for a second to rub his face against her hair, "in case you haven't noticed, I'm getting off on this."

She could feel herself getting physically sick. She didn't have to use her imagination to know what the man had in mind for her.

"I'm not," she said, hoping that might make him view this Neanderthal action differently.

But instead, he just laughed at her, enjoying this unexpected turn of events. "Too bad. I am."

The inmate looked over his shoulder to make sure he was going in the right direction as he continued to drag her off with him.

The next part happened so fast, neither Maggie nor the inmate realized what was going on until it was almost over.

In the inmate's case, it wasn't until he felt a wire going over his head, around his throat and then tightening in one smoothly executed movement, deftly robbing him of the ability to get air into his lungs.

"Let her go, you brain-dead jackass," Jonah ordered.

Furious, he tightened the wire even further. "Now!" he commanded.

Because he was suffocating, the inmate dropped the knife he was holding to Maggie's throat. A gurgling sound was coming out of his mouth as he desperately tried to suck in some air.

The second the knife was away from Maggie's throat, Jonah loosened the wire that he had gotten around the inmate's throat, although he still held it in place to show the man who was in control.

With Maggie free, Jonah stepped back and let the guard take over restraining the inmate. Warren was quick to jump in.

"You're not going anywhere," Warren snarled at the inmate when the latter struggled, then sank down to his knees. Warren yanked him back up to his feet. "You're going back to your buddies. And then you're all going to be getting what's coming to you," Warren informed the would-be escapee.

It was over as quickly as it had begun. All the prisoners were being herded back to their cell block, although they were all going to be kept separate from one another until the responsible parties were singled out and properly dealt with. It was clear that some heavy restrictions were going to have to be put in force.

Jonah was oblivious to all this going on. His only concern was Maggie.

"Are you all right?" he cried as Maggie all but collapsed into his arms.

He held on to her for a long moment, incredibly relieved that he could. There had been one really scary moment back there when he was afraid that this whole scenario was not going to end well for her.

Jonah upbraided himself for ever having brought her

back here, but at the same time he knew it was futile to feel guilty about it. Maggie was stubborn. She would have come here on her own and if he hadn't been with her, who knows what might have happened?

"I'm fine," Maggie assured him in a somewhat-shaky voice.

But he wanted to see for himself, to check her over and make sure that the deranged inmate hadn't cut her or left any kind of a mark on her from that knife he'd been holding against her throat.

Because if he had, if the prisoner had left even the tiniest scratch on her, he was going to come back and make the man pay for that.

"I just want to make sure for myself," Jonah told her.

Satisfied that there wasn't so much as a scratch on her, he took Maggie back into his arms, embracing her as if he had been separated from her for an entire eternity. It certainly felt that way to him.

"When I saw that lowlife holding that knife to your throat, I swear my heart froze. I just wanted to rip *his* heart out with my bare hands," Jonah told her.

Holding her to him, he kissed the top of Maggie's head several times over. He felt his own heart twisting as he relived the scene in his head. "I've never been so scared in my life, Maggie," he admitted quietly. "Scared that I was going to lose you."

"No such luck," she murmured against his chest, her breath warming him.

"Luck?" Jonah repeated, then held her away from him for a moment to get a better look at her face. "I wouldn't call losing you 'luck,' Maggie," he said, enfolding her in his arms again. "If anything ever happened to you, I really don't think that I could continue."

This time Maggie was the one who drew back to look

up at his face, confused as she tried to process what Jonah was telling her.

"Just what are you saying, Jonah?" she asked, afraid to think what she was thinking.

Jonah paused for a moment then, drawing in a breath and pulling his thoughts together as best as he could. This was a new concept he was dealing with.

"I guess what I'm saying is that I love you," he told Maggie.

It was hard to know who was more surprised to hear him say that, Maggie or him. But once the words were out, he knew that they were true. He found himself smiling at her.

"Yup," he said, "I love you. And I don't ever, ever want to go through anything even close to that again."

Dazed by his revelation as well as by what had happened earlier, she nodded. "All right, then I guess I'll cross off prison riots from my list of preferred activities," she said with such a straight face, for a second she almost sound serious.

It took Jonah half a minute to realize that she was kidding. He laughed then, the sound echoing with almost-tangible relief.

"That's just fine with me," he told her. And then he looked her over one final time "You're sure that you're okay?"

"Jonah Colton," Maggie said, threading her arms around his neck, "I have never been so okay in my whole life. Really."

"Then let's go home," he told her, putting his arm around Maggie's shoulders. "There's nothing we can do here now that Corgan's dead."

"His 'suicide' is still rather fishy to me," she told Jonah as they began to walk toward the front desk.

He had no intention of disagreeing with her. "I guess we can just add that to the list of things that need looking into," he told her.

Their escape from the prison grounds was delayed when Warren, the guard who had brought Jonah to the corridor that intersected with the one the escaped inmate had taken returned. He placed himself in front of the couple to momentarily prevent their exit.

Jonah instinctively positioned himself between the guard and Maggie just in case something else was about to happen.

"Hey, in all the excitement," the guard said, "I forgot to ask you if either one of you wanted to press charges against Waylon."

"Against who?" Jonah asked, not recognizing the name the guard used.

"Waylon Roberts," the guard said, "the guy who held a knife to your girl's throat."

"Absolutely," Jonah responded. "But can we come back tomorrow to do that?" He looked toward Maggie. She nodded her agreement. "I think we both just want to get out of here for now."

"Sure. I understand," the guard said, much friendlier now with the riot quelled than he had been just less than a half hour ago. "You want an escort out?" he offered.

Jonah looked at Maggie again and she nodded. "Sure, that would be good," he agreed for both of them. "Thanks."

The guard accompanied them not just through the first set of gates, but he also came with them when they picked up their personal possessions.

Warren seemed impressed when he saw Jonah's handgun. "That's a beauty." And then he asked, "You have everything you came with?"

"That, plus a whole lot of adrenaline I didn't even realize I had coursing through my veins," Maggie replied, speaking up.

"Yeah," the guard said as if he was accepting partial blame for that. "I'm really sorry you had to go through all that."

She appreciated the apology. "All that matters is that it ended well."

The guard stood and waved them on their way, which surprised them.

"That was pretty gracious of you," Jonah remarked as they left the man behind them, "considering that if someone at the prison hadn't dropped the ball, you would have never had a knife pressed against your throat." He took her hand as they left the building. Then, glancing at her face and seeing her expression, he had to ask, "What are you smiling about?"

"That guard, he called me your girl," Maggie answered.

"All right," Jonah responded, still waiting to hear why she was smiling like that.

Her eyes met his. "And you didn't correct him."

"No," he agreed. "I didn't. Because he was right—unless of course, you don't want to be," he interjected. Maybe she'd been offended by that, he thought. "I guess that is rather an adolescent term," Jonah admitted, watching her expression.

"And just what's wrong with using a term that adolescents use?" she asked. "All my best friends were adolescents once upon a time."

He put his arm around her shoulders and pulled her to him, laughing. "Funny you should say that. Mine were, too."

Chapter Eighteen

By the time Jonah had pulled his truck up in front of the cabin, he had put everything else out of his mind except for one all-consuming thing. He desperately wanted to make love with Maggie. After almost losing her in the prison riot, he had realized just how very precious she was to him.

If there was anything else even remotely on his mind, it was trying to come up with a way to rearrange his life so that he could come back to Whisperwood on a permanent basis and live here. But he intended to tackle those logistics *after* Donovan and Bellamy's wedding had taken place.

Right now, all he wanted was to lose himself in Maggie. Everything else was a distant, *distant* second.

Looking back, Jonah was certain that if he hadn't been so terribly preoccupied, he would have noticed that something was off even before he approached the front door.

Which he discovered was slightly ajar.

He turned toward Maggie, puzzled. "Did you leave the front door unlocked?" He didn't think it was like her, but he had to ask.

"No, and besides that, you were the last one who left the cabin," she reminded him. Maggie stared at the door. This didn't feel right. "And you always lock the door after you." She bit her lower lip. After the prison riot, they were both admittedly a little paranoid. "Maybe there's something wrong with the lock. It is old," she pointed out.

"Get behind me," Jonah ordered. "Maybe it's nothing, but there might be an animal in there. If there is, it's most likely foraging for food." If it *was* an animal, Jonah wanted to make sure that it didn't attack Maggie.

Maggie just thought that Jonah was focusing on an animal getting into the cabin to put her at ease. Had there been someone here?

She didn't hear any sounds of movement coming from inside. This *wasn't* an animal.

"You know any wild animals that 'almost' close the door behind them?" Maggie asked. She nodded at the door that they had found ajar.

Jonah shrugged. "First time for everything." His hand on the doorknob, he carefully turned it and then slowly pushed the door open.

The moment he looked inside, adrenaline blasted through him like an exploding grenade. Why hadn't he seen this coming?

His grandmother's rocking chair had been moved and positioned so that it was just a foot away from the door. Sitting in the rocking chair was James Corgan, Maggie's ex-husband.

He was holding a large handgun, which was now aimed right at Maggie. "Sure took you a long time to get back from the state prison, Mags," James commented.

"What the hell are you doing in my cabin?" Jonah demanded.

"Waiting for you, obviously," James replied curtly. "Or rather, for my winsome ex-wife here." His eyes slowly traveled down the length of Maggie's body with the air of a man who felt that he still owned her. "I see you managed to make it out of the prison riot in one piece." He shook his head bemoaning the fact. "What a pity."

Maggie was instantly alert. "How do you know about the prison riot?" she demanded. Had her ex-husband orchestrated it?

James appeared to be bored by the question. "I'm a Corgan. My family practically owns this area. Nothing happens around here without me knowing it."

"The riot wasn't 'around here,'" Jonah informed the other man coldly. "It took place in Randolph State Prison. That's in Austin."

James's eyes darkened. "I *know* that. But since dear old crazy uncle Elliott has been in that prison for what amounts to decades now, I consider Randolph to be part of the family's sphere of interest, as well," James answered with the air of someone who felt he was entitled to everything and anything he wanted.

On his feet now, he continued to study his ex-wife like someone trying to find the answer to a riddle. "If you don't mind my asking, how did you manage to get away from that hulking drug addict? He was at least twice your size if not bigger."

Incensed, Jonah suddenly demanded, "Did you have anything to do with that?"

James's expression mocked him. "Do I look like the type to kiss and tell?" he smirked.

"You worthless piece of garbage," Jonah spit. He didn't know how yet, but he would bet anything that James was somehow behind that riot *and* behind that addict getting a knife so he could attack Maggie. "That addict held a knife to Maggie's throat," Jonah shouted angrily, taking a step closer to James.

The latter cocked his gun. "Too bad he didn't plunge it in up to the hilt. That was what he was supposed to do, not grandstand and draw the process out," James informed them, lamenting the inmate's failure. "Don't take another step, Boy Scout," he warned Jonah. "You might be good when it comes to digging through dirt, but you're not fast enough to outrun a bullet." His smile was positively chilling. "Although you're welcome to try," he taunted, aiming his gun at Jonah.

"Jonah, don't," Maggie warned, putting her hand on Jonah's arm to keep him back. "He's a trained shot. He likes to show off for his friends at the local firing range."

"I'd listen to her if I were you, Joe-naw," James said, deliberately drawing out Jonah's name and ridiculing him.

"What is it you want from us, James?" Maggie asked her ex-husband angrily. "Why are you in Jonah's cabin, playing these games?"

"No games, Mag-pie," James denied, taking a step closer to Maggie. "You were the one who liked to play games, remember?"

She looked at him as if he was crazy. "What are you talking about?" Maggie demanded. "What games?"

The cold-blooded smile vanished, replaced by a look of sheer hostility. "Then what would *you* call marrying me for my money?" he demanded.

"I didn't marry you for your money, James," Maggie denied passionately. There was hatred mingled with pity in her eyes. "I married you because I loved you. Until I didn't."

"You loved me," James mocked, his hand tightening on the handgun. "Is that why you took me for half my money?" he demanded.

Jonah watched the other man's every move, bracing himself to jump in and defend Maggie if the need arose.

Maggie's eyes were blazing. "Call it a consolation

prize for putting up with all your womanizing," she retaliated. "And it wasn't half your money. I just took what I felt was due me," she told the man she had come to loathe. "I wanted to give the money to my parents to help get them out of debt, but they died before the terms of our divorce were even drawn up."

"So I was right. You were just a greedy whore," James accused.

Maggie held on to Jonah's arm again, restraining him. She had no doubt that he wouldn't think twice about beating the living daylights out of James, but she didn't want Jonah hurt and James was still holding on to his handgun, aiming it at them.

"I gave the money to Bell to buy our old house," she told her ex.

James's complexion turned a bright shade of red. "You used my money to buy your sister a house?" he shouted, livid.

"No," Maggie calmly corrected, her voice the complete opposite of her ex-husband's, "I used *my* money to buy my sister our old house."

Instead of screaming curses at her, James surprised them by laughing. It was the laughter of a man who was coming unhinged.

Regaining control over himself, he wiped away the tears that had rolled down his cheeks.

"Who would have ever thought that someone with such a gorgeous face and killer body could actually be able to think things through like that? Such a surprise," he told her, nodding to himself. And then he sobered. This time the hatred was back in his eyes. "Why did you have to leave me?" he asked, fury mingled with self-pity vibrating in his voice.

"Why did you have to cheat?" Maggie countered, refusing to be intimidated.

"Because I'm a man," James shouted into her face. "It's the way of the world. All men cheat."

Instead of Maggie, it was Jonah who spoke up. "No, they don't," he told James, looking at the man as if doing so turned his stomach and made him sick. "Not unless they're insecure."

Rage entered James's face. "What the hell do you know?" he challenged.

"I know a good thing when I see one," Jonah answered, still exceedingly calm as he glanced toward Maggie. "And I know how not to do something stupid to screw things up and lose her."

"So is that it?" James demanded, all but spitting out the question as he asked it. He turned toward Maggie. "He's your new boy toy?"

Maggie raised her chin proudly, a woman who wasn't about to be cowed. "He's not anybody's toy, James. Jonah just opened my eyes and made me realize that not every man is a pig like you."

James seemed to go blind with rage, clutching his handgun. "I'd watch my mouth if I were you, Mag-pie. You won't be able to kiss your cowboy hero if I shoot it off," he warned.

Jonah curled his fingers into his hands, fighting the very strong urge to strangle Maggie's ex. "Don't threaten her," he warned.

"You're right," James agreed, underscoring his words with almost a maniacal laugh. "Besides, this dumb blonde can't be scared off with just threats anyway."

Maggie's eyes widened as everything fell into place. "That was you," she cried. "You're the one who's been sending me those awful anonymous email threats, aren't you?"

"And you're the one who's too dumb to pay attention to them," James screamed at her in sheer frustration.

Jonah moved in closer, intent on shielding Maggie with his own body. "Why did you send her those texts?" he asked.

"Why?" James echoed, stunned that the other man had to even ask. "Because if she wasn't going to stay married to me, I didn't want her digging into my family, not even into my loony old uncle Elliott for any reason. She doesn't get to do that."

"So you threatened her instead?" Jonah asked, stunned that anyone would think of that as a reasonable course of action.

"Hey, if she's not willing to be on my arm and act like my eye candy, then I've got nothing to lose," James responded. "Too bad that idiot addict botched the job. Just shows, if you want something done right, you have to do it yourself," he sighed, raising his gun and taking aim.

But Jonah moved farther in front of Maggie. He had to stall for time. "But why did you have your uncle killed?" Jonah asked.

James looked at him as if he was insane. "I didn't, not that it's any business of yours. As far as I know, that crazy old loon did away with himself. Well, good riddance. But I had nothing to do with that."

Jonah didn't believe him. "And I suppose you're also going to deny knowing anything about the person who killed Emmeline Thompson."

Fury washed over James's face again. Being accused of doing things that he had had no part in didn't sit well with him.

"How would I know anything about a woman who was killed almost before I was born?" James demanded. His eyes washed over the two people in the room with him.

There was nothing but pure hatred in his eyes. "You two are really made for each other, you know that?" he declared maliciously.

James's eyes narrowed as he pointed his gun at first one, then the other, wanting to make them sweat. It infuriated him that neither flinched. "And that's why it seems like some kind of poetic karma that you're going to die together."

"You don't want him, you want me," Maggie cried, shifting quickly so that her body was blocking Jonah's instead of the other way around. "You don't have any reason to hurt Jonah."

"Sure I do," James said mockingly. "I don't like his face. And neither will you," he predicted. "When I'm finished."

Maggie stared at the man who had once been her husband, horrified. How could she have ever been in love with this man, even for a moment? He was a disgusting, depraved, poor excuse of a man. Even his good looks were beginning to wane, a casualty of James's unbridled love for all manner of alcohol, it didn't matter what kind.

But even if he was still as good-looking as the day she had met him, it was his black soul that had pushed her away and made her not want to have anything to do with him.

"Leave him alone," she cried when she saw James begin to take careful aim at Jonah. "You want me? You have me," she told her ex. "But on the condition that you leave Jonah alone."

"Oh, how very touching," James hooted, turning his attention toward Maggie. "Maybe I don't want you anymore," he told her, the look on his face growing downright menacing and ugly as he shifted his gun to point straight at Maggie. "You're tainted goods now."

It was now or never, Jonah thought. And since he couldn't think of anything to distract James and get him to leave Maggie alone, he knew he had to do something drastic, something James wasn't expecting before the other man could follow through on his overwhelming, all-consuming hatred.

"Get out of the way, Maggie!" Jonah yelled. Ducking his head down, he dived straight for James, throwing the other man off and knocking him to the floor.

The handgun discharged, sending two shots into the ceiling.

"You son of a bitch!" James cried, scrambling to recover both his balance and his weapon.

But Jonah was faster and he managed to pull out the gun he had kept tucked in the back of his belt since before he had left his truck. A gut feeling had been responsible for his taking his gun along, and now he was really glad that he had followed that instinct. He had just been waiting for the right opportunity to catch the other man unaware.

"Don't move!" he warned James, pointing the handgun at him.

The expression in the other man's eyes was wild. "What the hell do I have to lose?" James cried, trying to reach for his own gun.

Jonah discharged his weapon, but it was only to shoot the butt of the other gun out of James's reach.

"Don't do it," Jonah warned again. "Leave the weapon where it is."

"Sorry, can't do that," James responded, once again trying to go for his gun only to have Jonah shoot it away, out of his reach for a second time.

James looked at Maggie. The look on her face was one of pity. That only incensed her ex-husband further. He was about to lunge for his handgun one last time when the sound of approaching sirens pierced the otherwise-still air.

A look of frustrated panic came over James's face.

Even Maggie was surprised.

"How would they know to come here?" she asked Jonah. It seemed like a highly unlikely coincidence and she had stopped believing in coincidences a long time ago.

With his free hand, his eyes never leaving James, Jonah reached into his pocket. "Maybe because I dialed Thompson when I saw that the cabin door was opened. He's been listening to you rave the entire time," he told James.

With a guttural shriek, James was about to launch himself at Jonah. But before that could happen, the chief and two of his men burst into the cabin thanks to the unlocked door. Their guns were drawn and all three guns were pointed at James.

James swung around toward his handgun, his intentions obvious.

"I wouldn't do that if I were you, son," Thompson warned James. "You don't want people knowing that the last thing you ever did on this earth was something incredibly stupid."

James was breathing hard like the whipped animal he had become. "I've got nothing to lose," he growled.

"You've your life and where I come from, that's still plenty big. Step away from the gun. Your daddy wouldn't want you to die this way."

At the mention of his late father, James looked subdued. Still angry, he reluctantly stepped back from his weapon on the floor.

"You win this time," he said grudgingly to Maggie.

But Jonah was the one who answered him. "You're wrong. She's won for all time," he informed Maggie's former husband. Then, looking at Thompson, he said, "Sorry, Chief." Before the chief could ask him what he was sorry for, Jonah hauled off and punched James square in the face, sending the other man flat on his back. "That's for pointing a gun at Maggie," he told the crumpled heap on the floor. And then he turned toward Thompson. "You can arrest me now, Chief."

"For what?" Thompson asked. "I didn't see anything. Get this piece of garbage back to jail, boys," he ordered. "Looks like he's got more of his uncle in him than his daddy," the chief added. He smiled when he saw Maggie sink against Jonah. "You can come in tomorrow to press charges," he said. "We'll see ourselves out. Be sure to lock the door." He glanced toward the man his officers were taking out between them. "Never know what can come slithering in when you least expect it."

With that, Thompson closed the door behind him.

Chapter Nineteen

"You know, I was really starting to doubt that this day would ever get here," Maggie confided to her older sister.

She and Bellamy were looking themselves over in the full-length mirror one last time. The wedding ceremony was only minutes away from beginning.

Maggie found that she was *really* nervous for Bellamy. It surprised her that the latter looked like calmness personified.

"I know what you mean, what with first the hurricane, then the flood, it felt as if we were never going to find an island of time to have this ceremony in front of our family and friends," Bellamy agreed, adjusting her headpiece. It seemed a little lopsided to her.

Maggie was about to add the prison riot and James showing up at Jonah's cabin with his gun to that list, but then decided that, at least for now, she would keep those things to herself. There was no point in possibly ruining Bell's day with talk of what *might* have happened if things had gone badly. What counted was that they *hadn't* happened.

And more importantly, what mattered was that they were all finally gathered here to see her sister and Jonah's brother exchange their vows in front of all their loved ones.

Maggie's eyes met her sister's in the full-length mirror that had had been brought into this small room just for this occasion.

"I really wish that Mom and Dad had lived to see this," Maggie told her.

Bellamy's eyes became misty. "Yes, me, too," she agreed quietly.

Maggie squeezed her sister's hand, silently offering support.

"They've got a front row seat in heaven, watching over you. And if you ask me, I think they're going to be crazy about their new son-in-law," she confided.

Bellamy smiled. "I think so, too. All I know is that I'm glad you're here."

"And Donovan," Maggie reminded her, tongue in cheek. "Don't forget Donovan."

"No," Bellamy said with a wistful, faraway tone, "I'm certainly not about to forget Donovan," she told her sister with a laugh.

"Hey, how's it going in here?" Rae Lemmon asked, sticking her head into the room. Her expression looked resigned as she took a look at Maggie. "Well, maybe I should drop out of the wedding party."

"Wait, what?" Bellamy cried. "Why?" Her calm exterior instantly threatened to crumble. At this point, she couldn't bear the idea of facing even a thimbleful of stress, much less anything else. She just wasn't up to it.

"Well, we're supposed to be co–maids of honor and I don't look anywhere near as good as Miss Beauty Contest Winner over there," Rae said, jerking a thumb in Maggie's direction. "Compared to Maggie, I look like one of Cinderella's ugly stepsisters," Rae complained. "Or a least the plain one."

"You think that's something—how would you like to

have grown up with her? People would take one look at Maggie and then they would look at me again and ask, 'What happened to you? Were you adopted?'"

Having been a beauty contest winner had its downside, but Maggie had never become vain about those so-called "crowns" she had won. She had never been that shallow.

"Stop it, both of you," she ordered. "Beauty is in the eyes of the beholder and as far as I'm concerned, both of you are gorgeous. Besides, I hate to be the one to tell you this, Rae, but nobody's going to be looking at either of us. Every eye in the place is going to be looking at the bride here." Maggie gestured toward Bellamy. "Thinking how beautiful she looks."

"Terrific, now you've finally made me nervous," Bellamy complained.

Maggie gave Bellamy a quick hug, taking care not to wrinkle her sister's wedding gown. "There's nothing to be nervous about, Bell. You are going to be marrying the love of your life. Just remember to say 'I do' when the Reverend feeds you the line and everything will be just great."

Overwhelmed for a moment, Maggie hugged Bellamy again, this time harder. "You look just beautiful, Bell," she whispered. "Really." Releasing her sister, Maggie stepped back and looked at Rae. "Is everybody ready?"

Rae nodded. "Quick," she urged, "let's do this before anything else happens."

Maggie laughed. "Amen to that," she told her sister's best friend. Turning toward Bellamy, she said, "C'mon, big sister." Maggie gathered up her sister's long train. "Let's get you married."

Taking a deep breath, Bellamy smoothed down the sides of her gown and nodded.

Maggie cocked her head, listening. The beginning

strains of The Wedding March could be heard echoing through the air.

"And there's the music, right on cue," Maggie commented.

Rae opened the door and all three of them filed out of the small back room.

"I CAN'T BELIEVE she's really married," Maggie said again. She had lost count of how many times she had voiced that thought.

They were all at the reception. Dinner had been served and eaten, although some of the slow eaters were still at it.

Despite everything the town had just gone through, somehow they had managed to put together a band to play at Bellamy and Donovan's reception. Hearing the music somehow made everything seem brighter and hopeful.

Taking advantage of having a live band there, Maggie had gone up to Jonah and asked him to dance. She was actually prepared to have to drag him onto the small dance floor, but to her surprise, Jonah had gone along with her willingly.

The first dance was a relatively fast number, but the next one was slow. It felt perfect to have his arms around her.

"I don't think either one of them quite believe it, either," Jonah said, nodding toward the bride and groom, who were also on the floor, dancing.

"I guess it's going to take some time to sink in," Maggie commented. And then she turned her attention back to her partner. He had really surprised her. "You dance well."

Jonah laughed at the stunned expression on her face. "You were expecting me to trip over my own feet, weren't you?"

"Well, not exactly that," Maggie quickly corrected.

"But, well, you're a Cowboy Hero, you spend all your time looking for lost people and rescuing them," she explained. "That doesn't exactly leave much time over for any dancing."

"Sure it does," he told her with a straight face. "My team and I do a little victory dance every time we find someone."

"You don't have to make fun of me," she told him, although she had to admit that probably from his point of view, she did have it coming.

"Oh, but it's so much fun to do that," Jonah confessed—just before he stole a quick kiss.

The slow song they were dancing to ended, but another one quickly started, taking its place. Because it felt so utterly right to be holding her like this, Jonah just continued dancing with Maggie.

"You know I'm just kidding, right?" he asked her. The last thing he wanted was to hurt Maggie's feelings.

She lifted her shoulders in a quick, fleeting shrug. "Everyone's got to have a hobby, I guess."

That made him think. "Well, if we're going to be talking about hobbies, I guess this is the right time to tell you that I've been thinking about taking up a new one," he told her.

Listening, she wasn't sure just where he was going with this. "Oh?"

"Yes." Now that he had gotten started, he was determined to push through this, even though he felt as if his gut was tying itself up in knots. "I've been thinking about this for a long time now and unless you have any objections—"

"Me?" Maggie cut in, confused. "Why would I have any objections to your new hobby?" she asked.

He looked down into her face. "Because my new hobby is you."

Maggie stopped dancing. "Excuse me?"

"I said my new hobby is yo—"

She shook her head, waving away the rest of his sentence. "I heard what you said, but how can I be your new hobby?"

"Because," he continued, smiling into her face, his courage growing, "I intend to learn every little thing there is to know about you." he told her.

He still wasn't being clear, Maggie thought. "Why would you want to do that?"

"Because," he told her, playing with a stray lock that had worked its way out of her carefully arranged hairstyle, "I think that a husband *should* know everything about his wife."

To say that she was stunned was a colossal understatement.

"Wait, hold it," Maggie cried.

Grabbing his hand she led him away from the small area that had been designated for dancing and drew him over to the far side of the rec center, away from all the other wedding guests.

Only when they had finally gotten clear of everyone did Maggie let go of his hand and turn around to face him. "Did you just miss a step? Because I know that I did."

His expression never changed. "I thought we were dancing very well."

"I'm not talking about dancing together," she insisted, feeling disoriented, not to mention more than a little confused.

"But I am," Jonah told her, then added very seriously, "I am talking about dancing together for the rest of our lives."

"Wait," Maggie ordered, putting her hand on his chest as if to underscore the instruction she had just managed to utter. Her pulse was racing so fast, she was certain he could detect it. "Back up here."

Maggie felt as if she was having a total out-of-body experience, which, considering everything else she had been through recently, didn't really surprise her as much as it should have.

But maybe she was just reading too much into this. Maybe there was another meaning entirely to what Jonah was saying to her, but if there was, for the life of her, she couldn't find it.

"Are you asking me to marry you?" she questioned Jonah very slowly, afraid that she had gotten her signals crossed somehow. She watched his face to see if he would suddenly start to laugh.

But he didn't.

There it was, he thought. There was the question. The answer could either make him or break him entirely, not to mention that the wrong answer would suck up his soul.

But now that it was out on the table between them like this, there was no running from it, no stalling to buy more time so that when Maggie finally gave him her answer, it was the one that he was hoping to hear.

"Well, Colton?" she pressed, waiting for him to answer her. "Are you?"

"In my own halting, totally mixed-up way, yes," he answered. "But in my defense, I've never done this before."

"You've never asked a woman to marry you before?" Maggie asked incredulously.

How could someone as handsome as Jonah have gotten to this stage of his life without asking someone to marry him? It didn't seem possible—unless he wanted to be a bachelor forever.

"No," he admitted, "I never have. And before you ask me why, it's because I never found anyone I *wanted* to ask, never found anyone I wanted to spend the rest of my life with—until now," he said, cupping her cheek for a moment. His eyes all but made love to her as he looked deeply into hers.

Maggie stared at him, afraid to believe what she was hearing. "You mean me?" she asked haltingly.

"Of course I mean you. Unless," Jonah qualified as it occurred to him that maybe she hadn't already said yes because she didn't want to, "the reason you haven't said yes is because you're trying to find a way to turn me down."

"After that prison riot and then coming home to find yourself looking down the barrel of my ex-husband's gun, I'm surprised you even want to talk to me, much less marry me," she told him.

"Oh, trust me, I want to do much more than that to you," he told her. She still hadn't said what he was waiting to hear. Taking a deep breath, Jonah resigned himself to the disappointment that was coming. "But if you'd rather I just walked away and left you alone, I will."

Maggie could only stare at him as she shook her head. "Amazing."

Jonah didn't understand what she was saying. "What is?"

"That a man like you who is so incredibly clever that you can pick up a trace of a clue at fifty paces can be so unbelievably thickheaded when it comes to seeing what is blatantly right in front of you," she marveled.

It just made her love Jonah that much more, she thought.

"And what is it that's right in front of me?" he asked

Maggie, afraid that he was going to get it all wrong after all.

She turned her face up to his. "Me, Jonah, Me. I love you, you big dummy."

Relieved beyond belief, Jonah smiled into her eyes as he wrapped his arms around her waist. In the background, there was another song beginning to play, but he remained where he was, in the recesses of the rec center, content to be there with his girl in his arms.

"Good answer," he told her just before lowering his mouth to hers.

Lord, but he could get lost in that kiss of hers, Jonah thought. But this wasn't the time or the place to let that happen. He owed it to his brother to stay here for at least a large part of the reception even though every fiber of his being was begging him to just sweep Maggie up in his arms and go home with her. To make love with her until there was nothing left of either one of them but desire.

He was torn between duty and desire.

Maggie drew her lips back, afraid that with any more provocation, she was going to forget where she was and allow her crumbling barriers to just fall to the ground without an ounce of care.

But there were things that had to be settled. She couldn't just let all this happen blindly.

"Where are we going to live?" she asked him. She felt his arms tightening around her.

"Here." And then he explained why he'd changed his mind. "Your sister's here. My family's here. It only makes sense to put roots down here."

She wasn't going to let herself rejoice until she was absolutely sure he knew what he was doing—and why. "But what about your job in Austin?"

"After that hurricane and that flood, my organization

is going to need an outpost here. There's no reason why I can't get transferred to Whisperwood," he told her.

"And what about making your name apart from the Colton name?" she asked. He had been pretty adamant about that.

Jonah shrugged as if that no longer mattered. "I did that. There's no point in proving myself over and over again. You have any more details to get in the way?" he asked her.

Her eyes crinkled at the corners as she smiled. "None that I can think of."

"Good. Then it's settled," he declared. "Except for just one thing," he reminded her.

"Oh?" She looked at him, a little confused. "What's that?"

"You haven't given me an answer."

"Maybe because you haven't actually come out and asked me that question," she countered.

"All right, let's do this the right way." Before she could ask him what the right way was, Jonah dropped down to one knee, took her hand and said, "Magnolia Reeves, will you marry me?"

"Yes, but if you ever call me Magnolia again," she warned him with feeling, "the wedding is off."

He rose to his feet, still holding her hand. "Duly noted," he said, pulling her back into his arms.

It was the last thing he said for a while. He had been raised right and knew it wasn't polite to talk when his lips were otherwise occupied.

Epilogue

"I guess you must feel really relieved to finally be able to give your sister a proper burial, Chief," Mitch Cameron, one of Thompson's longtime police officers said. Cameron had come by to check with his superior before he called it a day and left the police station.

"Not as relieved as you might think, Cameron," Thompson answered. He'd been going through old paper files for the better part of the day. "Whoever killed my baby sister is still out there. The bastard needs to be made to pay for his crime."

Trying to comfort the chief, Cameron said, "You never know—maybe the guy's dead. That's always a possibility," he added hopefully.

But the chief shook his head. "My gut tells me he's still out there, Cameron. And," he added grimly, "I don't think that Emmeline was his only victim."

Cameron looked at the stack of files on the chief's desk. "Is that why you've been going through all those old missing persons case files?"

"Missing *women* case files," Thompson corrected. That same hunch that told him the killer was still out there also told him that the killer had a type.

"Maybe the way he buried your sister, mummifying her body and burying her deep in the earth, shows that he regretted what he did," Cameron suggested, watching the chief's face for a reaction.

"Or maybe he just didn't want her body found by a cadaver dog," the chief countered.

Cameron laughed dryly. There was no humor in his laugh. "You sure aren't giving this guy any points, are you?"

"No, I'm not," Thompson all but growled at his officer. "You have anything else you want to say?" he asked, indicating that if he didn't, then Cameron should leave.

Cameron lingered by the door. "Just that I'm sorry about your sister, Chief."

Thompson sighed. He was letting all this get to him and he knew that an emotional crime investigator was a sloppy crime investigator, one who was liable to miss minute clues.

"Yeah, me, too," the chief answered, his tone losing some of its anger. "Good night, Cameron."

"Good night, sir," Cameron answered, walking out of the police station. He eased the door quietly closed behind him.

Cameron hadn't been gone for more than two minutes before the phone on Thompson's desk rang. He put a pencil—his use of pencils had been a running joke at the station for a while now—into the file he was reviewing to mark his place.

He picked up the receiver on the third ring and cradled it between his shoulder and his ear. "Thompson," he announced.

"Chief?"

Thompson recognized the voice as belonging to another one of his officers, Michael Juarez. Juarez had been part of the police force for only a year and a half. He had pulled the night shift. Everyone knew that usually meant that it was a good time to take catnaps and get paid for them.

Thompson did his best not to lose his temper. "What is it, Juarez?"

"I think you're going to want to come down here, Chief. I found another dead body. It's wrapped up the same way that your sister was."

The young officer sounded scared, Thompson thought. He was already on his feet. "I'll be right there."

His gut instincts were right.

For once, Thompson really wished that he was wrong. But it looked like this case was far from over.

Maybe he'd finally get those answers about Emmeline's murder.

* * * * *

COMING SOON!

We really hope you enjoyed reading this book. If you're looking for more romance, be sure to head to the shops when new books are available on

Thursday 11th July

To see which titles are coming soon, please visit
millsandboon.co.uk/nextmonth